The Misfortunes of
John Bull

The Misfortunes of
John Bull
and Other Stories

by
Camille Debans

translated, annotated and introduced by
Brian Stableford

A Black Coat Press Book

ISBN 978-1-61227-411-9. First Printing. July 2015. Published by Black Coat Press, an imprint of Hollywood Comics.com, LLC, P.O. Box 17270, Encino, CA 91416. All rights reserved. Except for review purposes, no part of this book may be reproduced or transmitted in any form or by any means, electronic or mechanical, including photocopying, recording, or by any information storage and retrieval system, without permission in writing from the publisher. The stories and characters depicted in this novel are entirely fictional. Printed in the United States of America.

TABLE OF CONTENTS

Introduction

Les Malheurs de John Bull by Camille Debans, here translated as "The Misfortunes of John Bull," was originally published in book form by C. Marpon et E. Flammarion in 1884; it had probably been previously serialized as a feuilleton in a periodical, but I cannot identify any such publication. "Le Paralytique" ("The Paralytic") and "L'Angoisse" ("Anguish") were both published in *Le Science Illustrée*, each in four parts, the former in June 1900 and the latter in November 1901. "Graour le monstre" ("Graour the Monster") was originally published in the *Journal des Voyages* in eleven parts, from 5 July to 13 September 1903.

Les Malheurs de John Bull is one of a trio of significant future war stories published in France in the early 1880s; it appearing a year after the first version of Albert Robida's lavishly illustrated "La Guerre au Vingtième Siècle" (1883; the book version, with a variant text, tr. as "War in the Twentieth Century," appeared in 1887)[1] and a year before *La Guerre finale, histoire fantastique*, signed "Barillet-Lagargousse" (1884).[2] Camille Debans' contribution to the trio is, like Barillet-Lagargousse's, a relatively straight-faced satire—although Robida's text, too, is relatively sober by comparison with his caricaturish illustrations, as befits descriptions of mass slaughter. Debans' story is, however, distinctive in placing its principal focus on naval warfare, featuring battles between ironclad warships, assisted by various hypothetical inventions, which now seem very primitive but were innovative at the time. It is also distinctive in being unashamedly moti-

---

[1] Included in *Engineer Von Satanas*, to be released soon by Black Coat Press.
[2] tr. as *The Final War*, Black Coat Press, ISBN 978-1-61227-337-2.

7

vated by spite, not directed against the Germans, against whom the French had been bearing a sore grudge since 1870, but against the English, carrying forward a much older antagonism. Like the other two novels, however, it anticipates warfare on a global scale, recognizing that the dissemination of European colonies all over the world would mean that no major war involving European powers could any longer be a local affair.

French future war fiction was soon to take a much grimmer turn in a long series of jingoistic extravaganzas by "Capitaine Danrit" (Émile Driant) and similar endeavors by Georges Espitallier, *alias* Pierre Ferréol and Georges Bethuys, and "Colonel Royet," whose general tone makes the trio of which *Les Malheurs de John Bull* forms a component seem a trifle frivolous. The three earlier works remain very interesting, however, not merely because of their relative breeziness and sarcastic cynicism, but also because that attitude liberated the imagination of its authors to be more inventive in their anticipation of the manner in which technical invention would transform the nature and tactics of future battles. The inventions featured in Debans' novel are very modest, but that is a reflection of its early date, when many of the speculative devices that were to transform future war fiction in the 1890s were not yet on the imaginative horizon. Although Debans lacks the imaginative daring of Robida and the technical know-how of Barillet-Lagargousse, he has a similar grasp of the scope of future potential, and cedes nothing in terms of narrative brio and verve.

Perhaps somewhat implausibly, the war described in *Les Malheurs de John Bull* is not, strictly speaking, an international war, but rather a vendetta conducted by a single man—a Frenchman, naturally—who only invents a nation for himself as a means to the end of avenging an insult offered to him by an English nobleman, and then turns that improvised nation into a global empire by not merely defeating England but hijacking and improving upon her imperial ambitions. Although the author's tongue remains firmly in his cheek throughout, that does not prevent him from maintaining an earnest tone in his description of the tactics of the gradual but inexorable conquest wrought by the story's remarkable hero.

Debans, like all the French feuilletonists of his era, made up his stories as he went along, and whether or not it was originally published as a feuilleton, *Les Malheurs de John Bull* suffers markedly from some of the endemic weaknesses of that mode of composition, in that several of its plot-threads wither away without any proper denouement in an abrupt and seemingly-hurried ending. In spite of that flaw, however—particularly disappointing in respect of the fact that the hero of the novel misses out on his final personal confrontation with the villain—the story retains a robust continuity as well as a relentless pace. The story also suffers the standard fate of near-future fantasies—especially those dated as specifically as this one—of being very rapidly transmuted by the march of time into "alternative histories." The same thing happened to numerous British future war stories initially published as newspaper serials, which often used dates lavishly in order to create an impression of contemporaneity, but that "fault" fades into insignificance as the interval of time between composition and consumption extends.

This is not the first time the story has been translated—two different editions appeared very swiftly in the USA (the Americans had not forgotten 1776), but they remain extremely rare, so little known that they are not listed by Everett Bleiler in his otherwise scrupulously complete *Checklist of Science Fiction and Supernatural Fiction* (revised ed. 1978) or his account of *Science Fiction: The Early Years* (1990). Unsurprisingly, however, no such translation was published in England itself, then or later, although sufficient time has now passed for English readers no longer to feel any personal sense of injury in the events described, especially given the fact that the Empire stolen in the course of the plot has long been lost by other means. Although I. F. Clarke's classic study of *Voices Prophesying War* (2nd ed. 1992) describes Debans' novel as "violently chauvinistic," it is actually far less chauvinistic than most future war stories, making little attempt to trumpet the superiority of the French and employing a determined multiculturalism in its construction of the forces opposed to the overweening pretentions of English aristocracy and imperialism—an opposition with which the majority of modern British citizens would undoubtedly able to sympathize.

The fact that no translation appeared in England, however, does not mean that *Les Malheurs de John Bull* was unknown there; the *Pall Mall Budget* published a scathing article complaining about it shortly after its publication. Nor does it necessarily mean that it was entirely without influence on the development of British scientific romance. The plot has considerable similarities to that of M. P. Shiel's novel *The Lord of the Sea* (1901), and the naval battles have some affinity with those described in Shiel's earlier novel, *The Yellow Danger* (1898). The similarities might be coincidental, but Shiel did spend a good deal of time in Paris, and was able to read French fluently. All of his several future war novels—and many of his other novels too—are accounts of personal crusades in which heroes unsusceptible to intimidation are always ready to take on overwhelming odds, including entire nations, on a point of principle, in the same fashion as Debans' hero. Furthermore, the story that Shiel liked to tell about being crowned King of Redonda, for which he created a fanciful peerage among his friends, is strangely foreshadowed in *Les Malheurs de John Bull* in the assumption by its hero of the title of King of Pola and his gradual creation of a peerage by rewarding his associates.

Although Debans, born in 1834, was fifty when he wrote *Les Malheurs de John Bull*, it might still qualify as one of his earlier novels. He had been active as a journalist for some years before penning his first novel, *Octave Kellner* (1865), but published only three more before 1880, when he began to publish books on a much more prolific scale, most of them having appeared first as newspaper feuilletons. He averaged a book a year throughout the 1880s and 1890s, but none after 1900, although he did publish more feuilletons after that date and did not die until 1910. "Graour le monstre", which was his penultimate feuilleton in the *Journal de Voyages*, is too short to have been issued as a book, but the one with which he followed it, "L'Éléphant bleu" [The Blue Elephant] (30 episodes, 1904) was not. *The Journal des Voyages* was by then his primary market for fiction, the last two novels he published in book form both being taken from its pages. Previously, he had published seven items in *La Science Illustrée*—including one previously reprinted in the *Journal de Voyages*, originally published in 1869—although none was novel-length, and it is not obvious why the editor of that periodical, Louis Figuier, thought it appropriate to publish some of those stories in a popular science magazine. "Le Paralytique" and "L'Angoisse," in particular, do not seem to qualify as *roman scientifique* by any stretch of the imagination, although they do qualify as literary experiments, of a kind carried forward by "Graour le monstre."

Throughout his career, Debans was essentially a writer of popular fiction, and although he did write a number of "literary novels" with evident higher ambitions—including one item of non-speculative *roman scientifique, Boissat chimiste* [Boissat the Chemist] (1892)—he was essentially an entertainer, who had a considerable interest in the materials and techniques of melodrama. The three stories translated here are all deliberate attempts to wind up melodramatic pitch to a maximal degree, presenting intense stories of characters under unusual and extreme pressure of circumstance. The first two involve somewhat contrived but nevertheless naturalistic situations, but the third takes contrivance to an extraordinary degree, deliberately redeploying classic Gothic motifs in such a way as to try to extract the very last drop of narrative tension from them.

Although it does acknowledge one appropriation from H. G. Wells, the most conspicuous motif deployed in "Graour le monstre"—the human monster—is obviously carried forward from Victor Hugo, who did not originate it but did give it an unparalleled respectability as well as a uniquely fine pitch.

Debans makes no attempt to duplicate the unmatchable respectability that Hugo conferred on Quasimodo in *Notre Dame de Paris* (1831; tr. as *The Hunchback of Notre Dame*) and Gwynplaine in *L'Homme qui rit* (1869; tr. as *The Man Who Laughs*), but he does aim, not merely to match the pitch of narrative intensity attained in the relevant passages of those novels, but to exceed it, with the aid of a calculated garishness more reminiscent of the American "Weird Menace" pulps of the 1930s than any previous French fiction. The extent to which he succeeds might be debatable, especially given the strains imported into the story by the fact that it was obviously made up while in the process of serialization, but there is no doubt that the novella is an extraordinary piece of work.

Camille Debans remains a highly readable writer, and all four of these stories remain as engaging today as when they were originally published. If the first and the fourth seem a trifle quaint and old-fashioned by modern standards, that only serves to add an extra dimension of charm to their frank and casual extravagance. Because of their author's unusually attentive interest in the mechanics of melodrama, his most interesting works—which include these four items—were, in their not-entirely-modest fashion, significant stepping-stones in the development of the narrative techniques of modern melodrama.

The translation of *Les Malheurs de John Bull* was made from the copy of the Marpon and Flammarion edition reproduced on the Bibliothèque Nationale's *gallica* website. The translations of "Le Paralytique" and "L'Angoisse" were made from the Kindle edition of *Recueil de 7 nouvelles*, which collects all of Debans' contributions to *La Science Illustrée*. The translation of "Graour le monstre" was made from the serial version in the relevant volume of the *Journal des Voyages* reproduced on *gallica*.

Brian Stableford

THE MISFORTUNES OF JOHN BULL

I. Darnozan

It was the fault of an Englishman.

Maxime Darnozan had just been shipwrecked on the coast of New Zealand. The entire crew of the *Suzanne* had perished in the catastrophe, save for that extraordinary man, who was able to swim for more than five hours and come ashore in a safe place.

Having taken the precaution, before the ship sank, of putting all the money he possessed on his person, as well as a lifebelt, Maxime did not find himself devoid of resources in Auckland. He only stayed there, in any case, long enough to wait for a steamer, and three days later he left for San Francisco about the Pacific Mail Steamship Company's *Lapwing*.

The story has been inaccurately told of how, thanks to an extremely rare presence of mind, he saved the steamer during the crossing. It was the English newspapers that were the first to mention the fact, when Darnozan began to make them anxious, and, naturally, with their treacherous good faith, they had no scruple about depreciating his action—which was, moreover, the primary cause of what happened thereafter.

The *Lapwing* was making good progress. Four days out from Auckland, she was passing through the Kermadec Islands, traveling at twelve knots. The sea was sullen and the breeze stiff.

Long waves driven by the wind in the same direction as the ship seemed to be marching in step with her, and from time to time they fell in enormous masses on her stern, which groaned.

Maxime, enveloped in his overcoat, was sprawled on a bench on the poop deck, a short distance away from a group of three individuals who were protecting themselves from the splashes of sea-water with the aid of a huge umbrella. One has to be English to take the love of the umbrella to such extremes.

One of the three individuals was Lord Killyett, who was making a world tour in order to complete the education of his daughter, Lady Helena, Duchess of Wentworth. The second was James Wyndham, the *Lapwing*'s first lieutenant. The third was Sir Nathaniel Robertson, a brigadier-general in the British Army.

It was nine o'clock in the evening; there was no moon, nor even any stars. The ship had all her lights blazing. It would have been impossible to see land two cables away.

Having straightened up somewhat, Maxime leaned his elbow on the rail and searched the horizon with his gaze. Suddenly, he leapt toward the helmsman, knocked him violently to the deck, and, while applying his Herculean strength to the tiller shouted: "Hard to starboard! Damned ship!"

And almost immediately, an enormous three-master was seen advancing like a gigantic black phantom, with all sails deployed, about to cut the Pacific Mail ship in two.

Fortunately, the *Lapwing* was obedient to her tiller, and obeyed Maxime like a good horse. She turned abruptly to the right. The other ship had, somewhat hastily, made an analogous maneuver, and a frightful cracking sound was heard at the stern.

There were cries, oaths and *damns* from one end of the ship to the other. There was a moment of chaos. A few sailors, anxious for their skin, leapt into the boats, assuming that the ship was about to sink.

Three or four passengers, including Lady Helena Killyett, arrived on the poop deck uttering cries of desperation. The captain came running, while, from the bridge, the officer of the watch commanded a maneuver and ordered the fearful sailors to get out of the lifeboats, under threat of the lash.

In the meantime, the three-master disappeared into the night, and the same hubbub was heard aboard her as on the deck of the *Lapwing*.

Maxime Darnozan had returned the vessel to its course, and made summary apologies to the mariner he has so rudely thrust aside. Then he examined the damage.

"Much ado about nothing," he said, smiling, to the captain, who demanded to know the cause of all the racket.

"Thanks to this gentleman," said Lieutenant Wyndham.

"What?"

"The gentleman was the first—and, I dare say, the only one—to see the big ship that was about to cut us in two, and if, instead of taking action, he'd been content to shout a warning, we'd all have gone to perdition."

"You're exaggerating," said Maxime, modestly. "I didn't do anything out of the ordinary."

"You saved everybody's life!" exclaimed General Robertson.

Maxime was surrounded, he was thanked, he was fêted, and then everything aboard resumed its customary appearance.

Darnozan, certainly, had not given himself full credit, and there are many people, even among the English, who would have put on infinitely superior airs in his place. He remained modest and cool—but he thought that the passengers, without heaping him with praise, might have treated him a little more graciously.

Now, this is what happened the following day, in the afternoon. The weather was milder than the day before, and the sea not as rough. General Nathaniel Robertson, Lord Killyett, his daughter and two other passengers were having lunch on the poop deck, and chatting as they ate—for Englishmen, in spite of their stiff and surly attitudes, are inexhaustible chatterboxes, who are only exceeded in that regard by Englishwomen.

Lord Killyett was talking, and what he was saying doubtless interested his auditors, for they had drawn closer to him and were listening avidly. On the other hand, the narrator seemed convinced that important matters were at stake, because, in order to be understood by the able seamen or the petty officers, he was speaking French.

"Yes," he said, "Europe, and Bismarck himself, would be very astonished if they learned that the Egyptian campaign, from Arabi's *pronunciamento* to the victory of Tel-el-Kebir, has been nothing but a comedy, all of whose details were agreed and regulated in advance."[3]

"What! Arabi was..."

"An accomplice, nothing more."

At that precise moment, Maxime Darnozan arrived on the poop. He heard the last words and pricked up his ears. Either Lord Killyett was ignorant of Maxime's nationality, or he considered him a person of too little importance to hold back in his presence, and the conversation continued.

The noble lord was an important man in England. He had been Viceroy of India, and had served as Chancellor of the Exchequer twice. Reasons of a private and entirely respectable nature had distanced him from militant politics, but he re-

---

[3] The Egyptian Army officer who called himself Ahmad Arabi, or Arabi Pasha (nowadays more often known as Orabi or Urabi) led a mutiny in 1879 that escalated into a general revolt against the Anglo-French backed administration of Khedive Muhammed Tewfik. He was accepted into Tewfik's cabinet and started a program of civil and military reforms that worried the Europeans powers, before nationalist demonstrations in Alexandria in 1882 provoked a bombardment by British naval forces commanded by Admiral Edward Seymour; British land forces under General Garnet Wolseley eventually defeated Arabi's forces at Tel-el-Kebir and then marched on Cairo to take direct control of the government. The French, still weakened by the fallout of the Franco-Prussian War of 1870 and embroiled in the internal political squabbles of the Third Republic, did not participate in the military campaign and lost their influence over the Suez Canal in consequence. The story told by Lord Killyett is, however, a tissue of lies.

tained the closest links with the statesmen of the United Kingdom, especially with the diplomats who regarded him as an eminent man.

That elevated situation and the experience of the Duke, who had traveled the world in all directions and whom it was said that kings were pleased to consult, gave Lord Killyett an incontestable authority, and he was known to be too serious to state as fact something that he would not have been able to prove. That is why the declaration that he had just made acquired an indisputable importance in his mouth. The statement that he had just made could be considered as official.

"Every good Englishman," he continued, "every intelligent subject of Her Majesty, has known for a long time that the Suez Canal was bound to be ours one day. Slowly, but with prudence, the governments of Lord Beaconsfield, like that of Mr. Gladstone, have been preparing for that."

"Oh, yes—Cyprus!"[4]

"Precisely. England wants, before getting her hands on the Canal, to be in a position to protect it effectively, if necessary. She had Malta, she had Gibraltar; she needed Cyprus; she took it—you know how. All that, anyway, is ancient history—but what you might not know is that the Queen's government had made advances to Khedive Ismail[5] to know whether he would aid us, when the moment came, to take possession of the route to India."

---

[4] The British took control of the administration of Cyprus in June 1878 after making a secret deal with the Sultan of the Ottoman Empire. The British wanted the island to use as a base for possible naval operations in the Eastern Mediterranean, while Turkey—which maintained notional sovereignty—needed British support to protect her Asian possessions from Russian encroachment.

[5] Khedive Ismail, Tewfik's father, was deposed in 1879 on the insistence of the British, after his modernizing efforts ran up huge debts—which were partly reduced by selling Egypt's shares in the Suez Canal to the British government.

17

"Ismail refused?" queried Sir Nathaniel.

"The Khedive, who always needed money—on which we were counting to get him aboard—sold us, in return for a large sum, the shares in the Canal that he possessed, but he was too intelligent not to understand that once we were in his homeland, we'd be the masters; to the rest, he turned a deaf ear. We waited for his money to run out. You know what happened. Ismail was deposed, with the aid of France, which benevolently lent us her assistance, and naively, her collaboration, and we installed Mehmet Tewfik, a worthless idiot, on the throne, who became putty in our hands."

"Did the new Khedive put up any resistance once he was on the throne?"

"Not the slightest."

"What need was there, then, to put Arabi forward?"

"I'll tell you," said Lord Killyett. "When the moment came to seize our prey, we were bound to find our ally, France, indisposed to do as we wished..."

"Which is quite natural, Milord," agreed the General, laughing.

"So, we first had to embark on the adventure, thanks to the somewhat inexperienced good faith of Monsieur Gambetta.[6] It was then that we invented the colonels and their *pronunciamentos*. Monsieur Gambetta talked about putting down the rebels and was the first to suggest the expedition.

"That was only phase one of the affair. We knew that the Ministry might fall at any moment, and we gave the wheel at little push. When Gambetta was no longer in power we declared that we were ready to march with France, but she no

---

[6] The Radical Léon Gambetta was President of the Council and Minister of Foreign Affairs from 14 November 1881-26 January 1882, during a very turbulent period in the politics of the Republic; had he remained in office he would certainly have supported the British in Egypt; it was the government that replaced him, led by the opportunist Charles de Freycinet, which only held on until August, that shirked the task.

longer wanted to do so, as we knew full well. Arabi and his friends played their role so well that Egypt was really split into two parties. We went to fight Arabi. The French parliament, adroitly moved to suspicion by us, prevented the ministry from going with us."

People were listening religiously to Lord Killyett. In spite of the singularity of the revelations that his audience was hearing, they did not doubt their accuracy for a single moment, and they were right.

Maxime Darnozan had sat down on the bench in the same place as the previous evening, and he listened too, with a keen interest, without missing a word of what the Duke was saying.

Lady Killyett interrupted her father. "But if the French hadn't been afraid of embarking on an adventure," she said, "such as they had so often repeated, and had come to Egypt with the English, what would have happened?"

"What would have happened, Lady Helena, is that Bismarck might perhaps have taken advantage of the opportunity to make sure that there were still billions in France, and the cabinet in Paris would have been forced to recall its troops."

"All right!" said Sir Nathaniel Robertson, smiling. "And then?"

"The French didn't want to follow us," the Duke went on, "and they acted wisely from many points of view...especially ours. We went to Egypt alone, and as it was necessary to appear to be doing something, we bombarded Alexandria, but after having waited until Arabi had abandoned it. He had his orders, and they were carried out to the letter. You know that he hadn't cut either the railway or the Canal. You know that after a partial success obtained at Gassassine, which was designed to disturb Europe, General Garnet Wolseley fought the battle of Tel-el-Kebir, at the commencement of which Arabi, whose role was complete, went tranquilly to Cairo, where he allowed himself to be taken prisoner without putting up the slightest resistance, knowing that nothing would be done to him...unless..."

Lord Killyett stopped.

"Unless…?" interrogated his daughter, slightly anxiously.

"Unless imperious necessities obliged us to sacrifice him."

"Oh, Father!" sad Lady Helena, in a reproachful tone.

"What do you expect? That's politics, and sentiments don't enter into politics. Anyway, everything worked out well. Ceylon, rich and happy, is now our partner. Perhaps it cost us dearly, but monetary wounds, as the French say…"

"If I understand you correctly, Milord," said Maxime Darnozan suddenly, having risen to his feet and approached the group, "it's also necessary to count among the number of imperious necessities the massacres in Alexandra that you provoked."

Maxime had spoken in a tone of indignation. Lord Killyett turned round slowly, and then, having looked him up and down, picked up a saucer from the table that had contained butter and held it out to Darnozan. "My friend," he said, "you're doubtless a steward, to permit yourself to speak to us without having been introduced. Do me the favor, then, of taking this to the kitchen."

The Duke was short in stature, and Maxime was a tall man. Scarcely had the former finished pronouncing his insolent remark than the untimely saucer was in the sea. The Duke tried to stand up then, but did not have the time. Darnozan had seized him by the belt, lifted him up like a feather, and, in his legitimate and profound anger, was just about to send him to join the butter-dish, when Lady Helena, frightened, launched herself toward her father, crying: "Oh, Mr. Darnozan! Mr. Darnozan!"

She spoke English this time. Maxime looked at the young woman, and seemed to hesitate. Then he replaced Lord Killyett in his chair, sitting him down there forcefully, and said: "I don't know whether I ought to permit you to speak to me, Mademoiselle, for you haven't been introduced to

20

me…but your father should thank you—you've just saved his life."

Maxime bowed to Lady Helena and went down to his cabin. That evening, he did not appear at dinner.

The Captain of the *Lapwing* was very discontented with what had happened. He blamed Lord Killyett, and even went to see Maxime in order to ask him to come to the table.

"No, thank you, Captain," Darnozan replied. "I'm incapable of eating."

"Come, come! You can't hold the whole ship responsible for the insult that one old fool leveled at you. No one here approves."

"I believe you, Monsieur, but let me alone, I beg you; that's the best remedy for my ill-humor."

The Captain was obliged to withdraw. That evening, he approached Lord Killyett and did not hide the inclination of his thoughts.

"We're not in England here, where the most ridiculous customs are the most honored," he said.

"What does that mean?" asked the Duke, in a haughty tone.

The mariner was not a man to be intimidated, however. An American of old stock, he cared very little for the old formulas of the Three Kingdoms.

"I mean," he replied, "that when traveling, one ought to leave behind the prejudices and fashions that don't sit well with the mores of other peoples."

"I'm the sole judge…"

"Oh! Permit me to say that if Monsieur Darnozan had thrown you into the sea, I would have been very annoyed to have to put in irons and bring before a maritime tribunal a man who had saved us all not twenty-four hours earlier."

"Oh, saved…"

"Yes, sir, saved us all! You and your daughter along with everyone else, as you know very well!"

"You're taking the tone…"

"Of a master—yes, Milord, for, don't forget that you're only a passenger here, and since you've been a Commodore, you ought to be the first to set a good example. Repudiating a deplorable pride, you should testify to that young man some regret for a moment of impetuosity."

"Me?"

"Yes, you! Anyway, it's only an item of advice, but you'd be wrong not to follow it, because, either I'm much mistaken, or Monsieur Darnozan will harbor a grudge against you whose effects you might one day suffer."

Lord Killyett burst out laughing, like a man too highly placed for Maxime ever to be able to reach him.

The captain turned his back on him and the conversation ended there.

Darnozan nursed his wrath and ruminated his vengeance. He did not close his eyes that night.

In the morning, when he came out of his cabin, he went to see the Captain and said to him: "I want to thank you again, sincerely, for the kind words you brought me yesterday evening. I'm profoundly grateful to you, and I'd like to have an opportunity to prove it to you—but that will doubtless be for later. For the moment, on the contrary, I'd like to ask you for a favor."

"What? Speak."

"Do me the kindness of introducing me to Lord Killyett."

The Captain looked Maxime in the eyes.

"Oh, don't worry; I no longer want to throw him in the sea."

"All right! Come on—but on one condition, which is that I witness the conversation."

"I'd like nothing better."

The Captain assumed that Darnozan was going to make some cruel remark to the Commodore—which, deep down, he would not be sorry to see. That is why he did not even ask the Duke's opinion. He merely had himself announced by the steward.

Lord Killyett had a small apartment at the rear of the ship, composed of two large cabins and a small reception room, very nicely furnished. It was in that reception room that he received the visitors.

As soon as they had come in, the Captain made the introduction, as he had promised. Needless to say, Lord Killyett was not a little surprised by the incident. His astonishment gave birth to a malicious smile on the Captain's lips; he could not wait to hear what Maxime was about to say.

Darnozan had dressed with a certain care, and was looking very dapper.

"Milord," he said, "I am full of gratitude to the captain, who, having introduced me to you, has out me in a position to make a request that, I hope, will be very welcome."

"I'm listening, sir," said the Duke, with rancorous iciness.

"Milord Killyett, Duke of Wentworth, peer of England, I beg you to listen. I was born of a French father and a Russian mother on an American ship, which means that I don't know exactly to what nationality I belong. If I consulted my tastes, my choice would soon be made..."

"I don't suppose, sir, that you've come here to tell me your life story?"

"Perhaps..."

"In that case, sir, get to the point."

"I'm getting there, Milord. Yesterday, you insulted me gratuitously and boorishly..."

"Boorishly? I beg you to choose your expressions carefully."

"It is because I am choosing them very carefully that I am employing them. But let me continue: I have avowed a durable hatred for you."

"Ah!"

"And the hatred of a man like me is not one that a prudent Englishman should disregard."

"Really?"

"It is as I have the honor of telling you," Maxime added, smiling with the expression of a man completely in control of himself. "There is, Milord, a means for you to avoid the vengeance that I have the intention of exacting."

"And that is?"

Maxime bowed profoundly, straightened up again, and, looking directly into the Commodore's eyes, still smiling said: "I have the honor of asking you for the hand of Lady Helena, your daughter."

The Duke was a diplomat and a mariner; he believed that he had familiarized himself with the most improbable emotions and the most unexpected events, but such a pretention on the part of a man he did not know took him completely aback. For some time he was unable to reply, so much was indignation stifling him.

As for the Captain, he was expecting something enormous, but he had never imagined such a demand, and his smile disappeared to give way to the most visible amazement.

Maxime was still planted before Lord Killyett like a question mark, awaiting his reply.

After a few minutes, the Englishman found his voice again. "Sir," he said, "you're a witty man and I compliment you: the joke is full of humor. You have a fine manner of disarming my anger, and I don't bear you any grudge."

Lord Killyett did not bear Maxime any grudge!

The Captain nearly fell over, but Darnozan did not give him time.

"It's good of you to forgive me," he said, "but I wouldn't like you to labor under an illusion any longer. My request could not be more serious, and you know my conditions. I implore you to give me a response, affirmative or negative."

"Sir," said the noble lord, "my daughter belongs to a family that, if it does not make its alliances in England, wants princes or kings for its heirs. You're not even noble!"

"Oh, my God," said the young man, negligently, "by putting an apostrophe after the *d* in my name, I'd make a very presentable gentleman."

"I said princes or kings," said the Duke, with a cold fury.

"Don't let that hold you back, Milord," said Maxime. "I don't insist on marrying immediately. In six months, if you require it, I'll be a prince—even a king, if necessary, not to say an emperor. Does that suit you?"

Lord Killyett and the Captain stared at Darnozan, who added: "Word of honor, Messieurs!"

"I can't hear any more," said the Duke, "and I thank you for your visit."

That was a dismissal.

"So you refuse, Milord?"

The Commodore assumed an expression of disdainful condescension and replied: "Yes, sir, I refuse."

"You heard that, Captain!" Darnozan exclaimed. "Lord Killyett refused me the hand of his daughter, and you can bear witness to that fact, can you not?"

"Certainly!" said the Captain, with conviction.

"I wish that God gives you a long life, Captain, for you're a worthy man, and you may count on me in future if circumstances become difficult for you. *Salut*, Milord!"

Maxime withdrew.

When the Duke and the Captain were alone, the Master of the *Lapwing*, after God, impressed by Maxime's attitude, said to Helena's father: "You've made a mistake, Milord. That fellow is some prince of the blood in disguise."

"That fellow is insolent," replied the noble lord. "Give me the pleasure of not mentioning him to me again."

Between a fortnight and eighteen days later, the *Lapwing* arrived in San Francisco. During the crossing, since Maxime had made his singular marriage request, there had been no further incident. Only once had Captain Ellis said to Darnozan, laughing: "Well, do you still want to marry Lady Helena?"

"Still!" replied the young man, also smiling. "And you'll see that one day, Lord Killyett will come to offer me her hand, with all manner of respect—but perhaps he'll be too late."

"She's very pretty, Lady Helena."

"Yes, not bad—but there's better, even in England."

"She'll be very rich."

"Oh I don't care a flying fish about that. By asking for Lady Helena's hand I wanted to offer her father an opportunity to repair the outrage he caused me, and since he didn't agree, things will take their course. I assure you, Captain, that he'll regret it very bitterly."

There was no more mention of it until the ship docked. The Duke, the young lady and General Robertson, who formed a clan apart, had maintained a considerable distance between them and the other passengers.

Maxime had not changed his ways in the slightest. He neither avoided not sought out the Duke or his daughter, and when, by chance, he had an opinion to offer, he did not hold back.

Lord Killyett—who, in spite of everything, remembered very clearly being suspended over the sea, from which he probably would not have got out again—had softened his arrogance and drawn in his claws.

At the moment of disembarkation, Darnozan stepped aside to let Lady Killyett, the Commodore and Robertson pass. The last-named, who doubtless shared the other's confidence, saluted Maxime with a hint of irony. "Adieu, Monsieur," he said.

"Oh, General, we'll see one another again, perhaps imminently. Yes, yes, we'll meet again, I hope. That's why I shan't say adieu myself."

Lord Killyett went pass stiff and haughty. The young woman looked at Maxime with a very amiable gaze, and the trio went to take up residence in Montgomery, where a house had been rented and furnished for the Duke and his daughter.

Darnozan, for his part, booked a room in the first hotel he came to. On leaving Auckland he had had no intention of staying in San Francisco for twenty-four hours, but the adventure aboard the *Lapwing* had modified his plans. He booked the room for an indefinite stay.

San Francisco is the ultimate city of adventurers. One cannot count the number of people who have disembarked in California during the last thirty years with the formal intention of making a fortune by hook or by crook; it would be impossible to imagine the courage expended, and the sum of physical and mental energy brought to that corner of the earth. And the historian who could recount the acts of heroism, the infamies, the follies, the temerities and the crimes that have been committed in San Francisco and the surrounding areas during a quarter of a century would need more than a hundred volumes to write the most curious book ever.

Yes, it would be more gripping than the *Divine Comedy* itself, more interesting than *Pantagruel*, the theater of Shakespeare and the gigantic oeuvre of Balzac. Remember that the city has been founded, destroyed, rebuilt, destroyed again, developed and solidified, and has become a powerful metropolis in less than twenty-five years. Imagine, if you can, what must have happened in an alembic where all the constitutive elements of a society are combined in such a short time, and have produced a city as honest as any other.

It is nonetheless true that the sons of the men who founded San Francisco had the blood of adventurers in their veins. It cannot, therefore, be difficult to find among them those whose father have not succeeded as well as others, or who have seen their own efforts turn out badly: men capable of any audacity, who are not frightened by the great filibuster, and who seem expressly made for attack.

Maxime knew that, for, during his career as a mariner he had often come to California, and he had made a great many acquaintances here. The doors there on which one can knock with the greatest certainty of finding bold companions were known to him.

He did not waste any time. Within a fortnight he had assembled a little troop of fifty men, no more than twenty five or thirty years of age, the least valiant of whom had made himself famous in the city by means of three or four notable exploits.

It was not enough to have men, however; to do what Darnozan wanted to do also required money.

Fortunately, he knew the adventurous temperament of those Americans who know how to risk a hundred to gain a thousand. He therefore presented himself in the office of a banker with whom he had once gone to Europe and encountered thereafter in Paris.

After the usual compliments he asked the banker to listen to him, and said to him: "I need twenty thousand dollars. Can you furnish me with them?"

"Yes," the financier replied, "if you give me a guarantee, or allow me to glimpse a more or less considerable profit. In the former case—the guarantee, that is—I can give you them at eight, ten or twelve per cent a year, which is, as you know, the standard rate of interest in San Francisco."

"I have no other guarantee to offer you but my word and my signature."

"Very well. You'll tell me what your plans are, then, and I'll see if I can become a partner. In that case, you'll give me half the profit, or seventy-five per cent a year."

"Listen to me," Maxime continued. "I want to make war on England. Don't take me for a madman. If I explain my plan to you you'll quickly fall into agreement with me that success is possible."

"In America, we admit everything, so I believe that you can succeed. Except that it's not with a hundred thousand francs that you can undertake such a project."

"Obviously. But the twenty thousand dollars I'm asking you for are simply designed to facilitate the acquisition of the sums I need to commence hostilities. I ask you for two years to return that sum, and I accept the seventy-five percent interest."

"Would you care to enter into a few details, for which I promise you, of course, absolute secrecy?"

"I'm counting on it, for those I can make into my officers will only know in Europe, at the moment of action."

Maxime then set out, in half an hour, the details of the plan than he had made.

He had not yet finished when Mr. Thompson, the banker, stopped him. "The twenty thousand dollars," he said, "or even thirty thousand, are now at your disposal. I consider the operation to be entirely excellent. How much do you want?"

"Since you don't see any inconvenience in lending me thirty thousand, I'll take them."

"When?"

"Tomorrow."

Such was the definitive departure point of the astonishing adventure that changed the face of the world, and set against England, at the end of the nineteenth century, an enemy as prodigiously endowed as the gigantic man had been at the beginning, whose army had traveled from one end of Europe to the other. Except that Napoléon had never been able to reach England in his great endeavors—British soil, that is— while Maxime Darnozan was going to attack in Ireland, Scotland, and even London itself.

II. The King of Pola

The next day, Maxime, with the aid of the sums lent by Thompson, charted a steamship for a year and embarked his men, forty-two companions in all, eight of them having refused to serve at the last minute.

As soon as he was in the open sea, Maxime headed southwards for Ecuador and approached the coast. While passing through the mouth of the Guayaquil he assembled all his companions in the ward-room of the *Monterey*.

"Thus far, my friends," he said, "you've been relying on my word, when I promised you glory and fortune in a short time."

"That's true," said a big man, Russian in origin, who called himself Nicolas Ramine, and wore an enormous blonde beard in a fan, like a sun.

"I thank you for that confidence, and I beg you to listen to me.

"Some twenty-eight months ago I came to Guayaquil aboard the *Suzanne*, as first mate, and we remained here for three weeks, the time to load or ship.

"The idea came to me one day to visit Quito, the former capital of the Republic, and I'd been there for twenty-four hours, when, at nine o'clock in the evening, during the market, my attention was attracted by a quarrel. You know, I think, that in all these lands of New Granada and Ecuador, no one puts his nose outdoors between nine o'clock in the morning and seven o'clock in the evening, the heat is so suffocating, so the markets are held between eight and eleven in the evening.

"An Indian, who was selling those admirable straw hats to which the generic name of panamas has been given was surrounded by a dozen ragged soldiers, to whom one always takes care to show a pistol when one encounters them in an out-of-the-way place. They had probably seen the poor Indian sell a few hats, and had got it into their heads to rob him, without deigning to wait in a corner of the woods. A German quarrel was soon sought and found, and our fellows were soon closing in on the poor man.

"If the latter had been alone against one of the bandit soldiers the affair wouldn't have lasted long. He was about forty-five, with robust shoulders, a tall build and whose features respired a veritable majesty. He certainly appeared courageous, and was, for, in spite of the number of his assailants, he got ready to defend himself and gave a rude thump to the first one that laid a hand on him.

"That was the signal for a violent brawl, during which the unfortunate indigene perceived that his pockets were the objective of the rogues he was dealing with. Then he started lashing out more forcefully and shouting like a blind man. The crowd was watching the infamy, laughing. What was it, in fact? A member of the eternal oppressed in the exercise of his functions."

"Personally," said a young man named Pontins, "I would have broken the heads of three or four of the fellows."

"I'm delighted that you share my opinion, Pontins. I launched myself toward the group of soldiers, grabbed one by the back of the neck and shoved him so violently into another that they both fell down, bleeding from the nose, and they started squealing as if they'd been disemboweled. The others, momentarily nonplussed, let go of the Indian, ready to run away, but when they saw that I was alone they rushed me. I had a kind of walking-stick in my hand, a stout liana, to which I imprinted a rapid movement of rotation, and it fell heavily on the head of a soldier twice over.

"There was a marked hesitation among the assailants. They returned to the charge, but I gave them such vigorous blows of the fist and such remarkable kicks that the enraged mob, with whom the entire garrison had joined in, composed of twenty-three men, took to their heels.

"Oh, if the officers had got involved, I would have been doomed, for there were at least eight hundred of them, including a hundred and fifty generals and two hundred colonels— but they didn't, and my Indian was rid of his persecutors.

"The worthy man then came toward me, took my hand and raised it to his lips and his forehead. I advised him to quit the market and go home, but he shook his head. 'I wouldn't get there alive,' he said.

"'What! You think those cowardly blackguards will set an ambush for you?'

"'I'm sure of it.'

"'Well then, I'll go with you,' I said, showing him the pair of revolvers that I had in my pockets, and I left with my protégé.

"Some distance from the city we saw five or six people loomed up in front of us, at which I fired a few bullets. They all vanished, and we didn't have the slightest trouble thereafter with regard to the Indian.

"Like all the poor inhabitants of the region, he had a cabin constructed some four meters above the ground on a framework of four rather voluminous pillars. Underneath the hut three were some fifteen dogs, which barked furiously when they heard us coming, but the fellow called out to them, and they all shut up.

"A rope ladder thrown down by an invisible hand fell from the belvedere and we climbed up to my new friend's home. When we were inside the straw-hat merchant lit a branch of exceedingly resinous wood, which gave off a bright light. I then distinguished a woman, still young, in the one room that constituted the house, who had just woken up, and two children who were asleep.

"'Ata-Capac,' said the Indian, with a certain solemnity, 'is proud to receive here the generous man who protected him. Ata-Capac's hut, wife, children and Ata-Capac himself are at your disposal; you may dispose of them.'

"'Ata-Capac,' I said, 'I am glad to have been useful to you.'

"'Would Ata-Capac's friend like to take maté or *chicha*?'

"'Ata-Capac's friend,' I replied, 'is weary and would like to sleep.'

We had been walking through the night for some time, and I was tired. My host laid down several mats on top of one another, and I lay down.

"When I woke up the next morning it was broad day-light. Ata-Capac was there. When I stood up, he looked at me attentively, but when I turned to the dwelling's only window and the sunlight struck my face the Indian uttered a loud exclamation and bowed down before me.

"When he got up, he said: 'Yes, the man is brave, and he is handsome; he has the marks announced by the sun.'

"Ata-Capac was radiant. Taking three or four steps back, he struck a theatrical pose, inflated his voice, and said: 'Would you like to be a king?'

"I smiled, and told him that the supreme rank didn't tempt me.

"He smiled in his turn and said: 'The time has not come. When you want to be a king, remember Ata-Capac and come to find him.'

"*Good*, I said to myself, as I left, *I've fallen upon a madman.*

"When I got back to Guayaquil, at about half past nine in the morning—which is to say, the hour when there's no longer anyone in the streets but dogs and Frenchmen—I went to see one of my friends, who said, as soon as he saw me, with pointed irony: 'Well, what do you think of the Inca?'

"'The Inca?'

"'Yes. Ata-Capac is, or at least claims to be, the last descendant of the Incas, and he's waiting for the hour to chime to reascend the throne of his forefathers.'

"'Isn't he a little dotty?'

"'No more than anyone else. He's said to be a sorcerer. He reads the destiny of his people in the stars and is in direct communication with the Sun and the Moon.'

"'He has the appearance of a worthy man. What do they think of him in the region?'

"'Everything and nothing.'

"'What's the everything?'

"'The Indians obey him like a supreme chief, and if he wanted to urge them to insurrection tomorrow, it would soon happen, but it's believed that he's waiting for the favorable moment marked by destiny. There are intelligent and learned men who assume that he has the secret of the treasure of the Incas.'

"'What! The treasure of the Incas!' I exclaimed, repeating my friend's last words. 'That reeks damnably of legend. Tell me the story.'

"'You know that the Inca Atahualpa offered Pizarro a chamber filled with gold to the height of a line he drew on the wall as high and he could reach, on condition that his life would be spared. Pizarro took the gold, and murdered the Inca. Huascar, the Inca's brother, had offered on the same conditions a room containing gold from the floor to the ceiling, but when he saw that Atahualpa had been killed...'

"'Wait,' I interrupted. 'He hid his treasure, and the legend says that a family of Indians knows where it's buried.'

"'That's right.'

"'I read that, I think, in the works of the American historian Prescott.'[7]

"'Possibly. Well, it's believed that Ata-Capac is the custodian of the secret.'

"I smiled and didn't think any more about it...until recently. Messieurs, we're going to see Ata-Capac."

"Do you want to be a king, then?" asked Nicolas Ramine.

"Yes," said Darnozan.

"To do what?"

"You'll know when the time comes, in the right place, if you trust me and consent to keep following me."

"And you think," asked Pontins, "that Ata-Capac will give you the treasure?"

"I'm not assuming anything. To carry out the plans I've made, I need money. I have an idea that the worthy Indian can either give me millions, or good advice. That's why I'm going to see him."

A week later, Maxime Darnozan arrived in Quito and went to see the Inca, As soon as the worthy man saw him, he cried: "The time has come! You want to be a king?"

"Yes," Maxime replied.

"You did well to come and to have confidence. You need the gold, don't you? I have it—but before giving it to you, I have to demand an oath from you."

"What oath?"

"First, who are these four men?"

---

[7] William H. Prescott (1796-1859) was a narrative historian who appreciated a god story, but he had a firm commitment to scrupulous research and accuracy. The text that Darnozan read must have been *A History of the Conquest of Peru* (1847).

Darnozan had brought some of his companions with him.

"They're the officers who are going to aid me in my enterprise."

"Good," said Ata-Capac. "they're simply dressed; they're not adorned with gold or crushed by their epaulettes. I like them thus."

"What is it necessary to swear?" Maxime asked.

"Swear," said the benevolent Indian, resuming his emphatic tone, "that on the day when you are the most powerful sovereign in the world, you will reestablish Ata-Capac on the throne of his ancestors."

"I swear it with all my heart," said Darnozan.

"And you?" demanded the Inca. "Will you swear too?"

Each of Maxime's companions made the oath in his turn. Then Ata-Capac said to them: "Come."

He took them into the virgin forest by a path that seemed difficult, but which the Indian must have trodden incessantly. After half an hour's march, he stopped on the bank of a rather narrow stream, whose course—which is very rare—was not obstructed by any obstacle.

At the very spot to which he had led Darnozan and his four friends there was a waterfall ten meters high, coming from another stream.

Ata-Capac climbed up the rock from which the cascade was falling, and demolished two small walls to the right and left of the fall. The water, which had all been flowing through the center, stopped dead, in order to flow to either side through the outlets that the Indian had just opened.

The rock that the water had hidden as it fell a few seconds before was suddenly laid bare. The Indian applied a kind of ladder to it, which was already prepared, climbed up, and, shoving the wall violently, caused a section of basalt to rotate inwards, detached as if by magic.

Ata-Capac went in and invited Darnozan to follow him. The treasure was there. Maxime was not dazzled, for the good reason that the gold of vases, plates and chains had been tarnished by time, and it was necessary to know that it was gold in order to form an idea of the wealth that the mysterious hiding-place contained.

"Take what you wish," said Ata-Capac.

Darnozan could not make an exact calculation of the sum that it was necessary to take away for the sum that he needed. Knowing what a gram of gold is worth, however, he took away, or had taken, around two thousand kilograms of the precious metal.

"Is that enough?" he Indian asked.

"Yes."

"In any case, if you need more, you can come back. There's twenty times as much."

"Ata-Capac put the mobile stone back in place, reconstructed the little walls on each side of the rocky summit in order to force the cascade to pass through the middle and hide the opening of the hiding-place, and then he came back to Darnozan.

The latter was greatly encumbered by his treasure.

"How are we going to transport this gold?" he asked his wonderstruck companions. "It will be difficult—almost impossible."

"No," said Ata-Capac. "This is what will help you." And, taking hold of a long liana that was hanging within arm's reach, he tugged it like a rope. A perfectly constructed raft, of large dimensions and serious solidity, was then seen to move and approach the bank.

"Ata-Capac will be the Inca! I swear it again!" said Darnozan, enthusiastically.

The gold was embarked on the raft.

"The stream is clear as far as the Guayaquil," said the Indian. "Once on the great river..."

"We'll take care of the rest."

The adventurers embarked. Darnozan hugged the Indian effusively, and said: "How shall I ever repay such a debt?"

"There is no debt. You saved my life, and in any case, you have the announced signs in your face. Even if you had not rendered me a service, I would have obeyed the gods by giving you a part of my treasure. I am the last descendant of the legitimate heir of Huascar. But don't waste time. Go!"

Darnozan and is friends embarked, paddled into open water, and after seven hours of difficult navigation reached Guayaquil, where the *Monterey* was waiting for them.

They immediately put to sea again, and eighteen days later they reached the Navigators' Archipelago and took possession of the island of Pola,[8] where, without an hour's delay, Maxime had himself proclaimed king by the men who had accompanied him, and who, henceforth, were indissolubly attached to his fortune.

A ministry was immediately constituted. The cabinet was constituted by three departments: the Navy, attributed to a young man of Russian origin named Ivan Kasaloff, who as animated by a blind hatred of the English; War, whose title-holder was named Octave Kellner, an Alsatian;[9] and finally, Foreign Affairs, which was given to the only one among Maxime's bold comrades who bore an aristocratic name, Monsieur le Comte de Boislucas, the last descendant of a French family that had settled in Canada in the time of Montcalm.

Before leaving San Francisco, Maxime had had ministerial headed notepaper printed bearing the words:

KINGDOM OF POLA
Ministry of Foreign Affairs

---

[8] The Navigator Islands, or Navigators' Archipelago, was the name given to the Samoan Islands by the First Frenchman to visit them—the Comte de Bougainville, during his circumnavigation of the globe, in 1768—although it had fallen out of use long before 1885. Pola is a small uninhabitable islet off Tutuila, and is now part of the National Park of American Samoa.

[9] Debans' first novel was entitled *Octave Kellner*, but I have not been able to consult a copy in order to ascertain whether this is the same character.

37

Monsieur de Boislucas entered into his functions immediately, and signified the accession of Maxime-Jean I to the throne of Pola.

People still remember the fit of hilarity that took possession of Europe when it was learned that a new king had just been proclaimed.

The radical newspapers of France, above all, lent themselves to it with a joyful heart. One of them entitled its article: *Another King of Araucania*[10] and informed its readers, in very amusing language, that the new sovereign, doubtless to economize on the expenses of the voyage and the representation of his ambassadors, had simply sent the notification of his accession by post.

That extra-official document, sent by post, added a good deal of good humor to the carnival of 1885, and the newspapers of all shades exploited that mine of jokes with a veritable success.

In the meantime, the King of Pola set off for Marseilles. Before quitting the land that constituted his kingdom, Darnozan had written the following letter to Lord Killyett:

Milord.

In accordance with the promise I made you, I am now, since yesterday, a sovereign prince. A powerful party has proclaimed me King of Pola. I am asking you once again for the hand of Lady Helena. I can assure her, have no doubt about it, the highest destiny. Please let me know your decision by tele-

---

[10] The French adventurer Orélie-Antoine de Tounens assumed the title of King of Araucania and Patagonia in 1860, with the support of the indigenous Mapuche tribesmen, who were attempting to defend the region from in invading Chilean Army. He published his memoirs in 1863 after being deported to France by the Chileans; he returned to Araucania twice more in hopeless attempts to resurrect his kingdom and eventually came to be seen as a rather pathetic joke.

graph, addressed to M. Ivan Kasaloff, poste restante, Marseilles.

May God keep you in his divine protection

Maxime-Jean.

"Poste restante" was even more comical than "by post," but Darnozan did not care about being ridiculed for six months. He knew that if ridicule kills people, the terrible also kills ridicule, and even more promptly.

At the end of February the King of Pola disembarked in Marseilles with his forty-one companions. During the crossing, the forty-second having treated the king too familiarly and told him a few truths in the fashion of the old Aragonese Cortès, Darnozan had had him put in irons for forty-eight hours. A few days later, the same individual had tried to urge the others to revolt; Maxime had blown his brains out and had his body thrown into the sea.

When a man who is known to be honest takes it upon himself to commit murder, it is necessary that he feels his conscience to be square and calm for him to act in that way, and the energetic act probably costs him less than the moral responsibility he assumes.

The other companions were on the defensive for two or three days, ready to mutiny if the opportunity was offered, but the one that the malcontents considered as their leader having accidentally fallen into the sea, Maxime dived in without getting undressed and saved his life. From then on, all the men were devoted to him body and soul.

The man he had pulled out of the water, in his gratitude and after having conferred with his friends, even went so far as to confess that he had been on the point of heading a rebellion against him.

"I knew that," he said.

That reply stupefied the adventurer, who exclaimed: "And you risked your life to save me?"

"Yes, my friend. I had divined that you were all excited against me, but I know you; I've studied you and the others during the journey. I know now that there isn't one among you who is capable of an infamous action. You, in particular, Lamanon, I believe to be a valuable man, and I'm counting on you to accomplish prodigies when the time comes."

"But in sum, what are we going to do?"

"You'll find out in Marseilles. Just know this: I promise you a considerable fortune and an even greater glory."

Maxime spoke with such confidence, and had been seen to be so valiant in difficult circumstances, that not one of the men doubted his promises.

Several times, the King, as he was definitively called, joined in with his officer's games, and every time he proved to them that he was the most agile, the most vigorous, the most adroit, the most intrepid and the most intelligent of them all.

By the time the ship entered the Gulf of Aden, his people adored him.

It was him alone who, with an incomparable surety of gaze and a rare maritime expertise, had piloted the *Monterey* through the innumerable islands of Oceania. After having traversed the La Pérouse Archipelago he had navigated through the Louisiades, the Strait of Torres, skirted the Moluccas and the Celebes, reached the Sea of Java and the Sunda strait, astonishing his men every day by his knowledge and skill as a mariner.

When they entered the Red Sea he had charged Kasaloff, Kellner, Lamanon and four others in whom he had every confidence with landing on the isle of Perim.[11]

"I have the intention," he told them, "of conquering that island, which commands the Red Sea, at some stage. I need you to inform me as to whether it's necessary to land directly in front of the English fortifications, or whether it's easy to disembark at an undefended point. As you set forth on the

---

[11] The island of Perim, in the Strait of Mandeb at the southern entrance to the Red Sea, had been occupied by the British in 1857 (and remained so, in our history, until 1967).

mission, keep it in mind that I want to take the position by surprise."

The seven adventurers remained on the island for thirty-six hours. They found an inlet that could contain one or two vessels, and where a disembarkation could not be easier. The English garrison appeared to them to be sufficient, without being too numerous.

That was all that Maxime wanted to know.

As soon as he arrived in Marseilles, where he disembarked under an assumed name, as every sovereign who travels incognito knows how to do, the King sent Kasaloff to the telegraph office to see whether Lord Killyett had replied to his letter.

Lord Killyett had not deigned to telegraph a *yes* or *no*.

"So it goes, as they say in these parts," said Darnozan, when Kasaloff had informed him of the fact. "Council of war on board, ten o'clock this evening."

At the appointed hour, when all his people had gathered, Maxime-Jean spoke.

"You've understood, I think," he said, "that it wasn't only to take away Ata-Capac's treasure that I took you to Quito. That would be scarcely five hundred thousand francs each—less, because we have debts—and I'm sure that you nourish higher ambitions.

"We're going into action. On the road that I shall enable you to travel you'll reap a great deal of glory and huge fortunes, but have no doubt about it, there will also be blows to suffer. Several of us will probably not see the end of the epic of which I dream, and it's necessary that you envisage the future realistically. The enterprise that I'm about to undertake with you is gigantic; perhaps you'll think I'm mad, for what I want to do seems impossible. The world, at any rate, will believe us to be insane when it hears of our audacity.

"I want, as King of Pola, to declare war on England."

At these words there was a stir in his audience.

"That astonishes you," said Maxime-Jean. "I expected that. So, I leave each of you free to abandon me and return to

41

America. Let those who think me too bold not hesitate to leave me. I don't want semi-courages and flaccid devotions with me."

"Pardon me, Sire," said Zampironi.

"Keep calling my Commandant—you can call me Sire when we have a fleet—which won't be long."

"Well, Commandant, that's exactly what I was going to say. To make war on England will require a fleet. You can't buy a squadron of ironclads with four million."

"You're right, Zampironi; but with my four million I can conquer one."

"Listen, Messieurs," said Kasaloff.

"Here," the King went on, "are forty wads of cash, of a hundred thousand francs each. Except for Boislucas and me, each of you will take one."

Boislucas advanced and distributed the wads to Maxime's companions.

The King continued: "Now, you're still free to go, and anyone who abandons me will keep the hundred thousand francs, while those who remain with me—the faithful—must make use of every last sou for the purpose that I shall reveal to them."

There was a terrible silence. All the men looked at one another. Kasaloff, Kellner and Boislucas had grim expressions.

"No one has any intention of quitting," said Nicolas Ramine, finally.

"No one!" replied several voices.

"Good! And are you all determined to make war on England?"

"Yes!"

"All!"

"All!"

"All!"

"Thank you. During my sojourn in San Francisco I sent an agent to London to scout things out thoroughly. This is what I've learned.

"Two English ironclads are about to leave for the Bermudas. Nicolas Ramine, you'll take for lieutenants Messieurs Prytz, of Budapest and Joshua Klett of Chicago. You'll collect in the American ports all the sailors you can find in quest of adventures, and you'll take possession of one of those vessels."

"How?" asked Nicolas Ramine, quite calmly.

"You'll set fire to one of them, and when the crew of the other goes to its aid, you'll invade the latter and sail away at full steam."

"Yes, Commandant. What are the names of the two ships?"

"The *Achilles* and the *Valorous*."

"And which should we set fire to?"

"The *Valorous*. The *Achilles* has a far superior speed and her armaments are more modern. We'll find sufficient money, food and munitions aboard to go on campaign. Prytz, and you, Joshua, will obey Nicolas Ramine, whom I appoint as captain of the *Achilles*. I hope that it won't be long before you have the opportunity to command a vessel too."

"Will it be necessary to debaptize my ship?"

"No, my friend. We'll take a veritable pleasure in thrashing the English with ships whose names are familiar to them."

"What flag should we fly?"

"The flag of Pola, of course: sky blue with four golden swallows and the motto: *Everywhere*, with a negro's head at the top of the flagstaff."

"Very good, Commandant. When do we leave?"

"In one hour. Take this letter; it contains all your instructions and indicates the port of rendezvous to which it's necessary to go when you've succeeded.

"You, Pedro Cabanil, will depart for Valparaiso. There's an English squadron there. It might be at Callao or some other point on the Pacific. Do you know how to manufacture torpedoes?"[12]

"Yes, Commandant."

"Well, I leave it to you to choose between fire or explosion. If you can bring me two ships, that would be good."

"I'll try."

"You know that in the Southern Seas there are old two-deckers that have been transformed and are known as station ironclads.[13] They're the equivalent of French armored corvettes."

"I know them, Commandant."

"Take Ybarrondo, the valiant Basque, with you as second in command, and the American Fielding. If the three of you don't achieve prodigies, it's because I'm mistaken on your account. Come forward Weenix, honest Dutchman; do you know Halifax?"

"In Canada, yes, Commandant."

"There's also a squadron of station ironclads there, but it will need all your wisdom and your keen eyes to succeed. Plan the affair well. Use torpedoes or mineral oil, as you choose."

"But Commandant, it would be better not to sink your boats and bring them to you intact."

"Certainly."

"Give me Capmartin and Zampironi for companions—they're clever fellows, and I assure you that it won't go awry."

---

[12] As will become clear in the course of the story, the term *torpille* [torpedo] did not refer in 1885 to the kind of self-propelled device to which the word is applied nowadays, but to explosive devices that had to be planted or delivered, as it were, by hand. Most of those featured in the plot could be described as "mines" in modern terminology.

[13] I have translated the French *cuirassé de station* literally as "station ironclad," although the term was rarely used in English, which had no specific term for the class of armored cruisers in question.

"No, take Etchegoyen, the other Basque; I'm keeping Capmartin for a special mission. But don't be under any illusion; if there are more than two corvettes, use fore and torpedoes—the rest would be too dangerous, and I need you all."

"Very good, Commandant."

"Here are your instructions. You, Lamanon, know that there's an English ironclad—only one—at Salonika. One can find Greeks who make excellent corsairs on all the islands of the archipelago, and they're not demanding with regard to pay. It's necessary to steal that vessel by force."

"Yes, Commandant."

"Capmartin, you'll do the same at Smyrna."

"I'm ready."

"Perfect. Now, is there a man here audacious enough to attempt the incendiary coup under the guns of Gibraltar?"

"Me, Commandant," said a young blond man, who scarcely had a light down on his upper lip. He took a few steps forward.

"You, Pontins. Which companion do you want?"

"I'd like to operate alone."

"How will you do that?"

"I'll go to Salé on the Moroccan coast, where there are three or four thousand fellows who've been getting mightily bored for fifteen years and who'd do it for nothing—just think what they'll do if I give them twenty francs a head, in a country where three sous a day makes you rich."

"Go on, then, Pontins; I'm counting on you."

Maxime-Jean then designated three men for Malta and added: "Messieurs, the attacks must take place on the same day, at the same time. As soon as Lamanon, Capmartin and the Malta team have their prizes, they'll head at full steam for Gibraltar. Pontins having probably drawn the ironclads that he hasn't destroyed into the Ocean, the strait will be free. They'll head out. Let none of you forget, Messieurs, to hire double shifts of engineers and stokers."

"Of course!"

"Once in the Atlantic, you don't let any English merchant ship pass without imposing a tax of two thousand pounds sterling. Those that refuse are to be captured and taken to the rendezvous. They'll serve as supply-ships and squadron messengers."

Maxime-Jean designated seven more groups of three men, who were sent to Shanghai, Yokohama, Nagasaki, Singapore, Aden, Cape Town and Rio de Janeiro. They all had analogous orders.

He only kept five companions with him: his three ministers, Kasaloff, Kellner and Boislucas; and two of the boldest of his forty faithful, a Parisian named Robert who was bravery incarnate, and a man named Sancy, born in California of French parents.

When he had given everyone his task, he spoke again.

"Messieurs," he said, "we're about to undertake a colossal task. I want to found the Empire of the Seas. I want all the islands of the globe to belong to us one day. England, which has acquired the greatest maritime power in the world, once played an infamous comedy in order to take possession of the Isthmus of Suez, which she had coveted for a long time. She made a fool of Europe with the complicity of Arabi, and Europe remained calm. Europe didn't jib, and allowed the route of Oceania to be stolen. Well, Messieurs, what Europe dared not do, we shall attempt, with God's aid. We'll attack England on her favorite ground, on all the seas; we'll beat her—at least, I hope so; we'll diminish her, destroy her, and thus accomplish the greatest act of justice of modern times."

"*Vive le Commandant!!!*" cried forty voices, in unison.

"Now, my friends, listen to the most important thing. Today, it's the sixteenth of March 1885. It's on the night of the fifteenth and sixteenth of June that you must take possession of our first instrument of conquest, a fleet. The night of the fifteenth and sixteenth of June! Go, Messieurs; let all of you set forth this evening."

III. The King's Fleet

One month later, a ship bearing a sky blue flag with four swallows, and exposing, when the breeze deployed it, the motto *Everywhere* embroidered in the center, sailed into the Thames and moored in London. The next day, all the British newspapers announced, with the glacial gaiety particular to the English, that an ambassador from the King of Pola had just arrived.

The *Standard* entitled its article *The King of Pola Exposes Himself*, which made many readers laugh.

There was no longer gaiety, however, but delirium, when they learned that the ambassador from Pola had come to London uniquely to negotiate with Her Majesty's government on the question of the Suez Canal—and all of England was gripped by inextinguishable laughter when the *Times* revealed to the world that the King of Pola, in his capacity as a Oceanian sovereign, claimed to have the right to regulate the affairs of Egypt, and especially the Suez Canal.

Today, when events have occurred with lightning rapidity, and we know what has happened, the hilarity of England does not seem to us to be very witty, but at the time, as one can assure oneself by reading the newspapers, all of Europe joined in chorus with the English, and quips fell like hail upon the government of His Majesty Maxime-Jean I.

Monsieur de Boislucas, who was fulfilling the functions of Extraordinary Ambassador, was arriving from a general tour of Europe, where he had had the disappointment of finding that no government wanted to recognize his sovereign.

"They don't want to recognize me?" said Maxime-Jean, at that news. "Well, so be it—they'll make my acquaintance."

The wordplay was regal, and has become historic.[14]

---

[14] It qualifies as wordplay in France because of the identical roots of *reconnaitre* [to recognize] and *connaitre* [to know, in the sense of being acquainted with].

Endowed with an aplomb too American to be disconcerted, Monsieur de Boislucas solicited an interview with Lord Granville, who did not reply.[15] He did not experience any very extraordinary emotion in consequence. He was seen incessantly traveling the streets of London, costumed in sky blue velvet, successively visiting the representatives of all the great powers.

As he had an imposing appearance and his stare was not easy to sustain, people welcomed him politely, listened to him, bade him farewell, and that was all. He was soon well-known to all the idlers in Regent Street.

In the meantime, Maxime Darnozan and young Robert installed themselves in Woolwich, in the midst of the maritime population of that miniature city, and as they both spoke English admirably, they passed unnoticed. Maxime rented a large building close to the arsenal, empty or the time being, which had been used as a rubber factory. It was a quadrangular edifice three stories high, in the middle of which was a vast courtyard whose existence could not be suspected from outside.

When they took up residence they lived in a very retired fashion. In the early days, a few items of furniture, some large wicker baskets and a few other voluminous objects were moved in. No one paid any great heed; there was nothing abnormal in that.

From time to time, Maxime went into London and met Boislucas there in secret. Then he came back to Woolwich, from which Robert never budged.

In spite of his activity, his urbanity and his persistence, Monsieur de Boislucas was not received officially by Lord

---

[15] Granville Leveson-Gower, the second Earl Granville (1815-1891) was the Secretary of State for Foreign Affairs in the Liberal government led by his great friend William Gladstone, which was in office when the present story was written, and was, in fact, still in office in our history at the indicated date, although he was soon to be replaced.

Granville. He immediately addressed himself to Mr. Gladstone, but Mr. Gladstone showed no sign of life. In spite of his lack of success, Boislucas retained an affable, equable character and was certainly a personification of the ideal diplomat.

That went on for more than six weeks, at the end of which, he informed the newspapers that if the ministers did not wish to talk to him, he would be forced to resort to an unpleasant extreme.

His letter was published, and people were amused by it, as before.

On the third of June, he addressed an ultimatum to the Foreign Office, which he communicated to the press himself, on the fourth, the delay of the ultimatum having expired, he raised his flag and sent, via the lieutenant of the *Monterey*, a declaration of war drafted in the form customary in such cases.

The next day, the *Monterey* raised anchor before the eyes of an enormous crowd whose members had come to try to catch a glimpse the singular ambassador of a microscopic king who had just proudly issued a challenge to England. And they laughed!

"*Honni soit qui mal y pense!*" murmured Boislucas. "And, the proverb being equally apt, *he who laughs last laughs longest.*"

The next day, the weather was bad. The wind blew tempestuously, and although it was the end of spring, it was rather cold.

Toward the end of the afternoon, the rare inhabitants of Woolwich who were observing the state of the sky through their closed windows saw a series of small balloons rise into the air successively above the building in which Maxime was living and disappear toward the north-east after having floated over the arsenal.

They thought that the two tenants of the building had devised those minuscule ascensions to relieve the boredom. It would have needed a great deal of imagination to deduce the true motive for the little aerostats. Darnozan was launching them to make sure that they passed precisely over the construction yards, with the result that when dusk fell and the darkness thickened, one might have seen, if it had been possible to distinguish anything in the blackness of the night, another balloon—a veritable and large balloon—departing very slowly in the same direction.

There was a man in the nacelle, and a brave one, for it was not a good idea to risk oneself in an aerostat in such weather. Under the efforts of the gusts of wind, the balloon lay almost horizontal in the air, all the more so because it was solidly retained by a heavy cable unwound around a windlass operated by another man.

When the airship was directly over the construction yards, it stopped. The man dropped a rope-ladder, climbed over the edge of the nacelle and descended. Having arrived at the bottom rung, he gently slackened a cord that he was holding in his left hand, and which rose up to the nacelle. A sealed bucket arrived just above his head. He took it, and having opened it, spread its contents in a determined location over a fairly large area.

The he climbed back into his aerostat and made a signal, which was understood, for the balloon descended back into the courtyard again. Five minutes later, it set off again, and the same maneuver was executed, a little further away this time. The contents of the bucket were spread against the door and over the roof of a vast munitions store.

Two more ascents were carried out, with the same result.

Finally, at about one o'clock in the morning, the balloon went up again, but this time with two passengers in the nacelle. Four full and uncovered buckets were suspended outside. The first was lowered over the roofing of the yards and inverted there. Immediately, a rope soaked in inflammable liquid lit up in the darkness and snaked down to the ground, where fire burst forth over a wide extent. A little further on, the second bucket was released and ignited like the first, then the third and the fourth—and he balloon, which was no longer captive, plunged unperceived into the darkness of the night.

A gigantic conflagration had just burst forth in the foremost arsenal in the world. An hour later, all the construction yards were nothing but a furnace. An immense crowd, drawn to the scene of the catastrophe, contemplated the disaster. Two or three powder-stores blew up. It was frightful. The stocks of cartridges, grenades and shells exploded in the bunkers, which became utterly unapproachable as a result.

The violent wind that was blowing threatened to carry the flames toward the East End of the city, and all the efforts of the firemen had to be concentrated on private properties—which they did, in fact, succeed in preserving.

The next day, when England learned about the event, there was profound amazement everywhere.

What! Woolwich, the pride of Great Britain, the arsenal that seemed to contain, with all its engines of war, the security of the United Kingdom! Woolwich destroyed! Woolwich a heap of rubble and ash! People did not want to believe it.

It was, however, necessary to yield to the evidence—and then there was an explosion of fury. The Irish Fenians were accused, and the entire police force mobilized. It was not so much the material loss that afflicted opulent England, although it exceeded several million pounds sterling; it was the destruction of a enormous quantity of munitions, the annihilation of inventions of every sort, and innumerable vessels containing equipment and fitments that had been perfected over two centuries.

The majority of the English were under no illusion: it was an irreparable misfortune; and from one end of Great Britain to the other there was an enormous agitation. People went so far as to hold meetings, in which Her Majesty's government was held to blame because, it was said, it had lacked vigilance. Some orators, more impetuous than others were even talking about the dismissal of the minister responsible.

And yet, the English were not at the end of their troubles.

At the very moment when the emotion was at its most violent, in fact, the telegraph brought frightful, unexpected news from all parts of the globe, which drove the exasperation of the public to new heights.

On the morning of the sixteenth of June, before any newspaper had mentioned it, the rumor spread through the City that three ironclad ships—three of the most beautiful specimens of naval artistry, whose turrets were armed with thirty-six ton cannons with a range of seven to eight miles—had been set ablaze during the night in Portsmouth.

Soon, it was reported that another vessel had similarly gone up in flames in the harbor of Plymouth.

This time, there was no more doubt. It was not bad luck; it was powerfully-organized and systematic destruction. Again, the Fenians were accused, and then there was talk of anarchists and invincibles[16]—but the majority of the English openly accused the Irish and demanded that all those who were suspected should be massacred pitilessly. The population of England was going crazy.

And yet, they were still unaware of the most serious fact. At Portsmouth—or, to be more accurate, in the harbor of Spithead, which is where the conflagration had take place, only two vessels had burned, the *Inflexible* and the *Superb*, while the third, the *Monarch*, had disappeared, vanishing completely.

When the mariners of the *Monarch*, having set off in their launches with the pumps in order to bring aid to the two ships in flames, came back again, the ship was no longer there, having been stolen from them, with the height of audacity, almost before their eyes.

In Plymouth, things were worse. Only one vessel had been burned, the *Temeraire*, but two others, among the most

---

[16] The invincibles were a splinter group of the Irish Republican Brotherhood (popularly known as the Fenians), most famously responsible for the "Phoenix Park murders" of 1882, when Gladstone, nephew, Lord Frederick Cavendish, the Chief Secretary for Ireland, and the senior civil servant Thomas Henry Burke were assassinated.

admirable vessels in the fleet, the *Alexandra* and the *Northumberland*, had been seized by force during the blaze, and had headed out to sea, where they had been lost to sight. At the same time, explosions of dynamite destroyed the forts of Plymouth, whose cannons remained mute.

In all, therefore, six vessels had been lost.

And that was still not all. Toward midday a dispatch was received from Halifax announcing that adventurers had tried to set fire to the gunboat *Cygnet* and take possession of a station ironclad, which was under steam.

Fortunately, the dispatch added, *the attempt failed, thanks to the energy and vigilance of Mr. Meyr, the captain of the vessel.*

It went on: *A large number of the sea-raiders with whom we had to deal escaped, but we captured about fifty, among them a Dutchman named Weenix, who had organized the act of piracy, and will probably be hanged tomorrow after being court-martialed.*

That was a setback for Maxime—but at Salonika the coup had succeeded, as it had in Bermuda, and at Malta too.

In Gibraltar, Pontins, with five thousand Riff pirates, had not deigned to employ fire. He took the *Warrior* and the *Defence* by boarding, having encountered them four miles out to sea under the cannon of the redoubtable fortress.

Each of these news items arrived in its turn in London during the sixteenth of June, increasing the exasperation further. When it was learned that two vessels had been stolen at Gibraltar, there was an explosion of rage—and yet the English still had to learn about the success of William Smith in Singapore. The latter, making use of a torpedo, had destroyed the *Valiant* and captured the *Repulse*.

Joe Green, at Cape Town, had also succeeded. His prize was the *Hercules*.

Pedro Cabanil had not succeeded in taking a ship in Valparaiso—he had not had enough men—but at least he had burned two, the *Condor* and the *Bittern*.

Finally, James Kobb, the big Kentuckian, on whom Darnozan was counting heavily, and who had delivered his coup in Shanghai, had put too much trust in his lucky star; he had attacked with too few men. The fire on the *Invincible*, poorly set, had been extinguished in a matter of minutes, and when Kobb had tried to take the *Lord Warden* he had been confronted by an enemy far superior in number. His followers had jumped into the sea while he, not wanting to retreat, had died heroically.

Nevertheless, the fact was that during that fatal night, the government of Great Britain had lost twenty-one ships in total, the flower of the navy. Of that number, eight had been burned or blown up, and thirteen were in the hands of an unknown enemy—but who, as the *Standard* put it so well, did not take long to expose himself.

Indeed, that same evening, the *Times* received the following letter addressed to the editor:

Sir,

I am sending you a copy of the letter that I have sent this instant to the government of Her Very Gracious Majesty Queen Victoria. By publishing it, you will inform your compatriots how and why England has lost a substantial part of her war fleet. You will also let the English people know that the King of Pola demands the return of his officer Weenix, or, at least, that he should be treated as a prisoner of war.
pp The Ministry of Foreign Affairs

Boislucas

The letter addressed to Mr. Gladstone was thus conceived:

I inform you, Milord, that it is my terrestrial and naval troops that destroyed Woolwich Arsenal on the fifth of this months, and your fleet on the night of the fifteenth and sixteenth. You have not deigned to listen to my ambassador. You can see that I am in a position to support his claims. I imagine that people are no longer laughing at the King of Pola in the United Kingdom. A dispatch from Halifax informs me that my officer Weenix, erroneously considered as a pirate, is under threat of a court martial. I demand that the brave mariner in question is treated as the prisoner of war that he is. On the third of June I had my ultimatum delivered to you, and of the fourth of May my declaration of war; everything is in order. I offer in exchange for Captain Weenix one of the high-ranking prisoners that I took aboard your vessels, but if you do not order the Governor of Canada by telegram to refrain from convening any court martial, I shall hang an English Commodore from either side of my mainmast.

May God keep and protect you,

Maxime-Jean

The King of Pola, in writing thus, was perhaps not acting in accordance with the rules and formulas of protocol, but he said—and clearly—what he meant to say.

That letter to Mr. Gladstone was sent from Portsmouth, and bore the postmark of that city. Maxime-Jean was, therefore, in England. That really was pushing audacity beyond the limits of plausibility.

Maxime had, indeed, remained in Portsmouth—or, to be more precise, had taken up residence in Southsea, which forms an integral whole with Portsmouth and is considerably larger than the original city.

He had waited there for news, and he knew now which of his lieutenants had succeeded and those who had failed.

The dispatch from Halifax had arrived at an early hour. After writing his letter, the King of Pola had then gone to the High Street, Portsmouth's main street, where he had met up with an Irish friend. The latter, a certain O'Regan, had volunteered to take Darnozan out to sea, and kept his word. Kasaloff, was waiting for Maxime-Jean with the *Monarch*, which immediately set a course for the port at which he was to wait for his lieutenants.

Not far from Madeira there is a group of islets—or, rather, rocks—known as the Salvage Isles. It was there that Maxime-Jean had arranged to rendezvous with all his forces. The Salvage Isles do not produce anything; they are uninhabited, but they form a series of channels that terminate off the largest in a large, comfortable and admirably sheltered bay.

The place was marvelously chosen for meeting up and waiting without risk for the arrival of the vessels that were to constitute the King of Pola's fleet.

Naturally, it was Pontins who was the first to arrive at the indicated anchorage. He left one of his ships there and set off in the other to lie in ambush for the steamers of the United Steamship Company.

There were two of them; one heading for the Cape, the other returning to England. At a stroke, Pontins informed them as to how serious the King of Pola's declaration of war was, took them prisoner, took cognizance of what they had aboard, took all the money they had aboard in cash or gold powder, and set them free.

Pontins returned to the Salvage Isles just as Maxime-Jean was arriving there. The *Monarch*, the *Alexandra* and the *Northumberland*, as well as three wooden ships, formed a very respectable squadron under his command. Maxime had put his flag on the *Monarch*, whose crew, like those of the other two ships, was exclusively composed of Irishmen.

The three months that had elapsed since the departure from Marseilles and the night of action had been utilized by Kellner and Kasaloff in a manner that denoted great qualities of activity and skill on their part. Scouring the ports of Ireland, they had found ten times as many sailors as they needed for the task they were preparing. Al those irreconcilable enemies of England had made their way individually to Portsmouth, Southsea, Stonehouse, Devonport and Plymouth, and when the moment came to act, they had hurled themselves at the English ships with all the fury that two or three centuries of hatred can give to a people.

That had facilitated the mission of Kasaloff, who, with Sancy under his orders, had sworn to capture two vessels and had kept his word.

Kellner, who had carried out the coup in Portsmouth with Maxime and Robert, had also employed the Irish, more than fifteen hundred of whom had come, four or five hundred of them diehards.

Boislucas, after having quit London with the *Monterey*, had not wanted to come back empty-handed; that is why he had captured the Royal Mail's *Tamar* and the Pacific Steam Navigation Company's *Aconguada*. He arrived at the rendezvous three days after the king's three ironclads. Nicolas Ramine dropped anchor the following day with the *Achilles*.

The English vessels were abundantly provisioned with everything: food, money and coal. Maxime-Jean was able to wait for the hour to act, prudently keeping under steam.

Only one thing worried him: the impossibility, in that mysterious anchorage, of receiving news.

England could, in fact, put a fleet to sea without him knowing anything about it. In order to get around hat inconvenience, he sent Boislucas to Madeira, with orders to come back if any grave news reached the island. Lamanon and Capmartin, one returning from Smyrna, where the Greeks had lent him powerful assistance, and the other from Salonika, soon arrived. They had encountered two vessels, before which they had manned battle stations—and it was as well that they had, for they had been attacked. The combat had lasted two and a half hours, after which the English ships had retreated eastwards, where the two adventurers had thought it best not to pursue them.

"We're only waiting for William Smith and Joe Green," said Pontins, "for Cabanil will be obliged to reach Europe by another route than he's hoped."

"There's also Vorides, who's at Nagasaki, and of whom there's no news; the Mexican Garcia, whom I sent to Yokohama; and Magese, to Hong Kong. Big Brown was in Rio de Janeiro, but I learned that there was only a single English ship off the Brazilian capital. Finally, we're also waiting for Paleieff, who, I hope, will bring us an ironclad from Malta, and who ought to be here already."

A cannon shot was heard; it was Paleieff, coming back with the *Minotaur*.

"Messieurs," the King went on, "we're now complete. If I can count, we have six first-class battleships here. Each of those who captured them will remain the captain, but I'm dividing our forces into three squadrons; the first, comprising the *Monarch*, the *Alexandra*, the *Minotaur*, the *Northumberland* and the *Achilles*, under my immediate command, with Nicolas Ramine as chief of the squadron; the second, comprising the five other vessels here, under the orders of Kasaloff."

Everyone looked at him.

"And the third?" asked Pontins.

"The third, Messieurs, is already placed under the orders of William Smith, and as I speak, ought to have taken possession of the island of Perim, which is the key to the Red Sea. He will hold it until circumstances permit him to leave a garrison there and join us here."

"And what are we going to do?" asked Paleieff.

"We," the King replied, "are going to organize the crews of our ships in such a way as to have no need of Pontins' Moroccans. Those worthy Muslims imagine that they're going to see the return of the great days of ancient Algerian piracy. Let's not lose any time in demonstrating the contrary, contenting ourselves with disseminating the best of them between the nine vessels and depositing the others on the Moroccan coast at the first opportunity."

"Good—but that doesn't..."

"Be good enough, Monsieur Paleieff, not to interrupt me. From this moment on, I am, definitively, your King." Maxime-Jean pronounced those words in a tone that admitted no reply. He continued: "I don't believe I'm mistaken in anticipating that Great Britain will equip a fleet in less than a month to hunt us down. We'll wait until our adversaries put to sea. Until then, let each of the officers carry out a triage of his matelots, allocating to the cannons those who know how to aim a gun, and training the others to man the ships."

Six days later, the *Monterey* returned to the Salvage Isles. As soon as the ship was within a few cables of the *Monarch*, Boislucas put a launch to sea and came to see the King.

"Sire," he said to him, "William Smith, Vorides, Magese and Garcia have taken Perim without firing a shot and are solidly installed there. England has put seven battleships and two frigates on a war footing, which are about to set out for the Red Sea."

"When is the fleet setting out?"

"The dispatches say that it will leave Portsmouth on the thirty-first of July."

"Very good, Messieurs; we'll go to wait for it off the coast of Spain, and I hope to show you that I'm worthy to be your King."

IV. The Battle of Pontevedra

The emotion in England had only increased.

In the beginning, the actions of Maxime's officers had been treated as piracy, but the taking of Perim, which seemed to indicate a well-conceived plan and a firm determination to attack the Suez Canal gave the English the first serious anxieties that they were to experience in the war for the empire of the seas.

People were protesting in the streets and holding meetings, in the course of which the government was invited to punish the insolent corsairs who had stolen the ships.

The Statesmen were, however, calmer. They judged, from the beginning, that the struggle might perhaps be difficult. They resolved to arm a formidable fleet to be placed under the orders of Sir Beauchamp Seymour, Lord Alcester,[17]

---

[17] Admiral Frederick Beauchamp Seymour (1821-1895) was created the first Baron Alcester after the bombardment of Al-

whose mission would be to purge the seas of the so-called King of Pola and the bandits in his employ.

In the meantime, though, it was necessary to recapture Perim and, above all, to guard the two entrances to the Suez Canal. It was necessary, finally, to exercise a severe surveillance over the Red Sea in order to protect the route to India.

Already, commerce was beginning to suffer; five or six English steamship lines had lost ships and almost all their captains had been forced, in order to safeguard the companies' interests, to pay excessive tributes to the Polans.

An energetic and prompt repression was loudly demanded. The government hastily assembled ten ships that were in a state to put to sea. Three of them were at Hull, two at Portsmouth; the others would come back in the interval. They were put under the command of Admiral Hopkins,[18] who took to the sea without delay.

Under Maxime's orders, Boislucas had returned to Madeira. On the twenty-third of July 1885 he returned to the Salvage Isles and announced that Admiral Hopkins' fleet had left England that same day.

During the capture of the vessels that composed the King of Pola's squadron, there had inevitably been a number of prisoners taken aboard each ship. Numbering approximately twelve hundred, they were deposited on the principal islet with food for ten days, and Boislucas was set to guard them. Darnozan only kept two senior English officers aboard the *Defence*, in order to hang them from the yard-arm, in accordance with his promise, if the English had not respected Weenix's life.

The preparations for sailing took place in the evening, and at seven o'clock the Polan fleet, with the *Monarch* at the head, emerged into the Ocean at full steam, and set a course for Spain.

---

exandria. When the story was written he was the Second Sea Lord, a post from which, in our history, he retired in 1885
[18] John Omaney Hopkins (1834-1916).

The events are too recent for anyone to be unable to remember the naval battle of Pontevedra, so called because it took place within sight of the pretty little Galician town of that name.

Once at sea, Maxime-Jean had summoned all the officers commanding the ships under his orders to come aboard his flagship.

"Messieurs," he said to them, "we shall be the first to carry out an experiment that Europe has not had the opportunity or the courage to attempt. Properly speaking, there has been no naval battle since Navarin. No one knows as yet what tactics are best suited to ironclad steamships. The question of wind, which was once everything in an engagement at sea, no longer has any serious importance. The big deal, today, is the cannons, and it's necessary not to hide from ourselves that the English gunners, much more experienced than ours, might be able to inflict serious damage on us. We shall thus be at a manifest and worrying disadvantage if we let the English engage us in a regular battle. I've summoned you here to discuss the tactics we ought to employ. What's your opinion, Kasaloff?"

"I have only one: boarding. Each English ship gas a crew of four hundred men. We have six or seven hundred, all solid mariners. There's no hesitation."

"And you, Kellner?"

"I agree with Kasaloff."

"What about you, Pontins?"

"I believe," said the conqueror of the *Warrior* and the *Defence*, "that we ought to run straight at the English ships and try to cut them in two, like Admiral Tegetthoff at Lissa."[19]

---

[19] Wilhelm von Tegetthoff (1827-1871) was in command of the underequipped Austrian battle fleet when an Italian fleet attacked the Austrian naval base at Lissa in 1866. Because of his dearth of firepower he tried to ram the Italian ships, and the tactic had sufficient success to force the Italians to retreat.

Each of the officers, interrogated in their turn, offered an opinion similar to one of those expressed by Pontins and Kasaloff."

"That's good," said the King. "I believe we're in accord. You can all return to your ships. Instruct your gunners only to fire when they're within range and almost certain of their fire; none of them should aim at the hulls of the English ships; all their shots must hit the superstructure: the masts, the funnel and the turrets of the vessels. You should always present yourselves head on and fire incessantly with your pursuit guns and the big cannon in the turrets. For the maneuvers to carry out in combat you'll receive my instructions tomorrow."

Two days later, the *Tamar*, commanded by the young Parisian Robert, which had been sent beyond Cape Finistère as a scout, returned at full steam to announce that the English fleet was advancing slowly.

Hopkins had put his flag on the *Black Prince*. According to Robert's estimate, the English were some fifty or sixty miles to the north. Maxime-Jean decided, for the time being, that they would not head toward them.

Night was about to fall. There was no moon. According to all appearances, Hopkins was not expecting to be attacked. An hour before dawn, they might be able to surprise him.

Two vessels, the *Achilles* and the *Sultan*, were detached from the fleet and set forth under the orders of Nicolas Ramine, to the great amazement of the other commandants, who could not understand that decision.

The expectations of the King of Pola were unrealized. The British forces moved more prudently than he had expected, and the sun had risen when the Polans found themselves in the presence of the enemy.

Maxime-Jean addressed the adventurers ranged under his orders with the simple words: "Officers and mariners, remember that you are fighting to found the Empire of the Seas."

At the head of the Polan fleet was the *Monarch*, followed closely by the *Alexandra*, the *Minotaur* and the *Northumber-*

land. Two kilometers behind, Kasaloff, on the *Defence*, preceded the *Warrior*, the *Agincourt* and the *Hercules*.

A cannon shot was fired by the *Monarch*, and immediately the eight warships and the steamers that were serving as the squadron's dispatch-boats raised the sky blue flag with four golden swallows: the flag that would soon be the emblem and representative of the greatest maritime power that had ever existed.

Hopkins had not believed that his adversaries, whom he qualified as "wretched brigands," would dare to confront him. Certainly, he was an energetic seaman and was not caught napping; everything was ready for battle, but he had not supposed that bandits devoid of experience would have the audacity to measure themselves against Her Majesty's navy.

In his opinion, Maxime-Jean had already committed one grave error in dividing his fleet into two squadrons. It would be sufficient for him, he thought, to do as Nelson had done at Trafalgar and place himself between the two divisions, beat one of them first and then come back at the other, to reckon with it easily.

The English vessels assumed their battle formation in two lines, with the *Lord Warden* as the head of the wedge to penetrate between the two parts of the Polan forces. It was in that order that battle was engaged.

At the moment when the first cannon shots were exchanged, however, two ironclads appeared in the north, which raised the sky blue flag as soon as they were within range. They were the *Achilles* and the *Sultan*.

The King of Pola's plan was now easy to understand. The two ships commanded by Nicolas Ramine had the mission of putting on a demonstration at the enemy's rear, in order to draw away a part of its forces, or at least oblige the vessels placed at the rear to slow their march in order to be ready for any eventuality.

That is what happened. While the *Lord Warden* headed straight for the Polans, the *Penelope* and the *Hector*, which were the last in line, reduced their speed at their steam. The

Condor and the *Victoria*, which were sailing ahead of the Penelope and he *Hector*, slowed down in their turn so that the distance between them and the latter would not become too great.

Admiral Hopkins imitated that maneuver himself, in more restricted proportions, with the *Black Prince* and the *Invincible*.

With a sort of fury, the Polan vessels, as soon as they received the order, headed at top speed for the *Lord Warden*.

The English, meanwhile, still believed that they were certain of victory. They had not factored into their calculation the fact that Nelson had had a precious auxiliary at Trafalgar in the wind, which had not permitted Villeneuve to help the Spaniards in time.

At Pontevedra, it was very different. No obstacle could prevent the two Polan divisions from assisting one another, and the breakneck maneuvers that Nelson had employed, within sight of Aboukir as off the coast of Spain, would have been pure folly in our day.

On the express orders of the King, the Commandants of the Polan vessels hardly bothered to riposte to the shells of the *Lord Warden* and the two vessels following her. They headed for the English at top speed, with fearful rapidity. In the meantime, Nicola Ramine was advancing on and seriously menacing the vessels at the tail.

Hopkins, therefore, penetrated audaciously between the two squadrons and immediately opened a terrible fire. Like volcanoes, the *Lord Warden*, the *Invincible* and the *Black Prince*, which formed the head of the wedge, send a blizzard of iron and fire at the enemy.

The latter scarcely replied, but the distance separating Maxime-Jean and his vessels from those commanded by Kasaloff was shrinking progressively.

The entire Polan fleet, in admirable order, fell upon the three ships just named, and the wedge suddenly found itself caught in a vice, which two sides were tightening, but in such a fashion as to leave the *Condor* and the *Penelope* room to join the first three.

Then commenced the most frightful tempest of shells ever seen. The enormous cannons that England had been founding for twenty years launched, along with projectiles as heavy as houses, the most deafening racket that had ever resounded at sea.

Within half an hour, the din took on the proportions of a paroxysm of madness. When, by chance, a second elapsed when the voice of the hundred roaring thunders fell momentarily silent, the splintering of the masts, the rebounding of shells from the dented or disemboweled armor, and the howls of the mariners urging one another on, could be distinguished.

As for the dying and the wounded, their cries of despair and blasphemies could only succeed in producing something resembling a murmur in the midst of that general tumult.

Oh, the English truly fought like heroes, and anyone who had been able to see them distinctly from a safe place would have been able to cry out, like the king who admired his valiant enemies: "What brave men!" They performed prodigies. But the two divisions of the Polan fleet continued to draw closer, imperturbably, like the two pincers of a mighty crab, and while Nicolas Ramine attacked the vessels that had turned to confront him furiously, the King and Kasaloff crushed Hopkins, who defended himself like a lion.

The English did not take long to perceive that they were doomed, if some miracle or inspiration of genius did not get them out of trouble. Each of their vessels, in fact, was receiving two or three blows for every one that struck the Polans, much superior in number. The *Lord Warden*, which had borne the initial brunt of the enemy attack, attempted a desperate action. Her Commandant, one of the bravest and most intelligent mariners in the United Kingdom, headed straight for the *Monarch*, which was pressing her most closely, and attempted to ram her amidships with her spur—but Maxime-Jean, divining the maneuver, administered a turn of the helm, and presented her bow. The English vessel passed by, and received, almost point-blank, such a discharge that she trembled from one end to the other as if she were about to rip.

With the speed she had put on she went past the *Monarch* without being able to do anything, and did not have time, two hundred meters further on, to avoid the *Defence*, commanded by Pontins, which fell upon her and opened her up a few feet from her engine-room.

A scream was heard, uttered by four hundred fearful voices, and the vessel started to sink, taking less than ten minutes to go under.

It was then that the King of Pola summoned Hopkins to surrender. The English admiral responded by sending all the shells and grenades he could muster, and the battle recommenced. The English were one against two because Ramine was still keeping the rest of the fleet busy, and terribly.

Not for a moment did the idea even occur to the British officers to seek their salvation in flight, let alone surrender. It seemed, in fact, that Her Very Gracious Majesty's Admiral was about to bring the favors of the god of battles back in his direction, by dint of valor and obstinacy. He sent signals that ordered all the English vessels to attack the *Alexandra*, commanded by Kellner and placed slightly apart.

The movement was executed with a rare precision, and the *Alexandra*, crushed, soon sank in her turn. But Kasaloff and Capmartin, with the *Northumberland* and the *Warrior*, launched grappling irons at the *Invincible*, and a whirlwind of Irishmen full of rage fell upon the English, who were defeated in twenty minutes of combat.

In the meantime, Pontins, who was to be seen everywhere there was a heroic deed to accomplish, went in person to stick a torpedo to the flank of the *Black Prince* and blew her up, along with Admiral Hopkins, who had just had an arm and half a shoulder carried away.

All that remained within the teeth of the vice were the *Penelope* and the *Victoria*. It would have been madness on their part to try to resist any longer. They surrendered—or, to put it better, no longer defended themselves, for their flag was not raised.

Four ships of lesser dimension were at grips with Nicholas Ramine, who was performing prodigies. When they saw that all was lost, they maneuvered in order to reach the open sea and at least take back to England the debris of the powerful fleet that had departed seventy-two hours before.

Three of them did, in fact, succeed in getting away, but the *Hector* was overtaken in time to be captured by boarding.

Maxime-Jean's victory was a triumph. He had lost one of his ships, the *Alexandra*, but he had captured four.

Such a defeat constituted, for England, a disaster whose moral effect was far more deplorable than the burning and theft of her ships accomplished several weeks earlier. Albion had finally encountered a redoubtable enemy, and her maritime prestige was dented.

V. England Collects Herself, as does Maxime-Jean

The Battle of Pontevedra made an incredible noise. The news penetrated everywhere that the English sent ships, everywhere that they had trading-posts—which is to say, all over the world. But it was in Europe, above all, that the effect produced by the disaster was immense. The "whale—to use Bismarck's expression, when speaking of the British government—had just encountered another marine monster, which appeared to have the stature to stand up to it. In the Chancelleries of the continent, everyone naturally strove to foresee the consequences of such an event. That is the ABC of the métier.

The various European cabinets certainly did not believe that England was beaten on account of a few warships burned and one battle lost. They knew Anglo-Saxon tenacity too well not to be convinced that England would have the last word, but everyone thought, at least, that the time had come to take advantage of a situation as new as it was unexpected.

The Italian government—or, to put it better, the Italian people—was the first, doubtless purely by chance, to wonder whether it might not gain something from the weakening of England. The development of Italy has only ever taken place thanks to the crushing of someone else. It was therefore quite natural that the cabinet in Rome saw in England's defeat a possibility of enlargement, without quite knowing how.

That is why, four days after the Battle of Pontevedra, the Peninsular newspapers were already insinuating that it was necessary to conclude an offensive and defensive alliance with Maxime-Jean I. As usual, the same newspapers declared to France that she would have done well to take a firmer line.

Spain, for her part, was dreaming about Gibraltar and Morocco. The French ministry, on the other hand, was only anxious to know what Bismarck might be thinking. Austria was casting a concupiscent eye at Constantinople, and her gaze crossed with that of Russia. The Sultan and his counselors nursed sweet illusions regarding Egypt. Finally, Germany was provisionally content to soar over all those ambitions in order to exploit them to her own advantage when the time came.

As we have said, however, England was not yet beaten; far from it. The blow she had just received was rude, especially for her self-respect as a naval power, but in sum, there was nothing thus far but the Battle of Pontevedra to strike at her prestige, and the success of the King of Pola might, after all, be the result of a fluke.

The worst of it was that England, for the present, had no ships ready to put to sea. She still had stationary or flying squadrons in all the seas of the world, but the ships making them up were not very powerful and they might be destroyed if they attempted to rally in the ports of the homeland.

With the decisiveness that is the best side of the English character, the London cabinet decreed that a revenge would be prepared as soon as possible. In a full parliamentary session the First Lord of the Treasury[20] dared to say that it would take

---

[20] The title of First Lord of the Treasury has fallen into disuse because the position is nowadays always combined with that

six months to be ready—but he added that victory would then be certain.

Lord Salisbury[21] made the remark that in those six months, Maxime-Jean would have time to ruin English commerce.

"There is something more respectable than English commerce," replied Mr. Gladstone, to the applause of the Chamber, "and that is the English nation itself." (*Listen! Listen!*) "In trying to form a new fleet in haste, we would be heading for a new disaster. We shall take our time; we shall act slowly and sagely, and, in consequence, reliably. If this adventurer captures a few merchant ships during those six months, and exercises his piracy, he will not escape by virtue of that the chastisement that we have in reserve for him."

The King of Pola let Mr. Gladstone threaten him. He had a respite of six months to organize himself and to do all the harm possible to the merchant navy. He was not a man to refrain from taking full advantage of that.

As soon as he had won the Battle of Pontevedra, Maxime-Jean, who now had a fleet of twelve first class ironclads under his orders, sent half his forces to take possession of Cyprus. After that he went to renew his supplies at Ferrol. It was from there that he addressed the famous proclamation "to all those who hate England," in which he invited all the seekers of adventure of the two worlds to join him, promising them a great deal of glory and the spoils of the English. He gave them a rendezvous in New York, to which, in fact, he went with Kasaloff.

---

of "Prime Minister;" the reference here is to Gladstone, who held both titles in the early months of 1885.

[21] Robert Gascoyne-Cecil, third Marquess of Salisbury (1830-1903) was the leader of the Conservative Party in the House of Lords from 1880 onwards; in our history he took over from Gladstone as Prime Minister following the latter's resignation on 23 June 1885, although it takes him a little longer to acquire that privilege in the alternative history of the story.

Pontins, who had been created Comte de Pontevedra the day after the battle, in recompense for the courage audacity and intelligence he had shown in sinking one vessel and blowing up the *Black Prince*, which was carrying Hopkins himself' received the mission of taking three ships to drop anchor in Diego Suarez Bay in Madagascar. He was to wait there for the return of the King, without neglecting, however, to lay his hands on all the English ships that showed themselves in the Mozambique Channel.

In traveling to New York, Maxime-Jean did not neglect, of course, to give chase to English steamers. He took two ships of the Anchor Line, one of the Cunard Line, one of the Inman Line, two of the Moss Line and three Royal Mail vessels.

The taking of the *Trent*, belonging to the Royal Mail, produced an incident that was totally unexpected, but rather curious.

Among the passengers on the *Trent* were Lord Killyett and his daughter. The noble lord and Lady Helena were taken before the King, who wanted to receive them with a certain solemnity.

Lady Helena was a little frightened, but still charming. When she recognized the King of Pola as the passenger of the *Lapwing*, she seemed suddenly reassured, to the point that she smiled. Maxime-Jean smiled too as he looked at her with a bountiful expression of which one would not have thought his energetic face capable.

As for Lord Killyett, the arrogant and somewhat sullen expression of his features had not changed. He looked Darnozan up and down like a man determined not to make any concession.

"You've doubtless recognized me, Milord," said Maxime-Jean. "You can see that I've kept my word. I'm a King, and your country knows that I'm a serious king, a warrior king, and an administrator king. In a year or two, I'll be a glorious king. Would you care to give me the hand of your daughter?" Bowing, the young man added: "Lady Helena would be a very beautiful queen, and I promise to offer her a throne that has no parallel in the world."

The young woman blushed. Her father's scowl did not relax.

"The proposition you are making," he replied, "appears to me to be as insolent today, on this vessel where you are the master, as it was on the Southern Seas, when you made it for the first time."

"And you refuse?"

"It goes without saying that I refuse."

"And you would refuse even if your stubbornness causes the irredeemable ruin of our country?"

"Yes, I would refuse even in that case—but don't flatter yourself. England is not a nation that can be beaten as easily as you seem to believe, and if the government wishes to entrust me with a fleet, I'll show you how one chastises an adventurer."

"You're repeating words already pronounced by Mr. Gladstone, and I congratulate you on the high opinion you have of yourself," the King replied. "I should like, so far as it is in my power, to give you the opportunity to do battle with me, and for that, I shall have you taken to England, as well as Lady Helena. You may arm ships. I shall expect you. We shall do battle, squadron against squadron, ship against ship, as you choose. It can be a battle or a duel. For that, I am entirely at your disposal."

Maxime bowed again. "Milady, I assure you of my respectful attachment. You are free."

And without waiting for the Duke to say a word, he turned to his Minister of War, whose ship had been sunk at Pontevedra, and who had been exercising since then the functions of chief of staff aboard the *Monarch*. "Kellner," he said, "let all the officers of the *Trent* return to their posts; let the passengers return to their cabins, and give the captain a guarantee of safe conduct, to make sure that nothing disagreeable happens to Lady Helena or to her father."

Somewhat ironically, the King added: "*Au revoir*, Milord. If I don't have the pleasure of meeting you at sea I shall probably have the honor of coming to ask you for Milady's hand again in London." And as Lord Killyett struck a disdainful pose, he added: "You're wrong to doubt me, Milord, after events have given you so much proof that I can keep my word."

An hour later, the *Trent*, carrying the sky blue flag—for Maxime-Jean had demanded that—resumed her interrupted journey, bound for Liverpool.

When the victor of Pontevedra dropped anchor in New York, he was received with royal honors. The governor knew that the majority of the King's companions were citizens of the United States. He wanted to be agreeable to them. As soon as Maxime set foot on American soil he was welcomed by a host of volunteers who requested to embark under his orders. For a fortnight, every liner coming from Europe and every train coming from the interior of the Union brought soldiers and mariners for the King of Pola. A singular event even occurred in the open sea. One of Maxime-Jean's vessels captured an English steamer filled entirely with Irishmen who wanted to enlist under his orders.

In going to New York, Darnozan had three objectives in mind: firstly, to collect volunteers, and it was evident that there was no shortage of them; secondly, to see his San Francisco banker, to whom he had telegraphed news of his arrival, and who arrived six days later; and thirdly, to hire engineers and workmen to establish construction yards in Madagascar and Santa Domingo,[22] for he had resolved to take possession of those two islands, which was not very difficult.

First of all, it was necessary to negotiate a State loan with the banker. Things would go of their own accord once that had been done. Maxime-Jean only had to speak to obtain

---

[22] The island here called Santa Domingo was more commonly known as Hispaniola, divided into the Dominican Republic and Haiti

the two hundred million he needed. And as soon as the telegraph had carried the news of that loan to Europe, the King of Pola received offers from Paris, Amsterdam and—who would have believed it?—London of larger capital sums at more advantageous rates. Maxime-Jean was, however, too serious a man to lose his head and allow himself to be carried further than he wanted to go. He refused or adjourned them, contenting himself with the American money, with which he took to the sea again.

As he passed through the Antilles he disembarked two thousand men on the coast of Santa Domingo. Under Kellner's orders, that small army, which was sufficiently provided with artillery and long-range rifles, effortlessly overcame all the native troops that Haiti and the Dominican Republic could oppose to it. Only once did the Haitian army, without winning a victory, succeed in delivering a battle of which the result was indecisive, but Kellner attached his enemies again the following day, and the latter, who had doubtless been expecting to rest for a while, finding the procedure too pressing, broke up, and it was all over. The entire island submitted in next to no time, and Kellner, after having decreed extremely severe laws, installed the construction yards and naval foundries personally. After that, he appointed a governor. That was Joshua Klett of Chicago, an authoritarian governor if ever there was one.

When everything had been well-regulated, Kellner departed for Madagascar, where the King had arranged to meet him.

William Smith, for his part, no longer had anything to do in Perim, which was occupied by a numerous and vigorous garrison of near-savage Malays. In response to a telegraphic order from the King, he too had set a course for Madagascar, and he arrived in Diego Suarez Bay a few days after Pontins.

Sealed instructions ordered them to disembark half their personnel and hire a considerable number of Malabar blacks to construct redoubts on selected summits, and to sanitize the coast as far as possible by draining the marshes.

William Smith and Pontins set to work immediately. The Queen of the Hovas[23] sent a small army against them. The Polans did not attack it, but every time it wanted to show itself or made any appearance of troubling the works it was severely received and cruelly driven back to a respectful distance. As Smith and Pontins did not spare the negroes who were working for them, and also hired all those who presented themselves, the works progressed with great rapidity.

When Maxime-Jean arrived, the hardest part had been done.

The King had not wasted his time *en route*. He had taken possession of an island whose loss was extremely sensible to the English: Ascension Island, the largest store of coal and provisions that Her Majesty's government possessed south of the equator in the Atlantic. After having occupied it, Maxime had renewed his supplies of coal, food and even munitions there.

Smith and Pontins went there in their turn with the same objective as soon as the King arrived, and the latter gave a new impetus to the works in Diego Suarez Bay.

On the solidified terrain he established a vast arsenal, where the American constructors commenced work. Workshops of all the industries associated with naval warfare were set up under the protection of the redoubts constructed by Smith and Pontins, and in less than three months an indescribable activity reigned on that previously-deserted coast.

That happened at the beginning of 1886. The French, who had been on the point of occupying the island, over which they had authentic rights, two years previously, had allowed themselves to be intimidated by England after the war in Sudan and had abandoned the game, so the Malagasies had be-

---

[23] Ranavalona III (1861-1917) was the last ruler of the Kingdom of Madagascar, acceding to the throne in 1883; she fought a long battle against colonization, ultimately lost in our history in 1895, when the French took over.

come distinctly insolent, and were impatiently intolerant of such an installation.

The population of the island is very numerous and brave, and became menacing. It would have been imprudent to delay, temporize or merely to repel the attacks that were becoming more frequent every day. It was necessary to strike hard, and promptly.

With the aid of a captive balloon, Maxime-Jean had a study made of the country, which is, on that coast, very rugged and cut by numerous ravines. Then he sent an ambassador to declare war on the Queen.

The Ministers of Ranavalona, the fifteenth honor, as they say out there, found nothing better to do than inform Maxime that if he had the imprudence to start a war, England would come to their aid. They even threatened him with the famous Commandant Johnstone of the *Dryad*, who was lying low in a nearby port, and whom Smith was charged with going to collect.[24]

The Malagasies realized that the British nation had other things to worry about at that moment than protecting them. Maxime-Jean attacked them without delay, beat them hollow in six encounters, penetrated as far as Tananarive, captured the Queen, who was put in prison, and a few important chiefs, who were hanged as rebels. That act of violence, which as a trifle sharp, nevertheless had the result of frightening he Malagasies to such an extent that submissions arrived from all over the island.

In any case, the Hovas, who are the only inhabitants of Madagascar familiar with war, having perished in large numbers in the six great battles, there was no longer any resistance to be feared on the part of the other tribes, delighted with what

---

[24] *H. M. S. Dryad*, commanded by Charles Johnstone, rallied to the support of the Kingdom of Madagascar during the Franco-Hova War of 1883, but in our history she passed to the command Edward Hulton in 1884 and went to help out in the Egyptian War.

had happened to their oppressors. The King of Pola remained master of that immense land, where he had himself proclaimed King of the Isles. His capital was the city he had just founded, which he called Villejean, after one of his forenames.

As soon as he had completed his conquest, Maxime-Jean gave an astonishing impulsion to the work of sanitizing the coast, and especially the construction of engines of war. All the intelligent workers, whatever color they were, worked on the ships or in the construction of machinery. All those whose physical strength was their only quality remained employed in earthworks.

The King wanted to have as many people as possible for those two sorts of labor; that is why he hired, at relatively high wages, several thousand Malabars, who, along with the Hovas and the other Malagasy prisoners, did extraordinary work in a very short time. Part of the land of Madagascar, whose coasts had been called the cemetery of Europeans, was rendered salubrious, or very nearly so. Eight months after the King's arrival, the entire region around Diego Suarez Bay had been sanitized; the marshy ground had been drained, a superb quay and a number of houses built; the King's palace was inhabited and the maritime endeavors had been driven so actively that fifteen engines of war of a new model had been launched.

In any case, there was no urgency; the English, instead of taking six months to prepare the campaign, devoted an entire year to that work. That permitted the King of Pola to import Chinese and Japanese workers. Those perfect imitators constructed warships for him, on determined models, and even steam engines.

In the meantime, Maxime-Jean's officers hunted down English ships and set up ambushes into which the fastest steamers fell. Those prizes brought extraordinary returns for Darnozan's treasury, and it was with resources provided by British ships that Maxime-Jean maintained and paid, regularly, an army that already consisted of ten thousand men, and an even larger navy.

IV. The Turtles

Meanwhile, people in England were beginning to lose patience. The majority of steamship lines, as many for North America as for India, Africa and the Southern Seas, were ruined. One company had lost as many as ten ships of their fleet. Another was reduced to putting to sea old obsolete steamers whose fate was uncertain.

One can afflict English self-respect, but English commerce is untouchable. It is easy to comprehend that if ships that went out did not come back, the prodigious grocers of London were beginning to run short of raw materials. Business was going very badly, and complaints were coming from all directions. The steamships and sailing ships laden with English products of which Maxime-Jean's mariners took possession were no longer bringing profits to anyone but the enemies of England.

A muted agitation reigned in the manufacturing cities. Manchester, Sheffield and Leeds were the first to complain loudly about the inaction of the government. No one was unaware that the King of Pola, thanks to his loan, was making considerable armaments on his own behalf, and the newspapers were no longer inhibited about printing suggestions that the English fleet would not be ready for two years.

Monstrous meetings were held everywhere, principally in London's Hyde Park. Demands were made there for a more energetic politics, the call of all English mariners to arms, the formation of a respectable land army and the creation of fleets composed of commercial ships that no longer dared leave port, and to which letters of marque would be given, in order to become privateers.

One orator even proposed paying Maxime-Jean back in his own coin, sending determined men to burn "that audacious bandit's" vessels. People still referred to him as a bandit.

The government then supplied an article to the *Times* to demonstrate to the English that it would be pointless to try to create fleets of small ships armed for privateering. The Polans did not possess any merchant ships that could be destroyed, and steamers transformed into corsairs could not have the astonishing pretention of battling Maxime-Jean's ironclads.

Finally, in the middle of May 1886, it was announced that the English fleet was about to put to sea. It counted eighteen formidable vessels armed with monstrous cannons, which could send projectiles weighing fifteen to twenty quintals the incredible distance of eleven kilometers. The Admiralty, who wanted to put an end to Maxime-Jean at a single stroke, simultaneously put to sea more than twenty torpedo-boats of various forms and sizes, which were to escort the ironclads and blow up anything that came before their prow.

Sir Beauchamp Seymour, appointed Commander of that invincible Armada, received the order to go, first of all, to retake the island of Cyprus, of which Kasaloff had taken possession.

Maxime's minister had installed serious garrisons at Famagusta, Limassol and Larnaca, composed of Greeks and old bachi-bouzouck Turks, who each considered the occupation of Cyprus and Egypt by the English as an abominable and intolerable usurpation of their rights.

After having reconquered Cyprus, Seymour was to go through the Suez Canal, traverse the length of the Red Sea, bombard Perim and take possession of it, and then head for Diego Suarez Bay—to which the *Standard* referred as "the pirate's lair"—destroy everything on the coast if Maxime-Jean could not be found there, or crush him, if he had the inconceivable audacity to offer battle.

The details given by the newspapers regarding the new vessels calmed the ill humor and impatience of the English, who looked forward confidently to the imminent end of the commercial anemia of which the Three Kingdoms were dying.

It is impossible to form an exact idea of the imposing forces that England sent against the King of Pola. The most extravagant imagination could not find anything comparable to the engines of destruction invented by the maritime genius of England.

One Colonel Scott had constructed strange ships with the form of a shell, whose bow was equipped with a pneumatic apparatus. Three men were sufficient to operate it and direct it at enemy vessels, to which it was designed to adhere by suction. Once the vessel was attached by the vacuum, it was only necessary to open a panel at the rear; sea water entered furiously into a watertight cage, the pressure of which caused a frightful explosion.

It was called a volcano-boat.

The three men who manned it had time to save themselves in a minuscule diving lifeboat with the form of a cigar, with only resurfaced two kilometers away.

There were fireships of a new genre, and mortars of an improbable caliber.

When Beauchamp Seymour set out to sea, an enormous crowd gathered on the jetties, in the windows and on the roofs, all the way to the neighboring hills.

Among those spectators, who were mostly inflamed by English chauvinism, there were, it must be said, many people for whom the hurrahs of their compatriots resonated sadly. More than one poor woman—mother, wife or fiancée—had a presentiment of disaster, and gazed at the formidable naval army with a dolorous anxiety.

Lady Helena Killyett was one of those. She remembered the man with whom her country had to deal. She knew that the hero in question had not needed more than eight months, with no other resource than his genius, to inflict a bloody defeat on the most powerful navy in the world, and she was fully convinced that, if Mr. Gladstone's government had worked wonders, Maxime-Jean, for his part, had not remained inactive. She feared a disaster, for her father had obtained a command under the orders of the Admiral whose fleet represented England and her fortune.

Lord Killyett, more arrogant than ever, not only could not admit that his daughter might marry an adventurer like Darnozan, but had strictly forbidden Lady Helena to mention the King of Pola's pretention to anyone, for fear that there might be someone, either at court or in the government, who might force the noble lord to sacrifice his daughter.

No one, in consequence, outside the three interested parties knew the means by which peace could be made with Maxime-Jean.

In the depths of her soul, Lady Helena did not see things with the same eye as her father, and if she had been invited to do so, she would not have refused to save her country by marrying the King.

A profound sadness was painted in Lady Helena's features, and yet, a melancholy that was not without charm filled her soul at the sight of the last vessels disappearing over the horizon.

Beauchamp Seymour and the innumerable ships that he commanded headed in admirable order toward the strait of Gibraltar. The Admiral had put his flag on the most redoubtable of his vessels, which had been given the significant name of *England*.

All the other vessels had been baptized with names that translated the emotion of the English people, and which were equivalent to a declaration that the Fatherland was in danger. One was named *The Queen*, another *The Prince of Wales*, one *Scotland* and another *Ireland*, and others *India, Australia, Mauritius, Egypt, Dominion, Perim*, etc.

Such names indicated the firm, unshakable resolution to defend, for many years, if necessary, the lands over which the British flag flew.

It is necessary to add that among the men making up the fleet—who did not include a single Irishman, so determined was the Admiralty not to take any risks—there was not one mariner who was not ready to die in Her Majesty's service.

It was the second of June when Admiral Beauchamp Seymour moved into the strait of Gibraltar. Until then, Maxime-Jean had not put in any appearance. Like Hopkins, the English Admiral was not far from believing that his enemy would not dare to confront him.

It did not take him long to revise that error. In the evening of that same day, the crews of the vessels traveling at the forefront of the English fleet heard a detonation of extraordinary violence and, almost at the same time, saw a projectile fall a few meters from one of the ships, which was out of all proportion to anything previously known.

Admiral Beauchamp Seymour—or rather, Lord Alcester—having been alerted, immediately sent two light dispatch-boats to take account of the forces that the English had before them, but night was falling and things were put off until the following morning.

During the night, a ship coming from Tarifa under the Spanish flag entered into communication with the British fleet, and the captain—who, in reality, was Scottish—asked to be taken to the Admiral, to whom, he said, he had grave news to report.

Introduced to the presence of the celebrated mariner, the Scotsman revealed to him that the strait of Gibraltar was literally blocked, and that no ship could pass through it without the permission of Nicolas Ramine.

"How many ships does this Nicolas Ramine have?" demanded Lord Alcester.

"They're not ships that he has under his orders."

"What are they, then?"

"They're floating fortresses."

And indeed, Maxime-Jean had taken advantage of the year to construct a dozen engines of war such as had never been seen. Taking his inspiration from an idea that the Russian Admiral Popoff had had twenty-five years earlier, and rendering it practical, he had asked American engineers to construct immense circular vessels some four hundred meters in diameter, able to contain a considerable garrison in their hull, covered by a steel roof of prodigious thickness, shaped like the shell of a turtle, in such a way that enemy shells could only ricochet from the smooth carapace.[25]

Admiral Popoff's vessels, which were known as Popoffska, were, we believe, hexagonal, and their inventor had designed them to navigate. In Maxime-Jean's thinking, by contrast, the formidable constructions that he had put to sea had no other mission than to moor in narrow passages and block them entirely. There were five in the strait of Gibraltar and seven west of Perim. In consequence, so long as they were not swept away, the Mediterranean, the Suez Canal and the Red Sea remained inaccessible.

On hearing that story, Admiral Seymour smiled. Evidently, he considered the report that had been made to him as somewhat exaggerated. Knowing how scant the Popoffska's success had been, the English mariner did not hide his scorn for the King of the Isles' steam-forts.

"So," he said, "you've seen these leviathans at close range?"

"Yes, Monsieur."

"They have artillery?"

"Extraordinary artillery. The cannons, placed in iron embrasures, are protected throughout the time they remain mute by an enormous mass of metal blocking the embrasure, which cannot be penetrated by any projectile."

"And how do these astonishing products of Polan industry hold their positions in the strait? Are they under steam?"

---

[25] Andre Alexandrovich Popov (1821-1898) came up with the innovative design of the naval defense vessels in question— which were circular, not hexagonal—in the 1870s; two of them were built, the *Novgorod*, launched in 1873 and the *Kiev* (subsequently remained the *Rear Admiral Popov*). They performed poorly in bad weather and tended to spin around when they fired their guns, but were not decommissioned, in our history, until 1903.

"No, they're moored by eight anchors with enormous chains, and constitute, I can assure you, Admiral, a force before which it is necessary not to smile."

"We'll see about that tomorrow. These fortress, as you call them, these new dragons of the Hesperides, if one might call them that, aren't so malevolent that one can't force the passage they guard."

"I believe that will be difficult, for each of the steam-forts is close enough to the next to cover with iron and fire ships that try to slip through the mesh of the net."

Lord Alcester dismissed the Scotsman, letting him understand that he thought him pusillanimous, and immediately sent orders to attack at daybreak.

All of Europe had eyes fixed on the strait. The turtles—that was what Maxime-Jean's floating citadels were called in the Polan fleet—had been moored by night forty-eight hours before, forty kilometers west of Gibraltar, and the telegraph had cried the news to the ends of the earth. Admiral Seymour, already being at sea, could not be alerted. In any case, the English cabinet had only one order to give Lord Alcester: attack, and get through regardless.

Everywhere in the world there was a telegraphic station, people knew that, but they also knew from the description of the turtles that the English, already intimidated by the disaster of Pontevedra, whose anniversary was approaching, would have all the difficulty in the world combating those vessels of a new genre.

"It's true," people were saying everywhere, "that the English have torpedoes, in the use of which they're very experienced."

In fact, Admiral Seymour was counting heavily on his torpedo-boats to rid the strait of the obstacles obstructing it.

As soon as the light of day appeared—it was three-thirty in the morning of the third of June—the English fleet advanced toward the turtles.

The latter remained immobile and silent in the current, as if Lord Alcester and the vessels he commanded did not exist.

83

One veritably might have thought them gigantic turtles asleep on the surface of the water.

The English seemed to have adopted the tactics employed by Maxime-Jean at Pontevedra. Six warships, escorted by torpedo-boats, headed at top speed toward turtle no. 5—which is to say, the one that was closest to the African coast. Evidently, the Admiral's goal was to crush it with superior forces and blow it up before the others could assist it—after which he would attack another.

The idea was not bad. No help could come to the Polans from the Moroccan coast, and the English fleet, in passing between the land and the steam-fort, would easily reach Gibraltar and the Mediterranean.

As soon as Lord Alcester's maneuver became clear, the King of Pola's heavy war machines appeared to emerge from their indifference. Two of them, thanks to their steam-powered capstans, had soon raised anchor and moved toward another mooring, in such a manner that four were sufficient to blockade the strait. As for the one the English were attacking, it also raised anchor and advanced slowly toward the enemy, which began to pepper it with shells and cannonballs.

You will recall the amazement that struck Europe during the War of Secession when the *Merrimac*, of the Southern fleet, had traversed a formidable Federal squadron, sowing ravages all around, without sustaining any damage. The same phenomenon was reproduced in the battle of Gibraltar. Turtle no, 5 came bravely to place itself in the midst of the enemy vessels, as if its intention were to be completely surrounded, and once at the center of the squadron it wished to destroy, it vomited masses of iron in all directions, with a prodigious violence.

The English projectiles that fell thick and fast on the carapace did not have any effect. Thanks to the artistry of the construction, every shell, not finding a flat surface anywhere, rebounded, with or without bursting, and fell into the sea. Better than that, when the steam-fort had placed itself at the center of the circle formed around it by the English ironclads, more than one English projectile, after having touched the back of the turtle, described a new parabola and fell on one of Albion's own vessels, where it did enormous damage.

While Nicolas Ramine—for it was Nicolas Ramine who was manning turtle no. 5—resisted more than a dozen ships on his own, six of which were torpedo-boats, the rest of the English fleet tried to force a passage. Never had such fury been seen in an attack, nor such vigor in the defense. Each of the turtles was surrounded at every minute by a circle of fire, and vomited terrible projectiles.

Already, the *Scotland*, the *Dominion* and the *India*, among the English battleships, had suffered a great deal.

Chagrined, Lord Alcester gave the order to beat a retreat, in order to prepare for another, better organized attempt. The English, therefore, abandoned the battlefield without being victorious or defeated, but with the shame of having failed in their first assault against Maxime-Jean's steam-forts.

Five engines of war of a new model had sufficed to stop the most formidable fleet in the world. Eighteen battleships and an incredible number of torpedo-boats and gunboats had just seen their efforts come to nothing against relatively mediocre forces.

People throughout Europe were astonished by such a result, and there was no shortage of drawing-room warriors and paddling-pool mariners to declare that they did not understand it at all. In Lord Alcester's place, not one of them would have failed to blow up the turtles with torpedoes.

To be sure, Admiral Seymour shared their opinion to a far greater extent that they thought; unfortunately, the matter had proved difficult. Maxime-Jean's engineers had, in fact, taken the precaution of protecting the turtles as much as possible from such an accident.

In order to do that, they had thought of providing the immersed parts of the hull with countless enormous iron spikes forty meters long and proportionately thick, whose sharpened points were shaped like spear-heads. Those tightly-packed bars extended beneath the entire ship all the way to the water-line, in such a fashion that any wooden vessel arriving at speed would be caught on them like a pike on a hook, and the impact of iron vessels, of whatever size, would be deadened sufficiently to become inoffensive.

In either case, the attacking ship, if it persisted in its assault, could be considered doomed. It was thanks to that inverted porcupine construction that the five turtles had so admirably resisted Lord Alcester

The King of the Isles had only left his steam-forts to themselves, in this instance, to test their strength of resistance. The experiment was decisive and conclusive.

VII. Egypt Lost to England

The English fleet had retired to a Spanish port, as much to repair its damage as to be able to enter into communication with England. Admiral Seymour informed his government of the unexpected incidents that had occurred. In order that there should be no error in his report, he sent it via one of his aides-de-camp, who took forty-eight hours to arrive in London.

In response to that news, the Admiralty ordered the construction of torpedo-boats of a new model and commanded the founding of gigantic mortars, which we shall see employed in due course. In the meantime, it instructed the Admiral that he was to remain completely on the defensive, the government having decided to leave nothing to chance in the campaign, and Maxime-Jean I having become an adversary at which it had no desire to laugh.

The latter awaited impatiently the time to act. Sure now of the solidity of his turtles, he intended to execute the rest of his plan, which was the destruction of the English fleet. For that, it was necessary to force Admiral Seymour to fight, and that was not easy.

With fifteen battleships and a huge strange ship devoid of masts, entirely armored, Maxime-Jean lay off the coast of Morocco, informed by his scouts of what Lord Alcester was doing—but the latter went an entire month without budging.

Who can tell how long his inaction might have lasted if William Smith, departing from Perim, had not arrived in Suez with eight warships and put to flight the few English gunboats that reached Ismaila and Port Said.

William Smith immediately engaged in the canal, but, as a wily strategist—and doubtless following the King's instructions—he sent reliable men by railway to cut the telegraph wires everywhere. He intended to prevent, as far as possible, the cabinet in London being informed as to what was happening, so that the English government would not have time to give orders to the troops stationed in Egypt.

Thanks to the extraordinary activity he deployed, William Smith arrived in good time, and that was very fortunate for Europe, for at the first news of Smith's entry into the canal, the English cabinet had not hesitated to order what even Arabi and his accomplices, those savages, had not attempted: the cutting of the Canal. But the order arrived too late. The cable no longer existed, or was under the control of the Polans.

Everyone knows that England, after the war in Sudan—which it had provoked in order to have a pretext to make Egypt a British colony—had not hesitated to break her word and had forthrightly violated the neutrality of the Canal by laying the foundations of fortresses that could cover Port Said on one side and Suez on the other, not to mention establishing smaller redoubts at Ismailia, Kantara and Toussoum.

William Smith, with his ironclads, devastated the works that had been commenced, reducing everything to dust, and issued a proclamation declaring the Canal neutral and accessible to ships of every nation, with the exclusion of British vessels.

The English army of occupation left Cairo to come and attack William Smith, with the intention, if it did not succeed in expelling him, of drying up the Canal by some severance.

At the same moment, however, large transport vessels, eleven in number, each carrying fifteen hundred men, arrived at Ismailia. A small army of between fifteen and eighteen thousand men disembarked, under the command of Octave

Kellner. Maxime-Jean's troops had been making war for an entire year against the Malagasy tribes, almost all unsubmissive, and had acquired during that struggle on uneven ground, beneath a terrible hot sun, a solidity that many old European troops would have envied them.

Exercised, in particular, in disembarkation maneuvers, they were soon established on Egyptian soil, and when Major-General Evelyn Wood[26] appeared on the banks of the freshwater Canal, coming from Cairo with the English army, he found Octave Kellner installed at Tel-el-Kebir, in Arabi's old entrenchments, but with soldiers absolutely determined to be victorious.

Sir Evelyn Wood did not allow himself to be intimidated, however, and as soon as his troops were rested, he attacked Kellner. The battle was rude, and the English acquitted themselves honorably, but the Polans, being solidly entrenched, killed a great many of the assailants, who nearly overran the first trench.

The next day, there was a new attack, and further losses, even more considerable than the previous day.

In brief, after four days, the English had covered themselves in glory but had lost half their troops. Wood beat the retreat.

That was what Kellner expected; he gave chase and sent cavalry to cut off the route. The English were following the railway tracks, pursued with swords in their backs by the Polan army. Nevertheless, they conserved a semblance of order, and discipline was not overly lax.

---

[26] Sir Henry Evelyn Wood (1838-1919), enormously experienced in campaigns in India and Africa, commanded a brigade during the suppression of Arabi's rebellion and took command of the Egyptian Army in December 1882. In our history he held the post until 1885 and then went to attempt to relieve the beleaguered General Gordon in Khartoum before returning to England in 1886.

However, the Bedouins of the entire surrounding region, for fifty leagues around, had mounted their horses on hearing that an unknown army was hounding the English out of Egypt, and when Her Very Gracious Majesty's general arrived at Belbeis, he found a numerous Arab cavalry there, which charged him furiously.

The small contingent of Polan cavalry, which had made a large detour in order to outflank Wood, only had to fold their arms and let matters take their course. The English, utterly routed, hurled themselves into the desert left and right, and those who feared dying of thirst or hunger—which is frightful for an Englishman—surrendered to Kellner, who immediately sent them to Perim.

Lord Wolseley of Cairo had taken very little time to put on a semblance of ridding Egypt of Arabi and his troops; Octave Kellner took even less to destroy the English forces of occupation completely and take possession of a enormous quantity of war materiel.

The Polans merely had to collect, so to speak, more than seventy-two field-cannons, a considerable number of positional pieces, and a large quantity of Gatling machine-guns.

When William Smith was tranquil in that regard, he passed into the Mediterranean, where there were a large number of commercial steamships, which had entered before the strait of Gibraltar was closed, and which were now trapped, no longer able to go through the Suez Canal or to return to England. William Smith detached a dozen light ships, which captured a great many of them, especially ships of the Anchor Line, the Peninsular and Oriental Company, and the Moss Line. The *Sesostris*, the *Pharos*, the *Osmanli*, the *Magdala* and the *Mareotis*, of the Moss Line, fell into their power, as well as the *Justitia*, the *Armenia*, the *Ischia*, the *Anchor* and three steamers of the Peninsular and Oriental.

As for the ironclad fleet that Smith commanded, it headed for Gibraltar, leaving the squadron of its privateers to purge the Mediterranean of all the English ships that dared to show their bowsprits.

When that news reached England there was an explosion of fury. What! English commerce, for the first time in two hundred years, had experienced veritable disasters! The most productive seas in the world were closed to the merchant navy of the United Kingdom. No shipping company any longer dared send a ship to Africa, Brazil, India or Australia. Time being money, the sums that the British nation was losing, by not earning them, became more incalculable with every day that went by.

Under the impression of the events that had just transpired, an exceedingly lively current of opinion formed, which required the government to act, and act quickly.

Already, confidence in Lord Alcester was shaken; the masses, in their blindness, declared him incompetent. The bigwigs of commerce, irritated by a situation so prejudicial to their interests, began to form a chorus with the common people.

The City of London and its official organ, the *Times*, called on the British cabinet to show greater vigor and employ all the forces of the nation to crush, once and for all, the insolent corsair who had just stopped, so audaciously and so completely, the governmental mechanism that had been functioning for so many years.

The House of Commons became stormy at the slightest argument. Some member of Liverpool, Glasgow, Manchester or Sheffield, normally placid, would suddenly launch a violent attack on the First Lord of the Treasury, accusing him of ruining the nation with his procrastination and weakness—not to mention that the Irish members of parliament, Parnellists or otherwise, seeing England in disarray, put more ardor than ever into obstructing Parliamentary debates, and developed in the counties of old Erin an agitation that the government could no longer counter efficaciously. All of its attention and all of its efforts were directed to the struggle for the Empire, at sea on the one hand and, on the other, in Europe, which was beginning to show the English that any nation whatsoever is always wrong to allow itself to be beaten.

Under the pressure of public opinion, the Prime Minister, Gladstone, not without taking into account the misfortunes that precipitation might engender, decided to strike a terrible blow.

The Admiralty recalled all the warships that England still possessed in all the world's seas. It sent orders to all the station ironclads to go to Cadiz and immediately rally to Admiral Seymour's fleet. At the same time, press gangs were sent into the all the English ports in order to embark as many sailors as possible. The arsenals were working day and night. Prodigies had been achieved, for new engines to combat the turtles were already in production, and mortars of an incredible power were joining the fleet that was to employ them.

The English were committing the fault of believing that numbers were worth more than military talent, and were dreaming of a torrential attack in which, they thought, Maxime-Jean, his ships and his memory would be blown away.

Lord Alcester soon found himself at the head of an Armada such that he was frightened by the risks that the determination of the Ministry was making him run. He had, in fact, received the order to attach the turtles with all the ships under his command—ships which, including the station ironclads and torpedo-boats, rose to the number of forty-nine.

Oh, if it had been a matter of fighting a battle in the open sea, to be sure, it might have been easy enough to maneuver that large quantity of vessels and crush the King of the Isles, but Maxime-Jean had anticipated that circumstance a long time ago, and that was why he had thought of drawing the English into the strait, where their excessively considerable forces ran a grave risk of impeding one another.

At the place where the turtles were moored, the Strait of Gibraltar is about twenty-one kilometers wide. What can fifty warships be expected to do in such a restricted space, when half the battlefield is already occupied by enemy vessels that are very numerous themselves?

VIII. The Three Day Battle

It was two days before the anniversary of the battle in which, the previous year, Admiral Hopkins had lost the Battle of Pontevedra and his life, that Lord Alcester finally thought that he was ready to attack the turtles.

A council of war was held, in which all the officers in command of a vessel, of whatever kind, took part. It was decided there that Admiral Seymour would not be inconvenienced by the twenty ships of which he had no need, that he would attack with his original fleet, reinforced by the new engines that had recently arrived, and that the other vessels, remaining under steam, would come to lend their support as soon as the pass was breached.

The Admiralty had sent a plan that consisted of occupying each of the turtles with six or seven vessels, while the others, without firing except in case of necessity, would go through the strait at top speed and take refuge under the cannons of Gibraltar.

Admiral Seymour and his officers made the Ministry understand that if the turtles held out regardless, all the ships that passed through in spite of them would be lost to England, because William Smith was holding the Mediterranean with a powerful fleet. It was therefore necessary to persist against the steam-forts and destroy them by any means possible.

To begin with, before even firing a shot, small boats set forth that did not resemble anything known. They were like the apices of cones whose points, ten meters long, were cast in steel. The structure floated like a long buoy, and traveled very rapidly with the aid of an ingenious electrical machine enclosed in the flanks of the engine; two metal wires, as flexible as a watch-chain, were sufficient to govern the little boat from the deck of a warship and give it an enormous speed. It was no stouter than a strong lighter, and could be thirty meters long.

The prow of the thing, which did not carry a single man, resembled a powerful hammer fifty centimeters in diameter, and behind that prow, the engine tapered all the way to the stern, which might be eight meters in diameter.

That strange boat was designed to penetrate the iron spikes with which the turtles were bristling, moving them aside by deflecting them, and then to batter a breach in the ion that constituted the external wall of the steam-forts. Fundamentally, they were nothing but battering-rams. By dint of striking the metal plates of the turtles, they could succeed, if the hopes of the English were not deceived, in dislocating the bolts that held them together. If, by misfortune, the latter result could not be attained, the battering-rams would at least have the advantage of parting the iron spikes sufficiently for an audacious mariner to be able to place a torpedo in the breach.

Admiral Seymour, continuing the tactics of the first attack, again directed all his forces against a single turtle. The battering-rams, twelve in number, were launched against the steam-fort closest to the Spanish coast.

At first, things went marvelously. The first ram separated the spikes and was about to strike the hull of the turtles with incredible violence. Aboard the English vessel the impact of the steel hammer was heard to resound against the iron wall.

The second ram did not enjoy such a complete success. Lifted up by an abrupt wave, it leapt over the spear-heads and struck the turtle with an even greater violence—but it could not come back, and remained suspended on the iron bars. The other rams enjoyed various fortunes, but did not succeed in making inroads into the steam-fort in an efficacious fashion.

In the meantime, formidable detonations erupted from all the vessels, which were very close together. That was the famous mortars entering into play. Those masterpieces of ballistics launched seventeen-hundred-kilogram masses of iron into the air to an astonishing height, and when those projectiles had described a sufficiently acute parabola, they fell almost perpendicularly on to the roof of the turtle, producing a sound like a cracked bell, which was audible ten leagues away.

Thus, the English plan seemed as clear as the water in a rock-pool. They simply wanted to strike the steam-forts continually, like anvils, until their blows split the carapaces. And they were not so crazy in hoping for such a result, for if each mass of iron, in falling back, did not produce any immediately appreciable result, they soon divined, from the fashion in which the turtle defended itself, that the attack was succeeding.

In fact, something unexpected was happening inside the floating forts. Although the engineers who had constructed them had taken the precaution of lining the carapace internally with felt and wadding a meter thick, the noise produced by the English projectiles on that bell of sorts was so intense, so horrible and so murderous that several matelots went suddenly mad, and half the garrison was rendered deaf in less than forty minutes.

Admiral Seymour quickly perceived his success, without knowing exactly how it was being achieved. He increased his fire, and it was then seen that the other turtles were maneuvering to assist the one that was in danger.

At the same time, however, cannon fire was heard from the direction of Makabata Point, on the coast of Morocco. Maxime-Jean had arrived, with his entire fleet.

The English vessels that were not taking part in the action against the turtles, and which, on the Admiral's orders, were awaiting developments, having perceived the Polan fleet, went to meet it. A furious battle was engaged ten kilometers from the African shore.

Lord Alcester having taken his most powerful battleships to attack the floating fortresses, the remainder, although composed of a large number of vessels, was not capable of standing up to Maxime-Jean. The King of the Isles deployed his forces in a great arc, enveloping the second English fleet, and, driving it vigorously before him, soon obliged it to move in the direction of the turtles, all of which then began to vomit shells and cannonballs furiously.

That sudden intervention by the King changed the face of things abruptly. Admiral Seymour, caught between two fires, understood at a glance the danger he was in—the danger of being crushed between the turtles and Maxime-Jean's powerful fleet. There was no time to lose. Immediately renouncing his bombardment of the steam-forts, he turned round toward the Polans and raced to the rescue of his compromised ships. The veritable battle—the Three Day Battle, as it came to be called—commenced in earnest.

The King of the Isles, extending his right flank toward the turtles, with which he had succeeded in putting himself in direct communication, and his left toward Alboasa Punta, tried in vain to close the Atlantic to the English army with his fleet, as the turtles closed the Mediterranean. Lord Alcester, extending his right flank, had the intelligence to draw away as far as possible from the turtles, thus preventing his adversary to enveloping him. Better than that, he succeeded in taking the offensive, thanks to his enormous numerical superiority, and Maxime-Jean retreated.

Everyone knows that it was a battle of giants. The English opposed their most formidable ships to the Polan fleet. With regard to battleships of the first rank, the enemy forces were almost equally matched, but Lord Alcester also had a considerable number of smaller ships of every kind, which set about harassing the King's vessels in such a fashion as, not to do them any harm, but to distract and worry them.

Seeing that, Maxime-Jean gave an express order to Kasaloff, who was commanding his left wing, not to follow the English if they attempted to draw him out into the open sea, and to each of the captains of the ships on the right wing to continue lending solid support to the turtles.

Seeing that, in those conditions, he was expending effort uselessly without obtaining any definite result, Lord Alcester soon deployed against the warships the means of destruction invented to disable the turtles. The battering-rams were launched against the King of the Isles' ironclads, and went to shake them in the depths of their hulls, while the mortars launched the formidable weights that we have described into the air. Maxime-Jean's vessels were moving incessantly, though, and it was very difficult to calculate the parabola, in that new kind of fire, to cause the projectiles to fall directly on the deck of one of them.

The *Northumberland* had her funnel crushed and its engine damaged by one of the gigantic bullets, and was put out of action. Fortunately, the current carried it toward the turtles and it made contact with one of them.

That accident drove all the King's officers and mariners into a fury. A veritable madness took possession of the matelots, who demanded a boarding with loud cries—but Maxime issued a general order absolutely forbidding any such insensate action.

Needless to say, cannons of all dimensions were raging, and the rumble of those thousand thunders was incessant. The torpedo-boats of both fleets were attempting with the aid of the thick smoke that was covering the sea, to slide under the enemy ships in order to blow them up.

In that regard, however. Maxime-Jean was as well-equipped as the English. His men, manning special boats, mounted a strong guard around the battleships, and it happened several times that the torpedo-boats of both camps collided with one another and came to hand-to-hand fighting. Once, in fact, two of those ships, in the fury of attack and defense, blew one another up with the most frightful bang imaginable.

The battle, commenced in the early hours of daylight, lasted until nightfall, without either Lord Alcester or the King of the Isles having departed for a single minute from the plans that they had sketched out.

It appears certain that if Maxime-Jean had not had the turtles to support him, Admiral Seymour would have succeeded in the course of the day either in driving his enemy out into the Atlantic or under the canons of Gibraltar, and winning a resounding victory.

When night fell, the crews of the ships of both fleets were too weary not to seize the opportunity to get a little rest. Each of them, by a tacit accord, took advantage of it to repair their damage.

Then, in the darkness, another battle began: a muted battle, a battle of ruses and ambushes, a battle in the fashion of savages. Here and there, intrepid mariners, avid for glory or inflamed by patriotism, manned fireships or launches crammed with dynamite, and set out to try to blow up a frigate or an ironclad. Many of those acts of heroism were carried out in the gloom.

At the slightest alarm, however, immense electric searchlights lit up aboard Maxime-Jean's vessels. The sea was illuminated as in broad daylight. Lord Alcester did not judge it necessary to do the same, since the King of the Isles had rendered it impossible for him to move without being seen, and the torpedo-boats continued to search for one another, avoid one another, fight one another and destroy one another, without any major result on either side.

At daybreak, the great voice of the cannons caused the echoes of the Sierra and the Djebel to resound once again.

More than a hundred thousand Spaniards on one coast, and twenty or twenty-five thousand Moroccans on the African shore, had gathered on the mountain slopes to watch the terrible drama that was about to unfold there. With the Spaniards there were Europeans of all nationalities. It had been known for a long time that the fleets would come to grips at that very place, and from Paris as from London, from Vienna as from St. Petersburg, people had come in haste.

The representatives of all the European powers in Madrid had sent embassy secretaries. Wagers were made, especially between Russians and Englishmen, the former betting on Maxime-Jean and the later, naturally, backing Lord Alcester. It was a sport of a new kind: a terrible sport.

It was about four o'clock when the cannonade recommenced; twenty thousand pairs of binoculars were aimed at the battlefield from the Spanish side, and it is necessary to say that the general sympathies were not in favor of England.

Maxime-Jean remained backed up against the Moroccan coast, supported on his right by the turtles. Admiral Seymour kept to the opening of the strait on the Atlantic side, out of range of the turtles and sufficiently well placed to attack the King's extreme left.

And, indeed, by directing all his effort at the last vessel of the Polan fleet, that one could be sufficiently exposed for the others to come to her aid, thus abandoning the support they had from the steam forts. That vessel was the *Invincible*, one of those that England had lost at the Battle of Pontevedra. Its Commandant was Pedro Cabanil, the coolest of men, although he was a Spaniard, and the most courageous of adventurers.

Maxime-Jean's order was that the vessel thus attacked should fall back toward the rest of the fleet in order to draw the English under the fire of the turtles. Pedro Cabanil executed his maneuver of retreat while sending repeated discharges of his powerful artillery at the British ships, all of which shots struck home, so tightly packed were the English vessels.

Lord Alcester did not allow himself to be drawn toward the floating fortresses any more than he had the day before. The greater part of the morning was thus employed in an artillery duel in which the two adversaries inflicted approximately equal damage on one another. The advantage in the combat without a victor, however, remained with the King of the Isles—for after all, what did he want? To prevent the English passing through. Now, the English did not get through.

Toward midday, Lord Alcester drew closer to the enemy and recommenced the previous day's maneuvers with the battering-rams and the mortars. This time, however, the Polans threw themselves across the metallic wires, by which means they succeeded in neutralizing Lord Alcester's electricity, and the motionless rams floated like huge useless buoys.

Then the English sent monitors to free their rams; the Polans, for their part, brought forward the enormous ship devoid of masts that we have mentioned. The latter, which was named the *Vesuvius*, sailed ponderously into the vicinity of Admiral Seymour's monitors and stopped.

The spectators of the Homeric struggle then saw, to their great amazement, two battens of a door open abruptly in the bow of the ship, and a cigar-shaped boat emerge from that portal under steam, plunge into the sea and disappear under the water.

Twenty seconds had not gone by before the English monitor blew up, along with the ram, reduced to shards flying through the air.

The *Vesuvius* sank profoundly, as if she were doubling her draw of water, the doors opened again, and the torpedo-boat that had departed a little while before reentered with as much precision as she had merged. Reestablishing her original flotation line, the mysterious vessel veered away tranquilly, while innumerable shells fell upon her armored and seemingly invulnerable carcass.

The King of Pola was "exposing himself," as the London newspapers had once so wittily put it.

Almost at the same moment, a kind of raft that looked like nothing much, and which had also emerged from the flanks of the *Vesuvius*, advanced between the two fleets, heading for the place where the torpedo-boats and the smaller warships were positioned. It moved with a singular speed and seemed to be gliding over the water. Like Admiral Seymour's rams it was steered by mans of electric chains that unwound as the raft moved forward.

The English fired on it furiously, but it kept advancing. It came alongside a station ironclad to starboard, and a large iron arm was suddenly seen to reach up into the air automatically and fall down upon the vessel, which made vain efforts to extract itself from that terrible embrace; then there was a terrible explosion, a frightful ripping sound, and everything collapsed, fireship and ironclad alike, to disappear beneath the sea.

A hurrah erupted from the Polan fleet, and the battle was soon circumscribed between Lord Alcester's torpedo-boats and the mysterious obese vessel, the *Vesuvius*, which seemed to contain an inexhaustible supply of fireships and cigar-boats within her flanks.

Until then, the combatants had almost retained their composure, but there was soon something resembling madness in both fleets. Then it became frenzy, fury, and rage. Little was calculated. Maxime-Jean's officers fired at full blast into the massed English vessels, and the latter returned equal measure. The fireships sought victims, the rams struck redoubled bows at the Polan ironclads, and the torpedo-boats blew one another up.

But no one gave ground.

Neither fleet weakened. Neither Seymour nor the King was any further advanced than the morning of the previous day.

Night fell. They were too excited to cease fire. The battlefield then offered the spectators of the gigantic battle a sight of grandiose, sublime horror, if ever there was one. Throughout the breadth of the strait, and over a length of ten kilometers, there were incessant and deafening explosions. One could see as well as in broad daylight, so well was the battlefield illuminated by the lightning-flashes that the cannons were projecting, the conflagrations that the fireships ignited, and, from time to time, by the explosion of a vessel: a frightful firework display.

In the two fleets, people went insane. The leaders scarcely had sufficient rationality to watch over the salvation of their subordinates, but above all, the latter were scarcely capable of obeying them.

Toward midnight, Kasaloff, impatient at not achieving any result, gave orders for his squadron to head straight for the English ships and take them by boarding. He doubtless did not remember that he had already attempted that maneuver ten times in the past forty-eight hours, but that the mariners of Her Very Gracious Majesty's navy, suspicious of the numerous Polan crews, had carefully avoided such baneful contact. The new attempt almost cost Maxime-Jean the battle. Kasaloff commanded six ships. Vice-Admiral Sir Reginald Macdonald,[27] who had seven ships of various sorts under his com-

---

[27] In our history, Admiral Sir Reginald Macdonald (1820-1893) retired in 1884, but would doubtless have come out of retirement in the circumstances described in the story.

mand, threw himself upon the imprudent Muscovite and drew another squadron with him, commanded by Admiral Ryder.[28]

Kasaloff could not sustain the frightful impact and drew back. The English sensing victory, redoubled their efforts. The Polan squadron, swiftly retreating, threw itself chaotically into the bulk of the King's fleet, and, in spite of the heroism of Pontins, Lamanon and Kasaloff himself, who performed prodigies—though not so many as the King of the Isles himself, Admiral Seymour was able to profit very skillfully from the confusion to separate the Polan ironclads from the turtles that had given them such powerful assistance.

Maxime-Jean would have been lost if Pontins, Paleieff and Lamanon, sacrificing themselves, had not set forth at full steam to smash into the vessels at the head of the English fleet, with the aid of their spurs. Fortunately, they were followed, and in less than twenty-five minutes, the Polan ironclads were able to take refuge behind the turtles, while the latter opened an infernal fire before which the English were forced once again to stop.

The King of the Isles was saved, but not without sustaining damage. Three of his battleships were out of action. One of them, the *Defence*, manned by Pontins, had done her duty so valiantly that it was necessary for the crew to abandon her, and she sank.

As you can imagine, the English uttered cries of triumph—and yet, they were not yet victorious, for their objective, to penetrate into the Mediterranean, had not been achieved.

However, Lord Alcester expected that the attack against the turtles, with the means at his disposal, would succeed the following day.

Dawn broke, and Admiral Seymour was able to observe that the victory was costing him dear, for he had lost seven or eight torpedo-boats, two station ironclads and three battle-

---

[28] Admiral Alfred Ryder (1820-1888) had retired in 1882, but ditto.

ships, the *Australia*, the *Dominion* and the *India*, which Pontins, Lamanon and Maxime-Jean had pierced in the side.

Suddenly, however, an immense clamor resounded on the Spanish mountain, from which a hundred thousand people were watching the battle. And almost at the same moment, the Polan fleet was seen to reappear.

It was returning to combat, but singularly augmented.

As he beat the retreat, in fact, Maxime-Jean had encountered William Smith's squadron, of eight battleships. Thanking God for that providential aid, he had assigned each one its new battle position. He had transferred Pontins to the *Warrior* and Lamanon to the *Achilles*, with the rank of Rear-Admiral, and then ordered them to set a course for the English, which he was able to approach thanks to the terrible fire of the turtles.

The King of the Isles now had twenty-one vessels under his command, plus the *Vesuvius* and another ship of the same model. This time, he disdained the support of the steam-forts. His entire fleet, in two lines, went along the Moroccan coast as far as Malabatta.

The turtles, for their part, had moved forward, and while no. 4 took up a position near the little Tarifa isles, no. 5 guarded the passage of the island of Peregil.

That offensive return, with new and imposing forces, disconcerted the English. Having believed themselves victorious, they found it hard to be obliged to recommence in unfavorable conditions.

Lord Alcester deliberated for a few minutes with his officers in order to decide whether to accept the battle. In the meantime, the King of the Isles carried out his maneuver, gained the open sea and came around, to put the English fleet in the necessity of winning a decisive victory or giving way.

The English weakened.

The crews of Smith's squadron, who were entirely fresh, did not give them time to prevaricate. They headed straight for them, forcing them to recoil and driving them toward the floating fortresses which welcomed them in a terrible fashion.

An immense cry of joy went up from the Spanish mountain; the members of the crowd were thinking about Gibraltar.

Heaped up against the turtles, crowded together, in such a fashion as not to be able to maneuver without riddling one another with fire, the faithful subjects of Her Very Gracious Majesty were no longer thinking of anything but selling their lives dearly. They would have preferred to blow up or sink rather than surrender.

Sir Reginald Macdonald, a man of vigor and forceful action, tried to pass between two steam-forts. Of the seven ships he commanded, three entered the Mediterranean and, badly damaged, went to shelter under the guns of Gibraltar; the others were sunk.

Pontins, with the *Warrior*, William Smith, Joe Green and the Russian Paleieff each captured one vessel in good condition, and Maxime-Jean had the joy of boarding the flagship, the *England*, aboard which he took Lord Alcester prisoner, while Kasaloff, furious at nearly having spoiled everything, sank everything that came within his range.

In brief, of that immense flotilla, sufficient to deliver battle to all the European navies combined, nothing remained except Admiral Macdonald's three ships.

William Smith was immediately created Duke of Gibraltar.

IX. Gibraltar, the Archipelago, Malta

Three days later, Gladstone's government resigned. The cabinet that took power had Lord Salisbury at its head as First Lord of the Treasury; Sir Stafford Northcote was appointed Chancellor of the Exchequer; Lord Cairns the Lord Chancellor and Lord Privy Seal, etc. etc.; Mr. Cross became Home Secretary; Sir Gathorne Hardy was Minister of War; Sir G. Ward

Hunt became First Lord of the Admiralty; and Bulwer-Lytton the Viceroy of India.[29]

As soon as he arrived in power, Lord Salisbury resolved to organize a vast alliance of all the European powers against Maxime-Jean I. That was what England had done against Napoléon, and the new government wanted to attempt the same thing against the adventurer who, it was said, had so far enjoyed more good fortune than talent.

The new cabinet order construction of vessels to begin in every shipyard in England. Thousands of workmen were hired for the arsenals, and it was announced that the immense loss that Great Britain had suffered would be repaired.

Lord Wolseley of Cairo was charged, in concert with the First Lord of the Admiralty, to put the entire coast in a state of defense. Lord Salisbury had the courage to double taxes, after making a speech in the House of Commons in which he said that the nation must make every sacrifice, because this time, for England, it was a matter of a struggle for existence.

In the meantime, he sent instructions to all the ambassadors of Great Britain to the continental powers to demonstrate to them that their common salvation demanded the annihilation of the King of the Isles. "As long as that baneful man has not disappeared," said the chief of the English cabinet, "there

---

[29] In our history, although Lord Salisbury was named as Prime Minister when he formed a government in 1885, he was the leader of the House of Lords, so Stafford Northcote (the Earl of Iddesleigh), had the title of First Lord of the Treasury. Sir Richard Cross was indeed appointed Home Secretary, and Gathorne Hardy (Viscount Cranbrook) took over from William Henry Smith as Secretary of State for War in January 1886, but Hugh Cairns had died in April and was thus unavailable, while George Ward Hunt had died in 1877, so both are cited anachronistically. Robert Bulwer-Lytton (1831-1891), the son of the famous author, had served as Viceroy of India until 1880 but never resumed the appointment in our history, in which he became Ambassador to Paris in 1887.

will be no rest for Europe, for once he is master of the seas, he will impose a tribute on all European nations, and will want to conquer the world."

The ambassadors at the courts of Madrid, Rome, Paris, The Hague and Constantinople received orders to call the attention of those various cabinets to the fact that Maxime Darnozan had already proclaimed himself King of the Isles, that that was an indication, and that his intention was indeed—the London cabinet had certain proof of it—to conquer all the islands of the globe. In consequence, Spain, with the Antilles and the Philippines; Italy, with Sicily and Sardinia; France, with Corsica, New Caledonia, Réunion, the New Hebrides, Guadeloupe, etc.; Turkey, with the Archipelago; and Holland, with Batavia, Sumatra and her other possessions, were directly threatened.

To these propositions, Spain responded categorically with another: let England surrender Gibraltar, and the cabinet of Madrid is ready to enter into negotiations relative to an alliance. Spain was within her rights, and there was nothing about the claim that could surprise Lord Salisbury. Nevertheless, the latter refused point-blank, and broke off the negotiations.

Italy had no claim to make, but the situation was too favorable for her not to demand something. Her diplomats made it understood that Malta was, in reality, in Italian waters, that such a fortress was a threat to Italy, and that she was ready to make an alliance with England if the latter would surrender Malta to her.

The Depretis[30] cabinet pointed out that it had two or three vessels of a rare power, such that no other nation could put similar ones in the line: the *Duilio*, the *Affondatore* and the *Italia*.

---

[30] Agostino Depretis (1813-1887) began his final term as prime minister of Italy in 1881; in our history he died in office in 1887.

Sir Savile Lumley[31] smiled disdainfully and declared that Malta was England's. England would not cede that island voluntarily to anyone; if anyone wanted to try to take it by force, they were welcome to try.

The Italian cabinet retained that last word and, without delay, sent an ambassador to Maxime-Jean to offer him an alliance against England. The King of the Isles immediately promised to facilitate an Italian conquest of the Tripolitan, and the treaty was signed.

Marshal Serrano, then the chief of the Madrid cabinet,[32] also proposed an alliance to the victor of Pontevedra, the first consequence of which would be the siege of the powerful English fortress. The King of the Isles accepted that too, on condition that he would take various points on the Moroccan coast, including the little island of Peregil, in order to make it a sentinel charged with guarding the strait.

Spain accepted.

With Turkey and the Netherlands, Lord Salisbury was more fortunate. The Dutch parliament and the Sultan feared that, as England claimed, Maxime-Jean wanted to take possession of all the world's seas and all the islands with which they were strewn. They committed the imprudence of allowing themselves to be drawn.

In truth, Turkey, in acting thus, was remaining faithful to her eccentric politics, and hoped to recover Egypt directly from the Polans.

What was France doing in the meantime? As you can imagine, she was also warmly solicited, even more warmly than the other nations, to ally herself with England.

---

[31] The diplomat John Savile (1818-1896) was one of numerous illegitimate sons of the Earl of Scarborough, John Lumley-Savile, hence the suffix appended to his name here.

[32] In our history, Francisco Serrano, Duke of la Torre (1810-1885) had died in office as prime minister of Spain in November 1885.

Like all the diplomats in Europe, Lord Salisbury knew he inexhaustible depths if chivalric naivety of the French in general, and the astonishing absence of political sense with which they are afflicted at times. He hoped, therefore, to succeed in Paris, and his hope was based on the very particular situation of the Republican government at the end of the summer of 1886. Monsieur Grévy, who had died six months earlier, had been succeeded by Jules Simon.[33]

Toward the middle of 1885, the Opportunists had succeeded in having the scrutiny of lists voted. As soon as that result was acquired, they had proceeded with elections. One minister, apparently independent, fought that electoral campaign very cleverly, in spite of old Monsieur Grévy, whose health had deteriorated extraordinarily since his illness of November 1884.

The Opportunists believed that they held France in their hands; they were mistaken. Their budgetary imprudences were to cost them dear; they were beaten in many départements by the moderates of the center left.

The royalists, for their part, taking advantage of the opportunity, found themselves at the head of a significant minority, two hundred and forty-eight out of five hundred and thirty-seven, but they were not yet in a position to change the face of things. So, on the death of Monsieur Grévy, who survived until the following January, the opportunists had the chagrin of seeing all their maneuvers end in the election of Jules Simon, their mortal enemy.

---

[33] In our history Jules Grévy (1807-1891) did not die until 1891, having remained President of the Republic until forced by scandal to resign in 1887, and the Opportunist Republican Jules Simon (1814-1896) never held that position. The "scrutiny of lists" to which the next paragraph refers was a system of voting akin to the system of proportional representation used in many modern electoral systems, and it was indeed adopted in France in 1885.

The ministry that had called the election having fallen to a vote of no confidence, the Presidency of the Council was accepted by Senator Albert Decrais,[34] who simultaneously took responsibility for the Ministry of Foreign Affairs.

Lord Lyons[35] having made the propositions of the London cabinet to Monsieur Decrais, the latter took the news to the Council of Ministers. Immediately, the President of the Republic took the floor and declared that no hesitation was possible, and that it was necessary to conclude the alliance, thanks to which there was a possibility of regaining a little prestige in Europe.

The Minister of Foreign Affairs did not share that opinion. He did not hesitate to argue against the President.

"England is beaten, and for a long time," he said. "She cannot, therefore, give us any help in recovering our status. But if France cannot yet see the dawn of a new political and military grandeur, it is not foolish for her to hope for a commercial prosperity that the present circumstances and her geographic situation will make as great as possible.

"The English merchant navy has been annihilated and will vanish from all the seas. If we are clever, it is the French merchant marine that will replace it. Let us encourage the construction of commercial ships everywhere; let new lines of steamers be founded in our ports. Remember, Monsieur le Président, that there are ten or fifteen English shipping lines that no longer exist: the Pacific Steam Navigation Company, the Royal Mail. The West Indies and Pacific Steamship Company, the Royal Mail Steam Packet Company, the Guion Line, the Cunard Line and the Anchor Line, the White Star line no longer have a single vessel at sea. That is a fleet of more than a hundred ships that it is necessary to replace, and which we can create within six months, if we devote a great deal of

---

[34] In our history, the diplomat Albert Decrais (1838-1915) never held any major political office until he became Minister for the Colonies in 1899.

[35] The diplomat Richard Lyons (1817-1887).

money and activity to it. Even better, we have on our coasts two or three islands that are virtually part of the French fatherland, and which we can easily occupy—I'm referring to Guernsey, Jersey and Alderney, which England is incapable of defending."

"That wouldn't be generous at the moment!" said Charles Simon, the Undersecretary of State for the Interior.

"Isn't generosity, in this instance, stupidity?" exclaimed Monsieur Decrais. "Was England generous to France after the war of 1870? Has she even been honest, in the Egyptian affair? It's time, Messieurs, to decide what we want and act in consequence."

"I don't see any inconvenience, my dear President," said Jules Simon, addressing Monsieur Decrais, "in profiting commercially from England's ruination. You can see that you've converted me. But I'd be sorry to see France trying to take possession of Jersey, Alderney and the other islands. Don't forget that it would be necessary to declare war on Great Britain, and we don't know where that would lead."

Knowing looks were exchanged on all sides, and it was decided that although they would not make an alliance with England, nor would they make an alliance against her with the King of the Isles.

In the meantime, the Spanish army, under the command of Marshal Martinez-Campos,[36] came to lay siege on land to Gibraltar. At sea, a dozen of Maxime-Jean's turtles, under the orders of Nicolas Ramine, established a severe, real and absolute blockade.

Thus separated from the world, the old and powerful fortress had inevitably to succumb.

From one side, Martinez-Campos belabored it with heavy cannon fire, and had no scruple about demolishing that nest of smugglers, who had been inundating Spain with fraudulently-introduced English products for seventy-five years, one house at a time.

---

[36] Arsenio Martínez-Campos y Antón (1831-1900).

From the sea, Nicolas Ramine undertook to open a breach in the base of the famous rock with solid cannonballs, in such a fashion that the celebrated bunkers hollowed out in the living rock, so high-ceilinged that the officers could parade their horses there, were soon suspended over an abyss.

While Ramine actively drove that siege, Pontins forced the passage of the Dardanelles with seven ironclads, destroyed what remained of the Turkish navy—four or five vessels that came to meet him under the command of Hobart Pacha—and had the joy of beating yet another Englishman in thrashing that Turkish admiral.[37]

Once he was master of the situation, the young Admiral occupied all the islands of the Sea of Marmora, that paradise where Pachas go to dream of Mohammed's, and, turning to the Archipelago, did not leave a single island unconquered. He took possession of Crete, attacked and forced the submission of the Ionian islands and those which belonged to the Greek government.

Maxime-Jean offered to help the King of Greece to reconquer Macedonia in its entirety in exchange for what he had taken from him, and the offer was accepted with enthusiasm. After which, it was a question of going with the Italian fleet to lay siege to Malta, which Sir Reginald Macdonald had been able to reach with his three ships, all that remained to England of the vast fleet confided to Lord Alcester.

The Depretis cabinet, which had returned to power, had given Admiral Acton[38] secret instructions. The Italians' sole concern is to make others work for them and to pocket all the profits. Assuming, therefore, that all sorts of mechanisms must be disorganized in England, and, with even greater reason, in

---

[37] Augustus-Charles Hobart-Hampden (1822-1886) was a captain in the English navy before entering the service of the Ottoman Empire (with an immediate promotion to Rear-Admiral) in 1867.

[38] Guglielmo Acton (1825-1896) was Italian, but had an English grandfather, General Joseph Acton.

the majority of stations distant from the metropolis, the cabinet in Rome enjoined Admiral Acton not to wait for Maxime-Jean, but to set a course for Malta and try to take it before the King of the Isles arrived. If he succeeded, he was to hold on to the island and its fortified positions while waiting for some kind of *modus vivendi* to be negotiated with the vanquisher of the English. It was not difficult to divine Italy's intentions beneath those orders.

Admiral Acton acted in conformity with his superiors' wishes. He left Naples with his squadron, composed of five vessels, and reached Malta at full steam. Two days later, when Maxime Jean presented himself at Naples with is fleet to join up with the Italian vessels, he was told that Admiral Acton was waiting for him of Valletta, to which he had gone in haste in order to prevent the garrison receiving assistance.

Boislucas, who was aboard the royal vessel, and Maxime-Jean himself, were not duped by the explanations given to them, and regretted from that moment on having allied themselves with Italy, but their regrets gave way to more energetic sentiments when, within sight of Malta, they found the Italian squadron reduced to three ships in a poor state.

What had happened? Oh, nothing that was not perfectly natural.

Admiral Acton, having arrived off Valletta, had attacked without further ado. Sir Reginald Macdonald had thought at first that it was the Polan fleet, whose arrival he was expecting at any moment. In that case, he would have helped the place to defend itself, only making a reckless move when the position became desperate. When he saw that the Italian squadron was alone, however, and was sure that no other warship was in sight, he said to himself that an Englishman with three ships under his orders could well try his luck against five Italian ironclads.

And he had tried it so well that, the following day, he had inflicted a cruel defeat on his adversary, sinking the *Affondatore*—the second time that a ship of that name had experienced a similar misfortune—forcing another vessel to run on to the rocks of the little island of Cominotto and putting the rest to flight, while he, reaching the open sea, had headed for the Adriatic in order to reach the neutral port of Trieste.

After having made Admiral Acton comprehend that the Italian government had a singular manner of operating alliances, Maxime-Jean sent all his forces forward against the English fortifications, and bombarded Valletta in such a terrible fashion that it was not difficult to foresee the capitulation.

Rear-Admiral McCrea[39] put up a resolute defense, but his garrison, composed of mercenaries, like all the soldiers employed by the United Kingdom, threatened mutiny, as is often the case with the armies of vanquished nations. In the meantime, the new arrived that Gibraltar had fallen into the hands of the Polans and Spaniards. It required no more to provoke the final catastrophe. Malta surrendered.

The senior officers, seeing themselves abandoned by their men, would not consent to cease fire. There were abominable scenes, and the Admiral, with his entire general staff, fled into the interior of the island with the intention of reaching a small port from which they could go either too Tunisia or Greece, and return as quickly as possible to England.

Difficulties then commenced for the King of the Isles. The Italian admiral, without consulting with his ally, disembarked his men to occupy Valletta. It was necessary to go to extremes for the Italians to consent to leave Malta to its veritable conquerors. Although the Rome cabinet yielded temporarily on that point, however, it demanded that Maxime-Jean keep his word to attack and deliver the Tripolitan, and what while maintaining reservations on the possession of Malta, which, evidently being an Italian territory—so the diplomatic notes affirmed at least—was part of the claims of *Italia irredenta*.

It would not have taken much for Maxime-Jean, instead of heading for the African coast, to turn the prows of his vessels toward Naples or Venice, but he still had enough self-

---

[39] John D. McCrea, former captain of H.M.S. *Hibernia*.

control to believe that he ought to keep his word first, and see after that what he ought to do.

The Tripolitan, isolated from the rest of Turkey in consequence of the events at sea that had caused the Turkish fleet and all its islands to fall into Polan hands, was poorly defended, and it did not require more than a month for Maxime-Jean to take possession of it.

He gave it, as had been agreed, to the Italian government, and then returned to Madagascar, where a much more important expedition was being prepared under the orders of Kellner.

The King of the Isles had not had much joy, either, out of his alliance with Spain in the matter of Gibraltar. The redoubtable fortress, completely blocked, had not had time to renew its supplies beforehand, and food became scarce during the first weeks of the siege, all the more so because, as everywhere, there were monopolists, speculators and even simple sensualists who would not deprive themselves of anything when the rest of the population began to suffer. It was astonishing that a place like Gibraltar, which served as a warehouse for the English at the gate of the Mediterranean, had not been better provisioned. It was because the town, divested during the English expedition against the Mahdi in Sudan, had not yet received the usual stock of new provisions when the theft of the English vessels had taken place in all the ports of the world.

In any case, it was not famine that determined the fall of Gibraltar.

While Martinez-Campos had sent an incessant rain of projectiles against the fortress from the Spanish coast, not giving the English a moment's peace, Nicolas Ramine, with his turtles—between which a rowing-boat could not have passed, so strict was the surveillance—had applied himself, as we have said, to hollowing out the rock on which the town stood with his cannonballs.

When he had made a sufficient excavation in the granite for a number of men to be able to install themselves within it, he had sent sappers, who set about perforating the rock slowly but surely. The tunnels—or, more accurately-the holes were not extended beyond ten meters. A dozen of them were made, in the depths of each of which a formidable quantity of dynamite was placed. Then the sappers came back aboard the turtles, the dynamite was detonated electrically, and the old rock, the ancient pillar of Hercules, trembled in its foundations.

Oh, it was a cruel terror for the inhabitants of Gibraltar when, in the wake of the explosions, they experienced such violent quakes that the fortress shook as if it were about to collapse into the sea.

It is well-known what influence the civilian population always has on the remainder of the besieged in an invested town. The women and children, by their tears and their terrors, first soften their husbands' and fathers' courage; then, if the danger becomes fearful, all of them make out deadly reasons why, after all, the quarrels of nations are not their concern.

Any man who begins to be afraid, only asks to be convinced; he gradually communicates his impression to his neighbor, who is only waiting for that confidence to form a chorus. Soon, people dare to say aloud what they only whispered yesterday. Already, they no longer uninhibited; they go so far as to complain in their officers' hearing. The later become annoyed and threaten to have the cowards shot, but the soldiers too have understood. Undermined by the fearful, they have no enthusiasm for the perilous pass with which they are threatened.

In any case, Nicolas Ramine had recommenced his excavations; he was renewing his explosions. The terror reached its peak. On the other hand, Martinez-Campos' shells were claiming numerous victims—and finally, one evening, the soldiers, who no longer had enough tea and had run out of roast beef two days before, refused their duties and were obstinate in not manning the guns.

The civilian population marched to the governor's door and demanded that he surrender. The latter, indignant, came out of his house and tried to have the traitors whipped, but even the soldiers under arms supported the inhabitants. The governor and his officers then had the imprudence to fire on the crowd in order to intimidate them, and wounded an artilleryman. That was the signal for a bloody revolt. The Commandant and most of his officers were massacred in less than an hour, and the town surrendered to the Polans the same day.

It was then that a rather comical incident occurred.

In accordance with the instructions he had received, Nicolas Ramine handed Gibraltar over to the Spaniards, who entered it during the evening. The next day, the Admiral, taking his leave of Marshal-Campos, intending to head for the small island of Peregil in order to install his forces there, as had been agreed, and moor there with his turtles.

Then, however, a customs officer came to his ship—the same one who had operated with so much valor two years earlier at Irun.[40] That individual declared that the Polan vessels must communicate their bills of lading to him and pay a fine if everything was not in accordance with the regulations, the Spanish customs being unable, in any circumstances, to give up its rights.

Nicolas Ramine thought it was a joke and let it be known that he thought it mediocre, but that model administrator, who would have taxed the Devil himself, had the imprudence to insist that he was perfectly serious.

The Polan Admiral demanded a meeting with Martinez-Campos, who told him that it was nothing to do with him.

"In that case," said Ramine, "I know what I must do,"

And he went back to his ship, where the astonished customs officer was, and gave the order to arrest and tie him up, which was done.

He was brought before the Admiral, who said to him: "I do not like people to make fun of me. It's said that Spaniards,

---

[40] The Spanish customs officers at Irun, on the border with France, were notorious for their officiousness and rudeness. Debans had probably encountered one recently.

before dying, like to say their prayers; I invite you to hasten yours, for you're about to be hanged."

"Hanged?" cried the customs officer, utterly terrified. "Why?"

"I have no explanation to give to a man who does not understand that I have just given Spain a diamond equivalent to all the customs demands in the world. I'm going to hang you in front of your compatriots."

He made a sign; four sturdy matelots took possession of the customs officer and dragged him to a corner, where a greased roped formed into a noose had already been prepared.

The Spaniard started crying out like a blind man. From the top of the ramparts a few officers divined what was happening and alerted their general. Martinez-Campos sent a colonel to discover what had motivated Nicolas Ramine's preparations. Ramine had no hesitation in informing the general's messenger.

"But Admiral," said the Colonel, "that man is a Spaniard!"

"Oh, go to the Devil!" exclaimed Ramine. "I've just sat you down in Gibraltar, which I can blow up any time I like."

The Colonel asked the Admiral to wait a moment and returned to the General, who sent his apologies to Nicolas Ramine, asking him to release the administrator. Twenty minutes later, the later was free.

The affair caused talk, the customs officer protested, and Spain naturally fell out with the King of the Isles. The government even wanted to forbid Ramine to install himself on the Moroccan coast—but it was easier to announce that pretention than to sustain it. The King of the Isles' lieutenant took his turtles to Centa, which he bombarded and took by storm in a day, before the eyes of Martinez-Campos. He sent all the convicts back to Spain, furnishing them with small boats to cross the sea, and took possession of the coast, which he protected and fortified strongly, as he had been instructed to do.

That raid and audacious strike threw all of Spain into a fury. There was immediate thought of vengeance, and England, which knows how to forget her grievances if necessary, arrived just in time to renew negotiations relative to an offensive and defensive alliance.

Italy, for her part, did not conceal her chagrin

It is of little importance to us, said one of her most officious newspapers, whether England has Malta or not, *if Italy has nothing to gain by it. The adventurer who claims to be King of the Isles might well learn to his cost that one does not challenge great powers with impunity.*

Once again, the English cabinet did not want to remember that the Rome cabinet had just played a dirty trick on them and again offered an alliance. Great Britain was therefore able to count on the Netherlands, Spain and Italy, and the warships that she as building in her shipyards. But English ships could not penetrate into the Mediterranean, and the Italian ironclads, as well as a few Spanish boats, could not get out of it.

On the orders of his government, Sir Reginald Macdonald had returned to London. The Admiralty, informed by him as to exactly what had happened, at Gibraltar as well as Malta, congratulated him on his courage and energy. Then he was appointed commander-in-chief of a fleet that was to operate in the Mediterranean, composed of the three English vessels that had taken refuge in Trieste, five Italian ironclads under the orders of Admiral Mattei and a Spanish squadron.

Macdonald returned to Trieste, waited for his allies, and took to the sea.

At that point, the Polans only had in the Mediterranean, in addition to Nicolas Ramine's forces, a squadron of eight vessels, the general headquarters of which was in Cyprus, plus a few gunboats and one turtle off Malta. Pontins was in command of all these forces. Macdonald went to look for him at Cyprus and offered to do battle, Pontins accepted without hesitation.

The young Rear-Admiral had Capmartin and Paleieff under his orders as squadron leaders. He charged Paleieff, a man of uncommon audacity, to attack the three English vessels while Capmartin attacked the Spaniards and he took personal responsibility for the Italian fleet.

The battle which took place in view of Famagusta, was rude. Everything transpired, however, as Pontins had foreseen. Paleieff held firm against Macdonald, who had found an adversary worthy of him. Capmartin took possession of a Spanish vessel and Pontins was on the point of routing the Italia squadron when, just as the young Comte de Pontevedra was giving an order to run straight at the Italian flagship, the *Duilio* in order to take her by boarding, a grenade coming from God knows where exploded in front of him, killing him outright.

There was then great disturbance in the Polan fleet. Macdonald, redoubling his efforts, succeeded in retaking the offensive and had the glory, not of destroying the Polan fleet, but of obliging it to yield the battlefield to him. Rallied by Paleieff, it retreated in good order. The Englishman dared not pursue it.

In consequence of that demi-victory, a long cry of triumph resounded in England, Spain and Italy—especially in Italy. People congratulated one another from one end of the peninsula to the other.

The *Diritto* printed the following lines on its front page:

These insolent mariners are not invincible! It is evidence that they had as much conceit as good fortune in their previous successes. England, exhausted, only had to ask for our alliance for the face of things to change—for we can proclaim without false modesty that it is to Italy that Admiral Macdonald owes the victory of Famagusta. It is an Italian ship from which the fatal projectile was launched that killed Pontins. We ought therefore to rejoice in this victory and be proud of it from two points of view. In the first place, we have diminished the power and prestige of the so-called King of the Isles, and secondly, we have proved that the Italian navy has become one of the most redoubtable, if not the most redoubtable, in the world.

The article concluded, according to the newspaper's custom, with a few insults directed at France—which, however, remained tranquil.

Maxime-Jean was in the Red Sea, returning to Madagascar, when a dispatch-boat, traveling at full steam, brought him the fatal news.

On learning of Pontins' death, the King of the Isles could not hold back his sobs, but that initial moment of weakness soon gave way to the most violent anger that the man, ordinarily so self-composed, had ever experienced and allowed to be manifest.

Prey to a frightful nervous fury, his mouth pursed, his eyes wide and as pale as a corpse. Maxime-Jean paced up and down the deck of the royal vessel, the *Monarch*, uttering exclamations and threats.

"Pontins!" he said. "Three nations have united against me to kill Pontins! A hero! A boy that I made into a prince; a fearless mariner who would have married the daughter of a king. They've killed me!" Planting himself in front of the officer who had brought him the sad news, he cried: "First of all, who killed me?"

"No one knew when I left Suez to inform you of the misfortune."

"Oh, yes, a misfortune! The greatest that could strike our young monarchy. It's not the defeat that disturbs me, it's the loss of the man to whom I owe the victory of Pontevedra, and perhaps even more. Woe, woe betide whoever killed him! I'll guarantee that he shall know bad days."

It was with eyes full of tears that Maxime-Jean sent the signals necessary to turn the entire fleet around and retrace its steps.

"Messieurs," he said to his officers, "we're going to avenge Pontins, and neither you nor I will have any rest until it's done." Then turning to the second-in-command of the dispatch boat, who was awaiting his orders, he went on: "You, Monsieur, tell your captain to continue his route all the way to Villejean in Diego Suarez Bay. He'll find Kellner and Joe

Green there, who ought to have prepared the army and fleet of which I was going to take command. Tell them to come and join me at Cyprus, with all their forces."

The officer made a military salute and went back to the dispatch-boat, while the King of the Isles' ironclads returned at full steam toward Suez.

A week later, the allied fleet, which had made a failed attempt to land two thousand men on Cyrus, received the order to go to confront the King.

At Ismailia, Maxime-Jean read the Italian newspapers, including the article in the *Diritto*.

"Ah! It was them who killed Pontins! And they're bragging about it! They're bragging about it! They're direly mistaken!"

The brave Admiral Macdonald, one of the heroes of the Three Day Battle, knew by experience what Maxime-Jean was worth and was under no illusions about the probable outcome of the battle that was about to take place. He was not unaware of the extent to which he could rely on the Italian warships and the Spanish mariners, but he had received orders and he came to position himself off Port Said in order to prevent the King from emerging into the Mediterranean. That was the best thing to do. Maxime-Jean was too exasperated to retreat to take the slightest precaution or even to wait for twenty-four hours. As soon as he sighted the enemy he gave orders for his vessels to quit the harbor of Port Said and, as at Pontevedra, to go, almost without firing a cannon-shot to attack the enemy ships head on.

"Don't let a single one escape!" was his final word.

We shall not recount the battle of Port Said in detail. It was terrible, but it lasted no longer than four hours. The brave Macdonald, in spite of his talent and his energy, was crushed. His three vessels worked wonders, but did not succeed in bringing victory to the Brutish flag.

All the Spaniards were captured by boarding.

The Italians, knowing full well that Maxime-Jean would doubtless avenge himself in a fashion that history would not forget, defended themselves with a veritable rage. They deployed a rare valor in that circumstance. When two of their ships sank, Macdonald tried valiantly to come to their aid, but in spite of his courage, in spite of the ardor of his officers and in spite of Macdonald's support, the Italian Admiral had to concede to the force of numbers and, after having valiantly done his duty, he surrendered.

Sir Reginald did not want to surrender, and continued fighting until the situation was desperate. His vessel could do no more. It sank, but the brave English mariner succeeded in putting to sea in a torpedo-diver and returning to Trieste, from which he departed for England.

After his victory, Maxime-Jean came to Cyprus and asked to see Pontins' body, which had been embalmed. He wept once again for his intrepid companion, and then ordered solemn funeral rites.

The Italian prisoners were obliged to watch the funeral, in which the King lavished an indescribable pomp. All he said, by way of a funeral oration, was: "Pontins had all the virtues. He was the best and most worthy of us all. I shall take his coffin aboard my ship, in order to conquer a mausoleum worthy of him and of us."

The King did indeed take the bier on which Pontins was resting aboard the *Monarch*; it was deposited in a kind of chapel, where it was literally buried under flowers.

Al those ceremonies lasted a fortnight. As they were concluded, Kellner telegraphed from Suez, having just entered the canal. Three days later he was within sight of Cyrus with Joe Green, who had brought a squadron of twenty transport ships.

We shall not linger long over the details of that campaign, which is in all memories. Everyone knows how the King of the Isles threw an army into Sicily, which took possession of the island in a matter of days, exactly as Garibaldi had done, and better.

Sicily was decidedly not difficult to conquer. In the meantime, Sardinia suffered the same fate, almost without a shot being fired.

It was on entering Palermo that Maxime-Jean dared, for the first time, to reveal his ambition. In an order of the day that he issued in order to congratulate his fleet and ground troops he made the following pronouncement, which contained and explained all his politics:

The mission that we have imposed on ourselves is to extend our power over all the islands in the world. Today, Sicily and Sardinia are ours. Tomorrow, it will be the Balearics, the Spanish and English Antilles, the Philippines, the Isles of Sunda, the Celebes and all the islands of Oceania. Soldiers and mariners, we shall only rest when the supreme goal is attained. Then, we shall truly be masters of the world.

X. The Italian Incident and the English Maneuvers

That menacing declaration, which the telegraph carried to the four corners of Europe, would have been an act of signal folly if Maxime-Jean had not been ready to ensure its execution.

Two days before, the Governor of Haiti, the famous John Knox—who had been constructing warships without respite for two years and had trained an army of twenty thousand mulattos—had take to the sea with all his personnel and presented himself at Kingston in Jamaica in order to take it by force. The operation was not difficult. The English soldiers, less well-equipped since the defeats and also less well armed, only battled in the most ineffectual manner and ran away as soon as they found themselves confronted by troops slightly superior in numbers.

There is nothing astonishing in that; it is the case with almost all vanquished peoples. Commodore W. L. Brown, who wanted to resist and might have been able to do so, was deserted by his soldiers. Vice-Admiral McClintock,[41] who commanded the stations of North America and the Antilles, was in no state to oppose the intentions of John Knox. His best ships and station ironclads had long been taken away from him and had taken part in the Three Day Battle. Nevertheless, he tried his luck with a flotilla of gunboats, and was obliged to beat the retreat after a platonic manifestation.

John Knox took possession of all the ports of Jamaica, which, as is well known, number thirty, imposed a heavy war tax on the entire English population, and continued his campaign by attacking and taking the Spanish Antilles: Cuba, Puerto Rico, etc. After the Antilles he took the Bermudas, and only left Martinique and Guadeloupe untouched—not because Maxime-Jean had renounced their capture but because he was not at war with France, and adjourned that question for later, amiable negotiation with the cabinet in Paris, offering them significant compensation in the direction of Pondicherry.

In seas of the Indies, during the same period, Rear-Admiral Lamanon, Joshua Klett and Prytz, in command of the army, successively attacked the Philippines, the Celebes, the Moluccas, Borneo, Sumatra, Java and New Guinea, and succeeded in establishing garrisons everywhere composed of Hindus, Malagasies, Malabars and Malays. Lamanon had some difficulty disposing of the Dutch fleet, but eventually destroyed it after a series of five murderous combats, the last of which cost two vessels and earned him the title of Duc. Once victorious, Lamanon took particular care over the fortification of the Strait of Molucca, the Sunda Strait, the Bali Strait and the Pacific shipping routes in general.

In a cleverly-drafted proclamation the Polan Admiral explained to the indigenous populations that the King of the Isles was founding an Oceanian power and that he was offering them liberty by expelling the former masters, of whom even the best were worthless; that, in sum, they were neither Spanish, not Dutch, nor Portuguese, nor English, but Oceanian, and

---

[41] Francis Leopold McClintock (1819-1907).

that Maxime-Jean, their sovereign, had just founded in veritable Empire of Oceania.

Such good reasons, supported by thirty thousand men, a hundred cannons and a fleet of eight ironclad warships, won all the support that the new Duc had anticipated.

Prytz and Joshua Klett defeated Spanish and Dutch troops several times over, and all the islands of the large group obstructing the route to Japan and China were subjugated in a relatively short time.

There too England had Admirals and Commodores, but they commanded a insufficient navy, like McClintock, and could only watch, with rage in their hearts, the progress of Great Britain's mortal enemy. Unable to do anything to impede him at sea, they reached an understanding with the generals of the Indian Army to organize a defense of the Indian peninsula, at all costs.

They were well aware that the Rajahs of the interior were beginning to stir. The former Gaekwad of Baroda, deposed in 1873 or 1874,[42] had evaded the surveillance that was being exercised upon him and was seeking to incite the powerful kingdom of which he had been the sovereign to revolt.

On the other hand, it was known that since the Battle of Pontevedra, the Russian government had been incessantly moving troops into central Asia. General Ivanoff, the man most familiar with the populations of the region and the regions itself, a man of iron, had set up camps in the vicinity of Khiva, on the banks of the Amu Darya, near Tashkent, at Bukhara and on the frontier of Afghanistan. Those camps had gradually filled up with troops that were only waiting for a signal to come through he passes, take Kabul and move forward by three or four different routes into the kingdom of Lahore.

---

[42] The reference is presumably to Maharrao Gaekwad, who was deposed by the English and then put on trial for attempting to murder the English Resident in 1873, although his father had been far more famous.

Boislucas, the Minister of Foreign Affairs, was in Saint Petersburg. Russia had recognized Maxime-Jean I. France had done likewise, and Austria and northern Germany were expected to follow their example.

England, still powerful by virtue of her wealth and capable of constructing twenty fleets, nevertheless seemed doomed.

Obliged to assist their colonies and exhaust themselves in that, the Netherlands and Spain were incapable of doing anything to help Great Britain to regain the upper hand. The alliance they had had the imprudence to conclude—over which they were biting their fingers—was a dead letter.

As for Italy, she had too much to do on her own account. Maxime-Jean, with an army of fifty thousand men and thirty vessels—for Nicolas Ramine had joined him—had just attacked Naples, taken Ischia and Capri, which he intended to maintain as a perpetual threat, and had launched two armies, each of fifty thousand men, into Calabria, where small bodies of troops maneuver more easily than large masses.

The Italian government hastened to concentrate an army of a hundred and some thousand men in the foothills of the Apennines. The mobilization was decreed and the troops headed southwards—but then the King of the Isles and his lieutenants started running around the coasts, bombarding everywhere and simulating descents at various points. Genoa was threatened. Two thousand Polan marines occupied San Remo for a week, Paleieff peppered the fortifications of Ancona with shells and then headed for Venice.

A mad terror and complete disarray were the consequence of those events. The Italians were in a state of indescribable exasperation. The people accused the government of trying to come to terms with the enemy. Revolutionaries took advantage of the opportunity to rouse mobs in order to grab a little money, a position or a promotion. The army, harassed, went northwards and southwards, westwards and eastwards, searching for an enemy that showed itself everywhere but could not be found anywhere.

Octave Kellner, the Commander-in-Chief of the Polan army in Calabria, deployed an unusual activity and military intelligence. While skirmishing endlessly with Cialdini's[43] advance units or threatening his flank, for he transported his men from one place to another with astonishing rapidity, Maxime-Jean inundated the country with emissaries who carried out an active propaganda in favor of the former King of Naples. He even announced his intention of reestablishing the temporal power of the Pope and bringing down the house of Savoy in Piedmont and the Duchy of Genoa.

In the midst of all these events, Kellner, without fighting a single battle, forced his adversary to retreat incessantly and led to a battlefield on which, in spite of his numerical inferiority, he counted on fighting victoriously.

It was then that the Italian government, derailed by the anarchists and ceding to the pressure of public opinion, sent ambassadors to the King of the Isles to propose an armistice and implore peace.

Maxime-Jean, who had not lost sight of his principal objective—England—only made them beg him for the time necessary to demonstrate that he could have gone all the way to Rome.

"I consent to a treaty," he told the envoys, when he deigned to grant them an audience, "but tell your government that the ingratitude of a nation must have limits. If I were to ally myself with a power that there is no need to name, it would be a trivial matter for me to reduce you to despair. Will the lesson I've just given you profit your government and your people? I would like to think so, without being very hopeful."

It was necessary to accept those harsh words of a conqueror, and the peace was signed, on conditions disastrous for Italy. She ceded all her islands, was obliged to surrender what was left of her fleet, and promised in addition to pay a war tax of a billion. Maxime-Jean also stipulated in the treaty that fifty thousand Italian soldiers would be employed for as long as

---

[43] Enrico Cialdini (1811-1892)

necessary in the construction of an immense octagonal tower a hundred meters high, containing twenty-three floors including the terrace, on Mount Etna in Sicily, five hundred meters above sea-level, which would serve as Pontins' tomb.

Maxime-Jean wanted that gigantic monument for his favorite lieutenant to be visible for thirty leagues over the Tyrrhenian Sea, in order that his enemies would know how he punished felony in the fashion in which he avenged his people while honoring them.

The King had no need to leave an army of occupation in Italy. Sicily was sufficient to keep watch on his debtor. He established turtles in the Strait of Messina, in the Bocca Piccola, between Capri and the mainland, and in the Ischian Channel. He did not think it necessary to do any more. Naples thus served him as an open door to penetrate into the boot whenever he wished.

When all the islands of the Mediterranean except Corsica were in his power, Maxime-Jean went to take command of his fleet in the Indies, and it was learned with terror that it had just made a simultaneous appearance off Melbourne and Sydney. More than that; with the aid of rafts expressly constructed for the purpose, it disembarked twenty thousand men in the vicinity of the southern lakes and the province of Victoria. That army reached Gippsland and, without wasting a minute, and in spite of the mountains, headed for the Sydney-to-Melbourne railway, which Kellner had orders to occupy at Wodonga.

Australia has no more than three million inhabitants. No armed force worthy of the name is in any state of defend it. The ninety-six regular soldiers of the province of Victoria would not have any such pretention. As for the volunteers, they are brave and like parading, but one does not make war with such national guardsmen. Commodore Erskine[44] and Sir

---

[44] James Erskine (1838-1911) became Commodore of the Australia Station in 1882.

Henry Parkes,[45] the Prime Minister and Colonial Secretary at Sydney, wanted to oppose the disembarkation directed by Kasaloff, but the former had no ships and the latter had no men or cannons.

Since the commencement of the war, the Australians had created a maritime arsenal and shipyards. Sir Nathaniel Barnaby, the director of naval construction in England, had come to Melbourne secretly aboard a French ship with engineers and numerous workmen.[46] The chief engineer of machinery, James Wright,[47] had similarly gone to set up workshops. But things had moved slowly and the ships under construction had not been launched when Maxime-Jean presented himself at Melbourne.

Hasty works of fortification had been carried out on both sides of the pass, but the King forced a way through, penetrated into the immense bay, and anchored in front of the city.

The cosmopolitan population of Melbourne was not disposed to suffer a massacre. Maxime-Jean addressed a proclamation to them in which he promised the Australians not to touch their institutions. "However," he added, "my intention is to keep Australia, which is, after all, an island. Your country, which thus far has only been a colony, I intend to make into a metropolis, the metropolis of the vastest empire in the world: the metropolis of the Empire of the Seas."

Two ministers, the honorable Charles Young and Dr. L. L. Smith,[48] being unable to resist, handed in their resignation. The governor, representing the English crown, invited the principal citizens to an assembly in which the King's pro-

---

[45] In our history, Sir Henry Parkes (1815-1896) was temporarily out of office as prime minister from 1885 to 1887, but Debans had no way to anticipate that.

[46] In our history, Nathaniel Barnaby (1829-1915) retired due to ill-health in 1885, but ditto.

[47] James Wright (1824-1899).

[48] Louis Lawrence Smith (1830-1910)

posals were discussed. He had given the city twenty-four hours to surrender.

During those twenty-four hours they learned that the railway had been occupied by Kellner's army, installed at Wodonga and Albury, astride the two states of Victoria and New South Wales. Sydney, bombarded by Kasaloff, had surrendered. Melbourne was incapable of resisting the combined forces of the King of the Isles; it capitulated in its turn.

Maxime-Jean took possession of the governmental palace, declared Melbourne the capital of his Estates, and went to the Catholic church, where he had a *Te Deum* sung, after which, with no further ceremony, the bishop and his officers proclaimed him Emperor of the Seas.

It was on the day after his coronation that the English made their supreme attempt to get rid of their terrible adversary.

This time, they employed drastic means.

It was in the afternoon. Maxime-Jean emerged from the palace in order to welcome his land army, which was arriving by railway.

The Emperor's carriage had just arrived in the street when a man on horseback appeared, at the gallop, overturning all those who were in his way.

It was thought at first that the horse had the bit between its teeth and people scattered in all directions, but when he arrived in front of the King the man brandished a revolver and opened fire.

Maxime-Jean's hat was carried away by the bullet, and the murderer was about to fire again when the blade of a saber was seen to flash in the sun, and he fell from his horse, his head cut open.

It as the Emperor himself who, having divined the bandit's intention, had promptly unsheathed his sword and had just fractured his assassin's skull, saying: "If all sovereigns immediately struck down all those who attempted to assassinate them, the métier of regicide would soon become impracticable."

The man was not dead, however. He was given medical care, and, in the course of his convalescence he confessed that he was to have been paid two thousand pounds sterling by England for his attempted assassination.

The London cabinet denied the allegation, of course, but two or three Irish newspapers did not hesitate to declare that the English government had secretly put a price on Darnozan's head fifteen months earlier. And, indeed, several days later, the Melbourne police arrested several individuals who were convicted of plotting to kill the Emperor of the Seas.

The latter then embarked on the *Monarch* to go and obtain the submission of New Zealand and Van Diemen's Land. He had not been at sea three days, however, off an unapproachable coast, when incursions of sea-water were suddenly and simultaneously manifest on three of his ironclads, including the flagship.

The danger was perceived just in time to avoid a disaster, and they succeeded in repairing the breaches. Then an investigation was mounted and it was found that sailors recently embarked had gone down into the coal-bunkers and remained there for some time. The men had declared themselves to be Irishmen from Queentown. They were submitted to interrogation. They did not even know the county from which they were supposed to originate, and it was quickly perceived that their Irish accents were fake. Their bags were searched; they contained considerable sums in English gold and banknotes.

All three of them were immediately tried by a court martial presided over by Kasaloff, and two hours later they were hanged.

XI.

Lord Killyett, as you know, had taken part in the Three Day Battle, where he had acquitted himself honorably as the chief of staff of Admiral Hood,[49] who was in command of a squadron, but he had been taken prisoner by Maxime-Jean.

The King of the Isles had set him free for the second time. He had put him ashore on the coast of Spain after having said to him: "You would never forgive me, Milord, when you're my father-in-law, for having detained you. Present my honorable respects to Lady Helena, whom I have the intention of marrying in London itself. After what I have done, I can reveal my projects to you—which you will no longer, I hope, take for humorous boasts. Go!"

The noble lord, stiffer and more obstinate than ever, did not even deign to thank the King, and went.

Four days later he was in London and presented himself at the Admiralty.

There was no little surprise in England, when it was learned that Commodore Lord Killyett had just arrived, sent back unconditionally, by the King of the Isles. It was remembered that His Grace had already been taken prisoner once before by a Polan vessel, when he was returning to England with his daughter on the *Trent*, and that Maxime-Jean had released the ship, its officer, its sailors and its passengers— everyone aboard, in brief—as a favor to him.

Now, for a second time, he had returned safe and sound from the lion's claws...the lion with sharper teeth than the British lion, who had never, in other circumstances, let any prey escape, much less abandoned himself to any act of clemency toward Englishmen who had fallen into his hands.

When a people is humiliated by defeats, it easily becomes suspicious, and Lord Killyett was accused, at first in whispers, and later overtly, of high treason.

In England, Admiral Byng had been shot for having been beaten.[50] Nothing worse could happen to the noble lord, but

---

[49] Arthur Hood (1824-1901)

[50] John Byng (1704-1757) was shot for "failing to do his utmost" to prevent the fall of Minorca to the French after a naval battle; the incident gave rise the famous observation by a

after all, the same thing might happen to him, and there was already talk in the newspapers about a formal accusation when the rumor spread, without anyone knowing who had put it into circulation that if Darnozan—the Emperor of the Seas was never called anything else in England—was making war so furiously on Great Britain, it was because Lord Killyett had refused him the hand of his daughter, Lady Helena.

The news ran the length and breadth of the Three Kingdoms within forty-eight hours, without the newspapers having mentioned it, and a current of opinion of feminine origin was instantly formed that could not have been more favorable to Maxime-Jean.

Yes, that man, scorned yesterday by the entire English nation, represented in all writings as a coarse mariner, brutal and ill-educated, suddenly became a hero, one of those heroes of romance steeped in pure sentiment and refined delicacy.

That phenomenon, moreover, is not an exception. English women have been seen to become successively besotted with Garibaldi, Cetewayo, Arabi Pacha and the elephant Jumbo.[51] It is therefore not surprising that the shriveled hearts of all the aged spinsters whom fatal destiny had condemned to celibacy were stirred, beneath the ashes, in favor of the gallant mariner who was turning the whole world upside down an utterly ruining a powerful people, for the sole reason that he as in love with an heiress.

It was like a gunpowder fuse. From the Isle of Wight to the far north of Scotland, all disposable hearts began to beat

---

character in Voltaire's *Candide* that it is good to kill an admiral from time to time "to encourage the others."

[51] Jumbo, the first African elephant to reach Europe alive, was briefly exhibited in the Jardin des Plantes in Paris before being traded to London Zoo in exchange for a rhinoceros. He was the zoo's star attraction from 1866-1882, when he was sold to P. T. Barnum, initiating a massive public protest. He toured with Barnum until 1885, when he was killed in a railroad accident.

furiously for Maxime-Jean, whom Englishwomen called between themselves "the King." Yes, the King, simply the King; that was sufficient, for Darnozan appeared to them to be the only human being worthy of a throne.

In every boarding house in London, in every family in Glasgow, Liverpool, Manchester, Leeds, Sheffield, Edinburgh, etc. etc., there was at least one unfortunate woman who was incontinently obsessed with that victorious gallant. And from that moment on, the critical situation of England was a matter of secondary importance, by comparison with the merited interest excited by "the King."

One of those madwomen even proposed, one day, to organize a vast meeting, exclusively composed of spinsters—of all ages, of course—in which it would be declared that Maxime Darnozan was a perfect, adorable gentleman entirely worthy of his high destiny. A few newspapers, however, raised vehement voices against that complete neglect of "English decency" (*sic*) and the amorous supporters of "the King" were forced to resheathe their enthusiasm and expend it behind closed doors.

They made up for it by devoting all their time to the object of their amour.

Then commenced the sending of little gifts: *mains de justice,*[52] sword-knots, embroidered scepters and locks of hair; then they started sending "the King" everything that occurred to them. Some of them had teeth extracted—you know, those long teeth—in order to send them in homage to the hero.

Unfortunately, but understandably, the English postal service would not accept such commissions, and it was necessary to use subterfuges in order for all those presents not to remain on their hands. A few of the most passionate spinsters went to take up residence on the continent, at Boulogne,

---

[52] As the *main de justice*, a symbol of royal power, is uniquely French, it is perhaps unlikely that English spinsters would send them to Darnozan, although his patronymic might have encouraged the better educated among them to think of it.

Dinard or Tours, and generously took responsibility for forwarding the touching evidence of the submission of his conquests to the triumphant mariner.

But what did Lady Helena think?

The poor young woman, resolute in complying with her father's desires, tried not to think about the handsome young man who, she also believed, had only wanted so much glory and so much power in order to lay them at her feet to make himself worthy of her.

Deep down, she loved him, not in the fashion of her compatriots deprived of teeth or clipped of tresses that were already thinning, but as a woman who knows what the object of her love is worth, as a woman who would have been glad to give herself to that valiant individual unconditionally. And she was astonished that her father took pride and hatred to the extent of preferring the utter devastation of England to a marriage that, after all, was worth more than twenty others.

Lord Salisbury, who felt the ground trembling beneath his feet, would have given away all the amorous women in the United Kingdom without regret in order to have the time to create fleets, organize armies and retake the offensive against the conqueror whom the English continued phlegmatically to call an adventurer, a bandit or a brigand, but whom the French had baptized the Napoléon of the Sea.

The rumors running around with regard to Lord Killyett and his daughter reached the ears of the First Lord of the Treasury. He summoned the commodore and asked him whether it was true.

Lord Killyett replied that, indeed, Maxime Darnozan had once asked him for the hand of his daughter, but that he did not believe the adventurer capable of ceasing hostilities even if it were granted to him.

"It's although and not because he loves my daughter that the man is making war on us."

"That's what it's necessary to know, exactly," said Lord Salisbury, "and in the case that he'll consent to make peace, will you be obstinate in your refusal?"

"What, Milord!" cried Lord Killyett. "You'd bargain with that pirate? You want your name to go down in history..."

"Oh, no big speeches. That's fine for Parliament; here we're alone and have no need to impress one another. England, which wasn't ready for the savage war that that man has waged against us, needs two, three or four years to recuperate."

"What do you mean by recuperate?"

"I mean feverish activity in the arsenals, the shipyards, the ports, the barracks—everywhere, is sum."

"Which is to say that you'd be able to breathe long enough to recommence the struggle against Darnozan?"

"Yes."

"So it's a lame peace that you want to make?"

"Yes—but will you give your daughter to the man in order to make him wait? That's the real question."

"No!"

"Be careful—you're already under suspicion."

"I know, Milord. But I'd rather die than dishonor myself by throwing my poor daughter into the arms of that corsair."

"Word, words, words!" said Lord Salisbury. "I'll give you three days to think about it. It's a matter of saving your fatherland."

"So be it," replied Lord Killyett, "but in the meantime, Milord, don't forget that Darnozan has threatened to marry my daughter in London itself."

"Before he's in our waters he'll have encountered two of our fleets. As for the defense of the country, I'll take all precautions."

And, indeed, the First Lord of the Treasury, dipping both hands into the coffers of Great Britain, offered a high wage of four shillings a day to all the valid men in the world who wanted to take service in the English Army.

A veritable rabble, drawn from all the rogues in the two worlds, arrived in London in next to no time, and the streets of the immense city, already unsafe in normal times, soon became a veritable den of cut-throats.

It was necessary to take energetic measures, to construct barracks and install the whole of that cosmopolitan crowd in a camp at Aldershot under the orders of Sir Montagu Steele,[53] who tried to submit them to a severe discipline and teach them exercises—two pretentions that he did not have the joy of realizing completely, especially the former.

Meanwhile, the English government, with the aplomb of merchants who only really believe in one power—gold—made an extremely curious approach to Darnozan. One of the most expert diplomats in Great Britain was sent to him as a parliamentary envoy and, with an impudence that approached candor, dared to propose to Boislucas to buy the Emperor of the Seas.

We have said that the Empire's Minister of Foreign Affairs was possessed of a remarkable self-composure. He did not appear at all astonished by the proposition, and allowed the Englishman to go on until he had finished his speech.

Great Britain offered Maxime-Jean a billion to buy back Australia and her other possessions, and promised in addition to pay him two million sterling annually—which is to say, an annual income of fifty million francs.

When the famous diplomat had finished, Boislucas, who doubtless had no need to consult his master, stood up abruptly. "Monsieur," he said, "you're fortunate. The Emperor consents to respect your status as an ambassador, otherwise, you'd end your days in the depths of some dungeon. But after all, it's better that you return to your government, to tell them that your insolent proposition will cost them infinitely more dearly than the offer you've just made. Go, Monsieur, and leave Australia immediately."

---

[53] Thomas Montagu Steele (1820-1890) had been in command of the Aldershot Division of the British Army from 1875-1880, but from 1880-1885 he was in command of the British forces in Ireland.

The English ambassador, very surprised to find that there was anything or anyone on Earth that could not be ought, nevertheless did not have to be begged to take to the sea again.

In the meantime, it was known in England that Lord Salisbury had not persuaded Lord Killyett to consent to his daughter's marriage to the victorious adventurer. Only half of the three days that the First Lord of the Treasury had given him to reflect had gone by before it was being discussed frantically from one end of England to the other, and bets were being laid, in order not to lose the habit, as to whether the truly obstinate father would give in at the last minute or would persist in his refusal.

Even the newspapers were talking about it, and until the three days were up, nobody talked about anything else. The papers that represented more particularly big business and the people waxed indignant at the idea that a single man could have caused the misfortune of an entire nation in that fashion. The papers that were organs of the aristocracy and the clergy approved unreservedly of Lord Killyett's attitude and declared that the humblest and most wretched cockney ought to do as much, if the King of the Isles took it into his head to marry his daughter, under pain of rendering himself unworthy to call himself an Englishman.

And bets continued to be laid.

Lord Killyett, like many of his peers, only read the newspapers that shared his opinions. He thought, naturally, that everyone in England was encouraging him in his resistance, and persisted until the end in the firm resolution that he had made known to Lord Salisbury.

Lady Helena, of course had not escaped the chagrin of seeing her name in the public papers, and reading polemics by all and sundry, every day, dictating a line of conduct. The unfortunate child, whose thoughts went in spite of her toward the victor of Pontevedra and Gibraltar, was prey to the cruelest bitterness and the most profound discouragement.

Involuntarily, Lady Helena became indignant at seeing everyone permitting themselves to assume sovereignty over her and give her orders, almost insulting her. She said to herself that there was no one who had any thought of protecting her or defending her—not even her father.

Oh, if only Maxime were here! she thought. *I'm sure that he'd order all those people to shut up, and I'm even sure that they'd do as they were told.*

And in the somber solitude in which she lived voluntarily, in order to spare herself odious visits and stupid advice, the young woman, her memory always returning to the same memories and the same image, began to hate her compatriots, and was already appealing to the spouse in whose grandeur and glory she was already in haste to share.

By dint of talking about her, whether kindly or unkindly, her compatriots had given birth in Lord Killyett's daughter a supreme lassitude, and with every passing minute her desire increased to see the Emperor of the Seas arrive to snatch her away from the abominable torture that was being inflicted on her."

Then, however, Maxime-Jean, informed by telegraph of what was being said, done and written in London with regard to his fiancée, sent the following dispatch to the *Times*:

The Emperor of the Seas invites the English to cease all discussion on the subject of Lady Killyett. The newspapers that do not comply with this desire will be exposed to grave penalties when Maxime-Jean has conquered Great Britain.

It was insolent, but positive.

"He's read my thoughts!" exclaimed Lady Helena, overwhelmed by joy, on reading that singular dispatch. And while all England believed that it was a hoax, she did not doubt for a single second the affectionate intervention of the man she loved.

On the other hand, Lord Killyett was even more irritated by what he called the height of audacity, and immediately made the decision not to leave his daughter in England, in order that the brutal victor could not put into execution his project of marrying her in spite of everything.

Lady Killyett was sent to the continent, to a relative who lived in Nice in the winter and Paris in the summer. It was May, so it was to Paris that the young woman went to take up residence. She had scarcely arrived when news arrived of a further disaster for England.

Ceylon—the famous island of Ceylon, which was, according to Indian legend the earthly paradise; the pearl of India—had just been invaded by Lamanon, who was continuing his tranquil conquests in the Indian Ocean.

Before the disembarkation of land troops, there had been a naval combat that Rear-Admiral Gore-Jones[54] had attempted to deliver with wooden ships and two ironclads sold to England by Japan. The engagement, although serious, had still concluded to the advantage of the Polan admiral, who had infinitely superior forces and did not consider it a feat of arms worthy of him.

Prytz commanded the army of disembarkation. In the campaign he only encountered indigenous troops, which did not feel any need to resist. They broke ranks at the first cannon shot, delighted to shrug off the yoke of a master whose harshness scandalized the world, even though the British government had hypocritically undertaken to cease trading in negroes and transporting Chinese coolies.

Once Ceylon was submissive and sufficient armed to be able to resist a surprise attack, Lamanon departed to undertake the conquest of Japan.

For his part, Pedro Cabanil went with a squadron to subjugate all the islands of Polynesia and the various Pacific archipelagos.

Almost at the same time, Maxime-Jean and a retinue of only three or four officers quit Melbourne on a French ship in order to travel to Europe via the Suez Canal.

---

[54] William Gore-Jones (1826-1888) was appointed Commander-in-Chief of the East Indies Station in 1879.

The Emperor of the Seas, who was traveling under an assumed name, unrecognized by anyone aboard the steamer, did not pause in Marseilles; having arrived there, he took the first express train to Paris, where he was to spend two days.

For fear of being recognized, he only went out in a closed carriage, and, since everyone was far from supposing that the astonishing man with whom all Europe was occupied was in Paris, he was able to come and go without any great inconvenience.

It was during one of those excursions that, while passing along the Champs-Élysées, Maxime-Jean spotted Lady Helena going to the Bois in a caleche with her relative.

On seeing the woman he had once requested out of bravado and had ended up loving ardently, the Emperor experienced an extraordinary emotion. He almost let that unique opportunity to know if he had grounds to hope escape, but after a few moments of trouble and hesitation, Maxime-Jean asked the officer accompanying him to go back to the hotel and wait for him, and ordered the coachman to follow the caleche carrying Lady Helena.

An hour later, in the great Allée des Acacias, the Emperor of the Seas saluted the young woman, who, thanks to the liberty that young women enjoy in England, was able to converse with him without the relative thinking that there was anything extraordinary about it.

Needles to say, the two young people allowed one another to perceive the most profound disturbance. Lady Helena blushed to the hairline, and Maxime was pale—paler, to be sure, than during the combats on which he had staked his great destiny.

The young hero knew, however, what he had to say, and did not hesitate. They had both got down from their carriages and were walking side by side along the path beside the Allée, far from any indiscreet ear—for Helena's relative had remained, insouciant and tranquil, in the caleche that was following at walking pace.

Completely sure of the love that she inspired, the young woman was not astonished that Maxime-Jean was in Paris. She was convinced that the Emperor of the Seas had come exclusively to see her, as soon as he had learned of her departure for France.

"I thank God, Milady, for the good fortune that has granted me the joy of encountering you sooner than I had hoped."

"Have you been in Paris long?"

"For thirty-six hours, Milady, and not for much longer. I'm therefore very glad to tell you how much I love you and to be able to ask you, personally, if you would like to be my wife?"

Lady Helena raised her big profound blue eyes to look at Maxime-Jean and ask him, blushing even more deeply: "It's really true, then, that you love me?"

"Can you doubt it, after what I've done?"

"Oh, I'm not conceited enough to imagine that your exploits have all been accomplished for my sake."

"That speech, Milady, is almost that of a queen, and I thank you. Once again, would you like to be my wife?"

Maxime-Jean emphasized the words *my wife*, giving them a particular accent. He wanted to make Lady Helena understand that what he sought above all else in wanting to marry her was happiness."

"Your wife?" the young woman replied, with a gaze of sincere gratitude. "Yes, on one condition."

"What, Milady?"

"Will you grant me in advance what I'm about to ask you?"

"Yes, within reason. No, if your desire might be harmful to my glory and yours."

"Ah!" said Lady Killyett, suddenly saddened. "I wanted to ask you at least to leave Ireland and Great Britain to the British government."

"It's no longer in my power to satisfy your desire, Milady. At this very moment, William Smith, Kasaloff, Paleieff and Capmartin are delivering battle to the last English fleet, while Kellner is disembarking the hundred and fifty thousand men who will have conquered Ireland within a week."

"Wretch that I am!" murmured Lady Helena wiping away a tear.

"Why, Milady?"

"Because I'm betraying my country by loving you."

"Milady, I cannot renounce conquering England. That would be to stop within sight of the goal, but I can, in favor of my wife, treat gently a vanquished people that has never been mild itself toward defeated enemies. Tell me, do you want to be Empress of the Seas?"

"Oh, Sire, Sire!"

"Silence, Milady—don't call me that. No one in France suspects my presence here."

Lady Killyett turned into a lateral path, and showing her tearful face, said, explosively: "Oh, my love, how unhappy I am!"

"Milady," said Maxime-Jean, solemnly, "the archbishop of Dublin will celebrate our marriage in his cathedral within a week. I shall await my bride in Limerick on the twenty-fifth of May."

Lady Helena remained mute.

XII.

That same evening, Maxime-Jean departed for Saint-Nazaire. He was awaited there by a ship that was to carry him to Ireland, where events of extreme importance were already unfolding.

Six weeks before, and imperial fleet of twenty-four iron-clads and fifty-two transport ships had left Madagascar to go to attack Ireland. After having restocked with coal at Saint Helena, which had belonged to Maxime-Jean for six months, the vessels of the Emperor of the Seas had avoided getting close to any land whatsoever, wanting to get all the way to

Ireland without being seen, in the hope of taking the English by surprise.

The latter were on their guard, however, and they were waiting for their enemy with two respectable fleets, which Lord Salisbury had succeeded in assembling, in order to attempt one last supreme effort. The first of them, a dozen vessels strong, went to meet the Imperials and encountered them in the vicinity of the Cape Verde Islands. In the presence of the enormous forces of which Maxime-Jean disposed, however, the English fleet beat a retreat at top speed and came to rally with the remainder of the British forces, which were guarding the two passes of Galway Bay in Ireland.

They knew, in fact, that Maxime-Jean was going to attempt a disembarkation. All the available vessels and troops had been sent to the threatened county. Her Majesty's government had, in addition, sown torpedoes all along the Irish coast. Finally, with incredible activity, defenses had been established on all the vulnerable points.

Never had a vanquished people organized its last defenses with more ardor, more courage or, let us say, more calmness. But what can be done when fifty years of past errors are in combat against you? What can be done when it is a matter of battling internal and external enemies at the same time?

Maxime-Jean, who was fully expecting to find all the beaches on which it would be easy to disembark unapproachable, also knew the place where the British fleet showed itself would be the one where there were no torpedoes. He assumed, too, that along the sheer cliffs of the country of Galway, where nature has carved out the famous Giants' Causeway, there would not be any explosive devices, a descent in that locations being utterly impracticable.

His plan was constructed on precisely those suppositions, which were found to be exact—and that plan was simply to disembark his troops at the very place where all the English officers considered it to be radically impossible, to deliver battle to the enemy fleet, to follow it wherever it retreated, and, finally, to pay no more heed to the torpedoes then if they did not exist.

Thus, Maxime-Jean's twenty-four ironclads navigated directly toward the English fleet, which was supported by a formidable artillery placed on the Isle of Arran, half way up a steep little mountain.

It was the Duke of Edinburgh[55] who was in command of the British navy, with all the youth of England under his orders, who had come to do battle there *pro aris et focis.*[56] In every ten officers, seven or eight lords or sons of lords could be counted.

The battle commenced.

At the first cannon shots, the land batteries began to thunder, sending a rain of formidable objects down on the Polans. The famous mortars sending ten-thousand-kilogram projectiles came into play. Soon, the action was general.

The Emperor, however, kept a sufficient distance not to be inconvenienced by the land batteries, contenting himself with keeping the enemy fleet at bay. And while the artillery, the torpedo-boats and the machines of every sort raged, the forty transport ships headed for the Giants' Causeway as if they intended to plunge into the rock.

There was a redoubt at the top of the stairway, which began to bombard the transports, but the fire of that artillery suddenly ceased, and the amazement of the English mariners was immense when they suddenly saw the cannons, the gun-carriages and the artillerymen fall into the sea from the top of the cliff.

It was the Irish entering the lists.

More than six months previously, Octave Kellner had sent three or four hundred of his most determined and most intelligent men to Ireland. They were all among those who, with Kasaloff and Maxime-Jean, had taken possession of the

---

[55] i.e., the future King Edward VII, a.k.a. the Prince of Wales.

[56] Literally, "For our altars and hearths," but usually translated as "For God and Country."

English vessels at Spithead at the commencement of the epic that was about to conclude on the banks of the Thames.

Those three or four hundred mariners knew where to find thousands of men ready to suffer anything, on condition of striking a mortal blow against England. For six months, they had been training them secretly in marine maneuvers and soldierly exercises. They had been paid regularly as troops on campaign, and they were delighted.

As soon as Maxime-Jean appeared off the Galway coast with his fleet and his army, Ireland entire had risen up as one man. There was not a single corner of old Erin where some ragged wretch armed with a rifle, a dagger or a shillelagh was not searching for an Englishman to strike down. At the top of the Giants' Causeway, three or four thousand Irishmen, appearing unexpectedly, had just hurled the English gunners and their Armstrongs into the abyss.

In thirty minutes they had cleared the place, and then they established, without delay, machinery with the aid of which they began hoisting Maxime-Jean's soldiers, horses and cannons up to the plateau.

The Duke of Connaught[57] had wanted to take command of an army to defend the duchy whose name he bore, but his soldiers, attacked from all sides by innumerable bands of insurgents, were obliged to defend themselves against the Irish, were almost overwhelmed by weight of numbers, and were only able to save themselves by fraying a passage though country swarming with guerillas sending death from every bush, every marsh and every hut.

The Imperial Army was therefore able to disembark at its leisure. Squads of Irishmen, drunk with joy, carried cannons on their shoulders to the summit of the cliff, and guided the soldiers who had just landed as far as the plateau by means of steep paths that were thought to be impracticable.

---

[57] Prince Arthur, the third of Queen Victoria's sons.

As soon as his army was in possession of the summit overlooking the Giants' Causeway, the Emperor stopped fighting.

The English, very experienced and unaware of what was happening in Ireland, went back into Galway Bay, where the fleet remained, immobilized. By virtue of that maladroit retreat, the British Admiral put himself in the necessity of either forcing a passage or resolving himself to being taken prisoner on the day when Ireland was in the power of Maxime-Jean.

And that day was not far off, for scarcely had the Imperial Army commanded by Kellner set up camp in good order on the heights than the telegraph distributed all over the island a decree by the new sovereign of Ireland, by which the lords' lands were given to the Irish. A law was to be drawn up later to formulate the precise terms of that mutation, but in principle, the landlords were dispossessed—and that was the surest means of finishing with the English army within forty-eight hours, which could not resist for long in a country where there was a man ready to die for every acre of ground of which he had just been rendered the owner.

Three days later, Ireland entire belonged to Maxime-Jean. His transport ships, which had made a tour of the island via the north, came to Dublin to disembark a division. Twenty-four hours after that, Kasaloff took possession of the Isle of Man, half way to Great Britain, without firing a shot.

When the last Englishman quit green Erin forever, an immense acclamation resounded over that disinherited land, which had been struggling for so long in the claws of her oppressors.

Ireland, in its entirety, came before Maxime-Jean to bless him.

Millions of ragged individuals ran with laughter on their lips and tears of joy in their eyes to salute the liberator. From Galway to Dublin, the conqueror's horse marched incessantly over the flowers with which the Irish, finally free, had strewn the road. They came from every corner of Ireland. There were tender or unusual scenes at every step, of which the Emperor, his generals and his soldiers were the heroes.

Long lines of young women, as beautiful as only Irishwomen can be, came in their Sunday best to present their sons to the victor, and one of them, parting from her companions, said to the new sovereign: "We offer you our sons, Sire. They will be your devoted soldiers for the independence of Erin; we have the joy of thinking that you will make them men."

A few miles from Dublin, the clergy, dressed in their sacerdotal ornaments, came in procession to the Emperor.

The joy of the people then took on crazy proportions. It was more than intoxication or delirium. People who did not know one another embraced in the streets. An uninterrupted sequence of gunshots was heard in all directions. As in Spain, fireworks were even sent up in broad daylight. Never, anywhere, had such joy been seen. Already, that mercurial people had already forgotten the English, no longer thinking about anything but the present moment, full of joy.

Maxime-Jean, glad to see such felicity, advanced radiantly, waving to the crowd and enjoying for the first time the sweet métier of an acclaimed prince.

The cortege arrived thus at Dublin cathedral, where a solemn *Te Deum* was sung by two thousand pair of lungs, overflowing with effusion and gratitude.

The archbishop wanted to welcome the Emperor, in elevated language, and he ceremony concluded in the midst of a profound and general emotion.

The rest of the day was devoted to public rejoicing, and that evening, all Ireland was drunk. A considerable number of blows with the shillelagh were joyfully and robustly exchanged; a few heads were cracked and a few bones broken, but everyone amused themselves prodigiously, and even the wounded stoutly refused to complain.

It was at that moment that the Emperor remembered Ata-Capac and the oath that he had sworn to him.

A dispatch was sent to Joshua Klett in the Marquise Islands, enjoining him to go to Peru with ten thousand men and reestablish the Inca on the throne of his ancestors.

On the twentieth of May 1887, which was the next day, Maxime-Jean was informed that Lady Killyett had just arrived at Limerick. The Emperor left immediately to go to meet his fiancée. Her mere presence in Ireland was equivalent to a solemn consent, and on the twenty-fifth, as had been agreed, the charming young woman became the Empress of the Seas.

The imperial marriage was celebrated in Dublin cathedral. The archbishop officiated, and the joy of the people was even more immense, although a few unquiet minds were already remarking that Maxime-Jean was marrying an Englishwoman, and that she might one day have enough influence over her husband to return Ireland to her misery and the oppression from which the Emperor had just removed her. But those pessimistic prognostications could not trouble the delight of the people, and the lovely Helena, utterly confused and utterly gracious, but slightly sad when she thought about her father, was acclaimed in turn by her new subjects, whom she loved with all her heart, and who adored her in all sincerity, that day.

In England, the news of that marriage raised an incredible racket. The old spinsters were exultant, and made wishes that the conqueror would soon disembark, so that they might contemplate the features of such an amorous man, capable, into the bargain, of not forgetting, now that he was an Emperor, what he had promised as a mere commoner.

The other English people, of both sexes, especially the businessmen, caressed the hope of soon seeing an end to a war so fatal for commerce. But some did not believe that Maxime-Jean would stop at that. The latter secretly hoped that the Emperor of the Seas would start immediately on his English campaign, and that it would all be over rapidly. That way, business could be resumed before the other nations were able to supplant Albion completely, and perhaps there would be god days once again for the grocers of the United Kingdom.

Rule Britannia, anyway.

But there was also the government, which did not share that opinion. There was Lord Wolseley of Cairo too, whose courage and confidence had not been diminished by events in Ireland. It was always to be expected, he said, and for two months he had regarded the temporary abandonment of that part of England's possessions as necessary, or at least inevitable.

That generous soldier did not want to see that England was collapsing. One could have brought him the most disastrous news, and he would have remained serene. And when he saw that the Imperial Army was about to set foot on English soil, he cried: "So much the better! It's only here, on the sacred soil of Old England, that we'll come to the end of it, that we'll annihilate that army—after which we'll set out again to reconquer the Empire of the Seas, which the adventurer stole from us by surprise."

Lord Wolseley doubtless did not want to remember that the empire of lands was also escaping. On the one hand, Canada had just declared its independence, and was making eyes at France. Russia was in Lahore and her troops were slowly and methodically invading the Indian peninsula. Bismarck, who knew what Africa promised, was manifesting the intention of setting his sights on the Cape Colony and other British possessions in southern Africa. Austria was advancing on Constantinople.

Italy was reflecting, Spain could not get over her astonishment, and France was continuing not to budge, not being sure what the German chancellor would say if she permitted herself to twitch a leg or a finger, if she were imprudent enough to sneeze or wipe her nose. And yet, Lamanon was ready to give her his assistance if the colony of Pondicherry seemed too small to her. But no—she wanted to be very good, and she expended her activity internally, God knows how.

So, General Wolseley declared that England would be Maxime-Jean's tomb. Better than that—he proved mathematically that in two months, eleven days, seven and a half hours, he would have annihilated his enemies.

People have seen, he wrote to the Times, what I have done in Egypt. I promised to enter Cairo on the fifteenth of September and I entered it as I had said. It has been claimed that Arabi was in accord with me, to allow himself to be beaten, but those are inventions of the vexed French. In two months, eleven days, seven and a half hours, the famous Emperor of the Seas will have bitten the dust in some marsh of Old England.

English marshes are apparently dry.

In spite of the enrolments, forced or voluntary, that had been taking place for a year, and in spite of the appeal addressed to all the unoccupied scoundrels in the world, the English army was not extremely serious. Only the old army, the one that existed at the commencement of the war, formed a nucleus capable of some resistance, and even there, the majority of regiments had never come under fire, and lacked the aplomb and trim that the habit of doing battle gives to soldiers. The rest of the British troops formed a strange rabble, which a few cannon shots could disperse.

Perhaps the young volunteers, full of patriotism, might be able to render services on the flanks or in retrenched positions, but on conditions of being well commanded, and generals of talent were even rarer in England in the summer of 1887 than they had been in France in the Autumn of 1870.

Nevertheless, from one end of the United Kingdom to the other, there was a feverish activity. All sorts of positions were fortified; retrenched camps were installed on the edges of great cities where several railway lines converged—what the English call "junctions"—and sections of the rivers were guarded. Sappers installed near bridges were ready to blow them up at the slightest alert—which would slow the enemy down a little, but could not stop him.

At the same time, the government inundated England with reassuring proclamations. They wanted above all to tranquilize the people and the frightened bourgeoisie. Meetings took place every day in which crazy motions were proposed, pavement strategists developed fantastic and stupid plans, and strange inventors turned up to recount that they had found an infallible means of saving the country in forty-eight hours and destroying the Imperial army in less time than it takes to take a pinch of snuff.

In other popular assemblies, the government was blamed with the utmost violence. There was talk of indictment by decree, and the name of Lord Wolseley had already been out forward several times for dictatorship.

The Queen had returned to London with the court. The Prince of Wales had taken command of all the land and sea forces, with Lord Wolseley of Cairo as Field Marshal, placed immediately under his orders. The Queen's other sons and sons-in-law were also at the head of army corps.

In short, England seemed ready to receive her invaders—except that in high places, there was a prevalent vague anxiety, produced by a strange discovery that the Admiralty had made.

The geographical situation of England, so advantageous when the nation is powerful, becomes full of perils as soon as her fleets are destroyed. A continental nation on which war is declared guards her coastal frontier against attack and directs its arms in that single direction, but in an island, the frontier is everywhere, and when an enemy threatens to invade the island, the government and the generals find it very difficult to decide where to concentrate their personnel and their efforts.

Maxime-Jean might attempt his descent in any of two hundred different places, and one cannot maintain to hundred armies. In order to counter that inconvenience, Lord Wolseley organized four of them.

The first, the army of the North, under the orders of General Cameron,[58] was in a strong position at Gainsborough on the banks of the Trent, whose crossing it was to prevent. Cameron had strongly established communications with Lincoln to

---

[58] Duncan Cameron (1808-1888).

the south-east and Sheffield in the east, in such a way as to be able to move his troops in good order to either city, if necessary.

The second, the army of the East, was commanded by Major-General Radcliffe.[59] The latter, leaving a strong garrison of volunteers in Colchester, had set up his camp ay Bury St. Edmunds, ready to fall back to Cambridge in order to cover London of the enemy arrived via Norfolk.

The third army, that of the South, whose general was Edward of Saxe-Weimar,[60] was solidly established in Salisbury.

Finally, the fourth army, the most solid and battle-hardened, under the direct orders of the Prince of Wales and Lord Wolseley of Cairo, was guarding London, ready to move toward the threatened points, while a population of four hundred thousand poor devils enlisted by the engineers were digging earthworks all around the metropolis, in order to construct redoubts behind which they counted on resisting until the enemy army was exhausted and the English could take the offensive.

It was, above all, the suburbs north of London that it was necessary to fortify. The most distant line of redoubts on the left bank of the Thames began at Barking and extended all the way to Hounslow, passing through Romford, Enfield and Brentford. Behind that line, there were further redoubts, following the design of the first almost exactly, and finally, at the very gates of London, gigantic barricades, half earth and half masonry, obstructing the major roads and armed with formidable Armstrongs.

All the available positional cannons had been transported there and placed in batteries in order to defend the three principal lines.

---

[59] William Pollexfen Radcliffe (1822-1897).

[60] The German-born Prince Edward of Saxe-Weimar (1823-1902) was a career officer in the British Army, who, in our history, became Commander-in-Chief in Ireland in 1885.

On the right bank, there were only two lines of defense; the first passed through Greenwich, Woolwich and Richmond; the second was in London itself.

The second and third armies had orders to go to the assistance of the first, and reciprocally, the first was to support the second or the third, a soon as the pattern of the invasion was sketched out. The fourth army, although the retrenchments were defended by innumerable volunteers, was not to move away from London, but the Prince of Wales and Lord Wolseley were to move in person anywhere there was to be an engagement, a combat or a battle.

All these dispositions, in which a certain amount of panic was sensible, remained a dead letter because of one thing of which no one had thought—which often happens to people who have gone to earth. Maxime-Jean did what the English government had not anticipated; which is to say that he threatened the English coast at half a dozen different points simultaneously.

Eight warships flying the sky blue flag presented themselves at the mouth of the Clyde, and no one doubted that they had a whole fleet of transport slips behind them. Major-General Cameron, informed telegraphically, commenced a movement to cover York and Leeds, advancing northwards.

At the same time, however, a similar demonstration took place in the Bristol Channel. They knew full well that the invader would not land in Wales, where a few troops would be sufficient to stop an army, and, indeed, the imperial vessels headed toward Hatchet on the Somerset coast. The telegraph having alerted the Prince of Saxe-Weimar, the latter headed, at a forced march, for Bridgewater Junction, where he hoped to prevent Maxime-Jean from crossing the river.

A third squadron showed itself off Brighton, and Lord Wolseley detached a division of his central army to head toward that point.

All these alerts had the effect of drawing the first and third armies away from London, and, above all, of increasing the distances separating the four armies.

It was at that moment, while Major-General Radcliffe was requesting the help that he needed urgently, that the Emperor of the Seas, having gone around the north of Scotland with nine vessels and his forty transport ships, arrived on the Norfolk coast, disembarked at Happisburgh without significant resistance, and marched on Norwich that same day, which he occupied after a brief engagement with a division of volunteers who fired a large number of cannon shots without doing any serious damage to the Imperial forces.

After establishing his communications with his fleet and driving back into the marshes east of Norwich a small army composed of soldiers similar to the French sharpshooters of 1870, Maxime-Jean marched on Bury St. Edmunds, Mildenhall and Ely at the same time, in order to operate a vast turning movement and attempt, by occupying Cambridge before the English general, to cut off his retreat and force him to fall back to Colchester.

Seeing the danger that he was running, Major-General Radcliffe, fell back in a southward direction and went to wait for the Imperial army at Neyland, on the Stour.

The battle was not very serious. Radcliffe revealed his qualities as a tactician therein but, in addition to the fact that he showed himself to be a mediocre strategist, his soldiers, who had never fought against serious troops, were frightened by the hurricane of iron that Maxime-Jean's army hurled at them before even showing itself, and ran away to take refuge in Colchester.

Major-General Radcliffe then launched his cavalry—the superb English cavalry of which there is no need to sing the praises—but the Emperor also had cavalry, commanded by General Gwenteclob, the son of an Araucarian chieftain and a German woman from the province of Concepcion in Chile. Gwenteclob was a kind of Murat, who pushed courage to the point of madness, and who led his men so forcefully that they smashed the Queen's cavaliers, took eight thousand prisoners and entered Colchester with six thousand hussars at the same time as the fugitives from the Battle of Neyland.

The city fell into the power of the Emperor, and General Radcliffe, with the troops that he had been able to rally, beat a retreat toward London, pursued with swords at his back by General Prytz, who did not leave him a minute's respite.

In the wake of that defeat, all of England, which had not seen war on her territory for nearly two hundred years, was gripped by a frightful panic.

The most terrible fear took possession of everyone. A thousand horrors were related about Maxime-Jean's soldiers, almost all of whom were Malays, Malabars and mulattos. This dark-skinned men inspired an unimaginable terror in all the English women, and there was an epidemic of suicide that propagated rapidly throughout England.

Everyone lost their heads. It was the end of British power.

In the meantime, Octave Kellner operated a descent in Scotland with the Irish army, which his four hundred officers of that nationality had been preparing for six months.

It is at this point that it becomes evident how deplorable the English system of recruitment was. The enrolment of mercenaries can only produce, and only does produce, soldiers devoid of energy and any of the sentiments fundamental to victors. To be sure, Major-General Cameron's troops were better drilled and better disciplined than Kellner's Irish battalions, but the latter had two hundred years of oppression to avenge, and they fought like men who would rather die than be defeated.

The English earned their money and lost the battles, while their enemies were led to victory by their patriotism.

Octave Kellner annihilated the first army in three successive engagements, and advanced toward London at a forced march. All the country that he traversed submitted to the authority of the Emperor, and the first concern of the majority of commercial or maritime cities, once invaded, was to ask whether they could send their ships and merchandise to their trading outlets in all the countries of the world.

"Yes," Kellner replied, "on condition that they fly the sky blue flag with the four golden swallows and pay a war tax"

However, two English armies still remained, and numerous volunteers.

The Prince of Saxe-Weimar was ordered to rally to London before his communications cut be cut, and the Prince of Wales went to meet Kellner, who had just entered Warwick after having occupied Birmingham.

The two armies met at Stratford.

The battle began at daybreak on the twenty-seventh of June, and the Prince of Wales had the joy of beating his enemy, who was forced to retreat to Tamworth.

That was the only battle that the English won in that final campaign, and even then, the heir to the throne, who revealed great military qualities, was so grievously wounded as to be obliged to abandon his command.

On learning of his lieutenant's defeat, Maxime-Jean marched northwards and succeeded in reaching the English army, now commanded by Lord Wolseley, just as it was about to attack Kellner again.

The victor of Tel-el-Kebir, caught between two fires at Tamworth, was completely surrounded and obliged to surrender unconditionally.

The two Imperial armies did not encounter any further obstacles until they reached London, where all that remained were the army of the Prince of Saxe-Weimar and volunteers.

In order not to diminish his prestige and in order not to give the English time to reconnoiter, Maxime-Jean, after having assigned positions to each of his officers, commanded an attack on the first line of fortifications.

It was the eighth of August 1887. That first attempt failed. The Imperial forces were driven back, with enormous losses. But the Emperor of the Seas was a tenacious man. He recommenced the following night, with sixty thousand Malagasy and Malay troops, and stormed the redoubts, after three fruitless assaults and after having been forced to place himself at the head of the regiment on which he counted the most.

The most difficult part was done. Three days later, Kellner and the Emperor, combining their efforts, took the second line.

London's defenders would not consent to surrender, however. They took refuge behind the barricades of the third line of defense, and the combat continued for five more days without interruption. Finally, the Imperial army was victorious, and Maxime-Jean entered in triumph into London, which he made into a second-class prefecture.

Postscript[61]

After all these pages, more than one reader might say to me: do you hate the English that much, then?

If I were in the diplomatic service or a hypocrite, I would reply with attenuating circumlocutions, that one can execrate a nation without having any animosity toward the individuals who compose it. But that is evasive. I am neither a hypocrite not a diplomat, and since the word frankness has for its origin the very name of our country, I shall declare frankly: yes, I detest the English; I detest them as a government, as a people and as human beings.

I bear a grudge against them, firstly because they hate us cordially, and show it at every opportunity. I would hold a grudge against them without that, because they are cumbersome, incessantly meddling in things that are none of their concern; because once on the soil of a country that does not belong to them, they treat it as conquered territory; because they are dishonest, politically, commercially and humanly; because they are not polite, either in England or anywhere

---

[61] This postscript is not part of the story, and could easily be omitted, but as it casts some light, not only on the thinking behind this story but also the attitude tacitly adopted in the fourth story in the collection, it seemed best to include it.

else; and because, finally, any relations with the English are detestable, in our country, in theirs, and everywhere else besides.

Let us consider them in our country.

The English have spread out over all countries like sardines in all the seas, in shoals. In France alone they are legion; there is a shoal in Boulogne, one in Dunkerque, one if Fécamp, one in Dinan, one in Touraine, one in Nice, one in Cannes, one in Montpellier, one in Pau, one in Arcachon, etc., etc.

As soon as a subject of Her Very Gracious Majesty shows his equine teeth in a corner of Europe, that corner no longer belongs to the natives of the region; after that one come two, then four, the ten and then a hundred. It is like an eczema that starts to corrode the region.

And do you know why the English devote themselves thus to the exploration of stations virgin of visitors? To enjoy the cheap prices of foodstuffs that their presence immediately causes to increase—with the result that, gradually, with the aim of living comfortably on their small incomes, they are infesting and poisoning our country, in which there is no small village left in which an old captain can live in retirement.

And then, truly, there are too many of them, far too many. They multiply and pullulate like herrings.

In any case, they really do exercise a harmful influence on the French character, in this time of social laxity. They are the ones who introduced among us the politeness of the hat screwed to the head. People no longer know how to greet one another. Twenty years ago, when a man went into a public place—a café, a theater, an exhibition, casino, or a compartment in a railway carriage—he took off his hat and saluted the people present. The English came; they looked at us insolently and remained coifed. Then certain Frenchmen found that chic, and the rudeness passed into our customs.

Once, in France, men offered their arms to ladies, especially when walking with them. Because the English are unaware of that delicate and protective fashion of accompanying a woman, and, even when they are paying court to some young woman, march beside her like a beanpole, it is no longer good taste today to offer one's arm. Young people scarcely know of what exquisite sensations they are deprived by that wretched fashion, introduced to France by tradesmen from Manchester at the same time as cloth the color of droppings shed by a bird that has been dosed with medicine.

Oh, that's another thing for which I shall never forgive them: those fabrics devoid of probity, which have neither warp not weft, and have given birth to horrible thirty-five franc suits. If the French had the courage, they would form a league, all of whose members would swear never to buy a centimeter of that cloth, as perfidious as Albion itself.

While waiting for that league to be formed, tailors exist in Paris who declare with stupid pride that they have nothing but English cheviot in their shops. They probably blush at the fabrics of their own country. What is the League of patriots doing?

Nor will I pardon the English for having invented the ulster. They will not be worn in paradise. A people capable of imagining such a garment merits being banished from other nations.

And finally, I will not forgive the French for allowing their language to be infiltrated by expressions that no one knows how to pronounce and which obscure our limpid conversation: *high life, rally paper, five o'clock*, etc.[62]

That last expression, most of all, exasperates me. We have such a pretty expression in French to say the same thing: *le goûter*.[63] Is that not an expression truly made for ladies, in

---

[62] The author need not have worried about "rally paper," which did not even survive in English.

[63] The verb *goûter* mean to taste, but when adapted as a noun the word refers specifically to afternoon tea. When afternoon gatherings were integrated into the complex calendar of Parisiennes' social visits, however, it was thought necessary to pin such occasions down to a specific time, hence the borrow-

order that they might suppress the gross verb *manger*? And they have replaced it with the combination *cinq heures*—for "five o'clock" means *cinq heures*. And people think that more intelligent? No, but a few imbeciles imagine that they know how the language of Shakespeare is spoken. It's not enough to see the English; it's also necessary to hear their idiom flayed.

Don't you think that's enough to legitimate my hatred?

Besides which, that's not all. Who takes possession of the best seats in a railway carriage or on steamships, even when they have been reserved? The English. To whom are the employees of the French civil service gracious and obliging?—a phenomenon unknown to their compatriots. The English. Who go everywhere with aplomb, taking no account of customs, regulations or even laws? The English. Always the English.

It is necessary to see them in Paris. Everything belongs to them: the soil, the subsoil, the ambient air. I've heard one of them call Parisians "foreigners." Word of honor!

They install themselves in the museums and the monuments, everywhere, and put on airs with the attendants who try to keep them in order. They go to the Opéra in a jacket and soft hat. In the street they stop anyone to ask him, in unintelligible French, for information or directions. When they do that, they are all platitude, but as soon as you have naively put yourself out to answer them and enable them to understand, they go off impertinently without thanking you, leaving you on the sidewalk, bewildered by such rudeness. In one minute, they have covered the distance that separates obsequiousness from insolence.

On the railway, everything is for them. They snore, they shave, they change their shirts in tunnels. I won't talk about English women. They're redoubtable. If ever you show yourself in a carriage that contains two blonde girls from free England, get ready to suffer a horrible torture: that of hearing

---

ing of "five o'clock," which was imagined (erroneously) to be the time at which English ladies habitually took tea.

throughout the journey an uninterrupted conversation, in such a uniform tone that one could believe oneself condemned by Providence to submit without respite to the sound of a sewing-machine. Oh, I understand why Shakespeare insisted on the loquacity of women. The cackle of his female compatriots is surely superior to all other forms of cackling.

In their own country.

I am not, of course, talking about the relations of the English with one another. That is not my concern. What interests me is their attitude toward me when I go to London.

In Paris, I have racked my brains to divine what they are asking of me and done everything possible to oblige them. On the other hand, as they have made no bones about stopping me in the street and interrogating me, I believe I can act in the same fashion there. Well, yes. I address myself politely to people I suspect of being obliging and well brought up, and:

"I don't know..."

"I don't understand..."

Such are the responses they send to you on the wing, without looking at you or showing any sign of pausing. And if you finally succeed in getting hold of one who consents to listen to you, that one doesn't want to understand you. The same people who want information in Paris about the "Roo Rivelly"—that's the Rue Rivoli—and who are understood, do not hesitate to send you packing when, instead of "Lester Square," as it's necessary to pronounce it, you say "Leicester Square," as it is written.

That is, therefore, flagrant ill will. They are disagreeable for the pleasure of being so.

Certain people, even in France, feel the need to excuse the English and claim that if the passers-by do not listen to your questions in the street it is because they are afraid of being robbed. There is, therefore, no one in London but thieves? I dare not say so.

Others, equally well-intentioned on behalf of the English, inform you seriously that they genuinely do not understand.

What! That's as far as their intelligence goes? I dare not believe it.

But would you like them to demonstrate the contrary themselves? If, in Paris, an islander addresses you in his own jargon, reply that it's impossible to grasp a word of what he's saying, and speak to him in the English that is not understood in London, and you'll see that he grasps all of its beauties.

Or, better still, do as one of my friends did, who replied to one of the citizens of the United Kingdom: "I cannot inform you, because you have not been introduced to me." Put the children of Albion on that diet for ten years, and it would smooth their rough edges.

English is, in any case, a wretched patois. It is a bastard tongue put out of the range of other human beings. One can learn it without difficulty, but one can never speak it. One surprising particularity of the language is that the letter a is pronounced their successively like all the other vowels of the alphabet, as *a* in black, *é* in table, *i* in dear, *o* in yacht and the *u* that has the value of *ou* in Stewart. But if you ask to what rule these astonishing variations are submissive, the English reply that there is none. What phenomena!

Why don't they get rid of all the other vowels? It would be simpler.

As I am not telling anyone anything new, I shall skip lightly over certain details, like this one: those gentlemen who present themselves at the door of the Opéra in a reefer jacket demand that one is better dressed than the Prince of Wales when one wants to go into one of their theaters.

What can I say about the oppressive custom that consists of closing all the shops of Sundays, including those most necessary to the maintenance of the life and health of foreigners, while those puritans shut up in their homes on the pretext of savoring the Bible carry out comparative studies of claret, sherry, port, gin and whisky until the extinction of natural reason.

Need I recall that, under the cover of the respect that the English have for their ancient laws, they ambush our books, our operas, our comedies and our dramas in order to loot them from top to bottom? Which does not prevent them from putting on prudish airs when one reproaches them for that literary, dramatic and musical piracy. A little more and it would be them who cried thief, and we should be glad that they do not have the pretention of selling our best books back to us as a higher price.

But that will come.

When we are inconvenienced in our country, oppressed in theirs, and robbed almost everywhere by people of that nation, who tend to replace the old Jews that have now been absorbed and assimilated in all countries, we can expect in return, can we not, that they will leave us tranquil in our own civil, religious and political affairs? Well, no. They cannot; it is stronger than them. When we were a powerful people who did not allow anyone to tread on our toes without replying with a slap in the face, the sons of free England and their government kept very obligingly to their place—but since the destiny of battles has gone against us, that hero John Bull bravely imagines that he can make us feel the weight of defeats that he was incapable of inflicting upon us.

Do we want to move an arm? "Stop there!" cries John Bull. Are we tempted to look ahead? "I'm opposed to that," he declares, hastily. We go into Tunisia. "Oh, I don't know if I ought to permit that." We're in Egypt. "Get out so that I can install myself there."

We go to Madagascar; John Bull thinks it appropriate to throw Johnstone and Shaw[64] in our path. And the latter demands that twenty-five thousand francs be given to him. One of two things must be true, though: either Mr. Shaw, that man of God, has not played the role of spy and the reparation that is due to him could not be as paltry, or he has fought against us clandestinely and robbed us, and the Foreign Office has aided that clergyman in that deceitful operation.

---

[64] The Reverend George A. Shaw (1842-1917), nowadays remembered as a naturalist

But let us move on.

We have a quarrel with Tonkin. John Bull gets annoyed and declares that his interests will be compromised if we give China a thrashing. Do we want to send our recidivists to New Caledonia? "Not there!" cries John Bull. The sons of the former convicts of Sydney would be compromised.

Do we pierce the Suez Canal? John Bull filches it from us, and he accomplishes that gigantic act of pocket-picking like a sacerdote. It's in his blood.

Six months ago, a French officer bought land in the New Hebrides. John Bull, in the form of Commodore Erskine, arrives in Australia, has the deal annulled, and France puts up with that!

Last week, a French steamship, the *Ville de Tanger*, broke her axle-tree in the Mediterranean, and asked for help from an English vessel, asking to be towed to a nearby port. John Bull demanded a hundred and twenty thousand francs to render that service, and left to perdition the ship that was unable to pay so dear for a three-hour tow. Honest people!!!

Is that not enough to execrate the English, a nation that does not have a single virtue, but only has interests?

When they rose up against black slavery, it was because they had millions of Indians to exploit, Only yesterday they were running all over Africa killing slave-traders, battling for the holy cause of black humankind, but the Sudan rebels, and Chinese Gordon, Gordon Pacha, races to Khartoum and proclaims the right to possess slaves the day after his arrival. "I'm acting in the interests of England," he says, to those who are astonished.

O virtue!!

Hewett and Graham cannot put an end to a hero named Osman Digna.[65] At the head of a few thousand other heroes,

---

[65] Osman Digna (1840-1926) was a follower of the self-proclaimed "Mahdi" Muhammad Ahmad, who prompted the revolt in the Susan that led to the siege of Khartoum. British forces under Gerald Graham (1831-1889) defeated rebels un-

without rifles and without cannons, the latter waits, attacks, shakes and drives back Her Majesty's armies. What does Hewett do? He puts a price on his adversary's head. He sends emissaries laden with gold to sow division among his enemies and buy troubled consciences. Not having the strength to vanquish when they do not have a collaborator like Arabi confronting them, those brave men foment cowardice, excite avaricious instincts and obtain their triumph by the most sickening of treasons.

And that is the honesty of those Carthaginians!

---

der his command at El-Teb and Tamai in 1884, but were eventually forced to withdraw. Admiral William Hewett (1834-1888) evacuated many of the British troops isolated by the revolt.

THE PARALYTIC

What a treat it was for me!

For five years I had been nailed to my armchair. From time to time, I was taken down into a closed carriage and, for an hour or two, I was driven around the town or the roads of the surrounding countryside.

My legs! It's unnecessary to say any more about them. One of my arms still worked, and it's thanks to that one that I could still feed myself. Otherwise...

But my eyes were still good and my hearing keen. I read avidly, until the rising level of fatigue laid me low. That did me harm, and my family often hid my books, in order that my mind could rest. I was irritated then, and I became malevolent.

Fortunately, there was an infallible means of calming me down, and people never failed to employ it. They played me a few of the old opera tunes that I loved, or some novelty of penetrating grandeur, and like King Saul, I recovered my serenity. As soon as the first notes sounded, I experienced a delightful sensation. And when it finished, I remained under the charm for a long time. One might have sworn that I had just taken some celestial bath, whose virtue had suddenly relaxed my nerves—those terrible nerves, in the grip of which I was dying, slowly and horribly.

I could no longer walk. My sense of taste was atrophying day by day, and I could hardly find any savor in aliments any more. Touch was becoming gradually less distinct. I was, in consequence, only living via the eyes and the ears. Above all, I could hear marvelously, and that was an incredible pleasure for me. My entire life gradually took refuge in my head.

One day, when time was cruelly heavy and I had been shaken pitilessly by a frightful crisis, an idea occurred to me that I might recover a complete and marvelous calm if I could hear an opera.

Oh, that would be difficult! It would be necessary to carry me to the theater; it would be necessary to install me in a box, where I would be a sad spectacle for those who had known me when I was young, ardent and excessive, for those who still remembered the joyful companion I had been.

It was, therefore, a big deal.

As soon as I mentioned it, there were protests—but I insisted. My legacy was not to be disdained. Other nephews would not have hesitated to take me into their homes, to submit to my whims, and for those who were caring for me at that moment, it would have been five years of devotion gone completely to waste.

I say that because my first response, when I was refused anything, was to threaten to go and live elsewhere. In brief, I was a tyrant. They ended up giving in.

"What's playing this evening at the Grand Théâtre?" I asked. This was in the provinces, as you can see.

"They're playing *Le Prophète*,[66] uncle," replied a sixteen-year-old brunette, who was burning with the desire to go with me.

"Excellent!" I exclaimed. "Go and book me a box."

They resolved to satisfy me. My nephew ran to the theater.

I can't describe how joyful I was. I was going to stuff myself with music, with good music. By an unexpected stroke of luck, they were playing *Le Prophète*, which had always been one of my favorite works.

---

[66] *Le Prophète*, with music by Giacomo Meyerbeer and a French libretto by Eurgène Scribe, was first performed in 1849, and was a tremendous success. Set during the religious wars of the 16th century, it is based on the story of John of Leiden, who transformed the German city of Münster in to a theocratic Anabaptist community and proclaimed himself king in 1534. In the final act, his palace is set ablaze by a vengeful woman, as a result of the kind of misunderstanding that only occurs in melodramas.

Like a child, I could rest until they had dressed me. Then I wanted to have dinner early, on the pretext of having finished digesting it before going to the theater.

They gave in to my caprices. I abused them. A man in good health isn't good; sick, he's very bad indeed.

Finally, the time came. My little niece, the sixteen-year-old brunette, was to accompany me. Two vigorous commissionaires carried me away in my armchair. Fortunately, we lived not far from the theater.

During the journey the passers-by looked at me with pity. A few neighbors greeted me, with expressions of commiseration and the faces of people thinking: *Wouldn't it be better to leave that poor man at home?* But I didn't see anything and I didn't hear anything; I was entirely given over to my pleasure, my child-like joy.

I was taken into the foyer of the theater. My nephew had been inept enough the reserve me a box on the first floor. No matter: my two Auvergnats installed me there. My armchair was placed there, with me in it.

I was right at the front of the box, directly facing the stage, and I had an admirable view of the whole auditorium, from the orchestra stalls to the fourth boxes, those legendary seats where the chandelier is no longer troublesome because one can see over the top of it.

I remained alone with my niece, who was as enchanted as I was. Except that I had arrived too early. In my haste, I hadn't thought about the interminable half-hour that precedes the raising of the curtain.

My little Jeanne, who had only been to the theater three times in her life, wasn't bored. The comings and goings of the spectators, the movement in the hall as it filled up, and the more or less elegant dresses of the women sitting down in the balcony or in the boxes, all amused her—including the opera-glasses sometimes insolently aimed at her adorable face, or my decrepitude, which procured her new sensations: pleasure, regret or anger.

Finally, the horrible grating was heard of all the instruments tuning up—which had the effect on me of an exquisite melody.

The three regulation taps resounded behind the curtain. The brief introduction to Meyerbeer's opera was very aptly executed.

My breast and head were full of joy.

The first act was performed. I don't remember ever having experienced such a complete, sweet, and seraphic intoxication in my life. That evening, I was certainly in the shirt of the happy man for which the legendary Persian king sought in vain throughout his empire.

The second act, the third and the fourth were sung in a fashion that I found perfect. It had been such a long time since I had had a similar pleasure!

Furthermore, I was entirely absorbed in my pleasure. I didn't see anyone in the audience—where my presence, however, was exciting a certain curiosity. Even during the entr'actes, my eyes were fixed on the curtain or the orchestra.

Then, between two cellos, I noticed a bizarre little individual who interested me without my knowing why. He was a poor devil, no bigger than a child, frightfully hunchbacked, immeasurably deformed, in front as well as behind, his limbs twisted, his arms interminable—but not ugly.

He had that unhealthy complexion that is not rare among hunchbacks, but his features appeared to me to be quite regular.

When he played, during the performance, his entire body moved, twisted and seemed to wind around the cello in an oddly amorous fashion. By a singular contrast, however, his face then took on a serious, almost austere expression, and a flame of enthusiasm lit up in his eyes.

I saw all that quite clearly, thanks to my binoculars, and I was carried away by enthusiasm to the benefit of the deformed companion.

Loving music fervently, I thought of becoming the friend of that little individual, who would come to see me from time to time to make his marvelous instrument weep, and I was already forging a felicity for myself.

The hunchback, I could not doubt, was fanatical about his art. What more could one want?

I truly admired that strange individual, and I was already burning to know him, because I imagined that there must be something other than music in that extraordinarily pensive head.

From one entr'acte to the next, the interest I took in that twisted little man grew to excess. I can't describe the extent to which he excited my curiosity.

In brief, with the imagination typical of invalids, which can travel so far in such a short time, I first made the hunchback my fellow, and by the time the fifth act began, he was my friend—for the moment, my best friend.

Meyerbeer's vigorous music extracted me from my reverie, but I could not help saying to my pretty niece Jeanne, who could scarcely have been enjoying herself with her silent companion: "Have you noticed that little hunchback playing the cello?"

"Where, Uncle?"

"In the orchestra, of course, behind the bassoon."

"Oh! My God, how ugly he is!" the girl exclaimed, naively.

That exclamation shut my mouth and rendered me sullen. I didn't say another word until the moment when Jean de Leyde thought he ought to reveal to his accomplices that they were about to die with him. It was then that white smoke began to rise up to the stage through the cracks in the boards. No one paid any attention to it. It was no thicker than the regulation smoke projected from below.

Suddenly, however, there was an explosion and a flash that dimmed the lights of the auditorium, and the dancers were seen to rush into the wings, all on the same side. The tenor, who seemed at first to be nailed to the spot, soon picked up the hem of his white robe and literally took flight. All the others, singers and members of the chorus, disappeared in their turn.

"What's happening?" some of the spectators, inclined to alarm, were already demanding.

But then a young woman reappeared, running across the stage. The most hideous fear was painted on her features. Her eyes were bulging. She seemed to be searching for something, with mad haste.

"What's wrong?" people in the hall shouted to her. Without suspecting the reality, everyone was holding their breath.

The poor distraught girl leapt into the orchestra pit, shouting in a strangled voice: "Fire!"

Fire! At that word, the entire audience bounded to their feet with a single surge. Oh, I can recall it all is if it were still passing before my eyes. The musicians stopped abruptly, but not all at once, for isolated notes faded away into the air here and there.

There was a sort of lamentable bellow uttered by the trombone; two or three violins threw forth and sinister and false mewl; a harpist's arpeggio flew away joyfully; the shrill note of a *cor anglais* ripped through the horrible chaos that was erupting. But it was the cello that resounded last, on a penetrating F sharp. And that was my hunchback, my little hunchback, who, entirely absorbed in his part, had not heard or had not understood what the young woman had shouted.

Then, all the musicians, crazed with fear, launched themselves toward the door of the orchestra pit—but only two or three of them got out, who soon came back. The retreat was cut off; they had to escape through the auditorium.

Needless, to say, all of that happened with a magical rapidity.

The auditorium! Oh, it was there that everything was frightful, horrible, unimaginable.

The auditorium was a battlefield.

At first, I couldn't make out very much—in any case, I was trembling myself, shaken by a fear beyond the possible.

Alone with Jeanne, with that child who could do nothing for me and who was motionless, without an idea, without a gesture, the thought occurred to me that I was going to stay there without being able to move, at the mercy of the fire, which would come to lick me slowly, to burn me alive, to consume me.

I didn't lose my head, though.

No, I'm astonished even today by the composure that took possession of me, so to speak, and to which I was by no means accustomed.

"Quickly," I said to little Jeanne, "save yourself, my girl, and run to find someone who can get me out of here, if there's still time."

A young man who had undoubtedly noticed my niece, and who was not too frightened, ran toward her.

"Come, Mademoiselle, come," he said to the child.

Without further ado, he took her by the hand and drew her away.

"But my uncle, my uncle!" the good little girl cried.

"Eh! Let him come!" riposted two or three individuals who were crushing one another pitilessly at the overly narrow door of the gallery.

Let him come! That terrible phrase still rings in my ears. *Let him come!* I could not get up, nor move anything other than one arm.

Let him come!

They left me there.

And in the meantime, the battle of the orchestra stalls—all the stalls—was furious. There were four doors in all, each ninety centimeters wide, for that torrent, which had become a flood in two seconds. It was in the vicinity of those doors that all the effort of the panic-stricken people was expended. Everyone wanted to go through first. They pushed, they shouted, they howled, and they fought furiously.

In one, two vigorous men were braced back-to-back against the opening, which they each wanted to get through before the other—and in the meantime, neither they nor anyone else could escape. Behind them, there were cries of male-diction, imprecations, sobs, and everyone was shoving with a blind rage.

I saw two young men, who could already feel the heat of the flames, leap on to the banquettes first, and from there on to the shoulders of those who were nearest the door. They dragged themselves over their companions, curbing heads beneath the weight of their bodies, hanging on with their clenched fingers to the clothes and hair of anyone at all, dig-ging their fingernails into the flesh of women's shoulders and man's faces.

Eventually, the human mass on which they were count-ing to carry them outside, opened up, and they fell heavily between two banquettes, where they were trampled and crushed, carelessly, pitilessly and without remorse.

I can assure you that there is no spectacle more terrible.

Meanwhile, the fire was gaining ground. The sets were beginning to burn. The flames were approaching the auditori-um rapidly. The heat was becoming more sensible.

I was sweating, but more from fear than heat. There was already something grandiose in the spectacle that I had before my eyes: something grandiose and joyous.

That last word astonishes you?

I can't explain it. I'm simply relating and depicting what I experienced, what I felt.

In spite of the frightful anguish that was squeezing my throat, gripping my chest and constricting my abdomen, I found...yes, I found something insolently cheerful in those enormous tongues of flame dancing before me and coming to caress the proscenium.

That delight on the part of the scourge overwhelmed me, imposed itself upon me. I saw myself doomed. I had a frisson in the marrow of my bones at the thought that I was about to be burned alive where I was, without any possible resistance. It was horror pushed beyond its limits, and yet, in a corner of my mind, there was an acute obstinacy in finding that flame cheerful.

Another thing astonished me: the relative slowness with which the fire progressed.

It's true that I was thinking twice, three times or ten times as fast at that moment, and that time seemed to be indefinitely multiplied, as if it wanted to savor the atrocious torture to which I was condemned without appeal. The seconds, in fact, were flowing so slowly that I was able to make all the reflections you have just read before the auditorium emptied...what am I saying?...before half the spectators had got out.

The riot at the doors was becoming more intense, more compact, and ever more furious.

As the flames spread and the smoke thickened, the rage of those who were still inside took on the proportions of utter madness. It was a veritable struggle for existence, in the most absolute and most brutal sense of the expression.

Everyone wanted to get through first, and everyone lashed out pitilessly to the left and the right, in front and behind.

Oh, woe betide the weak! Woe betide the good! Woe betide all those who had not yet consented frankly to being ferocious beasts.

And there were children there—little children, who were screaming, while their pale, torn, scratched, bloodied mothers were begging men to be charitable, to be humane.

Well, yes, humane. It was certainly not a matter of that. Not being roasted in the furnace: that was the whole of it.

I saw one tall, dark-haired devil with the enormous nose of a bird of prey, his eyes wide with fear, hold out his hand—an immense hand, the vision of which has remained in my mind—to seize the young woman in front of him by the shoulder and pull her backwards, in order at least to take her place. The clenched fingers of that giant hand must have dig into the lady's flesh and turned the skin blue, if they did not rend it. But she resisted frenziedly, fighting with all her might, trying in her turn to dig her fingernails into her tormentor's face. Horribly, though, that wretch pressed his two hands down on the poor woman, weighing upon her desperately, until she fell between two seats, and he passed over her with a triumphant snigger.

I knew that coward by sight. He passed in society for a well brought-up man. Perhaps he knew his victim; perhaps he had danced with her in the town's drawing rooms the previous winter.

He did not get the benefit of his horrible egotism, however, for, when he reached the door, he was shoved so violently against the wall of the ground-floor boxes that he was knocked unconscious, and he too fell.

In the midst of all that effort, all that terror, all that flight, frightful cries rang out. Some were calling out to a relative or a friend; others were screaming without knowing why. Women were weeping and succumbing to nervous crises.

Suddenly, I saw a fireman appear. Where had he come from? I started shouting to him. He heard me. He looked at me, seemingly wondered what I was doing there, and disappeared.

I thought that he was coming to rescue me. Not at all.

Gradually, however, the auditorium emptied. A few of those who had kept their heads—they were not numerous—and who had remained until last, still had the courage to drag those vanquished in the combat, who had been trampled, out into the corridor. They were just in time. The fire had reached the orchestra pit.

There, everything testified to the stampede in which everyone had fled. The music-stands were overturned; violins, oboes, flutes and clarinets lay on the ground. Hardly any of the artistes had had the presence of mind to take their instruments with them. In the midst of that disorder, the harp could be seen standing up, straight and solemn, and then the long shafts of the double basses, and finally the cellos, which were les easy to make out.

On a few of the music-stands that were still upright, and on the conductor's lectern, the scores still sat, already turning brown under the action of the heat.

The smoke, thick at first, had been drawn toward the ceiling by some effect of the ventilation system—of which, of course, I had taken no account.

It was the flame alone, the white flame, that now burst forth in the hall, where the light of the chandelier was becoming ridiculously yellow and dull with every passing minute.

The flame! First it caressed the music-stands. An immense tongue of fire penetrated the proscenium, doubtless drawn by some open door, but withdrew almost immediately. The paper of the scores twisted slowly, the heat becoming intolerable; a violin string broke audibly under the effort of the fire. That note, yielded by the instrument that was about to die, had something heartbreaking in its melancholy.

But the nucleus of the fire was growing. It was soon the strings of the harp that were snapping, one after another. The admirable, delightful instrument seemed to be singing its swan song in the anguish that resounded like hiccups, and yet still found the means to be harmonious. A melody flew up into the flame with its soul.

After the harp, it was the doubles basses whose powerful chanterelles broke with a sound like revolver shots.

And finally, in the right-hand corner, an explosion rang out, and then another, and a third. They were the skins of the kettledrums and the bass drum, bursting under the pressure of the superheated air.

At that moment, I saw something that terrified me. Through the left-hand door of the orchestra stalls, a head appeared.

It had to be a child's head; I couldn't make it out very clearly. The smoke was recovering its intensity, and beginning to blind me. I could still see, though, as if through a fog.

In the movements of that head there was something akin to curiosity, mingled with an astonishing resolution.

Soon, though, the entire body moved into the auditorium.

What could that unfortunate child be coming to do? What idea was going through that head?

The face turned toward the orchestra it, and remained motionless. Suddenly, however, he took two steps forward, and I uttered an exclamation.

It wasn't a child: it was the hunchback, the little hunchbacked musician, my future friend of a little while before, the friend that I would never know, because I was surely about to die.

But what did he want? What had brought him back?

Tortuously, but deliberately, he moved toward the orchestra pit. A jet of fire stopped him dead. He recoiled, but did not appear to renounce whatever crazy plan he had doubtless made.

It was then, seizing a favorable moment, that the little man leapt forward.

He reached the first row of the orchestra stalls and, still running, his arms curved over his body to protect him, he drew closer to the place he had occupied among the musicians.

I had divined his thought, his desire. The poor hunchback had saved himself, like everyone else, at the first alarm, but after reflection, he had come back to look for his friend, his companion, his cello, the benevolence of which doubtless consoled all his troubles, all his bitterness.

Yes, that was it! I saw him pick up the instrument in both hands, and attempt to lift it over the balustrade that separated the orchestra pit from the stalls.

What folly!

The fire was beginning to rage, and I could not imagine that the unfortunate fellow could hold on for another minute without being mortally burned. I experienced an anxiety that shook me from top to toe. Involuntarily, I shouted, in a terrible voice: "Get out! Get out! You're tempting God! Get out, you poor fool! Get out!"

In all probability, he didn't hear me, because he continued wrestling with his instrument. The more I shouted, the more he persisted. The swirls of flame were already reaching down as far as his head.

All around him the fire was spreading. He climbed on to a seat and, standing on it, setting one of his feet on the barrier, he drew up his cello.

"You're insane!" I shouted, again.

In fact, I almost forgot my own situation in being moved by the hunchback's insensate action.

Poor little fellow, so singular, to whom I would never speak, and who must have been so good and intelligent...I can still see him, before my eyes, standing on that banquette, making mighty efforts.

Then, all of a sudden, it seemed that he succeeded. The cello, detached from the chairs that were impeding it, was finally coming toward him—when, almost at the same time, all the violins and cellos, whose light wood was overheated, caught fire at the same time.

The hunchback's burst into flames like all the rest. It was terrible. An explosive flame suddenly rose up to a great height. The little man immediately let go of the instrument he was holding, tottered, and fell forward, head first, into the orchestra pit, on top of his burning cello.

I cannot even try to depict the frightful horror that overwhelmed me when I saw that frightful denouement. I uttered something akin to a howl of despair.

By a secret instinct, moreover, I saw in the fate of that poor devil, whom I had just made my friend, the destiny that awaited me.

I sat there open-mouthed for a few seconds, with my arm—my only arm—extended toward the place where I had seen that strange and somber figure stand up, lit by the excessive glare constituted by the fire. I saw him move once again in the midst of the flames, extending his arms, blackened by so much radiance, and collapse into the blaze.

Pitiless were the instruments that had just caught fire, more joyously than ever. Their light flame danced around the fragile sounding-boards that were twisting and reddening, and which still seemed to be performing a frightful symphony, to the power and the horror of which I, perhaps alone in all the world, can testify.

I would really have liked to know whether the poor devil of a hunchback...but what madness to hope that he might have survived!

In any case, I could no longer see; the smoke was thickening; the flames were becoming more intense; the center of the conflagration was a furnace.

Rapidly, now, the cornices and the projections of the proscenium were lighting up. It was almost impossible for me to distinguish anything any longer. The smoke was blinding me and choking me. My turn had come; I was about to die.

No one in the world can have any idea of the innumerable thoughts that can be born and succeeded one another in a human mind in a few minutes. It's unimaginable. Thus, for me, between the death of the hunchback and the moment when I lost consciousness, it was certainly less than three minutes that went by, but what went through my mind during that brief lapse of time is incalculable.

My first impulse was one of utter resignation.

I considered myself condemned. Before the overwhelming heat in which my body was roasting had reached half its intensity, I wondered whether it might not be better for me to die in that fashion, frightful as it was, than to continue seeing my faculties wither one by one until death claimed me.

Whether I was burned alive in that blazing theater or I continued to drag out a miserable and declining existence in a hard armchair, wasn't it all one to me? Wasn't I bound for a lamentable end either way?

But one only makes those reflections when the supreme moment hasn't yet come, and while you're separated from that truly psychological moment, if only by an interval of three minutes, you envisage the present torture with a certain serenity.

On the other hand, as soon as the atrocious suffering begins to play its part, as soon as one reaches the second in which it's necessary to support the extreme pain, the soul becomes anxious, the mid jibs and the flesh revolts. You can't go on.

To save oneself, to escape death: the cry of the fabulist escapes your lips. Impotent, lame, crippled, mute and motionless—what does it matter, provided that one is alive!

There are terrors before which the bravest recoil, and cease to be impassive.

Death by fire is the domain of those terrors.

I was still nailed to my seat. The enemy was advancing, not without a certain relative slowness.

Had I lost all hope of salvation?

No; I have to confess, no.

Oh, there is a singularly vibrant and tenacious gleam of hope that shines in the depths of human being.

Yes, I hoped, I still hoped. My hope was built on the very death of the poor hunchback.

Since he had been able to come back in search of his instrument, others might be capable of reaching me, of picking me up and carrying me away.

And then, there was the fireman I had seen; I imagined that he was thinking about me, and nothing but me.

Ah, hope! But while I was building that castle of illusions, reality—which is to say, the fire—was continuing its path, surely. Gradually, the woodwork was catching fire.

The singed velvet of the seats was emitting an opaque smoke. It enveloped me, that smoke, it swirled around me; it got into my eyes, my nose and my mouth, and made me cough. From time to time, a current of air swept it away, and I breathed in—and I seemed to be alone, a frightened, motionless victim of an ineluctable catastrophe.

Then, like an immense wave, a new jet of smoke came to swallow me up and stifle me. One might have sworn that some infernal spirit wanted to savor the martyrdom to which I was prey, by prolonging it cruelly until it was sated. Thus, negro kings in the heart of Africa drown their enemies by plunging their heads into water and taking it out again, alternately, until they die after several hours of suffering.

Soon, though, it was no longer only the smoke that was besieging me. Although the fire had not yet reached the wood paneling of my box, the heat was so intense that I was beginning to feel the blood boiling in my veins, and in my brain.

Then the sensation of burning became terribly appreciable. I was able to calculate that at the point I had reached, I certainly could not remain conscious for two minutes more. The furnace was intensifying further. Sweat was pouring down my brow, from my temples on to my cheeks, into my beard. My entire body was inundated. I tried to put my hand on the varnished leather sill of the box; I snatched it back precipitately; it was burning.

A lick of flame, detached from God knows where, described a parabola in the auditorium and came to fall in the box next to mine,

My resignation could no longer hold. Decidedly, I didn't want to die. Save me! Save myself! I no longer had any other desire, any other rage.

Save myself! But how? It was too late to try, even if I were capable of doing anything toward such an enterprise. Save myself? Oh yes, save myself. I wanted that, I wanted that, I wanted that...

Oh, how I cursed my resignation of a few moments before. Perhaps it was not as difficult as I had thought...

After all, I still had one arm, one semi-valid arm, whose strength, tripled by fear, might be able...

Certainly: by throwing myself bravely backwards, I might perhaps be able to drag myself, in jerks, clutching at everything, all the way to the corridor. Once there, there would be a respite. After a few seconds' rest, I would be able to continue my route, as far as the big staircase, where, undoubtedly, someone would see me from outside.

Yes, I thought all that, but I did nothing, and my numb body remained motionless, while a nervous agitation developed in my head, which, I sensed, would turn to madness.

And the pitiless heat was still increasing, incessantly, in direct proportion to the development of the scourge.

I was gripped then by a nervous wrath that must have been frightful. My eyes bloodshot, my teeth clenched, my hair and beard bristling, I waved my arm, my futile arm, in an atmosphere of seventy-five degrees, and I uttered a scream, one of those screams that are paroxysms, and under the effort of which it seems that one's breast ought to burst.

But my fury, my heart-rending scream, and my crazed gesture were all in vain. No one came.

And I still did nothing; I was stuck.

Imagine some unfortunate tied to a stake, slowly attained by a deliberate fire. Well, my torture was more terrible, more abominable, because I was not tied, since I would have been easily able to save myself if…if only…ah!

But I didn't want to be turned to charcoal there, before even being burned. It seemed to me that my flesh was already twisting under the effects of the incandescence that surrounded me.

I could no longer see anything, and no longer hear anything except a formidable din that the victorious fire was making in the vast cage of the theater. My beard had to be singeing and beginning to burn. I could feel pricking sensations in my face, on my head, and the root of every one of my hairs.

This time, I made and effort; I stirred in my armchair.

There's still time, I thought.

And I resolved to get up, to walk.

Perhaps, I said to myself, again, *the frightful state that I'm in, that abundant sweat and everything I'm experiencing, have rendered to my body and my legs the strength that they'd lost.*

Almost convinced of the possibility of a miracle, I put my feet on the floor and I tried. Having leaned forward, I made an abrupt movement. There was something like a flash of lightning in my eyes. I believed that I was about to walk.

Not for long. No, no—my legs didn't want to. They remained pitilessly paralyzed.

Any my fury became immense.

Then I tried again. I remembered the mute son of Croesus, suddenly rediscovering the power of speech at the sight of his father threatened with death by a soldier who did not recognize him.

Why should the same effect not be produced in me by a danger even more pressing, even more horrible?

But once again, no, no, no.

Except that I could feel myself dying now. It was no longer possible to support one more degree of heat. It was over, really over. The torture was about to become implacable. I could no longer think; I could no longer feel. It seemed to me that I was vacillating.

In front of my eyes there was blinding light; around me, everywhere, above me and beneath me, fire.

I was inert. Perhaps I fell.

I no longer knew anything. I was abandoned.

A week later, I woke up in my bed, with a grievous head wound.

My young niece, as she ran to get help, had fallen and had sustained a serious head wound. She had been carried away, unconscious, and it was only when she came round that she had been able to speak. Two men had launched themselves forward, and had snatched me from the furnace at the very moment when I was no longer conscious of anything.

ANGUISH

When we arrived at Carlemont, there was a veritable fury
of enthusiasm on all sides. Alongside the train, which had just
emptied, or nearly so, we stood there dazzled. The region was
celebrated for its beauty. Most of us were expecting a splendid
spectacle. Well, the expectation was surpassed. Everything
that we had before our eyes was admirable—everything, down
to the slightest detail.

First of all, a few paces away, the station—and what a
station! Imagine a construction affecting the exquisite form of
a Gothic pavilion that the hands of enchantresses, of whom the
country must be full, had embroidered at their leisure, and
decorated with bell-towers, turrets, awnings, and terraces that
were simultaneously the most varied and most graceful in the
world.

It was a thousand times more poetic than the engineer,
the man who had built it, but—an improbable phenomenon—
another poet had come along, who dreamed of hiding, beneath
a mantle of flowers and foliage, the marvel of the first, and
had succeeded, O miracle, in creating a marvel more astonishing still! Thus invited to collaborate, nature had expended all
her talent. Wisteria, virgin vines, clematis and climbing rose
covered it entirely—entirely, you hear—the façades, the sides,
the projections and the roofs. Around the gracious columns
that sustained the canopy, the broad leaves of aristolochia
were displayed, between which convolvulus and honeysuckle
slid their flowers. The dazzling and robust vegetation had tak-
en on the exact form of the edifice, giving it the aspect of a
flowery palace, a perfumed nest in which elves were asleep.

At one of the windows, framed with vine-branches, a
young woman was standing, vaguely blonde and mysterious,
her eyes drowned in a kind of ambient bliss. She was looking

at the crowd, smiling, with the expression of a creature who has nothing to require of Providence.

Behind that enchanted castle, a mountain rises up, almost abruptly, alternately—in accordance with the height—flowery, wooded or arid, but always insolently or superbly picturesque. On its lower slopes, villas of every style nestle in groves of trees, surrounded by girdles of roses which seem to emerge from the green satin of lawns. Two or three hundred meters higher up, the profound forest commences, with its larches boldly suspended on the edges of precipices. And finally, touching the sky, the bare rock takes on violet tints in the sunlight, delightful in their effect. There are massifs of porphyry, large and grandiose in their design, which sometimes descend vertically, sometimes launch delicate ridges toward the azure, and sometimes extend in a colossal peak. Huddled in the angles, into which the beds of torrents are beginning to bite, vaporous vagabond white or pink clouds are perceptible, which, weary of wandering in space, have settled there, in order finally to rest.

If you now turn your back to the mountain and the station, there is a shining lake before you, with waters as calm as happy days, and whose little waves come to kiss the shore, dying almost at your feet. That lake is, however, immense; and on sounding it with one's gaze, one would have the illusion of a sea, if one were not able to perceive, beyond it, pale blue or faded green summits, which change color and appearance in accordance with the time of day, furnishing, like the Ocean, a spectacle all the more interesting because it is continually renewed and its appearance one day never resembles that of the next.

To complete the landscape, imagine all of that on a magnificent day in June, the fecund warmth of which is tempered by an imperceptible breeze, arriving fresh and even from a nearby hill. Imagine a village in fête, and all the curiosity-seekers from elsewhere taking advantage of that day to contemplate that ideal land. It is as if the lake were speckled with boats that are heading toward a small harbor near the station.

The sides of the mountain resound with the little bells of horses drawing primitive carriages carrying clusters of peasants in their Sunday clothes. Whip-cracks resonate over all the slopes.

On the edges of ravines and under the arbors, songs are strung out. There is gaiety everywhere, a natural youthfulness that suppresses all sadness. And down below, to the left, as if it were marching over the lake while seemingly embedded in the green background of the shore, the train that has brought us draws away at top speed, mingling its joyful cry at intervals with the sounds of the valley and leaving behind it a white plume, without the sound of its wheels rolling along its single track being audible at this distance.

As we came out of the station in order to savor these splendors at closer range, the rural postman arrived at his heavy and monotonous pace. The young woman glimpsed a little while ago, svelte and ethereal, ran toward the distributor, unconscious of the intoxications and woes that his Pandora's box contained. She received a letter in her hand that made her radiant.

"Papa," she said to an individual in a hat with golden palms, "he's arriving this evening." Then she blushed to the hairline, doubtless at letting her happiness show.

The day went by like an adorable dream, and the fête, which would have been banal in another frame, left us delicate, sweet and durable impressions in the series of its anticipated ups and downs.

Several times, the hazards of conversation brought back—no one knew why—the name and image of the happy blonde.

She was, as you will have guessed, the station-master's daughter, Marguerite Latour. A few months before, a young man had saved her life on the lake and had fallen in love with her. For her part, Marguerite had given her soul to Georges. But when it was necessary to talk about marriage, the two families, each judging that it was a bad match, had been obstinate in a dolorous opposition. Nevertheless, after a time, the parents had perceived that they were both going to die of grief. Fundamentally, they loved them, and conceded on both sides.

Marguerite was therefore living that day in the expectation of a happiness that did not lack the seasoning of resistance and temporary despair, and everyone on the mountain, on the lakeside and in the valleys of the foothills, being interested in her as a friend, offered good wishes for the realization of her dream.

At eight o'clock in the evening—the sun had disappeared behind the crests that it set ablaze—we had gone down to the station to catch the penultimate train. The little station had never seen such a festival. More than four hundred people were waiting with us. A universal delight penetrated the crowd, which had not wearied of contemplating that paradisal corner of the earth. Enveloped in an atmosphere of good humor, everyone walked, smiling in a dream full of charm. The smallest incident was a pretext for merriment.

People were particularly amused by the dazed expressions of the railway employees and the station master, without thinking that they must have been undertaking superhuman labors all day. Two Englishmen, in particular, provoked amusement by the tenacity with which they were harassing Monsieur Latour in French pronounced in an Anglo-Saxon accent. To that group of questioners, as obstinate as mosquitoes, was added the flood of cheerful idlers whose obstruction of the platform rendered service difficult.

At that moment, we saw Marguerite Latour appear, even more beautiful than in the morning, her cheeks flushed, her eyes illuminated by an ecstatic gleam, as if she were in communion with some divine thought.

"Oh, Father!" she said, on seeing the station-master so tormented. "How hot you are, and how tired you seem."

A locomotive whistled behind a fold in the terrain, and, drawing a long chain of carriages, stopped in front of the florid house, with a metallic sound. The train was not the one that was to take us away. It was, on the contrary, going in the opposite direction in order to pass the train for which we were

187

waiting at the next station. As we said, the railway only had one track; the crossing of trains, very strictly regulated, was only effected at the appointed times at determined stations.

Great precautions had been taken at all times to avoid accidents. People expert in such matters even affirmed that any surprise was impossible, the line being equipped with an extremely ingenious apparatus with the aid of which every station-master notified his nearest colleague of the departure of a train, and made sure automatically that the way was clear; if there was any obstacle or the rails between the two stations were occupied, the apparatus ceased to function.

In brief, all of that was so well calculated that there would have been nothing to fear, if the human brain, on which one cannot rely in an absolute manner, were as perfect as the instruments it creates—if one could count on the inventor as well as the invention: a strange subject of reflection on mind and matter.

But the dull and repetitive sound was heard of doors being closed, with regular haste, by the conductor and a crewman. The last bags had been loaded into the luggage wagon. Monsieur Latour, his silver whistle in his hand, seemed pensive. In his tried brain, a vague instinct told him that he had forgotten something. And as people continued to bother him with questions, he left his place in order to regain possession of himself, heading toward the train-driver, who said to him: "Well, Monsieur, aren't we leaving?"

Monsieur Latour darted an anxious glance around to make sure that everything was in order; then he put the whistle to his lips. A shrill, continuous sound rose into the air. The locomotive responded to the signal by whistling itself. The ticket-inspector's horn proffered its own plaintive notes, and the train pulled away, *pff, pff, pff!*

It departed; it was gone.

But the final carriage had not passed over the points when a light came on in the station-master's head.

Abruptly, he went pale.

"What's the matter, Papa?" asked Marguerite.

Monsieur Latour did not reply. He tottered, afflicted by such an emotion that he had not heard what his daughter said. One of his employees passed within arm's reach; he grabbed him violently by the arm, and with frightened eyes, snapped: "Was it you, Renault, who signaled train 211?"

"No, Monsieur," the man replied.

At that response, the station-master felt a sharp sting at the root of every one of his hairs.

"Was it you, then, Brémont?"

"No, Monsieur."

A cold sweat broke out on the poor man's face; two or three anxious people were watching him, listening.

"Joseph, did you signal train 211 to Laroque station?"

The same response fell like a hammer-blow upon the station-master. "No, Monsieur."

He had not done it either. He had just remembered that. And the train had gone.

"But in that case," whispered one of the people who had been listening to Monsieur Latour's questions, "the two trains are going to run into one another!"

Those words were heard by two or three neighbors. They were repeated—and ran through the crowd with the cruel rapidity of disastrous news.

The station-master could no longer see, and he stood there, thoughtless and petrified. Marguerite uttered a cry of alarm. A few optimists—there are always some—claimed that the thing was improbable.

"For that to happen," she said, "it would be necessary for the two trains to leave at the same time—to the very second—from the two stations. Then again, the station-master at Laroque can't have forgotten to signal his train at the same time as the one at Carlemont. That would be too much. Besides which, the ticket-inspectors and the other railway employees..."

That reassuring demonstration was cut short by a cry: "The Laroque train is on its way! Look! Look!"

There was a dolorous, stifling contraction in all chests.

"Something has to be done! Something has to be done!" repeated the jerky voice of a young man whose nerves were already suffering from the commencement of a crisis. "The train that just left is only two hundred meters away. We have to shout—the driver or the stoker might hear us."

Like a gunpowder fuse catching fire, everyone understood. A frightful clamor went up and spread, carrying fear to the heights of the mountain and the horizons of the lake. Canes and umbrellas were raised and waved madly, while further shrill, unhealthy, terrible cries were uttered.

In the midst of that panicking crowd, the station-master, motionless, as if changed into a statue, looked straight ahead without seeing anything; his complexion was gray.

And yet, there was someone paler than him: his daughter. Mechanically, she murmured: "Georges! Georges is on the train! He's doomed, Papa, Georges!"

Then she ran along the platform, launched herself in front of all the other spectator, sketched unconscious gestures, mingled her cries with those of the crowd, and fell into a bleak despair, without being able to take her eyes off the locomotive and its carriages, which were about to kill her fiancé.

Train 211 continued on its way. The track described a curve along the shore of the lake that inclined to the right, in such a way that they were able to follow, without any effort, the phases of the drama.

Coming from Laroque, the other train advanced. From time to time one or other of them disappeared into a cutting—and it was that curve and those cuttings which prevented the two drivers from seeing one another's trains. The white smoke from each funnel was launched into the air with the same hasty regularity. People sensed that the two drivers were traveling to their deaths without any suspicion of it, with tranquil souls. It was the spectators at Carlemont station who were enduring suffering, a nameless torture.

They watched, impotently, the tragic progress of the two monsters going to smash into one another, and in spite of anything they could imagine, say or do, nothing could prevent the catastrophe.

There was no tunnel or steep slope, however.

"How is it that they can't see one another?" someone asked.

"Ah! One might think that one of the trains has reversed its engine!"

"No, no, you're mistaken."

And, indeed, they were still moving forward. The travelers at Carlemont were prey to an abominable anguish, an anguish that was weakening and extinguishing a feeble glimmer of hope with every passing second. At that distance, the two locomotives seemed to be moving slowly, and some people concluded that they really were slowing down, and that they were going to stop. But no: the drivers and the stokers, and the passengers aboard the two trains, were as blind as their machines.

In the compartments, people were laughing, making plans, thinking about their children, their mothers, or the future.

Georges was eager to get there; he was impatient with the slowness of the train.

And with an implacable regularity, separated by a fold in the terrain of only a hundred and some meters, the two machines continued to advance.

The crowd in the station had fallen silent. Its members were frozen by the horror of the inevitable catastrophe.

"So they won't see one another?" said a woman, translating everyone's thought.

Monsieur Latour seemed fixed in his granite immobility. There was not a twitch of a hand, a lip or an eyelid. He watched. His entire life was concentrated in his wishes.

They could now see the two trains traveling at full steam toward one another. All the same, it took a long time to happen, the collision that everyone feared so terribly. Time, in such circumstances, is subdivided into infinitesimal parcels, which nevertheless have an appreciable length, capable of further division.

Marguerite, standing there, her hair partly undone, so violently was she holding her head in her hands in order to assure herself that she was suffering from an unspeakable nightmare, cried: "Doomed! He's doomed! My God!"

She twisted her arms. She was visibly ready to launch herself forward in obedience to some insensate hope of catching up with the train and saving Georges—for she was not thinking about anyone except Georges.

Neither the situation of her devastated father, nor the numerous lives that were about to be lost, claimed her attention; they did not touch her. Could she think about them? Georges, the man she loved ardently, whose bride she had been unable to count on being only a two days before, was about to die at the very moment when all obstacles had been removed.

And she was the one who had sent him the telegram twenty-four hours ago, begging him to come!

An illusion sprang into her mind.

"What if he missed the train? If some obstacle..."

She dared not finish. An obstacle? What? He loved her to much to delay his departure by a second. He was there, surely; it seemed to her that she could see him.

And he was about to die. Oh! She had an immediate movement of revolt, and stamped her foot violently.

"And nothing! Nothing! I can't do anything! I'm here; I can see him, about to perish, and my voice is too feeble, my arms too short, my will futile. What torture! I'll die of it too!"

What she said, in the panic of despair, the four hundred spectators also thought. It is necessary to have been subjected to a similar fright to have any idea of what the shocked spectators were experiencing mentally.

People were holding their breath. Abrupt cries were uttered. One young man collapsed on the sidewalk, in an epileptic fit. And the nervous crises spread from one person to another. Those who resisted remained nailed to the spot, every gaze and every gesture extended toward the part of the track where the denouement was about to occur.

Scarcely eighty meters, on a bed, separated the two trains. And everyone was wondering how it was that they had not seen one another. Eighty meters! In the time it takes to formulate a thought, they were only sixty meters apart, then fifty. They were hurtling together.

No one, at that moment, thought any longer that they were moving slowly. The distance was diminishing by the second. It was horrible

The breasts of the spectators, crushed by the iron fingers of anguish, shrank with every rotation of the wheels. Even those who had no friend or relative on the trains were suffering mortally. What, then, must poor Marguerite have been experiencing?

Her life was at stake—more than her life; that of her beloved!

It was her heart that was about to be crushed by the impact of the two machines. She took another step forward, as if to get closer to the accomplishment of her horrible destiny, her eyes haggard, her mouth taut, her hands and lips trembling, her hair loose.

A cry of joy rang out in the midst of the crowd.

"They've seen one another! The Laroque train has reversed its steam! Look—it's no longer smoking!"

"But the other! The other!" someone replied.

The most mortal of tremors passed through the crowd. Women turned their heads.

A shrill scream—the kind of scream that must be heard in towns taken by assault and delivered to pillage—resounded. It was Marguerite who had uttered it.

A brief sound, like that of a muffled cannon shot, was heard. The impact had occurred. The two iron monsters reared up, furiously, embraced, climbing up one another, seemingly wanting to rise to improbable heights, and fell back in the midst of seething vapor, which enveloped everything.

Carriages collapsed to the right, at the bottom of a slope, and came apart. Others leapt over the rocks, and the horrible shattering was divined from afar.

The station-master, not having the strength to take a step, collapsed, in an attitude of defeat. The terrified spectators ran at random. On the lake, all the boats were rowing as far as possible toward the theater of the disaster. Two carriages had fallen into the water.

Without knowing what she was doing, Marguerite set off at a run. There was six or seven hundred meters to cover in order to know—for hope was still burning like a candle-flame in her crushed heart.

"There are some carriages intact!" someone alongside her had murmured. She flew over the cross-ties, which twisted her ankles, tumbling at every stride. Never, in other circumstances, would she have had the strength to attempt such a run, but she did not notice anything, not even that she fell two or three times. Ever more rapidly, her feet bruised, her knees skinned, she went on, and on...

Men and young women, moved by a sentiment of charity, had taken the same route in order to bring help to the injured, to the survivors, if there were any, but no one could catch up with her.

Oh, those six hundred meters! There is no way to describe how long they were...long, long, long...even though she did not slow her pace for a second. What torture! No one can have any suspicion of it. It is impossible to suspect the division of the seconds into endless hundredths, at such moments.

She arrives, however, out of breath, voiceless. The spectacle she expected was nothing by comparison with the one that strikes her. It is chaos. One of the machines has disemboweled the other. The tender and five or six carriages on either side are no longer anything but an impenetrable mass of wreckage. The ground is gouged out to astonishing depths. Half of one carriage is on its roof, its wheels in the air. From the middle of that inextricable tangle, howls of pain, desperate appeals for help, sobs and plaints emerge, dying away, from crushed breasts.

Horrible! A thousand times horrible!

Marguerite thinks: *Georges is among the victims, among those who are enduring that martyrdom!*

She is still running, trying to see, circling around that confusion of people and things, shouting: "Georges!"

Others arrive, begin to organize first aid.

"Georges? Georges?"

She falls to her knees, commences a prayer, but gets up again energetically, violently, shouting even more loudly. People look at her with an infinite pity. No one doubts that she has lost the man she loves...

She had traveled the length of the battlefield; she has circled around it; no voice has responded to her appeals.

"Georges!"

Then, she run to the carriages that are still intact, opens the doors.

Empty!

Well, of course, empty! One needs to be in the state into which anguish has put her not to realize that no one would have any desire to stay there.

"It's over!"

But in the distance, someone is already pulling a body out of the wreckage.

"He's not dead," says a voice.

Marguerite runs forward, parts the crowd with the authority of misfortune, and looks.

It isn't him.

She falls back into darkness. Her heart is beating abominably. Her blood flows away from her temples, dazing her. She is about to fall. But no—an effort restores her equilibrium. She hears crewmen saying: "It'll take twenty-four hours to bring out the wounded from under all that."

Twenty-four hours! she thinks. In her dementia, she wants to make the workman a liar. With her hands, her feeble hands, she begins pulling on iron bars, which yield at first, but then resist, proving her debility.

She has to accept her impotence.

Someone tries to draw her away; she resists.

Someone orders someone else to take her away, but she begs, bursts into sobs. She is about to be dragged away when she suddenly stops defending herself.

In complete immobility, she looks straight ahead, and listens.

Then, with a single effort, she pulls free of the hands that are retaining her, and takes two steps forward.

"Georges!" she shouts for the hundredth time—but joyfully this time.

A young man was coming down a path, out of breath. It was her fiancé, already returned from the station, to which he had run in order to reassure her.

Marguerite became even paler, smiled and held out her hands. They were about to fall into one another's arms when the poor child, strong enough a moment ago to support the agony of damnation, no longer had enough capacity in her lungs or her brain to contain the joy with which her entire being had abruptly filled.

"God be...," she murmured, in a stifled voice, unable to finish.

And, clutching both hands to her breast, she uttered a profound sigh and fell, mutely, into the arms of the man she had loved so much.

Georges uttered a cry: "Dead!"

And he was standing there, stupidly, in his immeasurable despair, when Marguerite's discolored lips quivered slightly.

She had a smile even before she opened her eyes. Joy had not been able to kill her, any more than dolor.

GRAOUR THE MONSTER

Brucolacas and Vampires

One of the most striking of all superstitions is, without fear of contradiction, the belief in the category of revenants that the Greeks of the Middle Ages called Brucolacas and which are known in western Europe, principally in France, as vampires.

In Illyria, Greece, Hungary, Serbia, Rumania and Bulgaria, only the word Brucolaca is currently employed. The excess of terror that it provokes is indescribable.

Consider this: a man—or a woman—has just died, and is buried. Soon, the rumor spreads that he emerges nocturnally from his tomb and goes to isolated houses to suck the blood of the living, especially that of young women and young men. In reality, he is not entirely dead. His heart, it is said, is still palpitating and he strives to renew life by gorging on that blood, which causes his arteries to pulse.

Among the fanatics for whom that horror is an article of faith, one hears it said that the brucolaca drinks so much human blood in a single night that when he returns to his coffin he sweats red droplets through every pore, and his mouth is frightfully polluted.

That being accepted, if one of those as-yet-unidentified epidemics ensues, against which physicians are temporarily disarmed, any unfortunate who succumbs to it is deemed, in the eyes of the terrified peasants, to have been killed by a vampire. If some beautiful young woman perishes of languor, it is the brucolaca that has stolen her blood. Any individual dying alone in a field, anyone found expiring in a more-or-less sinister corner—on the edge of a cemetery, for example—is undoubtedly a victim of one of those sanguinary phantoms.

And it is not a good idea to claim in front of a crowd of Serbian country-dwellers that vampires are the products of sick or excessively crude imagination.

Furthermore, one cannot disdain certain very troubling events, which, in twenty different countries, seem destined not only to root local superstitions more deeply, but insolently challenge the arrogance of travelers, who, not understanding them at all, are forced, if they are honest, to record them without explanation.

Charles Nodier, who lived in Illyria for five years[67] under the governments of Junot and Fouché, speaks about inexplicable deaths that cause one to shiver, of which he was a witness, and which everyone around him attributed to vampires. He was so impressed by them that twice over, in a book and in the theater, he put brucolacas on stage.

And Prosper Mérimée! He is difficult to pass off as a paragon of silly credulity, but he too has seen such things at close range; he too narrates stories of vampires whose appar-

---

[67] In fact, Charles Nodier (1780-1844) only lived in Ljubljana, now in Slovenia but then the capital of the recently established French Illyrian Provinces, for a few months in 1812-13, where he was briefly the editor of the multilingual newspaper, the *Télégraphe officiel des Provinces Illyriennes*. He might well have encountered vampire mythology there, providing background for his classic phantasmagorical story *Smarrra, ou les demons de la nuit* (1821; tr. as "Smarra"), although that is probably not the book to which the present text refers. The theater piece is certainly the 1820 production of *La Vampire* at the Port-Saint-Martin theater, an adaptation of John Polidori's *The Vampyre* (Black Coat Press, ISBN 978-1-932983-10-4) to which he made a minor contribution. He also wrote the introduction to the book *Lord Ruthwen; ou, Les Vampires* (1820; tr. as *The Vampire Lord Ruthwen*), Black Coat Press, ISBN 978-1-61227-004-3), but he did not write the text (actually by Cyprien Bérard), although the title-page implied that he had.

ent reality it is impossible for him to deny.[68] He has seen, and has been amazed. He tells the story—nothing more, but it is singularly astonishing coming from such a pen.

The brucolaca, therefore, plays an enormous role in the existence of peoples principally massed on the banks of the Danube, the beautiful blue Danube, which then becomes the lugubrious red Danube. It is accused of everything, even the most comical misdeeds.

Thus, when there is an eclipse of the moon, for the mountain men of the Carpathians of Rumania, it is vampires who are devouring the night star. Then all the men in the vicinity gather together, full of anger and fear. Can they allow the horrible drinkers of blood to eat the moon? No. That is why they fire their rifles into the air throughout the duration of the phenomenon, and have the pleasure of having delivered the chaste Phoebe when the eclipse is over.

Is it not singular to find in Europe, a short distance from civilized centers like Bucharest, a belief similar to that of the Chinese, who, as is well-known, also make a frightful racket with saucepans, gongs and other noisy instruments in order to chase away the evil spirits determined to destroy the sun's cousin?

One question must be on the reader's lips, as it came to ours on the day when the most amiable of Rumanians wanted to initiate us into these singular mysteries: how, after the unpleasantness of dying, does some poor devil become a brucolaca? For after all, not all dead people have the redoubtable faculty of rising from their resting place to the great detriment of the living.

This is how.

----

[68] Prosper Mérimée (1803-1870) published a collection of ballads ostensibly translated from Illyrian, *La Guzla* (1827) under the pseudonym Hyacinthe Maglanowich, which includes references to vampires, but he certainly did not take such tales seriously.

Originally, only people who had died excommunicated for reasons of magic became brucolacas. Thus, witches, sorcerers, werewolves, etc., had every chance of turning into brucolacas as soon as they were dead. At any rate, the word Brucolaca was invented for them by the modern Greeks.

Later, people who were guilty of a few other crimes were also suspected of playing truant from the cemetery. Finally, suspicion extended to those who were personally irreproachable. In Rumania for instance, a dead person is dimly viewed if, on the day of his funeral, his relatives are niggardly with the customary alms. That is a misdeed for which the unfortunate deceased can hardly be held responsible! No matter—he has every chance of becoming a vampire.

We are employing the latter word by design, because "brucolaca" was initially applied only to the excommunicated, and if it applies today to designated thieves of blood in general, it is because it is more widespread than the word vampire—which is, however, current in Hungary—in cases where excommunication is not an issue.

With regard to the fabrication of monsters and the phenomena to which we make allusion in *Graour*, it is in Serbia that they have been recently discovered.

Scientists—true scientists, but devoid of conscience—carried out operations and maneuvers there of which it is impossible for us to provide a glimpse because, in the first place, we cannot permit the perception of the odious machinations of speculators who are veritable monsters themselves, and secondly because, silence having descended promptly on the abominable case, it would be reckless to advance on that subject facts that would be difficult to prove. The fabrication took place. That is what is certain. Perhaps it is still taking place. That is all that we can affirm.

C.D.

I. Brucolaca!

Vidra is a small town in Rumania, situated picturesquely in the wildest valley in the mountains of Vranchea, the ultimate foothills of the Carpathians.

If civilization has made astonishing progress in the plain of that beautiful country in the course of the last thirty years, it has, on the other hand, stopped at the foot of the mountains, like an impotent flood.

Mores, customs and superstitions have remained in Vidra and the neighboring villages what they were two or three centuries before. Furthermore, neither mores nor customs, nor superstitions are trapped there by banality, as you will see if you take the trouble to follow the author of this story.

One evening, toward the end of May, on the scarcely-traced road that departs from the modest town to lose itself in the nearby forest, a frightened man was fleeing at top speed. He was a tall, thin individual, with red hair, long, yellow teeth, wearing a tight-fitting jacket of extravagant fabric—all of which revealed his British origin.

Night had just fallen, heavy and menacing, after a day in which suffocating heat had weighed upon the entire region. A storm was already rumbling in the distant gorges where it was testing its fury. Low in the sky—so low that one had the impression of almost being able to touch them by aching out a hand—enormous coppery clouds were coiffing the fire-trees, whose crowns were creaking under the first gusts of wind. A raindrop as big as a hazelnut fell on to the fugitive's hand.

"Damn!" growled the Englishman, launching himself forward with renewed vigor.

But the hillside was difficult to scale, the road was strewn with potholes, and, in spite of his long legs, he was doubtless not advancing as rapidly as he would have liked, for there was a black terror in the coming and going of his panting breath.

Why was he running like that? For fear of the tempest?

No. It was because behind him, also running breathlessly, was an improbable individual who was shouting in a powerful, terrible voice, one incessantly-repeated word:

"Brucolaca! Brucolaca!"

And every time that cry tore through the air, the islander thought he had received a lash of a whip, stinging his flesh.

"Brucolaca! Brucolaca!"

The voice of the individual in furious pursuit of the fugitive resonated clearly and distinctly, with no apparent indication of fatigue.

Someone who chanced to find himself there, an involuntary witness to the scene, and who, in the profound darkness, had succeeded in making something out, would have fallen from a height on seeing a fantastic form pass by, sixty or sixty-five meters behind the Englishman. It was about a meter high, or even less, as broad as it was tall, and was surely running, in spite of astonishingly short legs, more rapidly than its prey, whom it seemed bound to overtake in a relatively short lapse of time.

"Brucolaca! Brucolaca!" that strange phenomenon continued to howl.

And down below, in the direction of the town, there was an increasing murmur, drawing closer, becoming louder, and then finally bursting forth in a furious din. A human whirlwind was precipitated on the heels of the dwarf, composed of men of very tall stature—almost giants—who went past like a hurricane, uttering the same cry as the other:

"Brucolaca! Brucolaca!"

Among the latter, a grimmer tone was audible than on the part of the enraged dwarfish individual running ahead of them. The blind hatred of superstitious or fanatical crowds was detectable therein, pitiless and murderous. And the Englishman was surely not unaware of the mortal danger that was threatening him, for he was, so to speak, flying before the deformed being whose footsteps were resounding on his heels.

Now the rain became torrential. The enormous clouds burst in sheets. To the east, the whole sky was ablaze with violet flashes succeeding one another, overlapping and doubling up, with the result that for thirty or forty seconds the entire region—mountains, ravines and valleys—seemed bloodied by a paroxysm of horror and terror.

By that light, however, the Englishman had been able to see, not far away—scarcely a kilometer—a square house, solidly set on a little plateau, with the appearance of a fortress, three windows of which were brightly lit, as if someone inside had lit a beacon in order to guide and encourage the fugitive.

Undoubtedly the latter belonged to the category of gentlemen who build the most solid of muscles in the practice of sports, for, on perceiving the dwelling in which he expected to find salvation, he forgot all fatigue and set off like a bullet.

"My God!" he murmured, between his long teeth, not without sketching a smile reminiscent of a grimace.

A hundred meters from his goal he uttered an appeal that would have cast a chill into the marrow of those who heard it, if his cry of anguish had not been covered by the formidable rumble of a thunderclap, or by the hissing of the hailstones as large as cherries that had started falling an instant before.

But the dwarf too had redoubled his energy.

"Faster! Faster!" he roared, to excite the others.

In fact, there was no more than forty meters between him and the islander. If the latter should stumble or mere lose a couple of seconds for one reason or another, it would be all over for him.

In the house, the lights were now passing from one room to another, disappearing only to show themselves again on a lower level, and finally on the ground floor. They seemed to be behind the powerful oak door, behind which was shelter and an end to terror.

Another twenty-five meters...fifteen...no more than ten...five...one—the door was open. The Englishman was plunging through it when he felt something grab his leg.

"Brucolaca!" shouted the dwarf, in a triumphant tone.

But from inside, six or eight arms had grabbed the islander and were pulling him irresistibly—so effectively that they dragged the stump of man, possessed of too much momentum, with him. The later doubtless did not have the presence of mind to grab the door jamb or to wedge himself in the doorway, in order that his companions, who were no more than a stone's throw away, could come in with him.

The enormous batten closed abruptly. The giants of Vidra ran straight into its broad-headed nails and remained momentarily crestfallen, while their leader, imprisoned, saw five or six Herculean Scottish servants loom over him. A word or a gesture on his part might have sufficed to strike an imprudent individual dead on the spot, if the sight of him had not frozen them with terror.

II. The Barbarian Invasion

When the improbable individual was brightly lit by lamps, their visages expressed a fear that confused the profound amazement by which they were assailed.

Imagine, in fact, a monster with a human face, who would have had the almost perfect appearance of a meter cube if the legs had not left appreciable voids in the base, even though their dimensions were incredible short. Like formidable balusters, his calves, scarcely a handspan long, measured at least twenty-five centimeters in circumference. One could without exaggeration compare his thighs to the knotty trunk of a centenarian oak, all the more so as, in order to attach themselves to the monstrously thick body, they broadened out unimaginably toward the pelvis.

As for the shoulders and the chest, the abdomen and the back, they were a mass of muscle and bone a meter broad and deep in every direction. And above that the head of a man that was surely powerful, in spite of its smallness by comparison with the enormity of the back and the torso.

The arms, much larger proportionally than the legs, displayed biceps that would have been sufficient in themselves to honor five or six fairground strong men, if it had been possible to divide them up.

As soon as he saw that he was caught in the trap, so to speak, Graour—that was his name, Graour the monster—carried out an unexpected maneuver, wedging himself in a corner of the antechamber so that he was not at risk of being attacked from behind. There, compact and terrible, he faced up to the enemy—which is to say, the servants who were about to try to subdue him. But to reach that battle station he had had to push past two or three of the gigantic Scotsmen charged with mastering him, and they had been so rudely knocked down that they had difficulty getting up again, so painful had the impact been.

The Englishman, however, made a sign, and the flunkeys, who were courageous, launched themselves forward in a simultaneous assault.

There was a brief moment of chaotic struggle. Ribs were heard cracking.

Two men fell again, which a third croaked, half strangled by Graour, who threw him with a thrust of his arms into his master's breast.

After which the dwarf found himself alone in his corner, calm and almost smiling. The effort he had just made to free himself did not seem to have cost him excessively.

"Dr. Mathews," he said, "I haven't sought you out, even though I have a rude score to settle with you, but you've placed yourself in my path, and that will cost you dear—very dear..."

Graour had pronounced those words in very pure English, although his accent denoted that he had learned the language of Mr. Chamberlain[69] in the United States.

"Well, what do you want with me? What have I done to you? You owe me your fortune..."

At that moment, the fury of the storm arrived at its peak, mingling around the house with the vociferations of the mob that had been marching behind Graour a few minutes before, and whose disappointment must have been frightful when the

---

[69] The statesman Joseph Chamberlain (1836-1914).

door was closed, separating them from the one who had drawn them after him with his lugubrious cry of "Brucolaca! Brucolaca!"

There were about forty of them to begin with, and others were arriving gradually, in spite of the hail and the lightning that was falling at intervals on the nearby trees. Nothing seemed to be able to distract them from the task for which they had quit their hearths in haste.

Undoubtedly, the peril against which they had departed so hurriedly surpassed anything one might suppose, for, after less than a minute of deliberation they decided to break down the door behind which Graour had disappeared. Immediately, twenty of them dispersed into the forest in search of a tree that they could make into a battering ram.

That did not take very long.

On the edge of a ravine they found a beech tree in unstable equilibrium, of which one a few roots were preventing the collapse, and which, under the enraged gusts of the tempest, was threatening to fall at any moment. They assisted it to uproot itself; a noise of broken branches and stones rolling to the ravine informed the others that the implement was in their possession.

They all flew toward the spot where the uprooted tree was lying. They all harnessed themselves to its branches, its roots and its trunk.

It was not an enormous beech, but as a battering ram it was more than sufficient—except that when they had transported it to Dr. Mathews' door, it was necessary for them to take account of the fact that even if there had been five hundred of them, they would not be able to make use of it effectively without stripping it of its roots and branches.

"How long is that going to take?" exclaimed one of them.

"We need axes," said another, "And unless we go back to Vidra to fetch them..."

"Yes, and Graour will be dead by the time we get back."

"Dead, little father? They won't kill Graour as easily as that."

"They'll kill him like anyone else, with rifles, and there are ten of them to shoot at him."

"How are we going to get in, then? How do we help him?"

There was a prolonged silence. Those hirsute individuals were greatly hampered but their useless tree.

"It's not useless," said one of them, in the one of authority that one adopts when one has just found a triumphant solution. "Let's try to stand it upright, as if we wanted to replant it in front of the house, very closely."

"What do you want to do?"

"You'll see." Those last words had only just been pronounced when a gunshot resounded inside.

"They're murdering Graour!" howled three or four voices.

But the one who had had the idea repeated: "Quickly! Quickly! Stand the tree up like a mast."

"It'll still be necessary to cut off its branches."

"No, no—on the contrary."

Behind the door, outbursts of Dr. Mathews' voice resounded; he appeared to be prey to an extreme anger.

That was because one of the more ham-fisted servants—the one that, half-strangled by a preliminary suffocation, had been launched at the doctor as if by a catapult—had gone away momentarily, drunk with rage, and had reappeared with a revolver in his hand in order to shoot at the dwarf.

The projectile had hit him in the middle of the forehead, between and slightly above the two eyebrows.

Mathews, bounding toward his servant, had immediately snatched the weapon from his hand with a rare violence and had yelled into his face: "Are you mad, Tommy?"

Graour had tottered. His forehead had reddened with blood, which was running from the wound—but he had not fallen. Better than that: as he shook his head like a dog trying to get rid of a tick, the bullet, somewhat flattened, dropped at his feet with a dry click.[70]

The frontal bone had not even broken. If there was an effusion of blood, it was only because the skin had been torn and crushed.

Nevertheless, that attack caused a prodigious anger to burst forth in the dwarf. His heavy mass was lifted up by a mighty leap of which no one would have believed him to be capable.

The imprudent Tommy, both his wrists seized by hands of iron, uttered a howl of pain; he was seen to spin around above Graour's head, and he was sent crashing into the wall.

"Whose turn next?" asked the monster, careless of the precautions that he had exercised a few moments earlier.

No one budged.

"It's a misunderstanding, Graour," said Dr. Mathews, with rare phlegm. "Your life isn't threatened."

"Oh, really?" riposted the dwarf, bursting into nervous laughter. "What would you do if it were?"

Mathews did not reply to that. He explained to his servants that he was determined that no murder should be committed under his roof, but did it in a Highland patois that the formidable adversary, whose eyes seemed to be searching for a new victim, no longer understood.

"Oh, I understand," said the monster, in an ironic tone. "You don't want the law poking its nose into your operations. And you're right. Anyway, it isn't me who'll go to fetch them.

---

[70] Author's note: "For readers tempted to accuse us of exaggeration, it is sufficient to recall that under the Second Empire, one could rub shoulders every day in the Faubourg Montmartre with the journalist M. L***, a sort of colossus who, in a duel, having received his adversary's bullet in the middle of his forehead, had experienced only a slight shock. The projectile, in fact, had been unable to pierce the frontal bone; it was content to crack it like a starred window, and M. L*** lived for twenty years with the scar."

I take care of my own affairs. But there's a brucolaca here. I want to know where it's buried. So much the worse for you if it puts us on the track of one of your new crimes."

The Englishman was about to retort when a door opened rather violently and a young woman appeared, whose amazing beauty inundated with a gilded light the tragic scene in which Graour was evidently playing the role of an administrator of justice.

"Father," she said, "the house has been invaded by the savages from Vidra."

"What? How?"

"Through the windows. They've stood a tree up against the façade..."

"Oh, the demons!"

"And then they've climbed up, by means of the trunk and the branches. I heard the panes shatter..."

The young woman, whom Graour, immobile and calmed down, was devouring with his eyes, had no need to say any more. The eternal cry of "Brucolaca!" could be heard resounding, uttered by forty voices spreading out through all parts of the house, of which the Vidrans were searching every corner. Soon, one of them even set foot in the vestibule.

Mathews, who appeared to have been plunged into terror by the appearance of his daughter, swiftly took her by the hand and, shoving her toward a door dissimulated in the woodwork, whispered something rapidly into her ear. He added, still in a low voice: "Don't come out, Beatrix, until I assure you personally that you're safe. Do you swear?"

"Yes, Father."

"Good! Come on. It'll only take a few moments!"

They both seemed to plunge into the wall.

A few minutes later, the doctor reappeared—very boldly, in truth, to face up to the invaders of his domicile and a danger of whose gravity he was under not the slightest illusion.

III. The Fire

The house was still resounding with the cries and appeals of the Vidrans, more excited than ever. However, the majority of the invaders had grouped around Graour, forming a platoon, the sight of which engendered terror. The Rumanian mountain men bore not the slightest resemblance to peaceful peasants.

We have already said that most of them were of giant stature, but what gave them an even more terrible appearance was their ferocious faces, their resolute, implacable eyes, their long hair and, most of all, heir unkempt beards, broad and infinite, into which no comb had ever intruded, which departed from their eyes, swallowed up the entire face and extended half way down their bodies.

A distinctive sign particular to those populations: they all had their chests uncovered between the armpits, and from the Adam's apple to the waist.

This was happening in the month of May, to be sure, and they were not running any risk of catching a chill. But if, in the mountains where everything is excessive, the heat of summer is intolerable, the winter frosts are recorded by the thermometer at an average between twenty-five or thirty degrees below zero—and whatever the season, in stifling temperature or in the snow and ice, they go about thus, sternum bare, breast to the wind, without being unduly discomfited, so solid is their carcass, so triumphant their rudeness.

One can easily imagine that, thus built and naturally brutal, they did not attract the confidence of people to whom they were appearing for the first time. So the doctor's servants, although chosen from among the most redoubtable and least civilized in the Scottish Highlands, did not put on a bold front before those men, exasperated by a superstitious fury and also armed with rifles or large cutlasses passed through their belts.

Mathews was too much a man of his own nation not to bluff as much as possible. It was in a serene voice, without apparent indignation, and a man who knows to what one is exposed in those extravagant lands, that he spoke.

"Now," he said, "what do you want? What is this about? What can I do for you?"

The islander was doubtless aware that Graour had personal reason for mortal hatred against him, but the others were only thinking about vampires, for "brucolaca" means vampire, and the accusation of concealing a vampire in his house—which is to say, a cadaver that roams the night in order to such the blood of virgins—could engender innumerable inconveniences, primarily death to the brucolaca, the vampire with which the fanatics believed that they were dealing. In consequence, the living were only in danger of ricochets.

"I've told you. There's a brucolaca here. I saw it coming out of the house where Kaçandra Landru was found dying, with the imperceptible little hole near the jugular through which the vampire had just sucked his blood to the last drop."

"I beg your pardon, but it was me who went to Kaçandra Lambru's house."

"The vampire followed you there or preceded you," retorted Graour, and added, slowly: "And who knows whether or not you had arranged a rendezvous?"

"A rendezvous?" said Mathews, who sensed the danger increasing, but had the strength to laugh loudly.

"Yes."

"Come on, Graour, you've traveled, you've been in twenty different countries...France, Germany, America. Are you seriously accusing me of entertaining relations with the dead—with vampires? Do vampires even exist?"

A scandalized murmur cut through the doctor's words. To deny the existence of vampires before the brutes that were surrounding him was a blunder."

"You certainly entertain relations with the devil!" Graour retorted, profiting from Mathews' imprudence.

The latter only laughed more loudly. "With the devil!" he repeated.

But the Vidrans were not laughing. There was even a movement of hostility in their mass, which would have chilled the heart of someone less brave than the doctor. He was seen to tremble, and then to collect himself. Maintaining his audacity, he said: "All right. If there's a vampire here, I'm unaware of it. But I'd be delighted to be rid of it if there is, and since you've come to find it and reduce it to impotence, you'd be doing me a favor. Let's look for it."

Mathews thought that is words would destroy the bad effect of his preceding remarks, and, in fact, if the dwarf had not been there, the others would have been content with that resignation and would have resumed their search of the house without any further malice.

"Search for it?" retorted Graour. "What's the point? You must know where the vampire is, and it's probably because you haven't given it a Christian sepulcher that it's become a brucolaca."

"So," said the doctor, "you're accusing me of having murdered someone, and of buried them somewhere in my house...?"

"Yes and no," replied the monster.

"What, then? Explain yourself precisely," demanded the Englishman, who felt Graour's implacable enmity weighing upon him and was afraid that he might be driven into some frightful situation.

"Listen to me, then," said the strange individual, who was not himself either a fool or a brute.

The Vidrans drew closer, also, and especially, avid for enlightenment, for Mathews surely suspected that Graour was about to lead him on to slippery ground, to say the least.

"Fort twenty years," Graour continued, "you've been practicing an abominable métier here. Abusing your real—even extraordinary—knowledge, you take little children from the cradle, little children constituted normally, born to become men and women like any others, and you apply yourself to making monsters of them: monsters like me, or phenomena; Siamese twins, for example, human torsos without arms or legs..."

"You're joking!" the doctor dared to say, beginning to sweat.

"I'm joking! Do you dare to say that Raveloff, the unipedal dancer, isn't of your fabrication? That you haven't joined his two legs together and only left him one foot—and that you didn't sell him for forty thousand francs to a German barnum who took charge of making him into a dancer with a great reputation?"

"But..."

"Do you dare to sustain that the man with four hands didn't emerge from this house, which he entered at the age of thirty-five days with two hands and ten fingers? And the two little girls joined at the back, who have only ever seen one another in a mirror?"

Mathews made a few gestures of negation.

"And me! Me!" added Graour, explosively, quivering with anger. "Isn't it you who made a normal infant, elegant in form, destined for a tall stature, the frightful, monstrous, crawling, implausible creature that I am?

"But it's not a matter of that, at least for the moment. Of the subjects that you transform, that you mutilate, there are some who can't support the audacious and cruel operations...and they die. What do you do with their cadavers? Isn't it one of them who, having become a vampire, sucked all of poor Kaçandra's blood just now?"

"No one has died in my house," Mathews replied, with a hint of professional pride that would have made a less rustic audience quiver with indignation, because such words were tantamount to a confession.

"No one? You're lying, because you can't have forgotten little Stephan Malecou. That one, you tried to gratify with three noses, three mouths and three chins, but your science remained impotent. Gangrene devoured the poor devil..."

"Who told you that?" cried the satanic doctor, parading his suspicious gaze over his staff.

"What does it matter? It's true. That one, you didn't dare to have buried publicly. It would have been necessary to explain how he came to have the frightful face that you had built for him."

"You're mad!"

"The madman is you—the dangerous, atrocious madman—and if I didn't think so, I'd already have laid you out dead at my feet, although a quick death would be, in my opinion, insufficient punishment for so many horrors. You merit some new, unprecedented torture. Anyway, we'll see about that. For the moment, it's a matter of the vampire. Where have you buried Stephan Malecou?"

The Englishman remained silent for a few moments, waiting for an inspiration. They his eyes lit up fugitively. He suppressed a smile of satisfaction that was already distending his lips. He had just found one.

He knew better than his staff the most varied details of the superstition that had brought his ferocious neighbors to his house. He knew that, for these mountain-men with the obscure souls, two or three infallible means existed of rendering a vampire impotent. One was to pierce the heart of the dead man with a sharpened stake; the second was to plunge the cadaver into quicklime; the third was to crush it beneath an enormous cube of granite so that it could no longer budge—but the last procedure was not very certain.

"Oh, well, it's true," Mathews admitted, "Stephen did die here—not as a result of an operation but of smallpox. And then, to cut short the contagion, in the interests of the locality, I buried him in a shroud of lime."

"You did well," said one of the Vidrans."

"That one can't be a brucolaca."

"Obviously not," said the same voice.

"All right," said the dwarf, who sensed his strategy compromised. "It's another one, then. We need to find him."

"But since I've offered to help you search..."

At that moment, a newcomer made his entrance. He was a short, round man, very blond, with a humble, blissful expression, with large dark blue eyes whose harsh expression contrasted with the rest of his sanctimonious and unctuous physiognomy. He was dressed in a yellow check suit over which an apron with a bib, like those worn by medical students, was spread. He looked exactly like a surgeon's aide or male nurse.

"Go away, Joe!" said Mathews, imperiously. "What are you going here? You know I don't approve of curiosity."

Joe, however, did not have the look of a curiosity-seeker. But for the criticism he would doubtless already have explained his presence as a matter of some urgent communication. What is certain is that he had not expected to emerge into the midst of such a crowd. He looked at Graour and his companions in total bewilderment.

"But someone's set fire to the house," he said.

"Fire?" exclaimed Mathews and the dwarf, simultaneously.

"Who has started the fire then?"

"Probably one of the bandits one encounters at every step," replied Joe, in a blank voice, in the tone that one employs to speak in a sickroom.

"That's not the means to find or destroy the brucolaca," said Graour, impetuously. "Dmitri, Vlad, Stan, all of you—go and extinguish the fire, if it's possible,"

Graour enjoyed a considerable authority over his companions, firstly because he was rich and secondly because he had the advantage over them of an intellectual superiority. Dmitri, Vlad and the others obeyed immediately, and launched themselves into the interior of the house almost in unison.

"My daughter!" cried Mathews, with an expression of anguish so poignant—for the malefactor, perhaps conscienceless, certainly had and extremely well-developed sentiment of paternal love—that the dwarf, on whom the marvelous beauty of Beatrix had made a profound impression, muttered: "His daughter! That's where it's necessary to strike to punish him as he deserves."

Whatever consequence he attributed to those words, however, and precisely to ensure them of a consequence, it was necessary for the ravishing young woman not to perish, miserably asphyxiated or reduced to ashes in the hiding-place where her father thought he had sheltered her from the brutalities, insults or familiarities to which she might have been exposed on the part of the redoubtable invades of the house.

The doctor was no longer there; he had followed Joe to find out where the fire was.

Graour followed on his heels, determined not to lose sight of him, but equally ready to do the impossible in order to put the fire out without delay.

In addition, the monster was determined to maintain everyone in confrontation with the original question, that of the vampire, knowing full well that on that terrain his companions would remain intransigent, and that beyond that, those formidable but fundamentally benevolent individuals would not attach any great importance, as he did, to Mathews' surgical crimes—as we shall see in due course—whereas the mere word "brucolaca" unhinged them, gave them gooseflesh and could drive them to the most horrible ferocities.

IV. Graour's Hatred

Imagine that! There was not one among them who did not believe in the frightful faculty that certain dead people had of quitting their tombs, even if they are buried a hundred feet underground in order to go by night to habitations to such the blood of young women—or, in their default, the most beautiful, strongest and most beloved young men.

That odious superstition is spread through the majority of the countries, still unenlightened, that are watered by the lower Danube. In Serbia it is rife to the point that Belgrade can be called the Vampire City.

Among the Bulgars a large part of the country—I am talking about the lower classes—firmly believes in brucolacas.

It was the same in Rumania fifty years ago, but, we repeat, because it is just, civilization has penetrated today into all the regions of the plain and hardly anyone but the semi-savage mountain people confined to the ultimate chain of the Carpathians who get excited—but excessively so, of course—

when someone cries "vampire," as people once did in our rural regions when someone cried "wolf."

All of them come out of their homes bearing arms, and we have seen how easy it is to lead them by means of such a cry.

What, then, had happened in Vidra to justify the emotion of which Graour had cleverly taken advantage in order to draw half the neighborhood into the pursuit of Mathews?

A young woman, Kaçandra Landru, who was quite well that morning, had been found dying in her bed at about ten o'clock in the evening. After examination, a tiny, seemingly-insignificant wound had been discovered over her left breast, near the neck, through which, the experts said, a brucolaca must have fed on her blood. It was the usual mark of the murderous contact, the trace of the hideous suction that revealed the horrible posthumous crime of an unknown dead man, henceforth redoubtable because he might return and continue his ravages at every hearth,

Immediately, cries for help had rung out, and everyone had come running, trembling or furious. Graour, whose house was next door to the contaminated dwelling, had been the first to go into room of the dying girl, whose parents, overwhelmed by grief, could do nothing but moan.

But he, accepting or pretending to accept the vampire's crime as an undeniable fact, had immediately roused the entire neighborhood, declaring that he had seen the vampire flee, that he had taken the road up the mountain, and that it was necessary to run after him right away. At that moment, Dr. Mathews had just passed by, marching with great strides in the darkness in order to get back to his isolated abode, where he devoted himself to his horrible endeavors—for it was perfectly true that the islander fabricated monsters and phenomena.

The matter was notorious in the region and the mountain men were no longer indignant about it. Not that they would have pardoned him if it had only made money for him, but it was well known that the majority of his subjects, prodigies of deformity or extravagance, generally made fortunes by exhibiting themselves in fairgrounds or circuses, and in truth, they felt more envy than horror.

Graour himself, one of Dr. Mathews' most extraordinary subjects, whose paradoxical form engendered as much amazement as fear among the spectators, had harvested in the United States, in less than two years, such a rich crop of dollars that he had been able to abandon his career and come back to live in his homeland with a respectable income.

His compatriot did not hide the fact that they thought him very lucky to have been transformed into a miniature mastodon, and that he owed a fine candle to the Englishman. Unfortunately for the latter, that was not the opinion of the dwarf. On the contrary, Graour had vowed a terrible hatred against him. Rich now, he was devoured by the despair of not having human form.

When he saw one of those superb mountain men passing by, tall of stature, with a harmonious and powerful stride, handsome, supple and admirably equilibrated—especially when he was present at a marriage in which the magnificent and triumphant husband was head and shoulders taller than the charming bride—he entered into black rages all the more maddening because he had to hide them in order not to become the butt of sarcastic remarks.

The poor devil had a heart. The monster would have like to be loved, and perhaps he had been in love. One day, when he had dared to let that be understood, a young woman at whom he gazed, while speaking timidly, had smiled scornfully, and another proffered in an insufficiently low voice, the cruel observation: "Is Graour in love? That's enough to make one die laughing."

Wounded, he had been very careful, since then, not to allow any glimpse of the state of his soul. What? That obese dwarf, that deformed being, only *so* high, as broad as a barrel, would have liked to be adored!

To be sure, he knew more than one father capable of giving him his daughter because he was the richest man in the neighborhood, rich to the point of superfluity, but that was not what he desired, for after all, he was young—twenty-seven years old—and he was not a beast.

But the bride with whom he could savor the delicious moments of tender confessions, the exquisite sensations of the initial conversations, all the adorable, precious, sweet puerilities that make one hope, and suspect, that delight is mutual, that one can scale heaven in an atmosphere of joy, nevertheless remained impossible to find.

All of that it was necessary to renounce—necessary because Mathews, when Graour, as a child, had promised to be the handsomest man in the region, had taken him away and, enclosing him in a special apparatus, a kind of iron cage designed to prevent him from growing, had striven to make him a dwarf.

For that he had dressed his shoulders in a heavy metallic cope, linked by inflexible bars to a tiny platform from which the patient's feet could not move, with the result that his growth was arrested without remission.

But there had been such a sap in the body thus tortured that if Graour could not develop in height, by way of compensation, he spread out in width and girth, becoming as strong as an oak, and finally, when he was twenty years old, constituted the monster that he was to remain for the rest of his life.

Then, Mathews had sold him, very dearly, to a barnum—not at his real value, however, for Graour, already unique as a phenomenon, soon demonstrated that he had no equal in physical strength, and performed exercises such that he became all the rage in Europe and North America. He bought his liberty and, leaving his barnum behind, exhibited himself on his own behalf, amassed a fortune as rapidly as a singer or a boxer, and returned to his homeland with the formal resolution of making Mathews expiate the crime against nature that he had committed in crippling him with his deformity.

The hatred he bore toward the Englishman was limitless. While traveling the world he had learned many things, among others that if he wanted to bring Mathews before a tribunal the wretch's trial would cause a worldwide sensation.

It did not seem sufficient, however, that the islander should simply be hung one morning, painlessly, so to speak. He remembered all too well the physical tortures he had endured during his horizontal growth, and when he added to that the mental sufferings in which he had felt steeped since he has measured the distance that separated him from a wife, he trembled with fury, searching for some atrocious vengeance into which to pour his imperishable hatred.

That is why, when someone had shouted "Brucolaca!" and he had seen Mathews passing through the neighborhood, he had thought of setting the horde of superstitious and Vidrans on his heels.

To be sure, Graour did not know yet in what sauce he would accommodate his enemy; for him, the important thing was to get inside Mathews' house. And when the doctor's servants, drawing him into the vestibule, thought that they had caught him in a trap, it was in reality the dwarf, confident in his unlimited strength, who had allowed it to happen. He knew that the horrible surgeon was continuing his abominable commerce and he wanted to see at close range what perfection he had bought to his odious industry.

Determined to search the house in its most secret recesses, under the pretext of discovering the vampire, he was counting on finding the subjects in gestation in Mathews' house.

After that, he would see.

It is, therefore, easy to understand why he objected violently to the stupidity of his companions in setting fire to the doctor's house. That could not lead to anything, even with regard to the pretended vampire—on the contrary—whereas the unfortunates whom Mathews mutilated and transformed were in danger of being asphyxiated or burnt, and in the depths of his heart, without knowing them, Graour nourished a profound pity for them, divining that they were suffering and considering them as brothers, whose frightful misery might be eased by his protection, and even his purse.

V. In Which the Monster Seems Inconsequent

Unfortunately, the fire had rapidly taken on a considerable extent. The madmen who had ignited it a few minutes before had attacked, without any attempt at finesse, hangars backed up against a wing that was somewhat isolated from the rest of the habitation—which, we ought to have mentioned earlier, covered a large surface area, including as many courtyards of various dimensions as solid constructions, sturdy and offering more resistance in consequence.

The hangars, in which resinous woods furnished by the neighboring mountain had not been spared, were blazing like torches. Save for the roofs, still inundated by the storm that was now drawing away, everything was burning, crackling in a furnace against which the restricted resources of the establishment would surely remain impotent.

Mathews and Graour measured the magnitude of the threatened disaster at a glance.

Only one strategy offered a chance of success: to let the hangars burn, which were only linked to the actual buildings on one side, and try to preserve the latter at all costs.

The doctor seemed to be mad with terror and despair. Large drops of sweat were running down his forehead. A door, very heavy, in truth, but very close to the place where the fire was raging, was beginning to smoke and might burst into flames at any moment.

It was toward that point that Mathews was directing his fearful gaze.

His daughter is behind that! Graour thought, quivering with commiseration in spite of his hatred. And for a second, the dwarf had a very clear vision of the splendid beauty that had appeared to him in the vestibule.

To be sure, the father did not merit any pity, but her, Beatrix!—he had remembered her name—of what was she guilty?

Furthermore, the monster was determined that the Englishman's torture would be enduring, would last for as long as the torture that he had endured in that same house.

Then again, there was something new in his breast and in his head, which had just awakened, without him knowing exactly what name to give it.

His powerful voice rose above the tumult: "How many wells are there?" he asked the doctor.

"Four," the other replied.

"Where are they?"

"Here's one. You'll find two others in the next courtyard. The last is some distance..."

"A chain! Form a chain! I can't see your domestics."

"Only three of them are still fit."

"Tell them to bring buckets." Addressing his compatriots, Graour said: "As for you, inundate that door and prevent it from catching alight. There must be axes in the house...?"

"Yes," the Englishman replied, in whom hope was returning, without his being able to explain the dwarf's new attitude.

"Have them brought right away, Doctor—go fetch them yourself—and you too, Joe, damn it!" Graour added, rousing the fearful assistant and sent him after Mathews, who was running toward an unaffected corner of the courtyard...

But now, frightful screams were beginning to ring out behind the overheated walls.

Their fearful tone could be distinguished in spite of the rumbling noise of the conflagration and the shouts uttered by the Vidrans who were organizing the chain, and already hurling bucketfuls of water, one after another, over the threatened door.

It's in there that the lamentable children are locked, on whom Mathews' avid and cruel art is being exercised. Damn! O horror! Is this, then, nothing but Destiny? And his daughter?

The doctor and Joe came back with the axes. Graour seized an enormous one, the cutting edge of which he examined, which probably seemed perfect, and immediately advanced toward the burning hangar in order to try to sever the vertical beams forming its angular support at the base.

"Water here! Floods of water!" he shouted to the Vidrans, who were no longer thinking about anything but the task in hand, and who, with their muscular strength, were performing their function with a prestigious rapidity.

The first corner beam having been half-extinguished by five buckets emptied almost simultaneously, Graour approached, handling his axe like a toy. It was heard to hiss though the air around him, and the wood was split to half its thickness by a single stroke.

"Get that pole, the rest of you. Set it against the beam high up and push hard when I strike more blows with the ax."

With a single stroke of the ax Graour smashed the enormous pillar supporting the hangar, which crashed down in a shower of sparks that sprang forth like a firework display, on top of the burning debris. That was one aliment less for the fire.

The blaze was nevertheless giving off such an intense heat that Graour, as a result of having approached it for the two fleeting seconds that he had needed to undermine the beam, had singed his eyebrows and his hair. And it was not over yet; there was more to be done.

Cross-beams embedded in the wall quite deeply, and probably in contact with interior joists, were still ablaze, so powerfully that they might communicate the fire to the wing that it was necessary at all costs to preserve—because, once that part of the edifice was attained, not only would the rest infallibly be destroyed, but the poor wretches whose desperate cries for help could still be heard from inside would perish, and with them, doubtless, Mathews' daughter.

Mathews was tearing out his hair. And it was surely not the phenomena, interesting as they might be in his eyes, or the fate with which they were threatened, that were drawing cries of grief from him.

"We have to extinguish the cross-beams!" he shouted, half-suffocated by anguish. "Or cut them! A ladder, William! A ladder!"

"To do what?" demanded Graour, rudely.

"To lean against the wall and go to cut..."

"Are you out of your mind? You'd have to put the supports in the middle of the fire, and it would catch alight before you'd climbed ten rungs..."

"It doesn't matter. I must at least try to save my daughter."

His daughter! Graour was not mistaken. For Mathews, the others counted for nothing.

"My daughter and my son!" added the Englishman, increasingly agitated.

"Ah! There's a son too," muttered the dwarf, his eyes shining with a ferocious joy.

A ladder had just been brought, but there was no possibility of leaning it against the burning, unapproachable wall. Graour snatched it from William's hands and, searching for a section of the façade sufficiently distant from the fire, made sure that it was long enough to allow him to climb on to the roof. Seizing a coil of rope that was nearby—God alone knows for what frightful usage—he launched himself forth and soon reached the top of the house

The others were throwing water on to the burning debris that was furnishing the three beams. Mathews was now looking all around with a bewildered gaze, but soon saw Graour on the edge of the roof, leaning over to calculate the distance of the beams that were perpetuating the danger.

Then he let himself slide down slowly, in a direction contrary to the wind, and was soon suspended by the rope, which he had attached to a chimney. Holding on with one hand to the cable, looped around him in such a way that he could sit on it, the other brandishing the ax, of which he had not let go, he felled the first cross-beam from the same level of the façade—but he was literally being grilled.

Throwing the ax away, he climbed back to the roof and there, almost suffocated, sat down in the shelter of the chimney in order to get his breath back. It was a miracle that he had not fallen, asphyxiated, into the incandescent furnace.

Scarcely had he regathered his thoughts than he saw Mathews in front of him. The infamous doctor had also climbed the rungs of the ladder.

"There are still two dangerous beams," he said. "I'll detach them in my turn."

"You, man?" the dwarf replied. "If you want to be grilled in two minutes, you only have to try it. As for me, I wouldn't do it again, even if there was every joy and intoxication at the end of a further attempt...even if you gave me your son to torture and your daughter in marriage."

Those last words would certainly have made the doctor jump if he had heard them at any other time, but Mathews could not occupy his thoughts with anything but the blaze and the immediate danger that his children were in. Graour's menacing words did not trouble him.

In any case, Joe, the medical student with the doll-like face had just climbed on to the roof in his turn, with one of the Vidrans, by the name of Bran, whose courage and audacity as a bear-hunter was famous for twenty leagues around. The latter was the one who spoke immediately, saying: "Futile to try Graour's mortal exploit again. Tell them to pass up as many buckets of water as possible, making a chain up the ladder, and we'll inundate the beams that are still burning. They'll be out in no time."

The doctor's face lit up.

"Excellent idea!" he said. "Do it, quickly!"

Bran and Joe gave the orders. The chain was rapidly established. Graour wanted to place himself on the edge of the roof in order to throw the masses of water on to the incandescent beams, but Mathews pushed him away.

"Me! Me!" he said.

The first bucket was passed to him. He leaned over to see where the joists were that it was necessary to cover with water. Either because the conflagration, still fearful, sent up an unbearable wave of heat, however, or because Mathews missed his footing, he was seen to lose his equilibrium and tumble into the heart of the furnace.

A cry of terror emerged from all throats.

Graour, as quick as lightning, raced to the ladder, allowed himself to slide down the supports and arrived on the ground of the courtyard before the doctor was sprawling on the red-hot brands forming the debris.

Fortunately, as it fell, Mathews' body had collided with one of the burning cross-beams and had been pushed out of the perpendicular by the impact. The place where he had fallen was in no way comparable to a bed of roses, but the fire was less intense there. If he had fallen three meters to the right, he would have been asphyxiated before having the time to say *oof*.

"He's burning!" cried the dwarf.

And without reflection, entering into an atmosphere of eighty degrees, followed by three or four Vidrans, Graour succeeded in grabbing Mathews by the arm and pulling him out of the fire.

"Quickly! Cover him with our garments to extinguish his!" said the monster, who did not seem to feel any pity, doing that instinctively, as a Newfoundland dog hurls itself into the water, as if it were his function.

Quantities of water were poured over the doctor, who was writhing, burned to the quick all over his body, and whose face, most particularly, was already swollen ravaged and terrible. He had no more hair or beard; his hands and arms were nothing but an unspeakable wound. He was taken away from the fire.

From the height of the roof, Bran had extinguished the two redoubtable beams. All peril had now been averted.

Mathews was transported into another part of the house. The domestics were out of their minds. It was necessary for the Vidrans, commanded by Graour, to improvise a bed in the coolest room in the building.

"My God!" said Joe, when his master, immobile and groaning, had been laid on it. "That's a doomed man."

And the assistant surgeon, his chin in his left hand, contemplated the horrible thing that the doctor had become in less than three minutes. In the manner and the eyes of the short plump man there was the expression of indifference and almost stupid resignation that the majority of the English have in the presence of death. But Graour pulled him out of that astonishing state of the British mind by shaking his arm vigorously.

"You must know how to cure burns!" he said to him. "It's necessary to save him, you hear?"

"Save him? That's easy to say."

"You must!" declared the dwarf, imperiously. "Not for his sake! That he expiate his sins, nothing better—but there's his daughter, his son and the others—the phenomena."

"Oh, the phenomena are no longer in any danger."

"Good. But Miss Beatrix and her brother—do you know where he's hidden them?"

"No."

"In that case, it's necessary to restore sufficient reason to him before he dies for those children not to die of starvation in their hiding place, which might become their tomb."

"Damn! Damn!" said Joe, still phlegmatic.

"Come on, get busy—do something, in the name of your God, in the name of your king, in the name of your sacred England!"

At those words, Joe emerged from his inertia. "I forbid you," he exclaimed, "to speak in that tone of old England. She *is* sacred, England. Yes, you're right, she's sacred."

Graour's only response was to place his heavy hand on Joe's shoulder, squeeze his flesh rudely, and say: "Will you, yes or no, try to save that terrible scoundrel Mathews? Answer me: one word, just one!"

In the same way that they remain insensible before death, the English are not pointlessly obstinate in confrontation with force. If an Englishman perceives that he is the weaker, he capitulates.

"Don't bruise my shoulder like that," he said. "Certainly I'll try to heal my master's burns..."

"Get on with it, then."

"Yes, right away—so let me go."

Graour withdrew his hand. And Joe headed, at a trot, toward the well-supplied pharmacy that Mathews had established, in search of medicaments and bandages, everything necessary to dress wounds. Then he set to work, very adroitly, in truth, like a man who knows his métier, only seeking aid from one of the Scotsmen, William, who was also skilled in lifting a patient and turning him over without inflicting too much pain.

The doctor was groaning unconsciously, already almost comatose, but Joe took no notice of his plaints. He had heard many others in that accursed house. In less than half an hour, he had enveloped Mathews almost entirely in sulfurated Vaseline, not without having washed the wounds with powerful antiseptics.

As a supreme precaution he injected him with an antitetanus serum, and finally measured out phenic acid expertly, in order to inundate the parts of the body where the burns were particularly terrible.

"Now," he said, when he had finished, "we wait. Unfortunately, it's very hot...and gangrene..."

"It's necessary to combat that too, and in advance."

"Of course—that's what I've done. But the heat...!"

"Well, so be it, we wait," said Graour. "But you're going to liberate the poor devils who were howling in fear just now during the fire..."

"Oh, that's not your concern," Joe declared, peremptorily—which unleashed mysterious and contradictory sentiments in Graour.

"You're mistaken—it concerns all honest people. If you don't do as you're told I'll summon the law, and we'll see."

The law! Another force with which Joe had no desire to come into conflict, or even into contact. He therefore shelved his insolence, since it served no purpose for the time being, and made no protest when the dwarf said to him, in a categorical tone: "Furthermore, from this moment on, I'm the master here—isn't that so, you others?"

"Yes, yes!" proclaimed the Vidrans, in unison. One of them, however, added: "All this is stupid. We came to find the vampire and we're wasting our time playing firemen."

"Whose fault is that? Why the devil did you start the fire?"

"Perhaps we made a mistake, but me, I need to find the vampire. I have two daughters, and as long as its body hasn't been reduced to ashes I won't sleep easy."

"We could have done that without the fire," Graour retorted.

"And then again," said the same individual, "why do you need to lavish so much care on that heretic dog. It's all the same to me whether he dies or not."

"But damn it, he's probably the only one who knows where the brucolaca is buried. I want to save him so that he can tell us. Otherwise, we might demolish the house without finding it. Anyway, it'll soon be daylight, and we'll be certain then that the blood-drinker is back in his tomb, since vampires can only go out at night. We'll have more chance then of finding it and reducing it to impotence."

"Graour's right," said three or four other citizens of Vidra.

"In the meantime, we're going to set Mathews' victims free, and right away. Show us the way, Mr. Joe."

The surgeon's aide, who was not curious to see the dwarf resume the arguments with which he had shown himself so prodigal, did not even try to protest.

"At your orders," he said, heading for the far side of the courtyard...

VI. The Other Monsters

On the way, Graour demanded of Joe: "How old is Mathews' son?"

"I don't know. I haven't seen him yet."

"You're making fun of me!"

"Not at all. Miss Beatrix has been here for a fortnight, but the boy only arrived yesterday. Usually the boss goes to England every summer to spend a month with his two children. This year, he had them come here."

"Why?"

"I don't know. Anyway, he doesn't like his servants or me to have anything to do with them, doubtless because he wants to avoid them finding out..."

At that point Joe paused, visibly searching for mild expressions in which to couch his thought, but Graour finished his sentence for him: "Finding out what a terrible industry the author of their days practices."

"Exactly," said Joe, phlegmatically.

"Where has he hidden them?"

"Ah! That's the question."

"You don't have any clue?"

"None."

"You don't have a suspicion? You're familiar with the house."

"Fairly—but there are cellars and underground passages that I've never been into."

"But you know where they are?"

"Not with any certainty."

"It's doubtless in one of those mysterious hiding places that he's shut them away."

"Probably."

"Without suspecting that a simple accident might make it impossible for him to let them out before they die of starvation—for that's the death that threatens them now."

"Yes, it's frightful."

"He must have had the keys to these cellars, these subterrains, on him..."

"Certainly," said Joe, "but they've doubtless remained in the fire with his clothes."

"That's true I didn't think of that. We'll see, when there's no more danger in stirring the debris of the fire..."

At that moment Graour the assistant surgeon and three or four of the inhabitants of Vidra went into the building where the phenomena were lodged. The latter were still crying out in terror, unaware that the fire was extinct.

Very somber, his mind wandering, Graour thought about Beatrix, whose radiant beauty loomed up dazzlingly in his mind's eye—profaned, to be sure, by the misfortune of having a father like Mathews, but so victorious all the same that the monster felt his flesh creep at the thought that the young woman might be destined for a frightful death, either inflicted by him in the excess of his vengeance, or because immanent justice would take responsibility for her torment.

Very surprised to find himself softened by the rapid vision that he had glimpsed a few hours earlier, the pitiful fellow made vain efforts to extract himself from the implacable obsession to which he remained prey.

By virtue of a strange but clearly psychological inversion, what charmed him the most in Beatrix was that, in spite of her appearance of health, she gave the impression of a soul rather than a body. There was a fluidity about her, something imponderable. And that block of flesh, that mass of matter and strength, was ecstatic, in spite of himself, in spite of everything, before the celestial elegance of the person who had appeared to him as a pure spirit.

Shivering, he marched beside Joe, under the eyes of the rude mountain men who were escorting him.

The latter were still very surprised by his attitude. They had known for a long time that Graour had a mortal grudge against Mathews, without understanding why, since, in the final analysis, the doctor had made his fortune. Their astonishment was all the more intense because they had seen the dwarf expending his strength and his money unsparingly for the benefit of his friends, his neighbors and even strangers.

On several occasions, a young man or a young woman had experienced the effects of his generosity, when a question of money had risen between their parents and seemed an obstacle to their marriage, although they were in love. Graour, reestablishing equilibrium, had become the artisan of their happiness.

To think that such a man nursed a hatred so ferocious, and then to see him save Mathews, exposing himself to horrible danger, surpassed their comprehension. We repeat that they could not understand it—but they would have understood it even less if Graour had revealed to them what was passing through his mind and the extent to which it troubled him.

They had arrived in the corridor where Mathews' fearful subjects were. The spectacle with which the dwarf was confronted immediately reignited all his wrath.

One of the doctor's victims, Bulgar by origin, had literally been changed into a beast, a talking beast.

For a long time, Mathews had wanted to enable a dog or some other quadruped talk.

"Not having been able to succeed," Joe explained, "he resolved the difficulty triumphantly by turning a child into an animal."

"And?"

"And he succeeded in giving him the approximate appearance of a young wild boar. He speaks three languages: English, French and Rumanian."

The dwarf looked at Joe with a furious stare, but the assistant surgeon did not perceive it. He was entirely given over to the pride of showing off the frightful product of Mathews' infernal science.

"Nothing better has been done or will be done," he said, triumphantly. "In truth, he was inspired in this particular case by a book by Mr. Wells, the celebrated and witty English writer.[71] But if Wells imagined and more-or-less explained such phenomena, Mathews has created one, which is priceless, for, believe me, this one's worth a million if it's worth a penny..."

Graour started. "A million!" he repeated, explosively. "That's a big word, a million!"

"Indeed!"

"It's not only time that's money for the English," the dwarf went on, at the peak of exasperation. "It's also blood; it's the tortures endured by that poor devil, whom Mathews has made an object of disgust; it's the suffering to which I was subjected myself for twenty years!" Furious, the monster was roaring more loudly with every word he pronounced. "Neither your master nor you," he went on, in a thunderous voice, "have ever asked what an infernal existence that damned soul will lead! A million!"

Then, abruptly, before anyone could stop him, Graour seized Joe's clothing at waist-height, lifted him up one-handed before the admiring Vidrans, and while he held him thus at arm's length, he spat these words in his face: "If you've ever conceived the project of succeeding our master in his frightful commerce, remember this well, torturer's apprentice: while I'm alive, you'll never exercise it with impunity! At your first attempt to transform a child into something hideous, I'll ram your head down between your shoulders, your shoulders into your belly and your belly down to your heels. Do you hear me?"

Having said that, he dropped the red-faced Englishman, who was trembling from head to toe.

"Now, bring all the unfortunates here."

In a matter of minutes, Joe had assembled the doctor's half-dozen more-or-less mutilated subjects. Graour said to them: "You're going to go to my house in Vidra and wait for me there. I'll take care of you. Bran, you're going to take them."

"Yes, but what about the brucolaca?"

---

[71] *The Island of Doctor Moreau* (1896).

"We're going to see to that momentarily. Joe, go back to Mathews, and I advise you to save him. You'll answer for his life with your own."

The surgeon's aide seemed to have lost the power of speech, but he reflected, and his reflections were far from rose-tinted.

What rotten luck to fall into the hands of this brute, he thought. *Anyway, I'll find some way to escape if the boss kicks the bucket.*

With that hope in mind, he went back to Mathews.

Daylight had dawned. It was a matter of finding the vampire. Graour, overheated, no longer knew whether he believed in it or not. The spectacle that he had just had before his eyes had put him into such a state of fury that not a shred of pity remained within him for Beatrix or the doctor's son.

"Wolf-cubs!" he muttered. "I was stupid to feel sorry for them. The misfortune is that their father might not be conscious of their torture."

And as the image of the young woman loomed up before him again, fluid, radiant and divine, he shook himself to expel it from his mind.

But a scruple occurred to him: *Have I the right to strike them, those children? Their father's crimes aren't their crimes. Heaven's justice has already struck the infamous doctor. Perhaps that's enough...*

Then, shivering in spite of himself at the thought of the long martyrdom of those two beings, whom the doctor's accident had perhaps condemned to die in the mysterious redoubt where he had hidden them, he added: *Who can tell where God's justice stops? It's no longer my concern.*

VII. How Certain People who have Committed no Crime Disappear

A few minutes later, under Graour's supervision, the search for the brucolaca commenced. Thirty mountain men

234

took part in it. Their task consisted of digging in the soil of the courtyards and a small garden to the north of the habitation.

Now that it was no longer a matter of crying vampire, however, but of taking action, the ardor of some of them had diminished significantly. The fear of discovering the cadaver gripped the entrails of the most superstitious, spreading from the least brave.

"How can one know," the latter said, "what the phantom blood-drinker is capable of? Are we sure that, even in broad daylight, it can't stick itself to my chest to drain me to death?"

Those fellows were certainly not cowards, for the most part. Confronted by a human, natural danger, they were capable of great courage, even temerity. Nine out of ten of them went out in winter, their vast chests naked, to hunt bears, armed only with a solid knife. And this is how they proceed:

Before going into the forest, they soak the left sleeve of their greatcoat in honey. Having taken that unique precaution, they go in search of the redoubtable carnivore, whose tracks and habitat they have discovered several days before. On seeing the man coming toward it, the bear stands up on its hind legs and heads straight for the enemy in order to stifle him— but when the hunter and the plantigrade are two paces apart, the man extends his honey-coated left arm toward the animal. Never, it appears, does a bear have the prudence to disdain that delicacy, the perfume of which renders it mad with desire. Avidly, it licks the delicious bait, uttering growls of pleasure...and at that very moment, the man's right hand opens its belly with his knife, and kills it.

In other circumstances, mountain men, having revolted for some futile cause, have been decimated by troops sent against them. And it is such brave men that lose all confidence when it is a matter of vampires, the cruel power of which none of them doubts, although none of them has ever seen one.

That they can be seen, of course, they are convinced. Thus, a certain number of the loudest only embarked on the search for the brucolaca with an enthusiasm stifled by the dread of the mysterious peril by which they thought themselves menaced.

On the other hand, others, more fanatical, went to it with a will, digging into the ground left, right and center, everywhere.

Graour told them that Mathews must have buried some of the victims of his abominable practices in the vicinity—and it was sufficient for a corpse to be buried without the aid of religion, especially if the parents have been stingy with the alms that it is customary to distribute when someone dies, for the dead person in question to become a brucolaca.

"Dig most especially in places where the earth has been recently disturbed," the dwarf insisted.

And everyone worked with a frantic ardor.

"What do you have to fear?" Graour added. "The sun has risen. No vampire has ever budged from its tomb in broad daylight."

But the excavated soil did not yield any cadaver, any object of the frightful research.

Once, Vlad, one of the most ardent, had cried: "Here's a bone! We have it."

Indeed, he had just disinterred something resembling a femur—but there was nothing else for ten meters around. As a cadaver, it was incomplete.

"Leave it!" said the dwarf. "It's a sheep bone."

And the digging resumed in earnest.

Midday chimed. Everyone was dying of hunger. It was necessary to go back to the village for a meal.

Kaçandra was dead. Her relatives and friends were filling the mortuary house with lugubrious and desolate plaints. The crowd was indignant that they had not got their hands on the demonic author of that lamentable death, but what could they do?

Everyone ate his fill, and the most determined went back up to Mathews' house, to continue their sinister labor.

The doctor's condition had deteriorated. Since eight o'clock in the morning he had been delirious, only interrupting his incoherent speech to utter cries of agony,

He must, in fact, have been suffering a frightful martyrdom. His hideously swollen head no longer had a human form.

Graour, who had stayed with him during the Vidrans' absence, had tried in vain to understand anything that he said.

Neither Beatrix nor her brother had reappeared. The fourteen hours that had elapsed since the moment when their father had so imprudently sequestered them must have filled them with terror and anguish.

"So they're buried alive in some dark corner of this immense dwelling, perhaps a few paces away from their agonized father," muttered the dwarf, returning to less frightful sentiments. "From their father, who loves them, and to whom they might owe a careful education in the principles of honor and virtue..."

And that was true. Mathews, prodigiously imbued with immense Anglo-Saxon hypocrisy, had had his children raised in the fear of God, respect for the law, and the practice of an elevated morality. He had personally preached virtue, charity and devotion to one's neighbor to them, like the proverbial priest who invites his parishioners to do as he says and not as he does.

That is why he would have been deeply ashamed of Beatrix and her brother had learned what sort of surgery he carried out in that insensate country, in the depths of that sinister house.

As a matter of precaution, and because, in the end, it was necessary to admit a little of the truth while putting on an honest front, he had let his compatriots understand that he was working on a surgical problem of the greatest importance, and that he had chosen that remote corner of Rumania because of the magnificent people on whom he was carrying out his experiments. Given that there was no question of operating *in anima vili* on English people, neither his friends not anyone else had seen any problem with it. Except that his son Evelyn and Beatrix had tormented him for a long time for him to allow them to undertake a voyage to Constantinople and Asia Minor. In the end, he had consented. The children had just arrived, and everything had been ready for their departure when Graour and the Vidrans, throwing a spanner into the works, had invaded Mathews' dwelling.

It was then that the infamous surgeon, seeing the dwarf shouting his accusations out loud and, fearing that his children might learn the monstrous reality, and also to protect them from the brutalities of the crazed mountain men, had hidden them in a part of the subterrains unknown to Joe, the servants or anyone else.

Almost without having time to look around, Beatrix and her brother had been shoved by Mathews and locked into a large cellar with vaguely whitewashed walls, in which there was no bed, no armchair and no furniture of any kind.

Beatrix was still holding an oil lamp, which she was obliged to place on the ground.

"But what's wrong?" asked Evelyn, extremely surprised by what was happening.

He was a boy of about eleven, dressed in a classic costume by which foreigners, and even cockneys, are amused: black trousers, a black jacket, a large white collar folded back over the lapel of the jacket and, to crown it all, a top hat that produced a singular effect summed up by the gibe of a London street-urchin planted before a child thus disguised: "Hat, what are you doing with that boy?"

Although he was surprised, Evelyn was also anxious. Beatrix replied to him: "The house has been, so to speak, taken by storm by a band of men looking for someone whom, so far as I could make out, they believe to be hiding in Papa's house."

"Oh," said Evelyn. "Who are these bandits? Are they dangerous?"

"No, they live in the little town of Vidra. There must be some misunderstanding, and Papa will prove to them that they're mistaken. They'll go away and we'll be let out."

"It wouldn't be pleasant to spend the night here."

"I agree that it wouldn't be very comfortable," said Beatrix, smiling.

The brother and sister started walking side by side at a slow pace, without saying anything more. An entire hour went by.

"It feels damp," said Beatrix, shivering.

"Papa's taking a long time coming to fetch us."

"Oh, the house is so big. Before those savages have visited every part of it to assure themselves that no one's hiding in it, it will take at least an hour, perhaps two."

Evelyn agreed, and said: "If we have to walk like this all night it will he hard."

"Yes," Beatrix relied, simply.

They fell silent again. Mathews had said to them: "I'll come to fetch you in a few minutes and we'll leave early for our voyage." They did not doubt that their sojourn in the cell of sorts would be of short duration. However, the minutes went by, and ended up making hours. No one came to open the door, toward which they darted covert anxious glances.

Naturally, they began to get nervous. The prospect of spending the night on their feet in that tomb was already haunting them.

Beatrix murmured: "As long as those vile men haven't done anything wicked."

"To Papa?"

"I don't know." After reflection, however, the young woman added: "When one's waiting like this, in fact, the time seems longer than it is."

Evelyn took out his watch—a recent gift from his father. "Quarter past midnight," he said.

"Oh!" said Beatrix, whose anxiety was becoming sharper. "We've been here for more than two hours."

And they resumed walking round and round the large room without saying a word.

Soon, however, in the great silence that enveloped them, they distinguished vague rumors, perhaps screams...but all hardly perceptible.

"Something's happening," said the small boy, who had been yawning incessantly for a while, and felt overwhelmed by an imperious drowsiness.

Beatrix, terribly weary herself, seemed to be searching with her gaze for somewhere she might rest. The damp ground was hardly inviting.

For children brought up in a cottage, where they enjoyed all possible security and comfort, the idea of sitting down on the ground with their backs against a viscous wall, exposed to contact with venomous creatures, was enough to make them shiver.

"I can't hear anything more," said Evelyn, whose anguish had become visible.

"What time is it?"

"Twenty past one."

"Oh, that's a long time! A long time!" murmured Beatrix.

"I'm hungry," said the little boy.

That was bound to happen. An English person who cannot sleep always experiences the need to eat. In the circumstances, in truth, it was not very important. Evelyn had had a good dinner—abundant, in fact—at seven o'clock, and he was certainly not about to starve. But what he said—"I'm hungry"—caused a feeling like an icy wind passing through Beatrix's hair, and an atrocious prospect unfolded before her.

What if her father was prevented by some accident, or simply by the will of the frightened men she had seen filling the house, from coming to open the door of the hiding-place, transformed into a prison, and the next day, hunger—real hunger—and ardent thirst became an unspeakable suffering for them?

The brave girl refrained from communicating such a cruel thought to her brother.

"Oh, I can't go on any more," she said. "I need to rest, at least for a moment."

She let herself fall, rather than sitting down, on to the ground next to the lamp, still straining her ears in the hope of hearing someone coming to release them. Evelyn did the same. In him, however, sleep was soon victorious, and he let himself go, with his heed on his sister's lap, while she, similarly exhausted, put all her energy into staying awake, ready to escape.

The time went by, pitilessly. No one came to liberate them, neither their father nor anyone else. A heavy fatigue overwhelmed Beatrix, whose eyes closed invincibly. At intervals, her victorious somnolence filed her with brief dreams, followed by abrupt awakening.

Something terrible must have happened to Papa, she thought.

At the end of a further fleeting interval of sleep, she thought: *It must be daylight.*

After parading her keen gaze around her searching for some ray of light from outside, she tugged gently at her sleeping brother's watch and looked at the time.

Ah! I thought so! It's five o'clock!

Fearful of the abandonment to which she already considered herself condemned, she uttered an involuntary cry: "Papa!"

The walls of the tomb sent back the sound of her voice and the accent of her fear. Then everything fell back into the horrible silence that added one degree more to the sensation of being doomed forever that she now experienced to the full.

This cellar, she thought, *has no ventilation shaft through which daylight can be seen. What if my father is dead? My God! We too will die in this sepulcher, in frightful agony. I don't want that...*

As she pronounced those last words, the lamp suddenly projected a more vivid light. There was no mistaking what it meant. The oil, entirely consumed, was about to refuse its aliment to the wick.

Careful not to wake her brother, the poor girl got to her feet abruptly, casting fearful glances around her in the hope of discovering a glimmer of light...but there was none. In a few more minutes, thick darkness would weigh out on two beings who had been so full of joy and hope the day before.

Evelyn suddenly came to his feet with a single bound, saying: "What? Where are we? What's happening?"

"It's been daylight for more than an hour; the lamp is about to go out, and we've been left here to die."

The little boy was scarcely awake—but not for long. "Die!" he exclaimed. "Of hunger, then?"

Mad with terror, the boy launched in his turn the desperate appeal that had emerged from the young woman's lips a little while before: "Papa! Papa!"

Then, in a fit of nervous fury, the poor boy started beating with his fists and feet on the wood of the implacable door that separated him from liberty. To think that those few planks were the sole obstacle to their salvation! For it seemed certain, now, to Beatrix that their father was unable to come to their rescue, either because he was dead, perhaps murdered by the horde she had seen invading the house, or for some other inexplicable cause.

Then she too ran toward the batten madly and started hammering it with all her strength, repeating the same cry as her brother.

After which they waited.

Nothing.

The light of the lamp was vacillating more. Gathering as much energy and self-composure as she could, she went to pick up the dying light, brought it closer to the door and set about examining the hinges and the lock,

"We need," she said, "to detach that stone bed in which it's sealed."

"With what?"

"With anything."

"We don't have anything."

"I thought you always carried a pocket-knife."

"Oh! Yes, that's true!"

"Well, try to dig into the stone."

The child opened his pocket-knife, a mere toy, and scratched the part of the wall in which the tongue of the lock was embedded. Derision! It was as hard as granite.

"However," said Beatrix, "it's necessary to get out of here. We only need to hollow out an inch in twenty-four hours. Let's try. That's the price of our salvation. Perhaps our father's salvation too."

Taking the little knife from Evelyn's hand, she started scratching the stone with an incredible vigor.

The lamp threw out its last light. It went out.

"We might perhaps have needed it at the decisive moment," she said.

Then she resumed her work—but the blade of the knife, too rudely manipulated, snapped in the middle.

"What bad luck!" cried the boy.

"No, on the contrary. We'll do more useful work with the stump."

Indeed, the fragment of steel adhering to the handle constituted, by virtue of its thickness and resistance, a more fecund tool than the point of which Beatrix had been making use thus far. For a long time, the young woman dug into the cement surrounding the tongue of the lock. If she stopped occasionally, it was to measure with her groping fingers the groove that she hoped—in vain, alas—to find deeper than it really was.

Soon, her nerves became exasperated. She tried the lock repeatedly, trying to shake it, but nothing budged. Her discouragement changed to despair.

"I give up," she said, suddenly.

"Let me try," said Evelyn.

And the child started scratching with all his might, only succeeding in slowly raising an impalpable dust.

"We'd need a week," said Beatrix. "And within three days..." She did not finish.

Toward midday, the two prisoners, exhausted and feeling their stomachs crying out with hunger, lit the lamp again, which was still capable of yielding some light. They saw that they had scarcely worn away two millimeters of the stone. Then, their nerves exasperated, they both emitted a furious clamor, striking the wood of the cruel door, howling, for a brief moment, like lunatics.

Then Beatrix resumed her work, injuring her hands, grazing the fingers, which were bleeding without her being aware of it.

Finally, at about five o'clock, the two unfortunates, utterly exhausted, stopped and let themselves fall to the floor, incapable of continuing that struggle for existence.

Beatrix felt the cold sweat of the dying welling up on her forehead, beneath her eyes and to her lips, and wiped it away with her bloody hand. Fortunately, fatigue held sway over everything else. Sitting on the ground with their backs to the accursed door, they fell into a heavy slumber, which at least interrupted their torment.

VIII. In the Midst of Darkness

In the meantime, events in Vidra took an unexpected turn. Bran, Vlad, Dmitri and the majority of those who had come back for the midday meal recounted what had happened during the preceding night in the doctor's house. In less than an hour, all the inhabitants of the little town had repeated it to one another, with the result that it reached the ears of the authorities.

Those were of two kinds.

Firstly, there was a senior functionary, with a rank corresponding to that of our sub-prefect. Secondly, and almost parallel, there was a chief of police, more-or-less seconded by four or five subaltern employees.

Both of them decided that their combined intelligence would not be too much to appreciate and settle as equitably as possible the misdeeds that the revelation had just brought to light.

"It's terribly complicated," said the sub-prefect, who, hierarchically speaking, had the right to speak first, and who was not sorry to show a little zeal.

"In what respect?" asked the policeman.

"In that everyone involved in this scuffle is guilty. For a start, that Dr. Mathews is a horrible blackguard."

"Agreed, but we've all know that for a long time, and we should have put an end to his abominable practices. The veritable vampire is him."

"You're right—except that, when we wanted to molest him, he went to complain to his consul, and I received orders not to create any embarrassment for the government."

"If he'd been expelled from Rumanian territory, quietly and gently..."

"Yes, yes, undoubtedly," agreed the sub-prefect, taking his chin in his left hand, "we'd have avoided the terrible scandal that will make all Europe leap with indignation..."

"Can't we hush the affair up? It isn't our savage adminstratees who'd hold it against us..."

"Difficult, difficult! There are forty or fifty malcontents in the town who'd write to the damned newspapers, and then you'd hear the charivari with which they'd regale us from here."

"What if we put all the blame on Graour...?"

"I'd like that—the monster inspires an indescribable revulsion in me. There's nothing more frightening."

"Fundamentally, he's the only guilty one. He's dragged fifty brutes to attack the doctor's house, under the pretext of vampires. But for him, there wouldn't have been any fire..."

"Yes, but the whole population would be against us, and the population of Vidra's not comfortable when it's angry. Then again, he's the one who fought the fire with superhuman courage, and pulled Dr. Mathews out of the fire, at the risk of his own life."

"Then let's strike everyone, pitilessly—Graour for having cried brucolaca, the others for the crime of arson, and the doctor for the crimes that he's committed over the last twenty years."

"Very embarrassing. There aren't twenty people here courageous enough to declare that the Vidrans who believe in vampires are imbeciles."

"Of course! They'd risk being lynched."

"On the other hand, if you try to arrest Graour, apart from the fact that seven or eight hundred mountain men would defend him, weapons in hand, are you quite sure that your five agents and you wouldn't be defeated, knocked over and reduced to helplessness by that phenomenal and formidable dwarf alone?"

The chief of police did not reply to that question.

"It would be necessary to send for troops then, and you know from experience that my administratees don't permit themselves to be intimidated by rifle or bayonets. Do you remember Captain Valescu, who wanted to treat them harshly as reservists, and whom they simply massacred?"

"Yes, you're right—it's very embarrassing."

"As for Mathews, he'll probably die. Arresting him would be arresting a cadaver. Our redoubtable Vidrans wouldn't fail to make a vampire of him—and everything would begin again."

"What if you were to ask for instructions from the Minister of the Interior?"

"Yes, perhaps…and while waiting for an answer, we could go to Mathews' house and carry out an investigation..."

"A serious investigation?"

"Of course! Can an investigation be anything other than serious?" the sub-prefect replied, smiling.

"Perhaps it might be better not to inform the minister until we've taken a closer look at things."

"In fact, they're probably exaggerated. You know how the simplest events are travestied as they pass from mouth to mouth."

"There's more than one way to skin a cat."

"Graour played the hero...someone tried to kill him... Well, let's go take a look for ourselves at what's happened out there. We'll still arrive in time to take severe measures...but in that case, no pity...for anyone..."

"Is it really necessary for us to go?"

"Yes, yes. What are we risking? As long as we don't contradict the vampire-hunters too openly... It's settled. We'll leave at six, when the sun isn't so brutal. Your men can escort us. In case of accidents, they can carry their revolvers, unostentatiously."

It was after that memorable conversation that the two principal administrative authorities of Vidra transported themselves to the theater of events, without judging it indispensable to inform the judiciary authorities.

"They're big enough to know what they ought to do," declared the sub-prefect.

"I assume, in fact," added the chief of police, "that the gentlemen of the Court have been informed about the incident. There's no need for us to make suggestions."

"And if they act of their own accord, well, so much the better. We'll leave them the responsibility they'll have assumed. As for us, people will know that we haven't remained indifferent, but that we've operated with the sagest prudence."

The two functionaries arrived at Mathews' house at about seven o'clock, or perhaps slightly later. When one is the primary authority in a locality, one likes to surround the slightest official steps with a sufficient solemnity.

That is why the sub-prefect told one of his men to go into the house and signal his presence. The man went into the building, stayed there for a god quarter of a hour, eventually reappeared, and said: "Sir, they're all insane in there. The men from Vidra are still looking for the brucolaca. Graour can't be found. The servants sent me packing.

"And Mr. Mathews?"

"I didn't see him."

"But there's also Mr. Joe."

"I didn't see him either."

"Let's go in," said the sub-prefect.

On the side, the house seemed to be abandoned. All the doors were open. Muddy tracks had been left all over the floor-tiles by the Vidrans when they had perpetrated their invasion during the storm.

In the distance, beyond a first courtyard, cries and oaths were resounding; one might have thought that there was a battle raging. The sub-prefect and his acolyte headed in haste for the place from which all the racket was coming.

There they saw the mountain men, who were arguing furiously, addressing a thousand insults to one another, ready to come to blows.

"What does this racket signify?" shouted the sub-prefect. "What are you doing in this house?"

"We're trying to find the brucolaca, and burn it!" replied a voice.

"There is no brucolaca!" proclaimed one of the mountain men, more exasperated than the others.

"Who said that?"

"We'd have found it long ago."

"What! Because it isn't buried in the courtyards? But there are the cellars. There are wells that it's necessary to empty."

"That's certain, Me, I'm not going back to Vidra until we're rid of it."

"Good—but now they want to demolish the house, because they say that the cadaver might be walled up in some redoubt."

"Demolish the house!" cried the sub-prefect. "What! You're all going to be dragged into court for having set fire to it last night. It's already very serious."

"We need the vampire, Mr. Sub-Prefect. It's a question of life or death for our wives, our children, and ourselves!"

The functionary knew only too well that he would be wasting his eloquence trying to demonstrate that the brucolaca was a myth, and perhaps it would have cost him with such an angry mob.

"Well," he said, "nothing is simpler than to solve the difficulty. Those who are obstinate in waiting to find the vampire have only to carry on digging..."

"We want them to help us."

"And the others," continued the improvised Solomon, "can go where they please."

"The sub-prefect is right!" howled the dissidents.

And the quarrel began again, more brutal than before.

At the bottom of it all was that half of the disputants were beginning to doubt the existence of vampires, and no longer believed it except by night, while the other half, for whom it was an article of faith, felt threatened by the skepticism to which their companions were abandoning themselves, and felt a violent indignation in consequence.

Only Graour might have been able to reestablish harmony, or at least to impose peace by liberally distributing a few blows. But he was not there...

At about six o'clock, thinking that Beatrix and her brother had probably neither slept nor eaten since the day before; upset in spite of his rancor by the thought of the torments that the two of them must be experiencing in being buried alive in a kind of tomb, Graour had separated from the crowd of mountain men and, equipped with a lantern he had found in a corner, he had searched for and found the entrance to the cellars.

They can only be in the subterrains, he told himself. *Besides which, if they were on the first or second floor, we'd have heard them crying out, shouting for help.*

The subterrains! The word, with all the fear it can contain, was a good depiction of the maze of corridors in which Graour engaged, and which extended under the entire house, at the least. From time to time, a door bearing a number, rigorously closed, appeared to the right or the left. Having no keys, he rapped on them with the flat of his hand and shouted, in his powerful voice: "Miss! Miss Beatrix!"

Those cries were succeeded by black silence.

"If they were there," muttered the dwarf, "they'd already have replied. And even if the sound of their voices couldn't reach me, they'd have had the idea of knocking on the door."

And he continued on his way, renewing his appeals at every cellar. Everything remained mute and sinister, to such an extent that he suddenly started.

"Oh no, no," he said. "It's not possible that they've died of starvation in such a short time. I'm being stupid!"

Everyone knows how long a route can appear to be when one is traveling it for the first time. With good reason, Graour's exploration of the interminable corridors seemed sempiternal. It had been scarcely twenty minutes since his search began, and he already imagined that he had been there for more than two hours. He was still walking soundlessly, as far as possible, in order to be able to make out the voices of prisoners if they shouted for help or even groaned, in their despair at finding themselves abandoned. What astonished him was that the corridors extended infinitely.

Why the devil has Mathews had another house built underneath his, even vaster than the other? the monster wondered.

Mathews had not had anything at all built. On the place where the doctor's establishment now stood, there had once been a kind of fortified castle, under which vast subterrains extended, prolonged for a considerable distance, doubtless with an exit to open country.

The castle had been razed in the course of a war, in the reign of Vlad IV—the one who carried out furious campaigns against the Turks, a ferocious battler celebrated for the fashion in which he got rid of his Mohammedan prisoners by having every last one impaled on spikes of various heights, according to their ranks in the Turkish army, the Pachas being honored with the longest ones. A rich merchant from Bucharest had bought it in the first half of the nineteenth century, built his house with the dispersed materials without touching the subterrains, and, having lost his taste for it, had sold it to Mathews.

For three hours, Graour wandered through the subterrains, gradually subject to a cruel discouragement, and realizing that only chance—an improbable chance—could guide him to the precise spot where Beatrix was groaning.

Legions of rats fled before him at times. One can imagine the frissons that he felt running through him on divining the excess of terror that a similar promiscuity would inflict on that young woman, so refined, so elegant and so delicate.

And the more he persisted in his vain search, the more he dreaded never being able to liberate Beatrix.

At the very moment when the sub-prefect and the chief of police set off to return to Vidra, Graour had just arrived at a kind of spacious junction from which three tunnels departed, one to the left, one in front of him and the one through which he had come.

That was a great embarrassment to him.

Which shall I take? he asked himself, hesitantly.

He was sounding the thick darkness in which they were plunged with a sharp gaze when a light appeared in the distance: a light that was moving slowly—very slowly—and which was manifestly heading toward him.

The dwarf shivered, not without fear. His self-confidence was unlimited, but he felt troubled by an emotion compounded out of heterogeneous elements. Then again, who is the man who, thirty feet underground in that blackness, believing himself to be all alone, wandering in the middle of a labyrinth, who would not be slightly afflicted by superstitious dread? Others, even the boldest, would certainly have felt themselves quiver to their very entrails.

The light was still advancing, becoming more distinct. At times it rose up to a certain height, and then fell back, as if mechanically, to pause twenty or twenty-five centimeters above the ground.

"What the devil can that be?" Graour muttered.

He had scarcely formulated that interrogation, however, than he became conscious of the fact that he was producing himself, with his own lantern, the same effect of terror and curiosity—and he extinguished it precipitately, after which he plastered himself into a recess in the wall, and waited.

"My God!" he murmured, almost immediately, "what if it's Miss Beatrix herself, lost in such a complication of tunnels, trying to find a staircase?"

The light advanced, renewing its movement of ascent and descent so regularly that the dwarf understood. Evidently, the person who was carrying it was looking at the numbers of each door, which were perhaps enabling him to follow his route reliably.

Then, for the first time, Graour thought that in marching straight ahead for two hours, he had not paid any attention to knowing how he could get back to the point from which he had started.

"What a fool," he whispered. "One has to be stupid not to think about that! It would be a fine thing if I had to stay here in my turn, to die of hunger like an imbecile."

The mysterious individual continued waking, with the appearance of a phantom, and without making any more noise than if he had been one of those brucolacas of which the Vidrans were so frightened. And as the other drew closer, the dwarf felt his emotion growing, either because he expected to see Beatrix appear or suspected some bandit of hiding out in those depths.

In the latter case, the presence of an individual familiar with the subterrains might be a great help to him in finding Mathews' children, and he had irresistible arguments at his disposal to make any bandit into a reliable guide.

But if it were Beatrix! Graour was too intelligent not to know that at the sight of him, in such place, the young Englishwoman would experience a fear so horrible that she might fall down dead in consequence.

And it would have been well worth the trouble of trying to save her!

IX. Both and Neither

The mysterious stroller's lantern—for the person carrying it really did seem to be strolling—was no more than fifteen
meters from Graour, who opened his eyes like the searchlights
of an ironclad ship. No matter how much attention he con-
densed, however, he could not yet distinguish either the statue
or the form of the individual.

He gathered himself, ready to pounce if necessary.

At ten meters, the hand that held the lantern appeared to
him, feebly illuminated, but enough for him to be able to say
to himself: *It's a man's hand.*

In fact, he thought, *if it had been Miss Beatrix, she
wouldn't be walking so slowly. She'd be calling for help.*

The man stopped at the junction, trying to get his bear-
ings. He raised his lamp above his head in order to increase its
range...and Graour had to make a violent effort to stifle an
exclamation of surprise, perhaps mingled with anger.

*Joe! It's Joe! What is the tormenter's servant, a torturer
himself, doing here?*

What was he doing? The dwarf had not a second's hesitation in answering his own question. He too was searching for
Beatrix, wanting to save her from the frightful suffering of
hunger and thirst...

At that discovery, Graour, revolutionized, sensed in the
depths of his painful being something unknown and terrible. A
thousand thoughts of every nature—tender, furious, pitying,
sickening—traversed his consciousness like a hurricane.

But for an atom of reason he would have leapt at Joe's
throat—but then, suddenly, he calmed down, like a runaway
horse that stops dead, trembling. A resigned smile floated beneath his dense moustache.

Am I mad? he thought.

Joe had made his decision. Without suspecting the danger he had just run, the surgeon's aide went into the tunnel

from which Graour had emerged, and continued his exploration.

He lied to me, the dwarf said to himself. *He knows these tunnels. He wants to save Beatrix in order to marry her.*

The monster could scarcely suppress a new surge of rage. But he thought that Joe was the only one who had some chance of discovery the young woman and her brother.

When she's free, he added, mentally, *when she's safe, we'll see.*

Having made that resolution, Graour started moving behind Joe, without making any sound, like a phantom, so lightly that anyone who had seen him would have thought it a miracle.

And if the adipose Englishman had conceived the suspicion that a phenomenal being like Graour was behind him, what atrocious terror would not have seized him!

They both went forward in the slow manner from which Joe had not departed, and which made the dwarf impatient, both straining their ears, ready to run to the rescue of the imprisoned unfortunates if they gave any sign of life by a plaint or a cry.

But then, the mastodon having put his foot on something that cracked, the Englishman stopped dead, and directed his light toward the place where the dwarf was standing, motionless and ill at ease.

And at that exact moment, from fifty or sixty meters ahead of them, two exclamations resounded, in which an accent of triumph could be distinguished, and also of indescribable relief.

At the same time, there was a dull click like that of a piece of wood colliding with something hard, and finally, repeated cries: "Papa! Papa! Help!"

The voices of a woman and a child were recognizable.

It's them! Graour thought, with the bitter regret of not having liberated them himself.

Joe also experienced a painful sentiment at the thought of not having had anything to do with their salvation—but he did not linger on superfluous reflections.

"They'll get lost in the maze!" he exclaimed, almost involuntarily.

And he was about to launch himself in their pursuit when he felt himself seized by the nape of the neck and perceived words spoken in a whisper, two centimeters from his ear.

"That one, Joe, will never be your wife. You're not worthy of such a treasure."

The assistant surgeon, on whose forehead a cold sweat had just sprung forth, recognized the voice of Graour. Indignant and furious, he struggled in the Herculean grip, and replied: "Will she perhaps be yours?"

And the islander put such an expression of scorn into the way that he pronounced that sentence that Graour released the little man and, utterly dejected, replied: "Even less..."

That deformed and fantastic being had character. If it was impossible for him to prevent his heart from beating and his soul from dreaming, at least he had the good sense to understand that, with his monstrosity, he had to hide even his most ardent sentiments. And he had just pronounced sentence on himself, irrevocably.

But Joe, recovering the liberty of his movements, shouted with all his might: "Mademoiselle! Evelyn! Be careful! Wait for me—you'll get lost."

Well, yes, but neither of them had heard him. Bewildered, they were running madly toward the staircase near their hiding place, continuing to call to their father.

Free! Saved! Oh, what joy! What! Get lost, them? When, for thirty mortal hours they had passed through their memory twenty times over the incidents of the fatal evening on which their father had led them toward the cellar that had nearly served them as a sepulcher. No, no. They would not get lost. In four or five strides they would reach the stairway leading to the upper floors. It was dark, but what did that matter? Were their eyes not accustomed to the most profound darkness?

It would not take long. In four or five minutes, they would reach the vestibule where Graour had seen Beatrix for the first time.

But how—by what prodigy—had Mathews' daughter succeeded in opening the door of her prison?

There was no prodigy, but simply an untiring energy, which, after several fits of temporary discouragement, ha reawakened, every time more tenacious and ardent.

And then a stroke of luck had come to the children's aid.

To begin with it had required incredible patience and a great deal of force to hollow out the groove that we have previously mentioned around the bed of the lock. The cement resisted victoriously. Toward ten o'clock, however, when Graour and Joe were already searching the subterrains, Beatrix felt the softer stone that the cement covered ceding more rapidly, and crumbling almost easily under the stump of the knife-blade with which she was persisting in her work of liberation.

To be sure, it still took a long time, but the labor, feverish as it was, had the legitimate hope of success for its auxiliary.

And at eleven-thirty, the slot of the bolt, already unsteady for twenty minutes, finally came away. The door opened. A cry of joy—and the two children ran toward the upper floor, scarcely suspecting that they were running toward new proofs, toward more horrible dangers, a hundred times more frightful than the one they had just escaped.

X. The Vampire Hunt

The house was still full of noise. In truth, only twenty Vidrans remained there, but they were absolutely intent on their brucolaca. They needed it. The sub-prefect and the chief of police had tried in vain to get them to go home. Neither persuasion nor threats could determine them to do so.

At one time, when the authorities showed signs of wanting to employ force and arrest three or four of them, they had gathered together, brandishing their formidable knives, and the policemen, too small in number to take on men thus armed, were obliged to take refuge in negotiations, in the course of which promises were extracted from the Vidrans not to set any more fires and to confine themselves to the search for the vampire.

They kept their word. Except that they were becoming increasingly frustrated, and, after having tried to begin excavations in some of the cellars within easy reach, they had returned to the courtyards and the little garden, uttering exclamations of anger. Ten or twelve of them, carrying torches, scrutinized the darkest corners. There was soon a question of going to dig at the foot of the fir-trees that surrounded Mathews' dwelling outside the walls.

They had not rested for a moment, and had scarcely taken any nourishment for thirty hours. They could no longer succeed in dominating their nerves.

And it was at that moment that Beatrix and Evelyn came up to the ground floor, and then to the first, calling for their father.

Midnight chimed. Midnight: the hour of brucolacas. The full moon was floating in the velvet of the sky, brightly illuminating the countryside and the exterior façades of the edifice where the various scenes of the drama were unfolding.

While the Vidrans came back, noisy but discontented by having been no more fortunate in the search at the foot of the fir-trees, and spreading out once again as the children moved through the house, where the light of their torches appeared and disappeared as they passed from one room to another, Beatrix and her brother arrived on the first floor, still running, in a long corridor whose seven or eight windows allowed the bright moonlight to enter.

It was at the end of that corridor that Mathews' apartments were situated. Their own bedrooms were also there. Naturally, they wanted to take refuge there, hoping to find their father, or at least to discover what had become of him.

Having perceived the savage mountain men in the court-yard, shouting incessantly, they had hastened to reach safety, already anguished by the thought that Mathews was the victim of the invaders. But their silhouettes were outlined, a trifle fantastically, in every window that they passed, and one of the most excited of the Vidrans, mechanically raising his eyes, saw them traversing the zone of lunar light, disheveled and phantasmal. That man, under the obsession of the sinister idea that had been dominating him for so many hours, uttered a kind of roar, pointing his finger at the unfortunates.

All the mountain men looked at the same time at the place at which their companion's tremulous arm was pointing. A frightful clamor went up from a dozen throats:

"Brucolaca! Brucolaca! There it is! Quickly!"

And they all rushed forward, crazed by emotion, and perhaps by horror, in order to cut off the retreat of the pretend-ed vampire, take possession of it and subject it to the fate re-served for it.

But one of them—he had not wasted his tine shouting, that one—had already gained a lead. The people in the house since the day before—one could say the previous two days—who had been moving through it in all directions, had become familiar to him.

In three strides he was at the foot of a wooden staircase, and, as if he had wings, he went up the steps four at a time. Certainly, he had no idea what he was going to do. His idea, no doubt, was to follow the brucolaca back to its tomb. After that, everyone would take action.

Young and full of energy, he arrived at the top of the stairs at the very moment when Beatrix as about to reach the same point—with the result that they almost collided with one another, and both of them scarcely had time to recoil, for they were both prey to an indescribable fear.

The Vidran, with his immense beard, his unkempt hair and his bare breast, had an appearance made to inspire an abominable terror in any woman in Europe.

On the other hand, in the gloom, her eyes widened by the terror inspired in her by the sight of the man who had abruptly surged forth in front of her, dressed entirely in white, as Englishwomen often do in summer, and furthermore, with her tall stature and the singular fluidity of her movement, Beatrix bore sufficient resemblance to a fantastic being for the big mountain man, imbued with superstition, to tremble on finding himself so close to what he believed to be a vampire.

There was, therefore, in both of them, a moment of arrest full of anxiety. And during that moment, the mass of the excited, ferocious Vidrans raced up the stairs, with a thunderous noise, uttering clamors so frightful that the young woman, terrified, took flight, retracing her steps, followed by Evelyn, who was even more frightened than she was.

To be sure, she did not yet fear that those redoubtable beings wanted to hurt her. It was by instinct that she was running away, in order not to have to come into contact with them.

"Where is it? Where is it?" repeated the Vidrans, jostling one another in order to be the first to lay their hands on the object of their irrational hatred.

"There are two," replied the man who had outpaced his comrades so urgently a few moment before.

"Look! There they are, getting away!"

"Ah! Damn it! As long we can catch them!"

"One of them," added the first, "still had blood on its lips. That was what frightened me."

Those few words, in the mouth of the fanatic, had a terrible significance.

In fact, among the articles of faith relating to vampires, there is one that brings that insensate believe to the peak of horror. It is repeated, during the long evenings in which people recount, while shivering, everything regarding their abominable murderous rage—and it is thus that children receive the seeds of that singular belief at the most tender age—that brucolacas suck the blood of their victims with such fury and in such great quantity that it emerges thereafter from all their pores.

If you recall that Beatrix, while she was working so doggedly on her deliverance, had grazed her hands, and that afterwards, in wiping the sweat from her face she had soiled her fresh face with bloody streaks, you will understand, with terror, the mortal danger in which the coincidence in question was about to place her.

Inhuman cries sprang from all the breathless throats. At the same time, the barbarian horde launched forth on the heels of the young woman—who, fortunately, had obtained a start.

Evelyn, his hair standing on end, his eyes bulging, with a frightful rictus on his lips, exhausted by lack of nourishment and abandoning himself to destiny, could do no more than thrown himself into a dark closet, which served as a lumber-room, and huddle there, more dead than alive.

As for Beatrix, to whom fear gave a new burst of nervous energy, she ran up another staircase, as lightly as a creature of dream, which she found at the other end of the corridor, and which went up to the second floor.

But the mob resumed its furious course, in the midst of howls, competing to see who would be the first to seize the fugitive—and when one of the fanatics reached her, that would be the end of her.

Let us repeat that she did not believe that they wanted to kill her. No, like anyone else unaware of the hideousness of the infamous superstition to which she was about to fall victim, Beatrix assumed that the human whirlwind was running after some unimaginable objective, and that it would be sufficient to let it pass by.

But she was very rapidly undeceived.

As she stopped momentarily, she heard the clatter of enormous boots on the staircase. One of the Vidrans appeared, gigantic, a few meters away, and, on perceiving her, shouted: "There it is! There it is!"

"Come on! Come on!" roared the others.

The man bounded toward the poor child. It really was her that he wanted.

A scream ripped through the air.

"Papa! Help!"

Then she ran on, flying along a long gallery that went all around the house, followed close behind by the boldest and most agile of the furious madmen.

Strangely enough, in that semi-darkness, with the white garments fluttering around her legs, she really did give the impression of a revenant. It was, therefore, not astonishing that the crazed mountain men were more than ever convinced that they were dealing with a vampire.

If she had not already been familiar with the bends in the corridors—which gave her an advantage over the Vidrans—it is certain that she would already have succumbed and that they would have grabbed her, but she maintained her lead. For how long, alas? While running, she felt frissons of fear running through her and chilling her.

And then she, too, wearied, weakened as she was by a thirty hour fast. Her respiration became labored. Oppressed since the very start, strangled by anguish, she perceived at that moment that Evelyn was no longer following her, and his disappearance distressed her even further.

The idea came to her of stopping, of facing up to her cruel tormentors, of demanding to know what they wanted—but she did not know a single word of Rumanian. They would not have understood her.

In the end, terror carried her away, and, breathless and bewildered, she continued her desperate flight.

The scene was nightmarish.

Picture a poor child of seventeen, exhausted by two nights and a day of struggling against a frightful death, her stomach and head empty, running away through that vast house before a crowd of vociferating brutes, whose are on the point of seizing her dress at any moment.

Add to that the fact that seven or eight of the fanatics were still carrying their torches, whose flames, stretched horizontally by the rapidity of their movement, were shedding a sinister gleams, devoid of brightness, in the midst of which they were agitating in an infernal chaos.

She ran breathlessly, going up and down stairways, fearing that she might find herself at any moment face to face with one of those demons, who had moved perfidiously to cut off her retreat.

And, then, where was her father? What was he doing? Why had he not run to her aid?

He must be dead, she thought.

But she scarcely had time to dwell on that dolorous conjecture. The Vidrans had resumed their refrain: "Brucolaca! Brucolaca!"

Their fury was becoming sharper by the second on seeing their prey incessantly remaining just out of reach.

That was because they too were exhausted, worn out. Since the evening of the day before last they had expended themselves in cries, in excavations and in disputes—and even though they were solid and redoubtable brutes, hunger, and most of all the lack of sleep, had sapped a fraction of their strength. That is why the race was almost equal—except that Beatrix was bound to end up collapsing, fatally. Already, she no longer had the lightness that had given her the appearance of a supernatural being, sufficient to justify the error of the coarse Rumanian peasants.

Several times, she had almost fallen. It was only when the eternal clamor of "Brucolaca!" resounded in her ears that she surged forward again, passing the windows again and again, in the light of the moon, which was floating placidly in space.

Always pursued, she heard the heavy hammering of boots on her heels.

Once, one of her pursuers succeeded in grasping the hem of her dress, which was fluttering around her, and thought that he had her. He uttered a roar of triumph—but the fabric tore from top to bottom, and she continued her flight, looking even more like a phantom agitating in its shroud.

All of that, of course, lasted no more than a few minutes.

Graour and Joe, emerging from the cellars, had hardly had time to find the staircase by which they could climb out. It was only when they set foot in the famous vestibule that they heard the odious racket with which the Vidrans were seasoning their atrocious pursuit.

Beatrix was now uttering the screams of a hunted beast. Like a stag at bay she was weeping enormous tears. Nevertheless, although she was on the point of collapse, further bounds still carried her out of reach.

Without understanding, Graour grunted an oath, and a few bounds took him into the courtyard—and from there he saw the horrible chase that was about to reach its conclusion.

For the fifth or sixth time, Mathews' daughter was making the circuit of the second-floor gallery. He recognized her. The word "Brucolaca!" revealed the terrible reality to him.

For a moment, he was nailed to the spot, disentangling from his consciousness the realization that, fundamentally, he alone had unleashed that tempest by rousing the mob of mountain men against the doctor.

In a rapid vision, he conceived the horror of what was about to happen.

Beatrix, he told himself, *grabbed by those madmen, will be pierced through the heart with a stake, and then thrown into quicklime. Oh, no, no! Wolf-cub she might be—but I don't want such a crime to be committed!*

The fugitive, worn out, could no longer even run. Completely out of breath, she was staggering around one of the corners of the corridor when one of her torturers loomed up in front of her.

Vanquished, knowing that she was about to die, she could not put up any more resistance. Her strength, if not her courage, failed her. The man grabbed her with an unspeakable brutality.

"I've got it!" he roared.

For him, as for his companions, there was nothing there but a vampire, a fomenter of death.

By means of one last effort, Beatrix struggled, but what resistance could she put up? The demon that held her, in whom no dread and longer subsisted, put his arms around her and held her against his breast, against his enormous hairy beard, and perhaps would have stifled her in that grip, when a thunderous voice suddenly resounded behind him.

"Let her go, Spiro, let her go! That's not the brucolaca, that's the doctor's daughter. She's alive, wretch!"

But Spiro did not let go. He replied with a burst of laughter.

The others also mocked Graour. Not a brucolaca! When the phantom had fled them for such a long time, evading all their pursuits!

"I tell you..."

"Pierce its heart first," a voice interrupted.

Joe arrived, coming to the rescue, in the state that betrays individuals impotent to prevent a crime, babbling, indignant, audacious and fearful at the same time.

Beatrix was about to perish.

One of the fanatics was sharpening the ritual stake with a sickle—but at that very moment, Spiro was seen to go pale, as if the hand of death had abruptly struck him down.

It was like a thunderbolt.

There was a powerful effort of resistance, a croak, and then nothing more. His face became congested. The crack of a bone resonated, lugubriously. He gripped the young woman more forcefully, and tottered.

"Let her go, wretch!" shouted Graour.

Spiro opened his mouth, closed it, and opened it again, but no sound emerged from his throat. He collapsed on the floor, dragging Beatrix down with him.

He was dead.

The Vidrans thought that their comrade had just been killed by the vampire. A frightful panic ensued. None of them dared throw himself upon the pretended brucolaca.

XI. The Greater Horror

It was Graour, irritated and formidable, who, losing his head, no longer knowing what to do to spare those madmen the regret of a futile crime, and also to save Beatrix, had seized Spiro around the waist and, squeezing him furiously, had just strangled him, without meaning to, for he had only intended to render him impotent. But could such a man measure the force of his muscles of steel? A machine for crushing, he had accomplished his function, thoughtlessly, without limiting the intensity of his pressure.

And Spiro, choked, lay at his feet, breathless and stiff.

Then something happened even more frightful that the chase that has lasted for such a long time: something monstrous, hideous and infernal.

Beatrix, incapable of tolerating the repulsive contact of Spiro, had fainted. Graour tried to pick her up in order to carry her away and put her in a safe place, in a room at whose door he would mount guard.

But no! The dead man, in dying, had not let go. His muscular arms had closed around her in their final convulsions, and held her imprisoned. Those two arms, in their implacable rigidity, resisted the exceptional strength of Graour, who looked around, wild-eyed, gripped in is turn by a mortal fear.

It would be necessary for the dwarf to lift up the bodies of Spiro and Beatrix simultaneously...

He thought of that, and the burden certainly did not frighten him, but it was not a solution. By virtue of a few precursory signs, it was detectable that the unfortunate woman was about to recover consciousness.

Graour, Joe and even the Vidrans, who had finally realized their frightful mistake, trembled at the thought of the horror that would grip the poor child when she found herself imprisoned by that cadaver.

It might kill her.

"You have to break the savage's arms," said Joe, recklessly.

The dwarf had thought of that, too, but the Vidrans would not have tolerated what they considered to be not merely a profanation, but as a danger of making Spiro into a vampire.

"No, no," said Graour. "Something else—let's think of something else."

After a moment's reflection, the dwarf bent down and, embracing the two bodied in a grip into which he put all his strength, he tried to stand them upright.

Beatrix came round. When she perceived her torturer, realized that he was dead, and understood what had happened, it was as if her eyes were about to pop out of her head.

She tried to free herself from the odious embrace. With both hands she shoved the breast to which she found herself stuck. Then something similar to a sob, traversed by glacial laughter, resounded.

"Help me! Help me!" roared Graour. "Can't you see, you stupid animals, that she's going mad?"

"What do you want to do?"

"Free her, of course!"

Then, without further ado, the prodigious little man grasped one of Spiro's wrists and, at the risk of dislocating it, he tried to separate it from Beatrix's body.

Even so, he dared not take things to the extreme. Ten minutes went by: ten long minutes of frightful torture for Beatrix; then, suddenly, the arms of the cadaver relaxed naturally.

Graour leapt forward to prevent the young woman from falling, lifted her up like a feather, and carried her away at a run into the part of the house where her father had already endured a thousand indescribable torments.

With an infinite delicacy, the mastodon deposited his light burden on a bed, and repeated in, English: "It's over, Mademoiselle; it's over; collect yourself..."

And after having Joe bring salts and vinegar, the enormous and ridiculous phenomenon soaked a cloth, with which he wiped Beatrix's face in order to get rid of the bloodstains. He did that simply, with an incredible lightness of touch, attentively, accompanying his cares with encouraging words.

Joe could not help thinking: *That monster has a paternal heart.*

But Beatrix, refreshed, opened her eyes. Graour's soft words reached her like caresses—but when she saw the dwarf, his enormous girth, his little head, and his implausible beard, she was gripped again by her dolorous terrors, imagining that the scene of damnation was about to recommence.

With the gesture of a madwoman, she pushed him away, uttering piercing screams. And he, saddened beyond belief, tried to make his voice very soft in order to say to her: "Don't be afraid. I'm a friend, a friend..."

He did not find anything else because, in spite of everything, he was forced to admit to himself that what had just happened, he alone had provoked...

Continuing to care for the young woman, while Joe went to see to Mathews, whose moans were filling the house, Graour thought, desperately, about his destiny, cursing the doctor and feeling anger rising again in his consciousness.

"Woe! Woe!" he repeated, without daring to complete his thought, which, in any case, remained tenebrous.

The young woman had not calmed down. Every time she reopened her eyes she fell back, at the sight of the dwarf, into a new crisis. And the latter, vanquished, went away.

"Not even her gratitude!" he muttered, as he left.

The Vidrans, shamed, were waiting in the courtyard for news. The sun had risen, superb and bright, so marvelous in its splendor that such beauty seemed ill-fitted to illuminate the abominations that had just unfolded.

Spiro's body was lying in a corner, carefully covered. On perceiving his victim, the dwarf was seized by a tremor.

"I've killed a man!" he said. "I've killed a man!"

"Yes, but what about the brucolaca?" demanded one of the most obtuse of the mountain men.

"What, still?" Graour could not prevent himself from roaring. "Don't you see that it came here to kill Mathews' daughter? It's in the cemetery, and the cemetery alone, that it's necessary to search for it."

And without waiting for a response, the dwarf, shivering, left the doctor's house, went to Vidra. After having made arrangements to ensure that Mathews' subjects, gathered in his house, did not remain as wretched as before their release, and having charged a neighbor with liberal alms to provide for Spiro's burial, he headed for the courthouse.

Presenting himself before a magistrate, he said to him: "I've killed a man. Arrest me."

XII. In which Graour demonstrates that, in believing himself to be implacable, he was mistaken

While Graour was in prison, awaiting his trial, Joe cared for Mathews and his daughter, with some nonchalance, in truth, but very skillfully nevertheless, for he had learned a great many things in the school of his wretched master, especially practical things.

Beatrix did not recover her normal state of mind. The blow had been too rude. Often, in the middle of the night, she woke up in a cold sweat and thought she saw the Vidrans pursuing her relentlessly. A chambermaid had to keep vigil beside her bed to reassure her, in order for peace to return to her soul.

And more!

Sometimes, it was the face of the dead man that appeared to her, grimacing, and also that of Graour, which frightened her even more. By day, she sometimes pronounced strange words, in speeches denuded of any meaning.

Nevertheless, from time to time, she spoke rationally, and at those times, no one would have suspected the ravages that the cruel ordeal to which she had been subjected had inflicted on her brain.

Evelyn, having been found, but having become almost stupid, went back and forth between the bed on which the implausible thing that had been his father was writhing and the chaise-longue on which his sister was babbling. Over and over again he asked Joe why all that had happened.

Embarrassed, the surgeon's aide could only find one response, which did not explain anything at all.

"They aren't men that inhabit this place, they're ferocious beasts."

If Graour had heard him talk in that fashion, with what violence would he not have turned his words back on him, proclaiming: "Was not Doctor Mathews the foremost and most ferocious of beasts?"

The law followed its course. The dwarf appeared at the court of assizes. Nobly and simply, he told the whole truth, accusing himself more than any witness did—even the English consul.

The two dozen Vidrans called to give evidence against him, on the contrary, sang his praises, testifying to the courage that he had shown during the fire, and how Mathews owed the fact that he was still alive to him. The question of the vampire was inevitably raised, before an audience that did not know, in the final analysis, exactly what to think. Among the jurors, there were probably some who believed firmly in it.

Graour was acquitted, in spite of the determination that the British consul, and he more than anyone else, had brought to the affair. What that functionary wanted, above all, was to prevent Graour and Mathews' subjects from revealing the surgical horrors of which the doctor's lair had been the theater, for fear that the odium might fall back upon Great Britain in its entirety—and he was skillful enough to obtain that result, approximately. Graour passed rapidly over the details himself, doubtless deeming that it was a personal matter between the Englishman and himself.

The dwarf was therefore set free about two months after the events had taken place.

He returned to Vidra, where he was received with open arms, almost triumphally.

Mathews had almost recovered, either because Joe had worked a miracle in snatching him from death, or because that spoiler of humans was reserved by destiny to serve as a scarecrow for those who had too much scorn for the life and health of others. For, although he lived, he did not resemble anything human.

269

To begin with, he was blind and repulsively blind. In the place where two agile eyes had once shone, whose gleam revealed in him, in addition to his excessive audacity, an ardent intelligence, one could only see two bloody holes, which inspired more fear than pity.

The deformed nose, half eaten away by the fire, hung sideways like a rag, ten centimeters from the twisted mouth, transported close to the left ear, of which almost nothing remained. And that mouth! It had the effect of an extravagant hole, with ravaged lips, which seemed to be trying to talk to the ear.

Clownish and sinister.

And with that, not a wisp of hair or beard. On the bare cranium, innumerable overlapping violet scars, provoking disgust or horror.

His right arm, fleshless, was completely paralyzed.

To cap it all, Mathews was lame.

Joe had advised in him vain to wear a mask before showing himself in his hideousness. Unable to take account of what he had become, he had refused obstinately.

When Beatrix, after the few days necessary for her to obtain a relative calm, found herself in his presence, it was impossible for her to recognize him. It would not have required much for the poor child, so sorely tried, to have fallen prey to a definitive insanity. Joe was obliged to tell her that the terrible transformation was only temporary. It required nothing less to tear her away from such a spectacle.

As for Evelyn, he dissolved into cries of terror, and nothing could be got out of him but the endlessly repeated words: "That's not my father! That's not my father!"

Even Joe could not go near his former master without his flesh being shaken by tremors.

How many times the little Englishman, doll-faced and adipose, stood in front of Mathews, and examined him with an incessantly-renewed amazement, while making ponderous reflections on immanent justice and murmuring: "It's definitely necessary not to interfere with God's work!"

One day, Mathews wanted to embrace his children. Evelyn simply ran away to hide.

Beatrix was no longer able to doubt that the strange and
repulsive thing was her father. The poor girl had tried many
times to imagine all the tortures that the poor man must have
suffered in becoming so frightful. She sensed that it would be
a great joy for that damned soul to give her the filial kiss for
which he was thirsty.

At that moment she was in one of her calm phases of
mental health. Having approach him she offered him her forehead, closing her eyes. She had the courage to murmur: "Poor
father!"

Then the doctor, taking her gently by the waist, said to
her in the viscous voice that remained to him: "Kiss me, my
dear!"

Immediately, all her valor abandoned her. To be sure,
she wanted to vanquish herself and obey, but it was stronger
than she was...

Like Evelyn, she ran away, panting...

Mathews, stupefied, made a gesture of disordered fury.
"What!" he cried. "Am I as hideous as all that?"

Joe, who was there, did not have the strength to reply.

What was particularly painful for everyone was that the
former maker of phenomena incessantly felt the need to go out
of the house. Guided by Joe or one of the servants he would
go into the forest of fir-trees and sit down on the trunk of a
fallen tree. And when, by chance, one of the women of Vidra,
or even one of the mountain men, passed by, he inspired such
a great repulsion in them that they fled as if they had a vampire on their heels.

It was in the course of one of those excursions that
Graour, his liberty restored, saw him again for the first time.

The enormous and powerful product of the doctor's science, driven by a mysterious and irresistible attraction, had
gone up the mountain. From a height, he had seen Mathews'
dwelling, and had stopped, examining it with a bitter gaze.

A white form went diagonally across one of the court-yards. He shivered, and resumed walking, in order to return to Vidra, but not by the same path.

Twenty minutes later, at a bend in the path, a short distance away from a gang of woodcutters who were felling trees, the doctor appeared before him.

At the sight of that terrible ruin, Graour took two involuntary steps backwards, and stood still in confusion.

What! That was his torturer! The fire had not even changed him into a beast! It had made him into a monstrosity, like him. Even worse!

The monster! There's the monster now! he thought. *Oh, how I'm avenged, avenged! I could never have imagined a transformation more horrible! Only one thing is lacking, and that's for Joe to exhibit him in fairgrounds.*

But in spite of the ferocity of his thought, an immeasurable pity was born in the soul of the dwarf, who was, after all, good.

"How God can punish!" he murmured, then. "Poor Beatrix!" The last word marked the evolution of his ideas.

In spite of everything, in spite of his formal desire to expel, we shall not say hope, but the slightest remnant of illusion, all the forces of his heart and mind returned, unconsciously, to the young woman whose radiant beauty had transformed his soul.

And decidedly, he no longer bore a grudge against Mathews.

"It's destiny," he said. "A misfortune. Yes, a misfortune that I was made like this, a misfortune that I've seen…a misfortune."

Pensively, he was still gazing at the doctor, but he could no longer see him. His mind was elsewhere.

Mathews had no suspicion that his former subject was contemplating him in an indescribable alarm. And the domestic, William, who was serving as his guide, was certainly not going to tell him.

From that day on, the dwarf came back often to wander around the accursed house. Two or three times, he nearly found himself face to face with the young woman, who was gradually recovering her sanity.

She too went out from time to time, and lost herself, desolately, under the great trees, trying to summon up the courage necessary to render her father the caressed of which he was starved.

Sometimes she came back to him deliberately, with the intention of covering him with kisses; then, when she had him before her eyes, scared and livid, his face frightfully ravaged, she turned away, quivering in horror, having great difficulty suppressing her sobs.

On the other hand, the day came when a newspaper or some other source revealed to her that the ridiculous and terrifying ape, the mere memory of whom threw her into an indescribable panic, had delivered her from the most frightful torture, and that, furthermore, Graour had exposed himself to great danger to save her father's life.

With regard to the monster too, she felt that she was unjust.

It came to her mind to thank him, to hold her hand out to him; that appeared to her to be a duty. Nevertheless, the impression of fear that she felt at the memory of that singular individual, who was barely as tall as her waist and was as broad as a hogshead, left her helpless.

Two or three times she had seen him coming back from the mountain, and had had to make a violent effort not to cry out.

One day, however, in the morning, when she had ventured into the great wood of centenarian firs what covered the flanks of the Vranchea, she found herself face to face with him.

Her first impulse was to flee, but she succeeded in overcoming it.

Graour discerning the first sensation, and also the small victory that she had just won over herself, saluted her, nothing more, and disappeared so promptly that it seemed marvelous that a man so voluminous could vanish so quickly, as if someone had killed him at that very instant.

After that day, Beatrix did not encounter the dwarf again. Perhaps the poor child, moved by Graour's discretion, would have given him a less painful greeting, for she was able, now, to think about him without overmuch disturbance.

Time, which, at length, scars the cruelest wounds, especially mental ones, did its work.

Mathews came and went. Evelyn played. Beatrix went through a melancholy phase. It seemed that nothing could trouble that pain-stricken family any further.

At any rate, the doctor had decided to sell the house and leave the country. He was waiting for a buyer. But as a practical man, an Anglo-Saxon, who does not neglect any source of wealth, he exploited the part of the forest that he owned, having the tall firs felled, which he sold advantageously. A great activity reigned there. Woodcutters, carters and sawyers made a continuous racket. That provided distractions.

Joe, having become a steward, and overseer, or whatever, watched assiduously over his master's interests. In the first weeks after Mathews' recovery he had tried to conquer Beatrix's sympathies, without the slightest success. The young woman treated him as a negligible person.

The fellow had judgment. *No illusions*, he said to himself. *She just doesn't like me.*

In fact, there was something more than that. Beatrix knew, now. She knew what her father had been doing in that locality for the last twenty years.

Someone had taken the trouble to tell her Graour's history. She knew about the martyrdom of the other phenomena. In consequence, she was not unaware of the kind of assistance that Joe had lent the sinister doctor.

To learn that her father, as a sort of vocation, and for money, had used such odious practices would have revolted her incredibly a few weeks before the fire and the terrors of the horrid vampire hunt. Now, however, she saw humanity in a different light. Mathews' hideousness, moreover, put him, so to speak, in harmony with the abominations of his infamous science.

In her soul, there was an immense scorn for the human species, for her father and for Joe. Perhaps she excused Graour. Who could tell? She scarcely spoke once or twice a day.

The only pleasure she appeared to obtain, she found in the midst of the noise that the workers in the forest made. The cracking of the gigantic trees falling from a height and smashing everything in the vicinity, the incomprehensible oaths of the cart-drivers, and the quarrels: everything that struck her senses was a relief of sorts. And she often came to the work-sites in order to occupy her eyes and her ears, thus to distract herself from the obsession of her despairing thoughts.

She sometimes got much closer than prudence would have dictated to the horses and the axes of the workers. Joe made that observation to her. Meekly, she moved to a safe distance. But she came back with increasing frequency and, inevitably, the danger became familiar to her, if not indifferent,

One evening, an hour before sunset, she was there, more somber than ever. There was an animation in her cheeks that had not been seen for a long time. Joe watched her from down below, with a curiosity mingled with dread.

She had just had an exceedingly painful conversation with her father. The assistant surgeon had overheard a few words.

The veil is torn, then, he thought. *In which case...*

He did not finish. A loud cry went up from the middle of the work-site, forcing him to turn round in order to see what had happened. Then he let out another cry, more vibrant. Then all the woodcutters also started shouting, some running toward Beatrix, the others trying to hold back and enormous tree, perhaps the largest in the region, which, eroded at its base by the axes, was already leaning over, about to fall, an incalculable mass, on to the path where the young woman was walking.

She, absorbed in her dolors, did not pay any attention to what that excess of disorderly clamors, full of mortal anguish, might signify

"Run, Mademoiselle!" howled Joe, his voice strangled. "Look out! Look out! Oh, damn, she's in a daze today!"

The fir, scarcely still retained by a thin sliver of wood, cracked. There was a tearing sound, and the branches and trunk oscillated for two seconds. Then everything leaned over, toward the young woman.

There was a whistling sound in the air.

"Damn! Save her! Save her, then!"

Well, yes. The men who were running to snatch her from that horrible death evidently did not have time did not have time to reach her and carry her away.

Only then did she see the danger. But fear gripped her so forcefully that she scarcely succeeded in running a few steps toward the interior of the forest, where other tall trees might have protected her. Her legs failed. She collapsed into the ferns. The fir's fall accelerated, directly toward her.

She seemed doomed, when a formless mass surged forth from God knows where, which hurtled with the rapidity of a galloping horse toward the immense and redoubtable log, which had reached the mid-point of its fall.

"Are you mad, Graour?" shouted one of the woodcutters.

"You'll get yourself killed, imbecile!" shouted another.

"No, no—he thinks he's too strong, that one."

But Graour did not hear any of it. Having arrived at the spot where he believed that his reckless intervention would be efficacious, he stopped, braced himself solidly on his legs, raised his arms in the air and waited for the frightful impact, with the intention, not of stopping such a mass, but at least of causing it to deviate, in order that it would not strike Beatrix.

No one said anything more. A deathly silence would have reigned over the insensate scene, if a few of the branches had not been striking those of trees still standing.

The contact took place before the frightened eyes of Beatrix and Joe. They saw then, implausibly, the monstrous tree pause for half a second in its fall, and then swerve, following the arc of a circle, and crash down a few meters from the place where the young woman, untouched, could not believe her eyes, so convinced had she been that she could not escape death.

The dwarf had succeeded.

In a surge of admiration and amazement, everyone rushed toward the place where the prodigy had been accomplished. Hurrahs rang out.

Beatrix too ran forward to thank her savior.

But when the woodcutters and the young woman arrived at the theater of that unparalleled exploit, they perceived Graour lying at full length, his head crushed by the trunk of the gigantic fir, which had also been victorious.

Graour the monster was dead.

Beatrix remained there for more than an hour, motionless and weeping, contemplating that deformed body, and remembering that if he was thus made, it was her father who was entirely guilty.

"His soul, at least," she murmured, "he wasn't able to mutilate."

Night enveloped the mountain and the forest with darkness. Beatrix asked Joe and the woodcutters to go and fetch a stretcher. And when she was alone with the dead man, she knelt down, took him gently by the hand, and, after a long meditation, leaned over to stammer a single word:

"Sorry!"

On whose behalf was she saying sorry? On her father's, or her own?

Who can tell?

At any rate, Graour's soul, scarcely detached from his body, still floating around the young woman he had loved until death, doubtless experienced a divine intoxication, and regretted nothing.

SF & FANTASY

Adolphe Alhaiza. *Cybele*

Alphonse Allais. *The Adventures of Captain Cap*

Henri Allorge. *The Great Cataclysm*

Guy d'Armen. *Doc Ardan: The City of Gold and Lepers*

G.-J. Arnaud. *The Ice Company*

Charles Asselineau. *The Double Life*

Henri Austruy. *The Eupantophone; The Olotelepan; The Petitpaon Era*

Barillet-Lagargousse. *The Final War*

Cyprien Bérard. *The Vampire Lord Ruthwen*

S. Henry Berthoud. *Martyrs of Science*

Aloysius Bertrand. *Gaspard de la Nuit*

Richard Bessière. *The Gardens of the Apocalypse; The Masters of Silence*

Albert Bleunard. *Ever SMalher*

Félix Bodin. *The Novel of the Future*

Louis Boussenard. *Monsieur Synthesis*

Alphonse Brown. *City of Glass; The Conquest of the Air*

Émile Calvet. *In a Thousand Years*

André Caroff. *The Terror of Madame Atomos; Miss Atomos; The Return of Madame Atomos; The Mistake of Madame Atomos; The Monsters of Madame Atomos; The Revenge of Madame Atomos; The Resurrection of Madame Atomos; The Mark of Madame Atomos; The Spheres of Madame Atomos; The Wrath of Madame Atomos* (w/M. & Sylvie Stéphan)

Félicien Champsaur. *The Human Arrow; Ouha, King of the Apes; Pharaoh's Wife; Homo-Deus; Nora, The Ape-Woman*

Didier de Chousy. *Ignis*

Jules Clarétie. *Obsession*

Michel Corday. *The Eternal Flame*

André Couvreur. *The Necessary Evil*; *Caresco, Superman; The Exploits of Professor Tornada* (3 vols.)

Captain Danrit. *Undersea Odyssey*

C. I. Defontenay. *Star (Psi Cassiopeia)*

Charles Derennes. *The People of the Pole*

Georges Dodds (anthologist). *The Missing Link*

Charles Dodeman. *The Silent Bomb*

Harry Dickson. *The Heir of Dracula; Harry Dickson vs. The Spider*

Alain le Drimeur. *The Future City*

Georges Le Faure & Henri de Graffigny. *The Extraordinary Adventures of a Russian Scientist Across the Solar System* (2 vols.)

Gustave Le Rouge. *The Mysterious Doctor Cornelius* (3 vols.); *The Vampires of Mars; The Dominion of the World* (w/Gustave Guitton) (4 vols.)

Jules Lermina. *Mysteryville; Panic in Paris; To-Ho and the Gold Destroyers; The Secret of Zippeliu; The Battle of Strasbourg*

André Lichtenberger. *The Centaurs; The Children of the Crab*

Listonai. *The Philosophical Voyager*

Jean-Marc & Randy Lofficier. *Edgar Allan Poe on Mars; The Katrina Protocol; Pacifica; Robonocchio; Return of the Nyctalope;* (anthologists) *Tales of the Shadowmen 1-11; The Vampire Almanac* (2 vols.)

Xavier Mauméjean. *The League of Heroes*

Joseph Méry. *The Tower of Destiny*

Hippolyte Mettais. *The Year 5865; Paris Before the Deluge*

Louise Michel. *The Human Microbes; The New World*

Tony Moilin. *Paris in the Year 2000*

José Moselli. *Illa's End*

John-Antoine Nau. *Enemy Force*

Marie Nizet. *Captain Vampire*

C. Nodier, A. Beraud & Toussaint-Merle. *Frankenstein*

Henri de Parville. *An Inhabitant of the Planet Mars*

Gaston de Pawlowski. *Journey to the Land of the 4th Dimension*

Georges Pellerin. *The World in 2000 Years*

Ernest Pérochon. *The Frenetic People*

Pierre Pelot. *The Child Who Walked on the Sky*

J. Polidori, C. Nodier, E. Scribe. *Lord Ruthven the Vampire*

P.-A. Ponson du Terrail. *The Vampire and the Devil's Son; The Immortal Woman*

Georges Price. *The Missing Men of the Sirius*

Edgar Quinet. *Ahasuerus; The Enchanter Merlin*

Henri de Régnier. *A Surfeit of Mirrors*

Maurice Renard. *The Blue Peril; Doctor Lerne; The Doctored Man; A Man Among the Microbes; The Master of Light*

Jean Richepin. *The Wing; The Crazy Corner*

Albert Robida. *The Adventures of Saturnin Farandoul; The Clock of the Centuries; Chalet in the Sky; The Electric Life*

J.-H. Rosny Aîné. *Helgvor of the Blue River; The Givreuse Enigma; The Mysterious Force; The Navigators of Space; Vamireh; The World of the Variants; The Young Vampire*
Marcel Rouff. *Journey to the Inverted World*
Léonie Rouzade. *The World Turned Upside Down*
Han Ryner. *The Superhumans; The Human Ant*
Pierre de Selenes: *An Unknown World*
Angelo de Sorr. *The Vampires of London*
Brian Stableford. *The New Faust at the Tragicomique;The Empire of the Necromancers (The Shadow of Frankenstein; Frankenstein and the Vampire Countess; Frankenstein in London); Sherlock Holmes & The Vampires of Eternity; The Stones of Camelot; The Wayward Muse.* (anthologist) *News from the Moon; The Germans on Venus; The Supreme Progress; The World Above the World; Nemoville; Investigations of the Future; The Conqueror of Death; The Revolt of the Machines; The Man With the Blue Face*
Jacques Spitz. *The Eye of Purgatory*
Kurt Steiner. *Ortog*
Eugène Thébault. *Radio-Terror*
C.-F. Tiphaigne de La Roche. *Amilec*
Simon Tyssot de Patot. *The Strange Voyages of Jacques Massé and Pierre de Mésange*
Louis Ulbach. *Prince Bonifacio*
Théo Varlet. *The Golden Rock. The Xenobiotic Invasion; The Castaways of Eros; Timeslip Troopers* (w/André Blandin); *The Martian Epic* (w/Octave Joncquel)
Pierre Véron. *The Merchants of Health*
Paul Vibert. *The Mysterious Fluid*
Villiers de l'Isle-Adam. *The Scaffold; The Vampire Soul*
Gaston de Wailly. *The Murderer of the World*
Philippe Ward. *Artahe ; The Song of Montségur* (w/Sylvie Miller) *Manhattan Ghost* (w/Mickael Laguerre)

MYSTERIES & THRILLERS

M. Allain & P. Souvestre. *The Daughter of Fantômas*
A. Anicet-Bourgeois, Lucien Dabril. *Rocambole*
A. Bernède. *Belphegor*; *Judex* (w/Louis Feuillade); *The Return of Judex* (w/Louis Feuillade); *The Shadow of Judex*
A. Bisson & G. Livet. *Nick Carter vs. Fantômas*

V. Darlay & H. de Gorsse. *Arsène Lupin vs. Sherlock Holmes: The Stage Play*

Séamas Duffy. *Sherlock Holmes in Paris*

Paul Féval. *Gentlemen of the Night; John Devil; The Black Coats ('Salem Street; The Invisible Weapon; The Parisian Jungle; The Companions of the Treasure; Heart of Steel; The Cadet Gang; The Sword-Swallower)*

Émile Gaboriau. *Monsieur Lecoq*

Goron & Émile Gautier. *Spawn of the Penitentiary*

Paul d'Ivoi. *Around the World on Five Sous* (w/Henri Chabrillat)

Rick Lai. *Shadows of the Opera: Retribution in Blood; Sisters of the Shadows: The Curse of Cagliostro*

Steve Leadley. *Sherlock Holmes: The Circle of Blood*

Maurice Leblanc. *Arsène Lupin vs. Countess Cagliostro; Arsène Lupin vs. Sherlock Holmes (The Blonde Phantom; The Hollow Needle); The Many Faces of Arsène Lupin; The Island of the Thirty Coffins*

Gaston Leroux. *Chéri-Bibi; The Phantom of the Opera; Rouletabille & the Mystery of the Yellow Room; Rouletabille at Krupp's*

Richard Marsh. *The Complete Adventures of Judith Lee*

William Patrick Maynard. *The Terror of Fu Manchu; The Destiny of Fu Manchu*

Frank J. Morlock. *Sherlock Holmes: The Grand Horizontals; Sherlock Holmes vs Jack the Ripper*

Jean Petithuguenin. *The Adventures of Ethel King*

Antonin Reschal. *The Adventures of Miss Boston*

P. de Wattyne & Y. Walter. *Sherlock Holmes vs. Fantômas*

David White. *Fantômas in America*

Pierre Yrondy. *The Adventures of Thérèse Arnaud*

Victor Margueritte. *The Bacheloress; The Companion; The Couple*

SCREENPLAYS

Mike Baron. *The Iron Triangle*

Emma Bull & Will Shetterly. *Nightspeeder; War for the Oaks*

Gerry Conway & Roy Thomas. *Doc Dynamo*

Steve Englehart. *Majorca*

James Hudnall. *The Devastator*

Jean-Marc & Randy Lofficier. *Royal Flush*

J.-M. & R. Lofficier & Marc Agapit. *Despair*

J.-M. & R. Lofficier & Joël Houssin. *City*
Andrew Paquette. *Peripheral Vision*
Robert L. Robinson, Jr. *Judex*
R. Thomas, J. Hendler & L. Sprague de Camp. *Rivers of Time*

NON-FICTION

Stephen R. Bissette. *Blur 1-5. Green Mountain Cinema 1; Teen Angels*
Win Scott Eckert. *Crossovers* (2 vols.)
Jean-Marc & Randy Lofficier. *Shadowmen* (2 vols.)
Randy Lofficier. *Over Here*

ART BOOKS

Jean-Pierre Normand. *Science Fiction Illustrations*
Raven Okeefe. *Raven's L'il Critters; Rave's Faves*
Randy Lofficier & Raven Okeefe. *If Your Possum Go Daylight...*
Daniele Serra. *Illusions*
Randy Lofficier. *Over Here*

HEXAGON COMICS

Franco Frescura & Luciano Bernasconi. *Wampus*
Franco Frescura & Giorgio Trevisan. *CLASH*
L. Bernasconi, J.-M. Lofficier & Juan Roncagliolo. *Phenix*
Claude Legrand, J.-M. Lofficier & L. Bernasconi. *Kabur*
Franco Oneta. *Zembla*
L. Buffolente, Lofficier & J.-J. Dzialowski. *Strangers: Homicron*
Danilo Grossi. *Strangers: Jaydee*
Claude Legrand & Luciano Bernasconi. *Strangers: Starlock*
Thierry Mornet & Juan Roncagliolo. *Guardian of the Republic*
J.-M. Lofficier & others. *Strangers 0: Omens & Origins*
J.-M. Lofficier, M. Garcia, F. Blanco & J. Pima. *Strangers 1: Strangers in a Strange Land*